The Sil...

*To Paul,
With very best wishes
Hope that you will find
Norway as interesting
as Greenland.
Sam Hall*

BY THE SAME AUTHOR

The Fourth World
Killer Fax
Blisters

First published in 1998

The right of Sam Hall to be identified as the
author of this work has been asserted by him in accordance
with the Copyright, Designs and Patents Act, 1988.

This book is sold subject to the condition that it shall not, by way of trade or otherwise, be lent, resold, hired out, or otherwise circulated without the author's prior consent in any form of binding or cover other than that in which it is published and without a similar condition including this condition being imposed on the subsequent purchaser.

First published in the United Kingdom in 1998 by
Global Syndications
Dorking Surrey

ISBN 0 9533404 0 6

Typeset by Global Syndications, Dorking, Surrey
Printed and bound in Great Britain by
Michael Heath Limited of Reigate, Surrey

To the 'Children'
Jonas, Ulrika and Mira Petra,
Benedict and Valentina
and Helen

Chapter One

June 18, 3.15 p.m. - 7.15 p.m.

Visibility was superb, the mid-afternoon sun still high above the glacier. The pilot routinely scanned the helicopter's windshield and instrument panel. Attitude normal. Speed one hundred and ten knots. Pressure and temperature in the green. He had been flying for so many years now that he absorbed the information automatically, his eyes darting beadily from instruments to outer airspace and back again.

Flying conditions were perfect. A fifteen knot wind and a sky the colour of forget-me-nots. A bank of puffed clouds gathered lazily along the horizon, as if trying to soften the visual transition between the ice cap and the blue backdrop.

Humming to himself, the pilot was content. The MBB twin-turbine Bolkow 105 was the ideal machine for the job, the top of its fuselage painted white, the belly and sides mottled green.

Maintaining an altitude of 6,000 feet above sea level, less than one hundred feet above the surface of the glacier, called for relentless concentration but that was how he liked it. Flying was his life, no aeronautical challenge too great for him.

Glancing at the map on his knee, he traced the route ahead with his finger and made a quick calculation. The southwesterly course was taking him along the centre of Jostedalsbreen, the largest glacier in Europe.

Soon, he would turn due south to Bøyabreen and Suphellebreen, the twin tongues of fractured ice that tumble chaotically down to the valleys above Fjærlandsfjord.

Deftly adjusting the balance and attitude of the machine, he glanced at the passenger beside him, next to the open door. He was a bull of a man with a neck the size of his thigh and a ring of thick, wavy hair flowing from a bald crown onto his shoulders.

The pilot did not know his real name, nor even what he looked like. For his face was perpetually hidden behind a drooping moustache and sunglasses, the silvered lenses encased in bright yellow, plastic frames.

The passenger glanced up.

'Time to destination?' he demanded.

'Twelve minutes.'

'Tell me when it's six.'

Nodding briefly, the pilot changed course to the south. Again, he scanned the horizon. Beneath him, the ice field was breaking up, the crevasses widening as the mass of ice moved at six feet a day towards the edge of the plateau. He grinned, quietly planning his next move.

Raising the collective lever with his left hand, he climbed until he had gained sufficient height. Then, maintaining balance with his left yaw pedal, he carefully selected a cluster of ice pinnacles rising from the floor of one of the wider crevasses.

His mind racing, he pushed the Bolkow without warning into a screaming dive, simultaneously boosting the power to maximum as he arced into a sixty-degree left bank turn. Centrifugal force and power were critical. With the helicopter flying almost on its side, the weight of the machine was effectively doubled, the stress on the rotor head tortuous.

Using his feet to adjust for torque reaction, he knew that the slightest error of judgement could flip the machine over and kill them both.

It was a dangerous game but the exhilaration and surge of Adrenalin as he guided the helicopter through the jumble of ice towers made it worth the risk. He powered out of the dive and levelled off, climbing and banking sharply to starboard to regain his southerly course.

It was all over in a few seconds. Elated, he increased speed to make up for the lost time and swivelled the microphone attached to his helmet closer to his mouth.

'Six minutes.'

'You trying to scare me?'

'Nope. Just adding a little excitement to the brochure.'

Nodding, the passenger gazed out of the open door, his face devoid of humour. The farrago of ice disappeared behind them. Below the snowline, stands of Norwegian spruce clung to the shoulders of the mountains, falling steeply to a narrow, fertile valley 5,000 feet below.

Beyond was the head of the fjord and their destination. The pilot maintained height for another two minutes, the camouflaged underbelly and sides of the helicopter merging with the vegetation.

He had planned the flight meticulously, studying each contour of the map and learning the names of all the mountain peaks, valleys, villages and hamlets. He had even calculated the likely effects of air currents at crucial points of the flight.

Now, he was regretting his rash deviation into the crevasse. It had been asking for trouble and could ruin everything. He checked his watch and glanced at the altimeter, his forehead wrinkling into a frown.

Three minutes and thirty seconds from the destination, the pilot lurched into a descent. No ordinary descent. Not like the helicopters seen landing at airports. This was desperate.

The Bolkow plunged earthwards like a high speed elevator, its rotors windmilling in full auto-rotation, the steep sides of the valley only feet from the open door. Even the passenger, who seemed to have no nerves, looked mildly alarmed.

The pilot sensed rather than saw his glance. Descending at 2,000 feet a minute with a forward speed of eighty knots, he was concentrating to such a degree that each millisecond seemed like an hour.

Correcting the helicopter's attitude, he dropped to thirty feet above the water, opaque and milky-green from glacial deposits. The pilot boosted the forward speed to 130 knots and slipstreamed into a ninety-degree turn to starboard. Flying due west now, he skimmed over the fjord towards the Glacier Hotel, a white clapboard building instantly recognisable by its circular wooden balconies, tiled steeple and weather vane.

'One minute. Destination ahead.'

The passenger lifted his thumb, took off his headset and folded the sunglasses into his pocket. Swivelling sideways, he eased his feet onto the Bolkow's float, his mind concentrated, the wind and the force of the down draught from the rotors tearing at his leather jacket and trousers.

Katrina Hagen, the manager of the Glacier Hotel, first heard the helicopter when she was standing before the full length antique mirror in the Piano Room. The reflection was gratifying. Tall and slim, she had a perfect figure for the finely tailored navy suit that she had bought the previous week in Balestrand, the small but lively town at the other end of the fjord.

The soft thwacking of the rotors and the high-pitched whine of the turbines again intruded into her thoughts, this time forcefully. Suspecting that something was amiss, she peered through the leaded bay window. The helicopter was desperately low, streaking straight for the hotel.

As it roared overhead, she stared in horror at the man clinging to its fuselage. It seemed as if the machine would hit the roof. Clearly the pilot was in trouble. Rushing to a side window, she half stumbled over a coffee table and chaise-longue. She watched the pilot turn sharply again, this time towards the village.

For a moment, the helicopter disappeared behind the trees. When she saw it next, it was flying at less than rooftop level. Then it disappeared.

Moments later, the valley was filled with a sound so deafening as to leave her ears ringing. Recovering from the initial shock, she rushed past the piano and through the main lounge to the front door, only vaguely aware that the window panes were still rattling from the blast.

Outside, about a mile away, a column of thick, oily smoke was curling from the head of the fjord up to the ice of Bøyabreen and Suphellebreen.

With typical efficiency and clear thinking, she ran to the Reception desk, her high heels clattering across the parquet flooring. She ordered the receptionist to raise the alarm and telephone the police in Balestrand, then shouted down the narrow corridor to her friend, Tor Falck, who was reading a cheap novel over a beer in the café.

'Quick. A helicopter has gone down. Get the fire extinguisher.'

For a journalist, he reacted sluggishly, a characteristic that irritated her constantly. Probably his bulk, she thought. She wondered if there were any fatalities. Urgently, she grabbed the first aid box, snatched her car keys from the front desk and pulled an ice axe and climbing rope from the stand by the hall staircase. Then she rushed out to the car park, Tor lumbering behind her.

Her red Mitsubishi Colt started without a hiccup. Shifting directly from first to third gear, she roared out of the drive, tyres protesting as she spun the wheel, overtook a tourist caravan and headed through the village to Bøyaøyri, the hamlet from which the smoke appeared to be drifting.

There was no other traffic on the road, which was just as well. At the best of times, her driving reflected an intrinsic impatience and irritability. When she was excited, it verged on the reckless, possession of the road belonging, in her view, to the driver with the strongest nerves.

She had almost reached the scene when the fire siren wailed across the valley, a call to Fjærland's twenty volunteer fire fighters - all farmers - to drop whatever they were doing and hasten to the building that housed the village fire truck.

When Katrina jerked the handbrake through its ratchets and leapt out of the car onto the dirt road, the fire was still burning vigorously. It would be some time before the fire fighters would arrive and they would then have to run the hose across several fields, a distance of several hundred yards, so that they could pump water from the river.

'Give me the fire extinguisher, Tor.'

'*Ja, ja*. Let the dog see the rabbit.'

She watched him struggle out of the car, his obesity hampering his movements, and snatched the extinguisher from his hands.

'Bring the ice axe and rope,' she ordered. 'We might need them.'

Racing up the gravel driveway, she directed the jet of foam at the heart of the nearest fire. Only then did she realise the extent of the damage. One house was demolished. Two others thirty yards away were ablaze. A knot of bystanders watched helplessly, moving like a flock of starlings whenever the black, acrid smoke blew in their direction.

She was about to shout at them, to gird them out of their stupor, when she caught sight of a pile of tangled metal on the charred grass and recognised it as once having been a wheelchair.

Appalled by the shreds of clothing and the charred flesh, she felt a numbness seep through her brain and arms and legs, as if she had been injected with a general anaesthetic. She fought to repel the tunnel vision that encompassed her, unaware that she had dropped the extinguisher or that the jet of foam was spraying uselessly onto the ground.

'*Herre Gud.*'

Hearing Tor's deep, baritone voice behind her, she turned to him and laid her head on his broad shoulders. She had no idea how long she stood there, fighting the nausea. Gradually her paralysed mind began to function again, irrationally seeking to place blame. Without warning, she wheeled round on the bystanders, screaming.

'How could you stand there, doing nothing? Just letting him burn to death?'

Some lowered their gaze. Others shook their heads in despair. She glared at them accusingly and swung back to the fires, angry that she had allowed emotions to overcome her natural pragmatism.

Shielding her face against the heat, she reached for the extinguisher but its force had dissipated. There was nothing she could do. She realised then that she was helpless, that they had all arrived too late. She turned back to them, tears and perspiration staining her face.

'I'm sorry,' she whispered. 'I'm so very sorry.'

She allowed Tor to lead her back to the car and leaned against its door, gazing at the flames and smoke, and the snow on the mountains beyond. Fire and snow. Even in tragedy, the combination was strangely beautiful.

'Best we go, Katrina.'

She could tell from the tone of his voice that Tor wanted to leave her, to interview the villagers and find out what they had seen. Tearfully, she picked a loose hair from his beard. When he spoke again, she was surprised by the hardness of his voice.

'Did you notice anything strange, Katrina?'

'Strange? How do you mean?'

He looked at her, his eyes hardening, the wide, sensuous mouth pinched with anger.

'Three houses. How many people, Katrina? How many were killed? And how?'

'*Hvor* ...? I don't understand.'

'Neither do I. Not yet. But do you not see? In all this ... this carnage, there is no sign of a helicopter. Nothing.'

She caught her breath. She realised now why he was so keen to leave her. For all his ponderous ways, he had seen something that no-one else had noticed and she knew that he would persist, slowly and methodically, until he discovered the truth.

For a moment, they remained silent, the only sound the sparks from the fires crackling in the warm, summer air. When she heard him speak again, it was as if he was thinking aloud.

'It couldn't have been caused by gas because there isn't any gas. It's all hydro-electric power here.'

She thought for a moment, puzzled. 'Then if there is no wreckage, what was the helicopter I saw doing?'

'Did you notice its registration letters?'

'There weren't any. It was military.'

'No. This cannot be. We never have military helicopters up here. Anyway, they are no different. They have registration markings like any other aircraft.'

'Tor, it was painted green and brown, like camouflage. It almost fell out of the sky. It was so low I think it was not more than two metres above the hotel.'

'I know, I heard it.'

'And the explosion - it came seconds afterwards. A minute at the most.'

He pushed a stubby hand through his blonde hair. 'If there is no wreckage, there could not have been a crash. And if the pilot did not crash,' he said, slowly, 'then he must have seen or heard the explosion. If that is true, why did he not land and help? More importantly, who was he and where did he go?'

Katrina shook her head. 'You are right, Tor. There is something wrong about this. Something evil. I can feel it.'

Precisely sixteen seconds after Katrina and Tor left the hotel, at 3.32 p.m., the switchboard operator at Balestrand police station transferred an emergency call to the sheriff's assistant. After taking preliminary details, he passed the receiver to Chief Inspector Odd Ingstad of the *Kriminalpolitisentral*, the National Bureau of Crime Investigation, known in daily parlance as Kripos.

Based at the Bureau's headquarters in Oslo, Ingstad and his colleague, Detective Sergeant Nielsen, had been investigating a bank robbery in the town, the first such crime to be perpetrated there. Fortunately, the robbery had been straightforward and a tourist was being held in custody.

Ja, ja. Some kind of explosion, you say?' The Inspector reached for a pencil. 'Are you sure?'

The caller assured him that she was. Ingstad's heart sank.

'*Ja*. I will arrange for the boat. We will be with you as soon as we can.'

Heaving himself from the leather executive chair, he struggled into his tunic and sighed. He would need twenty minutes to rally the boat crew, plus fifty minutes to Fjærland. They would arrive a little before five o'clock.

In fact, the launch docked at Fjærland at 4.57 p.m. Stepping onto the quay behind the general store, he was surprised and a little irritated to find that there was nobody to meet him. Nor were there any customers inside the store.

Returning to the launch, he ordered the assistant sheriff to take him as far as possible up the fjord, a delay he could have done without.

'Have to go in over there, sir,' the policeman said. 'It's the only place I can get in.'

'All right. Fast as you can.'

Ingstad leapt heavily onto the bank. A gaggle of villagers had gathered 300 yards further along the road. Beyond them, a wisp of smoke rose from a burned building. He rattled off a string of commands to the men on the launch. There were five of them, Balestrand's entire force, but they would have to manage. The first job was to move the spectators out of the way.

'Sergeant Nielsen, get this area sealed off,' he ordered. 'Bloody ghouls. I want them at least a hundred yards further back. Don't let anyone leave without making a statement.'

He surveyed the smouldering ruins. With no fire brigade at Fjærland, the flames had raged unopposed through the houses, feeding on wood that was tinder-dry.

'I'll put the men in now, sir.'

'All right, Nielsen. Tell them to take care. We don't want any casualties.'

'Right, sir. By the way, first reports confirm there was an explosion.'

'Yes, but what caused it Nielsen? What caused it?'

The inspector studied the remains of the three houses, kicking aside charred planks, searching for something, anything, that might show what had caused the blast.

Fumes from heating fuel stored underneath a house were normally responsible for house fires, but here the scorched grass and beech trees uprooted at the end of the gardens proved conclusively that there had been an explosion. The blast had partially blown over a telegraph pole thirty yards away. There must have been a vast store of fuel to cause that kind of damage.

Inspector Ingstad was no closer to finding a solution when Detective Sergeant Nielsen reported that the men had retrieved seven bodies.

'Never stood a chance, sir, poor devils. Died instantly, I should think.'
'Seven …' The inspector sighed. 'Any idea who they were?'
'No positive identification yet, sir, but it seems there are three adult males, two females and two children. We'll get a better idea of who they are when the statements come through.'
'Very good, Nielsen. Get the bodies on the launch.'

The dapper business executive snapped shut his gold Kendal & Dent Half-Hunter watch and returned it to his waistcoat pocket at exactly 4.58 p.m., one minute after the police launch had docked at Fjærland. Pushing open the door of the telephone booth opposite the ferry terminal at Oslo's Pier Three, he emerged, half smiling, into the sunshine.

A half smile was as much as he ever allowed himself. He was a serious man, obsessed with the acquisition of wealth and ancient coins. Today, he had much to be pleased about. Oslo was his favourite European city and he was about to purchase a set of ninth-century coins that would markedly enhance his collection.

He had even been able to revisit the Viking Ship Museum to feed his other lifelong fascination, Viking culture.

Gently swinging a Louis Vuitton briefcase, he ambled along the harbour front opposite the City Hall and turned into Kongensgate, heading for number thirty-one, the site of Oslo Mynthandel, a leading European coin dealer.

Adjusting the starched cuffs of his shirt to reveal his gold cufflinks, he nodded to the uniformed security guard and pushed open the double glass doors.

Inside, the salesroom was well lit, lined on two sides with counters of birch - dark, high quality woodwork that reminded him of a luxury yacht.

In the past twelve years, since he had pulled off the foreign currency deal that had earned him more than a million dollars and set him on the road to personal wealth, he had visited the salesroom many times.

Gunnar Thesen, the co-owner, greeted him like an old friend, leading him through a remotely-operated plate glass door into a room crowded with desks, reference books and cabinets fitted with tray drawers, each filled with rare coins.

Only select customers or more important dealers were invited into the inner area, where Thesen and his partner kept their most valuable coins and bank notes.

'So, you would like to see some gold dinari this time?'
'I would indeed, Mr. Thesen.' The collector retrieved a sheaf of papers from his briefcase. 'They're Arabian, I believe?'

'That is correct. From the Ab Asid Caliphat. They were minted by Sultan Al Motaz Bilar in 867 AD.' Thesen removed a tray from the safe and placed it gently on the desk.

'As you know, the Vikings brought tens of thousands of coins back to Scandinavia but only a few hundred have been found in Norway. Most of those were German and Anglo-Saxon, so it is a most important find.'

Thesen selected a coin from the tray and, balancing it delicately between thumb and forefinger so as to protect it from skin oils, held it under a desk light.

'Quite beautiful, is it not?'

The business executive took it from him, his heartbeat quickening. The coin was in superb condition, the Arabic motif almost untarnished. He thought of the hardship and suffering the Vikings must have endured in their quest for it.

They would have sailed their ships across the Baltic and south through hostile territory along river routes to the Caspian and Aral Seas, frequently hauling their shallow-draft vessels, which weighed eighteen to twenty tons, overland from one river to another.

Eleven hundred years ago, traders would have used this small coin in the great market centres of Tashkent and Samarkand. How many men, he wondered, had fought and died to bring it back to their Scandinavian homeland?

'As you say, quite beautiful. I am indebted to you for contacting me.' He handed the coin back to Thesen. 'How many coins are there?'

'Including the silver dirhem? Fourteen. Nine dinari, five dirhem.'

They discussed the weight, quality and price of the coins but the collector knew that he had little say in the negotiations. These men were experts. There would be little give and take here but at least they were scrupulously fair.

He knew that as a collectable coin, an average gold dinar weighing 4.2 grammes was worth about four times its meltdown value. A silver dirhem of the same quality weighing 2.9 grammes would be worth fifty times its value in weight. If a coin was exceptional, as most of these specimens were, the price could double. The haggling was a gesture only. Thesen smiled.

'So, 17,800 Norwegian kroner. Shall we round that down to $3,000?'

'As always, it's a pleasure to do business with you.'

Shaking his hand, the collector reflected that the price was much as he had anticipated. Three thousand dollars was bird feed compared with the privilege of owning such a collection. He would make up the deficit on expenses in no time at all.

Bidding Thesen farewell, he strolled out through the shaded pedestrian area that lies between the Norwegian Parliament and the National Theatre. The blue sunshades of the Grand Café on Karl Johansgate brought his mind back to more pressing matters.

His next appointment at six o'clock would be trickier. Reaching for the Half-Hunter, he noted that he had twenty minutes in hand, enough to place a quick telephone call and change into more casual clothing. A novelist, after all, would hardly be wearing a dark suit and gold cufflinks.

When he emerged from his suite at the Grand Hotel and entered the Grand Café, he was wearing grey trousers, a dark blue shirt and a spotted bow tie. The leather patches sewn over the elbows of his rumpled sports jacket had been a neat touch, he thought. Guaranteed to put a university lecturer at ease.

He had also washed his hair, normally slicked back, allowing it to fall loosely over his forehead. Only the expensive Italian shoes jarred with the overall image.

The professor was sitting by one of the huge windows that lined two sides of the room. Slim, fair and not yet forty, he looked more like an Olympic athlete than a university professor, but Professor Otto Berg was nevertheless the world's foremost expert on Viking runic script.

For the past three years, he had been trying to decipher the carvings on a runestone known as the Eggjastone, which archaeologists had found on a hillside farm overlooking Sogndal.

Signalling a waiter, the man in the rumpled sports jacket introduced himself and ordered two beers and smoked salmon sandwiches. 'So, are you any closer to a solution, professor?'

Professor Berg shook his head. 'Unfortunately, there are more than 200 symbols carved on the Eggjastone and several interpretations of what they say, but at least we know in general terms that they tell of spirits and magic powers. That is a beginning.' The professor sipped his beer. 'But tell me, what is the origin of your own interest in the Vikings?'

'Oh, it began with a school project, I guess. The Vikings were my heroes. I was intrigued by their courage and audacity.' A half-smile flickered across his face. 'Later, I became more interested in their art. Despite their pillaging, I figured they gave more to society than they took from it.'

He studied the professor's face. The high forehead and fine bones warned him that this was an intelligent man not easily fooled. He would have to be careful. He had run over the story in his mind a thousand times. There would be no mistakes.

'It was the Eggjastone that prompted me to study runic script,' he said, fishing from his pocket a small piece of paper covered with vertical and diagonal lines. 'After that, one thing led to another and I devised this plot for my novel. Hence, my presence here.'

'As I understand it, you have invented a runestone for your plot and translated its text into a runic script yourself.' The professor took the paper and glanced at it. 'And now you want me to translate it back into English?'

'Right. I need to test it out. That way, I'll know it's correct.'

The professor nodded. 'In that respect, writing novels is clearly no different from the academic world. What I don't understand is why you didn't just ask me to translate from the English directly into runic script.'

It was the question he knew the professor would ask and which, because there was no satisfactory answer, he feared most. He felt the blood rushing to his head but remained outwardly cool.

'Oh, come now, professor. That wouldn't have been nearly so much fun,' He smiled, his voice silver smooth. 'Besides, it makes life more interesting for you, does it not?'

'Well, perhaps …'

'And it gives me the chance to have the world's leading expert in the field test my knowledge. That kind of chance doesn't come along very often. I'm indebted to you.'

'Well, flattery is a powerful persuader. I will see what I can do. I will write to you with my findings in a few days.'

They finished their drinks and parted company then, the professor intrigued at the ingenuity of the idea, the man in the sports jacket immensely relieved, his shirt damp with perspiration.

Ever since he had found an inscribed piece of bone a month ago, during the initial geological survey above Fjærland, he had known that he would have to persuade an expert to translate the runes - at the same time persuading him that they were fictional.

His own knowledge of runic script and old Norse was hopelessly inadequate. But he did know that the Vikings used the word *Serklandi* to denote the land of the dark-skinned Saracens, which presumably meant Byzantium and the Arab Caliphate.

He also knew that the Old Norse words *fimm skip* meant 'five ships'.

And these, combined with the words *silfr* and *gull* - silver and gold - generated in him a surge of excitement that he had not experienced since his coup on the foreign exchange markets twelve years earlier.

Chapter Two

June 19, 8 a.m. - June 25, 3 p.m.

When Chief Inspector Ingstad arrived at Balestrand police station the following morning, his mood was not as benevolent as it might have been. He had not left the office until after midnight and he had slept only intermittently. By eight o'clock, he was back at the office. Staring out of the window, he sipped lukewarm coffee from the dispenser in the corridor, his foul mood matching the weather. Low cloud clung to the green-black mountains. The fjord was choppy and sullen grey, the rising wind slapping the halyards against the flagpole beneath his window. A knock on the door interrupted his thoughts. It was Nielsen, cheerful and efficient as always.

'Yes, what is it?' he barked.

'Morning, sir. Lovely morning. Just thought you'd like to know we've got the identifications now.'

'Right, who are they?'

'Seems there were two couples - the Oskarsens and Nygaards - each with a child under seven and an old man of eighty-three called Ragnar Larsen.'

The inspector sighed, cupping his chin in one hand and tapping the desk with the fingers of the other. 'Life's so bloody unfair. Does it make any sense to you, Nielsen?'

'Life or the Fjærland business, sir?'

'Either.'

'No, sir.'

'That's a great help. Thank you. What do we know about these people?'

'Not much. Seems the old man was confined to a wheelchair. Several witnesses say the Oskarsens helped him into the garden at about three-thirty every afternoon, so that he could have a couple of hours' sleep in the fresh air.'

'That means the explosion must have happened just as they were wheeling him out. Sit down, Nielsen, sit down.' The inspector gestured to a chair, rose from his own and stood by the window, watching the car ferry ploughing across the fjord.

'Coffee?' he asked, suddenly.

'No thanks, sir. Doesn't agree with my stomach. Gives me ulcers.'

'Probably give you worse than that, Nielsen. Disgusting stuff. Still, I might just have another. Must be addicted to it.' Opening the door, the inspector called to an assistant. 'Another cup of ersatz, would you constable?'

Nielsen shifted uneasily in the upholstered office chair. The inspector returned to the window.

'One other thing, sir. The position of the bodies suggests that the kiddies were playing together in the old man's garden.'

'What about the other couple?'

'The Nygaards? They were probably chatting to the Oskarsens over the adjoining fence.'

'What makes you think that?'

'Well, sir, apart from Larsen, the bodies of all four adults were found more or less equi-distant from the point where the fences separating the three houses intersected. That suggests that as soon as the Oskarsens had brought the old man out, they stopped for a chat while the two children played near the old man.'

'What about dependent relatives?'

'None to speak of. Neither of the Oskarsens had brothers or sisters. The little girl was their only dependent. Same with the Nygaard family. Fru. Nygaard was an only child. Her husband had a younger brother who's a successful lawyer in Oslo. I imagine their estate will go to him. Not that he'll inherit much. You don't get rich as a tenant farmer.'

'And the old man, Ragnar Larsen?'

Nielsen stood up and stretched. 'Ah, now he's different. He emigrated to America in the thirties but came back to Fjærland in 1955 after a drunken driver had killed his wife. Apparently, he'd made a fortune over there but after that he sold up and used the money to buy the house over at Bøyaøyri. He also owned a large tract of land behind the house and the Glacier Hotel, which he renovated. Too old to farm the land himself, though, so he contracted it out on ten-year leases to other farmers.'

The sheriff's assistant tiptoed into the room and placed a plastic mug of coffee on the desk.

'Excuse me, sir, Tor Falck from the *Balestrand Posten* is outside. Says it's urgent.'

'Right. Give me another minute.' The inspector glanced at the clock on the wall and sank into his chair again, swivelling from side to side.

'Did Larsen have any children?'

'Yes, sir. A son, Jan-Erik. The only one, apparently.'

'All right. Better inform the next of kin, where it applies. Tell the constable I'll see Falck now, will you?'

Ingstad sipped his coffee, forcing himself to concentrate on the Fjærland affair. Three houses, sixty-five yards apart, all catching fire at the same time. It didn't add up. Maybe the Forensic boys would provide some answers. Meanwhile, he was at a loss to know what to do. The constable reappeared, followed by Tor Falck.

The journalist eased his bulk into a chair. He was a big man, nearly two hundred pounds at a guess. Unfit, too. Even the simple exercise of lowering himself into the chair left him short of breath. He grunted and extended a hand.

Instad nodded. 'Welcome back to Balestrand. It's been, what, six years since the last time?'

'About that. Thought I'd check on your progress, if any, with the Fjærland explosion,' he said, pulling a notebook from the pocket of his anorak.

The inspector composed his words carefully.

'The investigation is proceeding normally. As you will have seen from the press release, the fires regrettably claimed seven lives, a man of eighty-three, a boy of eight, a girl of five and their parents. We'll release the names when we've informed the next of kin. Forensic experts are currently sifting through the remains of the three buildings to establish what caused the damage.'

Ingstad leaned forward, doodling with a ballpoint pen.

Maybe Falck could throw some light on the affair. He'd have to be careful, though. Falck's appearance was misleading. Inside that slothful body, there was the mind of a ferret. Like most journalists he would probably sell his grandmother for a couple of column inches and a byline.

'Look, Falck, I don't mind taking you into my confidence again but if I do it has to be on a basis of trust. Frankly, I'm puzzled and it may be that we can help each other again. That said, if I see a POLICE STUMPED headline tomorrow, I'll ban you from the station.'

'*Ja, ja*. Warning taken, Inspector. What's puzzling you?'

'Basically, I'm intrigued to know how three houses so far apart managed to catch fire at the same time. Leaking fumes usually cause this kind of incident but you'd need a hell of a lot of fuel to cause this kind of damage.'

'What about the helicopter? That's too much of a coincidence…'

'What helicopter?'

'The one with the military markings. You mean you don't know?'

'Tell me more.'

'It literally fell out of the sky. We - Katrina Hagen and I - we thought it had crashed.'

'Nobody mentioned a helicopter to me.'

'Fjærland's a small place and the three houses at Bøyaøyri are isolated from the rest of the village. Maybe they didn't see it.'

Falck recounted how Katrina had seen the helicopter in trouble, its military camouflage clearly visible.

'We reckon the explosion …'

'Incident. We're not saying it was an explosion …'

'… happened about two minutes after it flew over the hotel. I checked with the military. They say a helicopter normally flies at between eighty and 120 knots, depending on the type. If it was flying at 120 knots, it would take approximately one minute to cover the distance between the hotel and the scene of the explosion.'

'Incident,' the Inspector corrected again. 'What are you trying to say?'

'I am saying that we know the helicopter was flying north up the fjord because Katrina saw it. We also know it didn't gain height and fly over the mountains because she was watching and didn't see it. There was nowhere else for it to go except to the scene of the explosion. Katrina reckons she was looking out of the window for about a minute after it had disappeared from view. Immediately afterwards, the entire valley was shaken by the blast.'

'But it could not have crashed. There was no wreckage.'

Falck slowly stabbed the air with his pencil, as if to punctuate his words, the flesh of his arms quivering. 'Exactly. That means it either caused the explosion and flew off, or that the pilot was there when it happened and didn't hang around to help. Either way he's got a lot to answer for. I want to know who he is, Inspector, and one way or another I'm going to find out. I'd like to think we can cooperate with each other.'

The inspector drained the last of his coffee and sighed. 'I'll get onto the military right away,' he promised.

From the open bathroom window of his home on Quincy Avenue, David J. Larsen watched the Piper Cherokee head towards Runway 28 at Willmar Municipal Airport, Minnesota. There was nothing unusual about the 'plane. Its landing gear and flaps were down, although it was banking too steeply into the glide path, a common enough habit - but the new ILS system would doubtless enable the pilot to correct that. Not that David was a pilot. His interest in aviation stemmed solely from the Flight Simulator software programme that he had installed in his office computer.

He continued shaving, his deep blue eyes gleaming like beacons in the mirror, reflecting on his appointment later that morning with the manager of the First Kandiyohi Lakeside Bank.

For two years now, the demolition business he had set up on leaving the army had been running into trouble. A downturn in the national economy meant that companies were thinking twice about moving into new buildings, which in turn meant that fewer sites needed clearing.

Competition had been fierce and less reputable firms were not averse to intimidation to protect their territory.

As times had grown tougher, he had been forced to take out a sizeable loan to stay afloat, but during the past six months, he had been unable to keep up with the repayments. A week ago, his bank manager had demanded to see the quarterly accounts. He had taken one look at the bottom line and threatened, politely and in the most urbane manner, to call in the loan unless there was a significant improvement in turnover during the next quarter.

Downstairs, David scooped up the ginger cat patrolling the hallway. 'He's gonna give me a hard time, Septimus. I guess we're gonna need more than a little gentle persuasion and diplomacy, huh?'

He reached into the fridge for the cat's breakfast as the front doorbell rang.

'Morning' Dave. If you could just give me a signature for this.' The mailman handed him a ballpoint pen and a slip of paper. 'Letter from the old country, huh? Not from your grandfather, though, by the looks of it.'

David glanced at the postmark and signed the slip, perplexed. The letter bore an express delivery stamp and had been posted in Bergen, Norway, but the only person he knew in Norway was his grandfather. They'd written to each other twice a month since his father had died back in 'seventy-five. Thanking the mailman, he walked back into the house, opening the envelope with foreboding.

The letter was from a lawyer, Paul Stryn, advising him that his grandfather had been killed in an explosion.

The police, Stryn wrote, were investigating the accident but so far had been unable to ascertain its cause.

Although David had never seen his grandfather, the old man had become a surrogate father. They had shared confidences and the *minutiae* of each others' lives in regular letters to each other ever since his father had died of lung cancer.

His grandfather, Ragnar Larsen, was his last and only contact with Norway. He had emigrated to the United States immediately before the outbreak of World War Two in Europe and settled with his wife, Emily, in Willmar. Investing his savings in a Nordic gift store, he had imported directly from Scandinavia all the items he thought Swedish and Norwegian-Americans might buy to remind them of their roots.

The business had been phenomenally successful and his grandfather had subsequently invested the profits in a motel. This, too, had generated handsome profits.

But when a drunken driver had killed Emily in 1954, Ragnar was so heartbroken that he sold the motel and, in 1955, five years before

David was born, returned home to Fjærland. He had lived there ever since.

David sighed, an inordinate sense of loneliness and loss sweeping over him. His father had died of cancer in 1975 at the age of forty, when David was only fifteen, and his mother died of the same disease nine years later, a kindly woman of pure Norwegian stock who had brought him up until he had joined the Army at eighteen.

He gazed emptily at the trees swaying in the breeze outside, reflecting that his life seemed to be filled with death. In the Army, he had narrowly escaped being killed himself. Only a cracked rib and injured shoulder sustained while tackling an obstacle course had saved him. President Carter had given the order for his squad to be placed on red alert to go to Iran within hours of his being admitted to military hospital.

Three days later, on April 25, the news came through that eight of his fellow soldiers, all close friends, had been killed trying to rescue fifty-three diplomatic hostages held by the Iranians at the U.S. Embassy in Teheran.

Later, when a gloating Ayatollah held up their bones in a plastic bag at a press conference, he had been sickened and inexplicably consumed by guilt. Ever since, he had wished that he, too, had been killed. The incident had taken the soul out of him.

Shortly afterwards, an ear infection affected his sense of balance and he began to develop a fear of heights. Inevitably, he was transferred out of the Delta Force and he knew then that it was time to leave the Army. He was not particularly sorry. The deaths of his friends had affected him deeply. And now, his grandfather was gone, too.

It was as if he had been cut loose from his Norwegian roots. Financial realities had prevented him from travelling to Norway and he had neither seen his grandfather nor Fjærland, though from his grandfather's letters he knew everything about the place - each blade of grass, each snowfall, each family, who was doing what and why. He picked up Stryn's letter and continued reading.

'As the sole beneficiary of your grandfather's last will and testament, you will, upon proof of identity and signature of the relevant documents before witnesses, inherit your grandfather's house, approximately 200 acres of land and the Glacier Hotel at Fjærland. Owing to your grandfather's age, he had contracted out this agricultural land to local farmers.

"Under Norwegian law, if you wish to claim this land, you would be required to live on the land and take up Norwegian citizenship. If at some future stage you should decide to take this course of action, I shall of course be pleased to obtain the necessary documentation.

"Unfortunately, it will be some months before I can finalise the affairs of your grandfather's estate, which for the time being must remain frozen. However, as his assets excluding the hotel amount to approximately four million Norwegian kroner (about US$670,000), I suggest that you empower me to open a Norwegian bank account on your behalf, and enclose the relevant documents for your signature.

"Finally, I attach the telephone and fax numbers of Katrina Hagen, the manageress of the Glacier Hotel, who has advised me that she will make any local arrangements you consider necessary. Should you wish to visit Norway, please advise me and I shall make the necessary arrangements in Bergen."

David whistled quietly, his future suddenly assured. Instead of having to beg for extended credit and more time, the bank manager would now doubtless be on his knees, grovelling for his custom.

David visualised him, wringing his hands in gleeful anticipation. 'Nearly $700,000 you say? Well, naturally, this places a completely different light on the matter. Maybe we could interest you in our investment service?' He laughed. The guy had the brain of a gnat if he believed he'd go along with that.

No, he'd taken too much garbage from him. There were other banks. The First Kandiyohi Lakeside could stick its investment services. Right up the alimentary.

Unbeknown to David, events across the Atlantic were gathering like witches round a cauldron to convert his good fortune into a nightmare. At Balestrand, Chief Inspector Ingstad pored over the forensic report, stunned by the significance of what he read. He crossed the room and bellowed down the corridor for Nielsen.

'Sir?'

'Listen to this. Forensic report from Oslo.' He brushed the back of his hand across the two-page document. Balancing his reading glasses on the end of his nose, he read aloud, his index finger tracing the words:

"Evidence retrieved from each of the three houses shows that the extent of the damage was a direct result of fires spread by heating fuel. This was stored either beneath or close to the three houses. However, in none of the buildings was this fuel the initial cause of the fires. In the case of the Larsen house, the fire ignited at a point directly beneath the steps leading to the front door. Damage to the concrete base and supporting columns underneath the steps shows conclusively that this was the result of an explosive force.

"Traces of the explosive together with the force of the blast at this point indicate a charge of one to two kilos of Semtex explosive packed in an aluminium container. This assessment is reinforced by the discovery of a small spring, possibly from an alarm clock which may have been used as a timing device …"

Nielsen's jaw dropped. 'So it was a bomb? But who …?'
'I don't know, but wait. This is the really nauseating part.' The inspector continued, his voice hardening:

"Closer inspection produced fragments of metal scattered over a wide area. The bodies of each of the four adults contained pieces of fragments of this metal. These did not emanate from the explosive placed under the steps of the Larsen house. Tests on shrapnel embedded in the wheelchair proved it to be from a hand grenade manufactured in eastern Europe. Evidence suggests there were at least four separate explosions, all more or less simultaneous."'

Nielsen sat down. 'Several explosions, that puts a different light on things. But who would want …'
'I don't know, Sergeant. But it explains how three houses managed to catch fire at the same time.'
'It also means that we have a particularly nasty murder enquiry on our hands, sir.'
'Quite so, Nielsen. Whoever was responsible is obviously utterly ruthless. He must have planted the bomb by the front steps, walked round the house and calmly tossed hand grenades at the old man and the children, and then at the four adults talking by the fence.'
'And lobbed more grenades into the other two houses after that.'
'Right. Look, for the time being, I want to keep this quiet. If Tor Falck starts sniffing around, stall him.'
'Any particular reason for that, sir?'
'Yes. We haven't the remotest idea who did this. When the *Balestrand Posten* plasters the story all over the front page, we'll have every crime man in the country on our tails. The papers will go berserk. It's the biggest story for years and they'll want an instant arrest. When we can't give it to them, they'll make our lives a misery. We'll need the biggest headstart we can get.'
'Right, sir. By the way, the military came back with an answer to that query of yours. They said none of their helicopters was anywhere near Fjærland at the time.'
The Inspector groaned. 'Doesn't get any easier, does it, Sergeant?'

'No, sir, it doesn't. I also checked all the helicopter companies in the area. The only machine that's been anywhere near Fjærland is from a company at Leikanger. They rented one on a semi-permanent basis to an American pilot called Delius Greenwood.'

'Better check him out immediately.'

'Already have, sir. Understandably, the helicopter people were reluctant to rent a machine to someone they didn't know, but apparently he was very persuasive - said money was no object and that it was for a geological survey so he was keen to avoid any publicity. Anyway, they checked both him and his flying ability themselves'

'And?'

'Seems he's a very experienced pilot with excellent credentials.'

'Any description?'

'Caucasian, small, about five foot seven inches tall. Slender build, dark hair and beard. Oh yes, he's quite sunburned and has a deep white scar on his forehead. He's been staying at the Glacier Hotel - even gives the local kiddies a trip now and again.'

'Anything else?'

'Yes, sir. It couldn't have been him.'

The Inspector groaned. 'Why not?'

'The company say the helicopter is painted red and white with the call sign L-XRYA clearly marked. In other words, no military colouring. What's more, the pilot promised that if he left the Sognefjord area, he'd file a flight plan with the company at Leikanger. Well, he kept his promise. On the day of the explosions he was in Oslo.'

The Inspector sighed and buried his face in his hands, his thoughts in turmoil. 'Larsen's son, what was his name? Jan-Erik. He's the only person to benefit from all this, isn't he?'

'It would seem so, sir. There's some suggestion that he died, though, in which case the grandson, David Larsen, would inherit. As for the Nygaards and Oskarsens - they had no money to speak of. Ragnar Larsen was the only one who had any money.'

'What do you reckon his estate is worth?'

'Hard to say, sir. The Glacier Hotel must be worth a few million and he owned a lot of land. When we were in Fjærland, people were saying he'd made a small fortune in the States, so there's probably a fair bit of money in the bank.'

'I think we'd better take a closer look at the Larsens, sergeant. I'll put in a request for an FBI check.'

Like most boys, Jan Tystad was consumed with curiosity. Not yet ten years old, his captivating charm and impish face almost guaranteed that he would be among the first of the Fjærland children to be given a ride in the helicopter. Delius, the pilot was his hero. If anybody had asked Jan at this stage of his life what he wanted to be when he grew up, there could have been only one answer - a helicopter pilot. He spent every spare moment either waiting for the machine to take off or for it to return from the mountains.

When Delius was not around, he would play on the floating pontoon and jump onto the helicopter's floats so that it rocked gently in the water. Jan hoped that if he spent enough time there, Delius would ask him if he would like to fly in the helicopter as a reward for standing guard, but to his disappointment he had instead been told not to play near the pontoon because it could be dangerous.

Several days ago, the pilot had seen him again but this time he had ruffled his hair and said 'Hi, kid, how y'doin?', a phrase which Jan had practised every day since. It had been to no avail, for no sooner had Delius uttered the words than he started the rotors and flew off down the fjord.

Since then, he had not returned. Jan was on the point of accepting that his dream would not be realised when to his joy he again heard the helicopter's rotors chopping the still air. It was one of the most welcome sounds he could have hoped to hear.

When Delius appeared, the long hours of anticipation were instantly forgotten.

'Hi, kid. How y'doin'?' Jan mimicked.

'You're still here then, eh, kid?'

'Sure am, mister.'

They conversed mainly through sign language, for Delius spoke only halting Norwegian and Jan had not yet begun to learn English, although he knew a few words from watching television. This was no hindrance to their relationship. Whenever Delius spoke, Jan would nod vigorously and smile, his eyes gleaming happily.

'You wanna ride?'

Jan could scarcely believe his ears. The blood rushed to his head and his legs felt weak. He grinned, nodding enthusiastically, too thrilled to speak.

'Take it easy or your head 'll fall off. What's your name, kid?'

'Jan.'

'Okay, Jan. Gimme your hand.'

The pilot helped him into the front passenger seat, strapped him in and warned him not to touch the foot pedals. 'Otherwise we'll be in real trouble, okay? Now, let's see if we can make that headset a little smaller for you.'

Jan studied the pilot's face as he told him how to talk into the microphone attached to the helmet. One day, he thought, he would grow a black beard like that and wear a leather flying jacket. He studied the instruments. There were hundreds of dials and switches, even in the ceiling of the cockpit.

As the rotors began to whine, Jan felt his neck and stomach tighten with excitement. He pushed his legs backwards so as to be sure that they would not touch the pedals, though there was little chance of that given that they scarcely reached the floor.

Slowly, the helicopter rose from the water, its nose dipping slightly. Passing sedately over the wooden church next to the Glacier Hotel, it headed west along Mundal Valley, which ran at ninety degrees to the fjord.

The flight lasted only a few minutes. Yet to Jan, it seemed forever, each second a lifetime memory.

Deliriously happy, he pointed towards a collection of farm houses behind the church. '*Mitt hus, mitt hus*,' he shouted, craning his neck as the helicopter flew on towards the mountains.

Delius climbed to 4,500 feet, flying up to the glacier. Then, he turned gently and retraced his route to Fjærland. When Jan saw that the helicopter was going to land in the field at the back of his house, he could hardly contain his joy. He tried hard to look cool but could not help but grin. His entire body quivered with the thrill of it.

When they were safely on the ground again, Delius helped him down and told him to stand well clear as he took off again. Jan paused briefly to wave goodbye, then ran into the house as fast as he could to tell his mother and father. His father demanded to be told everything about his adventure. But his mother fussed, as she always did, scolding him because his hands and trousers were covered with streaks of red and white paint.

George Vito whistled quietly to himself as he headed west at a leisurely pace along U.S.12. He was in no hurry. The 'plane from New York had landed at Minneapolis twenty minutes ahead of schedule and the journey to Willmar was little more than a couple of hours driving.

He nosed the limousine through the downtown business area toward Pacific Avenue, right next to the Old Town. He had done his homework well.

There was very little that he did not know about David J. Larsen. Leaning on the bank manager had been a particularly smart move. With debts like his, Larsen would accept his offer with the enthusiasm of a drowning man grabbing a piece of driftwood.

Vito pulled up outside an austere building facing the Burlington Northern Railroad yards and climbed the stairs to a third storey office, his nose wrinkling at the musty odour, his feet echoing on the bare floorboards.

Immediately he opened the door, Vito recognised Larsen from the photographs taken by the detective agency, though he was taller than he had imagined, his blonde hair and muscular build classic Scandinavian.

Vito smiled, adjusted his cufflinks and extended a manicured hand.

'You don't know me, Mr. Larsen. My name's George Vito. I represent Schneider Barr Incorporated, a multinational corporation specialising in overseas property development and tourism.'

David shook his hand and grinned. 'Hi, how can I help?'

'Right now we are especially interested in a tourist expansion scheme in western Norway and - this may come as a surprise to you - were just about to strike a deal with your grandfather …'

'My grandfather? But he…'

'May I be the first to offer my condolences? I'm real sorry about what happened. That was a terrible accident …'

David moved from behind a desk littered with papers and rolled-up blueprints. 'You'd better come out back, Mr. Vito. Pete here will look after the office.' He nodded to a broad-shouldered individual in a chequered shirt and leather vest, and ushered the stranger into a back room. He gestured towards an armchair facing the window, cracked and grimy.

'Sorry, the place is a mess. Keep talking, I'll get some coffee.' He slipped through a door leading to a galley kitchen.

'That's very kind, I appreciate it. By the way, call me George.' Vito drew a sheaf of papers from his briefcase and casually tossed them onto an old pine table.

'You probably won't want to read them but these papers will verify our dealings with your grandfather. You're welcome to borrow them if you wish.'

He sank into the armchair, his eyes panning along the shelves crammed with files and ledgers, missing nothing. Beside a computer was a framed photograph of Ragnar Larsen, a tough, bearded individual clutching an ice axe, a rope looped diagonally round his torso.

'I see you have a picture of your grandfather. Taken before he was confined to his wheelchair. But a good likeness if I may say so.'

David answered from the kitchen. 'Yeah? I never knew him. Never seemed to get a chance to go over there.'

'I'm sorry to hear that. He was an impressive man. And Fjærland is a beautiful place. As a matter of fact I was there myself a few days ago, just before the accident. A bad business. No one seems to know how the fire started, although I understand it was probably caused by gasoline fumes.'

David poured the coffee and produced a couple of doughnuts from the fridge.

'I only heard he'd died two days ago and I guess it's too late to go to the funeral. You said you were going to do a deal with him?' He picked up the papers and flicked through them.

'That's right. You see, we were hoping to invest in the Glacier Hotel and your grandfather's land. You probably know that the area is rich in Viking history and that some years ago archaeologists unearthed the remains of a Viking ship there.'

'Yeah, I heard about that. He wrote me.' David replaced the papers on the table, picked up a pen and pad from the desk and sat on a hardback chair. 'We wrote each other every couple of weeks so I guess I'm about as up to date as you can be on events in Fjærland. They also found a small settlement there a couple of years later.' His eyes met Vito's, then dropped to the pad on his knee.

Vito seemed surprised. 'That's correct. And it's precisely why I am here, David. You see, Viking culture is a hobby of mine. You might even say an obsession.' He smiled. 'I've even picked up a smattering of Old Norse. Anyhow, we've been talking with the Norwegian government and the National Tourist Authority about a plan to reconstruct the village. Build a Viking farm with houses, equipment, tools, boats and models. Show people the way it used to be.'

'Sounds interesting.'

'In short, we hope to capitalise on the Viking traditions so as to exploit the tourist potential. Put money back into the local economy. We're also planning to build a tunnel underneath the glacier, three and a half miles long and a tourist attraction in itself.'

Vito brushed away a dusting of sugar that had fallen from the doughnut onto his suit and leaned forward. 'You're a portrait artist?'

David laughed. 'Oh, just fooling around. Bad habit. I draw people all the time, I'm afraid. Take no notice.'

Vito nodded. 'As you'll no doubt appreciate, all this requires a sizeable investment, a great deal more than the Balestrand municipality can afford. That's why we offered to extend the Glacier Hotel and buy your grandfather's land. He was about to sign the contract when this tragedy happened.'

'So you're here to do business, George.' David looked him directly in the eye. It was a comment rather than a question. 'I'm not sure I can help you. See, I haven't actually inherited the land yet.' He studied the sketch, frowning.

Vito craned his neck and watched him erase part of the mouth, extending the top lip to make it thinner. From what he could see, the likeness was remarkable.

'I understand. I hope you won't think of my coming here as being distasteful or unseemly?'

'Not at all but I guess it'll be several months before the lawyers transfer the estate to my name.'

'Never mind. I merely wanted to advise you of our interest. To let you know that if you do decide to sell, we'd be prepared to pay around $250,000 for the land and, say, three million dollars for the hotel?'

David pocketed the sketch and looked up sharply. 'Three million bucks?' He laughed. 'I'll give it my urgent attention.'

'Of course, we'd prefer to buy the land and the hotel as a package.'

'I understand. If I decided to accept your offer, I guess that wouldn't be a problem.'

'Becoming a millionaire never is, David.'

Chapter Three

June 25, 3.35 p.m. - July 1, 1.50 p.m.

As soon as George Vito left Larsen's office, he drove along Business Route 71 to the Viking Motel, a small but comfortable establishment, the name of which appealed to his sense of humour. He checked in, booked a table for dinner and took a shower. He had good reason to be pleased with himself. The meeting with Larsen had gone exactly as planned. Larsen's eyes had glazed over at the mere mention of $250,000. And when he realised he could get three million bucks for the hotel, they had nearly popped out of their sockets. The transition from relative poverty to potential millionaire status in the space of about ten seconds must have been some shock.

Vito towelled himself vigorously. Larsen would probably blow his inheritance in twelve months but that was his business. Just so long as he signed over the land. As for the Glacier hotel, he'd have to figure out what to do with that later.

The essential consideration was to convince Hans Tripp, the President of Schneider Barr, that purchasing Larsen's land was crucial to company plans. He knew he was playing a devious and possibly dangerous game, that if Tripp discovered the purchase was essential only to his own, private scheme, he could finish up feeding sharks in the Gulf Stream.

Vito flopped onto the bed and reached for the 'phone. The operator answered immediately. Hans Tripp was on the line in seconds.

'Yeah? Tripp.'

The brusque voice grated like gravel on soft skin. He was a rude sonofabitch with the manners of a New York cab driver. Vito pictured the domed head and stubby body slumped at the rosewood desk, the wide, sensuous mouth ready to spew vitriol at the turn of a phrase, the magnate's thick fingers smearing cigar ash over his clothes. The suit would be crumpled, like a burst cushion.

'Morning, Hans. All well?'

'Cut the crap, George. How did you get on with the Larsen dude?'

'No problems. He'll sell.'

'He'd better. I want no foul-ups over this.'

'You worry too much, Hans. That demolition business of his has been losing money for nearly two years. He's so deep in debt he doesn't know whether he's coming or going. I also pulled a few strings.'

'How so?'

'I had the bank lean on him a couple of days ago. Threatened to call in his loan.' He laughed, a thin metallic laugh with no humour. 'Don't you worry, he'll sell.'

'If you say so, George.'

'I say so. Look, he has no alternative. If he sells, he's a millionaire. If he doesn't, he's bankrupt. Which would you choose?'

'It's not my ass that's on the line, George.'

Vito tucked the receiver under his ear and pulled a small leather case from his pocket. He took out a nail file, fighting to control his frustration. Tripp was an ill-mannered megalomaniac, no expletive too grand for him. On the other hand, the job as his Personal Assistant enabled him to exert his own power and live in luxury. 'Did you get the final geological report?'

'Nope.'

'It's on its way. Iron pyrites and zinc sulphide all over the place. We put a fifty-yard grid over the entire mountain. There's no mistaking the magnetic and electromagnetic anomalies. We're not through yet, of course, but we've sunk one hundred and twenty diamond drillholes so far. Looks as if there's a sloping Gneises sequence extending for miles.'

'How about the core samples?'

'We've drilled thirty-eight millimetre cores for assaying. The abundance of chalcopyrites and chalcocites confirms what we suspected. There's a significant copper zinc deposit there.'

'How much are we looking at?'

'At least forty million tons of ore grading eight per cent zinc and two per cent copper.'

'Great. What next?'

Vito heard him spitting cigar tobacco from his tongue. I'll tell you what next, he thought. You finance my personal little venture, that's what's next. He eased himself off the table and paced back and forth.

'I'm flying back to Norway tomorrow. It's a sensitive issue. The deposit is right on the edge of a national park. I had a hell of a time persuading the government to let us have the exploration license. Now we need the exploitation license.'

'Make sure you get it.'

'I've been checking out the top man. We'll get it.'

'Call when you get a result.'

The 'phone clicked. There were no pleasantries. No 'Thanks' or 'Well done' or 'Have a good flight'. Vito replaced the receiver and thoughtfully continued to file his nails. Hans Tripp was an uncouth braggart who believed that opulence was a substitute for culture. He had about as much finesse as a rhino at a tea party. Unfortunately, as President of Schneider Barr Incorporated, the multinational mining, construction and property conglomerate, he was his personal passport to riches.

David Larsen flipped the sign on the door to "Closed" and was prancing euphorically round the dingy office like a warrior at a fertility dance before Vito had pulled away from the sidewalk. He pummelled Pete Henriksen, his assistant, friend and confidant, in the ribs, whooping with joy.

'Pete, as of now your salary is doubled.'

Henriksen, calm and brawny, looked at him quizzically. 'Great. The guy leaps about like a crazed weasel and offers me the world. What gives?'

'Triple it, Pete, triple it.'

'Would you by any chance have had some good news?'

David swept a pile of papers onto the floor and sat on the edge of his desk, grinning. 'Good news? Man, I am gonna be *rich*. A goddam millionaire.'

'Sure you are. And I'm gonna be President of the United States. You want coffee?'

'No fooling, Pete. That guy - he just offered me a quarter of a million bucks for my grandfather's land. And that's only a part of it. He's gonna pay me three million bucks for the hotel I told you about. Three million - how about that?!'

Henriksen whistled. 'I guess I'll take the triple salary. What are you going to do with the money?'

'Hell, I dunno, Pete. Buy me a Jaguar XJ220. A Lexus, maybe. Live life in the fast lane. How do I know?'

Henriksen stood in the kitchen doorway, making fresh coffee.

'Will you go to Norway?'

David thought for a moment. Ironically, he had not been able to raise the cash to travel to the funeral. He had written to Stryn regretting that he would not be able to attend the wake owing to financial reasons and asked if the woman who managed the hotel, Katrina Hagen, would arrange it for him. He had also authorised the lawyer to open a Norwegian bank account for him.

'Norway?' he repeated. 'I don't know, Pete. Why not? Except now my grandfather's gone, there seems no point. Anyways, I got too much to do here.'

Henriksen handed him a mug of coffee. 'You're a crazy bastard. Ever since I've known you, you've talked about going there. Now, you're gonna be a millionaire, you tell me you got too much to do.'

'Yeah, but what in hell am I going to do there? There are no effects to sort out. The house and everything in it were destroyed in the fire. Anyway, this is Fest week.'

David dismissed the idea. The Willmar Fest, a combination of four local festivals in the last week of June, was the highlight of the year. As an accomplished saxophonist and leader of the Kandi County Vanguard, he and the group were scheduled to perform eight concerts at various parkland locations. Almost the entire 18,000 population would turn out for the events, colourful affairs with thousands of Minnesotans of Scandinavian origin wearing their national costumes.

David shrugged. Not that he cared about that - he just hated to miss the opportunity of playing live concerts.

'I know it's ironic, Pete, but I guess I'd rather be a part of the festivals here than go back to the real thing.'

Henriksen poured the coffee and sat on the arm of a chair. 'You don't want to see where your grandfather lived? Find out how he died?'

'Sure, I do. But not right now. Shit, I can't let the jazz group down and, anyhow, I have to help the Nature Conservation Society out this week on the Foot Lake project …'

'The Nature Conservation Society …?'

'Yeah, we have to figure out a way to stop that Eurasian water milfoil spreading.'

'That's important?'

'Sure it's important. Darned weed is so dense it's killing all the native vegetation and destroying the fish spawning areas. You can't even swim in parts of the lake, any more.'

'Come on, Dave, quit making excuses. Jeez, for all you know, the hotel and the land could be worth double what this guy Vito is offering.'

David studied his friend's face. Maybe he had a point at that. If he did go to Norway, at least he would have no worries about the business. Pete was efficient, as expert with explosives as himself and a hundred per cent trustworthy. David drained his coffee.

'Maybe I'll go after the Fest,' he said, logging onto the office computer. He flicked the mouse arrow to the Flight Simulator program, gave the Cessna 182 full throttle and, checking that the flaps were up, took off from Chicago Miegs airport runway three-six, heading north.

'You gotta do it, Dave, and I'll tell you for why. You said this guy, Vito, was about to do a deal with your grandfather. Right? Okay, if that's true, how come your grandfather never mentioned it in his letters? Shit, he told you everything there was to know about Fjærland.'

Stunned by the simplicity of Henriksen's logic, David could not imagine why he had not thought of it himself. He swivelled round from the computer.

'You're right. That *is* strange.'

'I mean, here's an old man who writes to say he's seen a pair of red-breasted mergansers nesting, but says nothing about a deal that involves the government, the National Tourist Authority and the entire village. It don't make sense, man. If all that stuff was true, he'd have been shittin' himself with excitement. There's no way he'd forget to tell you.'

David nodded. 'Yeah, you're right.' He bit his lip, thinking hard. It didn't figure. Maybe Pete was right. Maybe he should go. He might even persuade the bank manager to give him an advance against Stryn's letter. Or maybe Stryn could wire some money on account. He grinned.

'Okay, Pete. I'll go right after the Fest.' He turned back to the computer. The Cessna had crashed on takeoff.

With no breaks and no leads to follow, Inspector Ingstad was frustrated, impatient and testy. When the telephone rang and the fax machine at Balestrand police station whirred into life on the final day of June, he could see by craning his neck that it was from Kripos headquarters. Tearing off the paper, he noted that it was a response from the Federal Bureau of Investigation to his request for a check on Jan-Erik Larsen. He scanned through it quickly. The report was terse and factual:

"Subject Jan-Erik Larsen, born September 5, 1935, Fjærland Norway. Arrived New York May 14, 1938 with parents, Ragnar Larsen, born March 6, 1910, and Emily Larsen, née Hartland, born July 6, 1911, both of Fjærland, Norway. Emily Larsen killed in automobile accident at Willmar, Minnesota, August 2, 1954. Ragnar Larsen returned Norway February 8, 1955 and has not entered United States since that date.

"Subject Jan-Erik Larsen renounced Norwegian citizenship when granted United States citizenship September 6, 1953. Subject married Eva Berg, United States citizen, June 14, 1957. Only child is David Jan Larsen, born March 29, 1960.

"Subject Jan-Erik Larsen died April 14, 1975 of lung cancer at Rice Hospital, Willmar, Minnesota. Wife Eva Larsen (née Berg) also died lung cancer, August 17, 1984."

Sergeant Nielsen peered over the Inspector's shoulder. 'At least they're thorough, sir.'

'Yes, but look at this, Nielsen.' He pointed to the next paragraph:

"Subject David Jan Larsen volunteered U.S. Army April 1978 and served with Delta Force. Achieved rank of Master Sergeant in record time. Specialist in helicopter warfare, hand to hand combat and use of high explosives. Army records show exemplary service. Subject D. J. Larsen terminated Army service with honorable discharge, April 1981, following attacks of acrophobia (vertigo). Description: Caucasian, six feet tall, 160 pounds, powerful build, blonde hair, blue eyes. Sunburned complexion. Extremely fit."

'An expert in helicopter warfare and high explosives.' The Inspector stabbed a finger at the report.
'This is the man we're looking for. No doubt about it.'
'It's beginning to look like it, sir.' Nielsen nodded at the report. 'He was desperate for cash as well, it seems.'
The report confirmed all the Inspector's suspicions. His problem was knowing how best to proceed. You couldn't apply for extradition proceedings on the basis of suspicion and the only evidence he had was circumstantial. Even that was slender. He read on:

"On leaving the army, Subject D. J. Larsen worked as roughneck on several oil rigs in Texas. Employers described him as restless, malcontent and introspective. Subject subsequently moved to Minneapolis, working in construction industry, before returning to his home at Willmar, Minn.

"Subsequent to death of Eva Larsen, mother, in August 1984, Subject Larsen inherited three-bedroom home on Quincy Avenue, Willmar. Subject currently owns and operates demolition business specialising in levelling high rise buildings in densely populated areas.

"Corporate profits reported down sharply during past two years, giving rise to concern among major credit card companies. Subject D. J. Larsen's credit rating currently under reassessment. On June 11, First Kandiyohi Lakeside Bank issued warning of foreclosure on $120,000 loan following delays in repayments.

"On June 26, Subject D. J. Larsen purchased round-trip ticket to London, England, from Northwest Airlines. Flight Number NW044 departing Minneapolis June 30, 18.15. ETA London Gatwick July 1, 09.15 local."

Inspector Ingstad tossed the report on his desk. 'He's our man. No doubt about it, Nielsen.'
'Pity the report doesn't give his recent movements,' Nielsen observed.

'I mean, if he was in America on June 18, he couldn't have blown up Ragnar Larsen's house, could he, sir?'

'True. We'll ask the FBI to check that, but he was here all right, Nielsen. I'd stake my life on it. An expert in helicopter warfare and explosives? A demolition expert up to his cranium in debt and the old man's only beneficiary? It's got to be him. Oh, I'll bet he has a solid alibi, all right, but he was here and he's coming back. I can smell him.'

'Yes, sir.'

The Inspector strode to his desk, his lips tight and his eyes narrowed. He re-read the report. 'July the first. That's tomorrow. I want every immigration officer in the country alerted, every port and airport in the country watched. I want David J. Larsen, Nielsen. And I want him fried.'

Tor Falck had routinely telephoned the Kripos men several times a day but beyond releasing the names of the dead, the police investigators had little to tell him.

He had tried to keep the story alive, but even exercising his journalistic inventiveness to the full, his task had grown more difficult. There was no one left in Fjærland to interview.

The *Balestrand Posten* had run lengthy profiles of everyone who had anything to say, although astonishingly there had been no eyewitnesses to the explosions. Nor could anybody enlighten him about the helicopter. Apart from Katrina and himself, no one seemed to have seen or heard it. The paper had run the 'Mystery Helicopter' story *ad nauseam* but, lacking any concrete evidence of its existence, the story had faded.

As a result, he had been obliged to write endless columns on the 'Leaking Fumes' angle. Now, the story had been relegated to the inside pages and he was reduced to writing features about the danger of storing gasoline and heating fuel beneath or near to houses.

Desperately in need of a break, he reviewed the story from every perspective. The complete absence of information from Ingstad aroused in him the first stirrings of suspicion. Experience from his days on one of the country's biggest daily evening papers had proved repeatedly that when police say they know nothing, they nearly always know more than they are prepared to reveal.

Perhaps, it was time for a little gentle pressure.

He picked up the 'phone and punched out the number for the police station. Ingstad was clearly not pleased to hear from him.

'What's your problem then?' The Inspector's voice was harsh.

'I don't have a problem, Inspector. You're the one with the problem.'

The man's arrogance was stunning. He deserved to get hammered. Falck took a deep breath.

'It's now twelve days since the explosions and you've turned up nothing. The public has a right to know if you're making progress and if you're not, they have a right to know why.'

'What's that supposed to mean?'

'It means this. Twelve days ago, we agreed to cooperate. I opened up a possible line of enquiry for you about a military helicopter. Since then, you've been as tight as nun's ass. Unless you can be more forthcoming, I'm putting a front page story out tomorrow morning asking why the police appear to be doing nothing.'

'I told you. If you do that, you're banned from the station.'

'So be it. But you said you were puzzled because you couldn't understand how three houses could simultaneously catch fire …'

'That was off the record, Falck.'

'It's a legitimate point, Inspector.'

There was a long silence. Falck could hear the Inspector breathing heavily. He knew something all right. He could sense him weighing up whether to tell him. It was the same old story. You could never trust the police. When they wanted your cooperation, they were as sweet as Afghan tea; when they didn't, cooperation was a one-way agreement. This time he had two fingers up the Inspector's nose and, as he had anticipated, he succumbed. Thirty minutes later, when they met in Ingstad's office, he was charm personified.

'Come in, Falck, come in. Coffee?' The Inspector beamed. 'I think we might have something to interest you at long last.'

'What a surprise, Inspector. You're looking better than when I last saw you. Does that suggest a breakthrough?'

'I think you could say that, Falck. Naturally, I would have let you in on what we've been doing earlier but unfortunately we've only just received the news ourselves.'

'Naturally. Did you say "news"?'

The Inspector sank heavily into his chair, his jaw cradled between thumb and forefinger. 'That's right, Falck. We've decided to put a watch on ports and airports throughout the country. Now, the man we're looking for is one David J. Larsen, American …'

Falck held up his hand. 'Wait! You are going too fast.' He fished his pen and notebook from a pocket and sat down. This was big. He wanted to get it down accurately. 'Now, first of all, why have you ordered a watch on the ports of entry?'

The Inspector explained how the forensic scientists had discovered fragments of a bomb and several hand grenades at the scene of the crime.

He added that David J. Larsen, the American grandson of one of the victims, was a prime suspect.

'We know from the FBI that this man is dangerous. He's an expert in helicopter warfare and the use of high explosives. Runs a demolition company. Mr. Dynamite himself. We also know that he's in deep financial trouble and that he's on his way to London, which probably means this country.'

Falck scribbled frenetically, taking down the man's description and background. This was the scoop of a lifetime, certainly the biggest story he'd ever covered in Norway. He glanced at his watch. Just after five o'clock. It would be a busy night.

First, he would have to feed the nationals and the international news agencies. They would pay well for a story like this. After that, he'd rewrite the stories for the *Balestrand Posten*. If he knew the editor, he would splash it over ten or twelve pages. Minimum. He sighed. It would be a late night.

Sitting in seat 14E, David Larsen gazed out of the right-hand window just in front of the MD-81's wing. He was exhausted. Sleep had not come easily on the transatlantic flight. Rather than spend a day in London, he had transferred to Heathrow Airport to catch the Scandinavian Airlines flight to Stavanger and Bergen. It was due in at Bergen at one-thirty-five.

He calculated that he would be in town by two-thirty, exactly twenty-four hours after leaving Willmar, which meant that he could see Stryn and snatch a couple of hours sleep before dinner and a good night's rest. Tomorrow, he would travel on to Fjærland, although quite what he would do when he got there was another matter.

His eyes grated like sandpaper on glue. Dozing, let alone sleep, was impossible. For below him was the land of his forefathers and this was the first time he had seen it.

Hundreds of granite islands clad with spruce and bracken stretched northwards, protecting the coast as far as he could see, each inlet sheltering an armada of rowing boats, cabin cruisers and fishing smacks. These were people of the sea - solid, dependable people like the granite upon which they had built their homes. Proud men like his grandfather.

He thought of the photograph in his office and imagined his grandfather working his way across the glacier that he had described so often in his letters, roped to other men, chipping at the ice with his axe, an outdoor man like himself. David closed his eyes, but his mind remained hyper-active, revolving endlessly around his company, its financial situation and Pete Henriksen.

He reflected on the success of his jazz concerts at the Fest. Seconds later he was worrying needlessly about Septimus and the future, about what financial wealth might do to him. He shifted his position. His back was aching after so many hours aloft. Worst of all was the knowledge that he owed his new-found financial security not to his own efforts, but solely to the violent death of a man he loved, but had never seen.

The increased power of the engines brought him out of his reverie. Moments later, the aircraft touched down at Bergen and rolled to a halt at Gate 22.

David disembarked and strode through the modern lounges, grateful for the opportunity to stretch his legs. Other passengers hurried past him. Eventually, he joined the queue at the passport control booths. The woman at the window seemed as if she was in a dream. He waited briefly, then stepped forward to the window.

Stella Kristenssen knew as soon as the alarm clock erupted that she should not have stayed up so late. Four hours' sleep was not enough for her but the party had been fun and her boyfriend had been in a particularly good mood. They had danced until two in the morning and she had asked him back to her apartment for a nightcap. After that, he had made love to her like a Greek God. She had lain awake, thinking about it until nearly four o'clock, trying to recapture in her mind each caress. Eventually, she had fallen asleep, warm and pleasured on his arm.

Despite taking two painkillers, her headache had not abated by the time she reached the airport immigration office. She had not read the morning newspapers and had read the notice about an American murder suspect in only the most cursory fashion. For a while she kept her eyes peeled, but after counting no less than eleven Larsen's among passengers off the first three flights, her usual alertness dissipated.

By one o'clock, she had slipped into automatic pilot. By one-fifty, when the passengers from Flight SK 516 from London began pouring out, her mind had again returned to the previous night's lovemaking.

Lost in memories of the way her lover had teased her, brushing his lips over her thighs and stomach, then turned her over expertly running his tongue up her spine, she routinely stamped the passport in front of her. Blissfully unaware that the man who smiled and thanked her was David J. Larsen, the most wanted man in Norway.

Chapter Four

July 1, 1.50 p.m. - 11.50 p.m.

Cutting through the quiet streets behind the Grand Hotel in Oslo, George Vito was in an apprehensive mood. Aware of the common Norwegian aversion to giving foreigners any form of control over their lives, he sensed that his meeting with the Superintendent of Mines, at least initially, might not be as satisfactory as he would wish. Not that it mattered. He had a full house to play.

Striding jauntily along a street dominated by the soulless granite and glass buildings of the government quarter, he turned into Pløensgate and headed for the Ministry of Industry. He sensed that hiring a detective agency to investigate the background of the Chairman of the working committee evaluating his application would almost certainly prove judicious.

Vito was not impressed by the Superintendent of Mines, a small ratlike man with a neatly trimmed beard, who liked to give the impression that he was constantly in a state of deep thought.

The Superintendent coughed, his eyes darting about the room so as to avoid direct eye contact. Even as the man drew breath, Vito knew what the man was going to say.

'Bad news, I'm sorry to tell you, Mr. Vito.' The high pitched voice underlined all that Vito had surmised about him. 'As you know, staking a claim correctly in accordance with Norwegian law gives you the right to exploration of the site. However, in the case of foreigners, that does not automatically guarantee that the Ministry will subsequently grant licences to extract and export any minerals that may be discovered.'

Vito watched him impassively. Whine, whine, whine. The man was pathetic. A flicker of a smile crossed Vito's lips. He almost hoped it would be necessary to play his ultimate card.

'So you see,' the Superintendent droned, 'it was only after the most careful thought that the Minister, most reluctantly and regrettably I should say, accepted the advice of the State Pollution Control Authority. I'm afraid he feels it advisable under the provisions set out in the Mining Act of 30 June, 1972, Number 70, to, ah, turn down your application.'

Vito slid his fingers into a side pocket and withdrew a small leather case, taking from it a nail file.

'And the specific grounds for refusal?'

The Superintendent stood by the window and sighed, as if

commiserating with him. 'Solely environmental concerns, Mr. Vito. I believe the experiences of the Greenland government after allowing your company to extract lead and zinc from beneath the ice cap had much to do with it.'

Vito inspected the nails of his left hand. 'I see.'

He had half expected the conversation to turn to the Black Wilf Mine. It had been an unfortunate business. Large concentrations of dissolved metals had seeped into a fjord, polluting it almost beyond recovery. What the hell did the jerk expert? Put in a mine and you get tailings. Simple as that. The politicians didn't complain when they took their share of the profits, though.

'Tailings do represent a problem, I agree, but there are many ways …'

'The Minister is aware of that,' the Superintendent interrupted. 'Unfortunately, he is quite adamant.'

Vito popped the nail file back in its case and looked directly into the Superintendent's eyes. 'Superintendent, I would like you to go back to the Chairman of the Pollution Control Authority and suggest that he re-advise the Minister.' Leaning forward, he spoke with the authority of a man unused to taking "No" for an answer.

'The Chairman can say that he's reconsidered, made a mistake, confused us with another corporation, whatever the hell he likes. Just so long as he does it. And I suggest that you personally persuade him that Schneider Barr has great experience in this field, that there will be no pollution in Fjærlandsfjord.' He paused to let the point sink in. 'We understand that this is a sensitive region. We're conscious that Fjærlandsfjord is on the edge of a national park. You have my personal guarantee that it will not be affected.'

'I understand what you are saying, Mr. Vito, but I have no influence over the Minister. I do not believe he …'

Vito ignored him. 'What is more, Superintendent, we have now completed our survey for the road tunnel under the Jostedal glacier. As you know, that will end years of lobbying by the people of Fjærland. It will link the village with Lunde, Skei and the outside world. Everything is ready. Construction work can begin in a couple of days.'

He leaned forward, menacingly. 'If we build that tunnel, it's going to save the Norwegian Roads Directorate the best part of fifteen million dollars. But get this, I represent Schneider Barr, not Santa Claus. I want a return on our investment and that means an exploitation licence for the mine. Fast.' He straightened his back, smirking. 'After all, I'm only asking for fair treatment, Superintendent. I don't think that's particularly unreasonable, do you?'

The Superintendent leaned back, stroking his beard, his hand shaking. 'Certainly, I will inform the Chairman of what you say, Mr. Vito. I do feel bound to tell you, though, that he is most unlikely to be swayed in his decision.'

'Then let me help you try to persuade him, sir.' Vito moved into top gear. There was only one way to deal with obstructive civil servants. 'Schneider Barr is a very powerful organisation. It is also the principal financier of Planet Watch, an equally powerful environmental organisation, as I'm sure you're aware.' Vito smiled, his lips pressed tightly together.

'Norway's decision to resume whaling is not exactly popular with the rest of the world. It would be a simple matter for Planet Watch to organise a worldwide ban on all Norwegian products.' Vito's eyes drilled the Superintendent into the back of his chair.

'Manufactured goods account for one-third of this country's exports, I believe. I doubt the Minister would wish to jeopardise that for the sake of one mining licence.'

The bureaucrat struggled for words, his jaw slack, dismay spreading across his face. 'I ... Neither the Chairman nor the Minister will succumb to threats, Mr. Vito. Never.'

Vito stood up, placed his briefcase on the desk and snapped open the locks. Taking out a bundle of photographs, he leaned forward and waved them under the Superintendent's nose.

'Then let me explain, my friend. I am not going to allow some jumped up little jerk of a politician to stop me sinking that mine. Understand? So you tell the Chairman of the Pollution Control Authority that unless he wants to kiss goodbye to his career, he'd better change the Minister's mind and change it fast.' He stabbed his finger at the photographs. 'As a senior member of the Christian Democratic Party, I'm sure he'll be more than keen to maintain his image as a good, clean-living Norwegian.'

Vito paused, his nerves as taut as a panther's prior to the kill. 'Drinking in a homosexual club full of National Front racists in London is hardly a stepping stone to an assured political future. Especially when he's on official, Christian Democratic business.'

Eyes narrowed, he leaned forward to within a few inches of the Superintendent's face. 'Now, if I don't have that exploitation licence in forty-eight hours,' he breathed, 'I'll see that this little bundle of pictorial sleaze goes to every publication in the land.' Slowly, he straightened his back and smiled. 'It'll be like throwing fresh blood to a shark, Superintendent.'

David Larsen collected his baggage and pushed his trolley through the green Customs channel, absent-mindedly sauntering into the terminal's spotless but impersonal main hall. He glanced briefly at the first editions of the evening papers, intrigued to note that he partially understood the 140-point headlines: '*Politiet søker Dynamitt-mannen*' and '*Hvor er Dynamitt-mannen?*' Had he guessed that they referred to him, he would have been mortified.

Nor did he realise, as he changed money at the Bureau de Change and walked towards the taxi rank, that he was fortunate not to have been arrested. For neither the police nor the newspapers had managed to obtain a photograph of him and few people in Norway took much notice of a written description, especially when it was for a six foot male with blonde hair and blue eyes. Indeed, the description could just as well have fitted the taxi driver who insisted on practising his English during the twenty-five minute journey to the Bryggen Maria, the hotel near the downtown area of Bergen where he had booked a room.

He was equally fortunate when he checked into the hotel. The receptionist, a slim woman of about twenty-five with dark, curly hair, noted his description but did not react in the way that Chief Inspector Ingstad might have wished. Jokingly, she merely asked whether he knew that he was notorious.

'Notorious? How's that?'

'You're in all the newspapers, Mr. Larsen. You look just like the man the police are looking for. They've nicknamed you the Dynamite Man.'

He smiled and filled out the registration form. 'The Dynamite Man, eh? That's very complimentary of them.' He glanced at her suggestively. 'Guess there's only one way to find out, huh?'

She laughed, tossing her head knowingly.

'Just the one night, Mr. Larsen?'

'Yeah. I guess so.' He smiled. She was an attractive woman. If he had not been so tired, he would have asked her to dinner that evening but he knew that it was pointless. He was jet-lagged and would have been poor company. Tomorrow evening, if he was still around, would be a different story.

Picking up his room key, he glanced at the man checking in next to him. His neck was as thick as a telegraph pole. Strange how some people never took off their sunglasses, even indoors. Not until the man had completed the registration form did David notice that the fourth and fifth fingers of his right hand were missing. The remaining fingers and thumb, he thought, moved remarkably like the mandibles of a stag beetle.

Upstairs, he threw his bag onto the bed and luxuriated in a steaming hot shower. When he returned to the lobby thirty minutes later, the receptionist had gone, replaced by a pimply young man who gave him a street map of the town.

Stepping into the sunshine, he strolled along the waterfront and turned into a narrow alleyway darkened by overhanging garrets that had once been the hub of the old Hanseatic trading centre.

More than twenty hours of breathing the recycled air of airports and aircraft had left him dehydrated. Driven by thirst, he paused at a bar for a glass of lager. For a while he sat with his face upturned to the sun, relishing its warmth. But when he realised that he was in danger of falling asleep, he rose to find the man with the missing fingers standing at the entrance to a souvenir store, obviously in need of fresh air like himself.

David nodded but received no response. With his bald head emerging from thick waves of greying hair, the man had the appearance of a circus clown, an effect enhanced by a General Custer moustache and the plastic yellow sunglasses. Except that the mirrored lenses reminded him more of the state police in Minnesota.

David hurried on, savouring the smells of Bergen's famous fish market. Paul Stryn's office was on the first floor of an anonymous office block in the business district, a short distance from the harbour. The lawyer looked at him quizzically.

'So you are here? Welcome. I was not expecting you. Not so soon.' He spoke in a clipped, fussy way, each consonant carefully pronounced. A correct, prissy man, more English than the English, David reflected.

'I'm sorry, I called from the hotel for an appointment …'

'Yes, yes, but have you not seen the police?'

'The police? No. Why?'

Stryn threw up his hands, then clapped and wrung them despairingly. 'My dear fellow. It's a miracle you're here. I'm amazed they allowed you into the country.'

'Sorry, I'm not with you …'

'The police. They've put a watch on every port and airport in the country for you. Look, old chap, you'd better come through to my office and we'll decide what to do.'

David followed him, weaving past desks strewn with paperwork, conscious that the typists were staring at him. His mind was reeling. This was the second time he had been told that he was wanted by police. What was it the girl at the hotel had said? The Dynamite Man?

As Stryn held open the door for him, he remembered the headlines at the airport. Something about police seeking a dynamite expert? He sank uneasily onto the hardback chair by Stryn's desk, a chill sweat breaking out along his spine.

Stryn sat opposite him and leaned forward, placing his elbows on the leather-topped desk and pressing his fingers together like church steeples.

'We must decide what to do, but first, tell me - how did you manage to get through immigration?'

David looked nonplussed. 'I didn't do anything. I just walked up to the passport control like everyone else.'

'You mean you actually presented your passport and nobody said anything?'

'Sure. Why not?'

Stryn leaned back in disbelief, shaking his head. He began to laugh. 'I think we must have the most stupid security forces imaginable. Let us have some coffee and I'll explain. You obviously haven't the faintest idea of what's been happening here.' Chuckling to himself, he rose from his desk and called for the coffee.

'I'm afraid this may be rather painful for you but it is important that you understand your position fully. You see, your grandfather was not the only person to die in the fire. Six other people, including two children, also lost their lives. At first, the police said the fire was probably caused by the fumes of heating fuel igniting, but this morning a completely different story emerged.'

The lawyer reached across to a side table, picked up the morning newspaper and tossed it across to David.

'According to these reports, the police subsequently discovered fragments of a bomb and several hand grenades at the scene. They say there were as many as four separate explosions, that your grandfather and the - how shall I say? - the two neighbouring families were murdered by a pathological killer'

David gasped. 'Murdered? I had no idea …'

'Neither did anyone else and I deeply regret having to break the news to you. However, the position is this. Unfortunately, you answer to the description of the wanted man. Moreover, the newspapers claim that he is an American citizen, allegedly in debt, who stands to benefit from the deaths. You will appreciate that your letter stated that you could not raise the cash to come here and that my firm provided you with credit pending the release of your inheritance, your bank having refused to do so.' Stryn paused as a secretary brought in the coffee and waited for her to close the door.

'Sugar?'

David shook his head. 'No thanks, I'd better have it black.'

Stryn handed him a cup and leaned back in his chair. 'The only remaining question is whether you were trained in the American army as an expert in high explosives.'

'Sure I was, but …'

'And you run a demolition company?'

'Right.'

Stryn waved an arm melodramatically, as if speaking to a jury. 'There you have it. Quite clearly, you are the man the police wish to question.'

'Look, this is insane ...'

'Nonetheless, you are unquestionably the 'Dynamite Man' to whom the press refer.' The lawyer held up a hand, bidding him to remain silent. 'Please, do not worry. If you can demonstrate your innocence, there is nothing to worry about.'

'My innocence? Of course, I'm innocent. I wasn't even in this country when my grandfather died.'

'Can you prove that?'

'Of course, I can. I was ... well, I'm not too sure exactly what I was doing. In Minneapolis, I guess. Levelling an apartment building to make way for a new superstore.' He yawned and paused to think for a moment. 'Anyway, we had a jazz session the night before my grandfather died ... was killed. On the seventeenth.'

The lawyer did not answer but waited for him to continue. David wiped the back of his hand across his forehead. He could scarcely believe that this was happening to him. A suspect? It was lunatic. The police had to be out of their minds to arrive at such a conclusion. Dazed by the impact of what he had learned, he asked for more coffee.

'Look, I play in a jazz band. The Kandi County Vanguard, y'know? That night, we played until way after midnight. I don't know what time my grandfather was killed but there's no way I could have flown to Norway to murder him, even if I'd wanted to. Anyway, you know the kind of relationship we had.'

The lawyer smiled. 'I believe you, but I think we have to knock this on the head immediately. If we don't sort it out now, anything could happen. The immigration authorities may never allow you into the country again. The police could start extradition proceedings - anything.'

'What do you suggest?'

'My advice to you is to let me arrange an appointment with the police and, if you agree, we will see them together. They may hold you for questioning while they corroborate your story but perhaps we can keep that period to a minimum.'

'Shit! You mean I'm to be locked up because some idiot cops have fouled up? That's really great.' David rose from his chair and paced up and down.

'I understand your feelings but I promise you it is the most sensible approach. Perhaps if you let me have the details of anybody who can corroborate your movements beyond doubt, I could ask the police to check them prior to the appointment. Do I have your approval?'

Reluctantly, David agreed. Racking his memory, he compiled a list of names, thankful that he had brought his address book with him.

When he had finished, the lawyer asked a secretary to contact the witnesses with an urgent request that they substantiate any verbal comments with written statements sent by fax.

That done, he turned back to David and opened a folder, dog-eared and tied with red tape

'Now, before I telephone the police, let us get back to the real reason for your visit here.' He extracted a handful of documents from the file. 'I really am most sorry about your grandfather. We acted for him throughout his life, you know. As a matter of fact, I came to know him quite well. He was a prolific writer.' He smiled. 'As a consequence, I know more about you than you could ever imagine. Now, if you could sign these, we can finalise the probate.'

Unable to suppress a yawn, David signed between the pencilled crosses that the lawyer had marked on the documents, exhaustion washing over him. He was past thinking. All he wanted was to sleep. The thought of hours of interrogation by police appalled him. He sighed, only vaguely aware of what the lawyer was saying.

'I presume that eventually you will be travelling to Fjærland?'

'Yeah, I'd like to see where my grandfather lived. He wrote me every couple of weeks, so I feel as if I know the place intimately already.'

'And do you have any idea of your plans?'

'Oh, I guess I'll sell the hotel and the land.' David raised a hand to his mouth in an attempt to smother another yawn. 'I need the money and I already had an offer from the company that was doing a deal with him.'

Stryn looked surprised. 'The company …? You mean that your grandfather was going to sell, anyway?'

'Sure. To a multinational property company called Schneider Barr Incorporated. Apparently, they want to extend the hotel and rebuild a Viking settlement to attract tourists.'

'But this is impossible. Most unusual.' Stryn shook his head, clearly puzzled.

'Unusual? How so?'

'Perhaps it sounds arrogant of me to say so, but I have heard nothing of any such talks. I cannot understand why your grandfather didn't consult me. He was a consummate correspondent on all matters remotely legal.'

'Well, all I can say is that this guy, George Vito, told me that his company, Schneider Barr Incorporated, was on the point of signing a contract when he died. He said the Norwegian government and the National Tourist Authority were also involved. I guess they'd confirm it.'

Stryn laughed, shaking his head again in disbelief. 'I cannot imagine that he would not have told me. I'll certainly contact them.' He scribbled a note on a pad and gazed out of the window. 'It really is most odd. If all this were true, it would have been all over the village. Fjærland is a very tiny place. I would have heard about it from Katrina - she's the manager of the hotel, you know.'

'Sure.' David noted that he called her by her Christian name. 'You know her well?'

'Indeed, yes. A delightful woman. Beautiful, too. A divorcee of great elegance.' He grinned, sheepishly. 'As you may have gathered, I'm rather fond of her. The strange thing is that she is something of a fanatic on the environment. Conservation, all that sort of thing. If anybody had mentioned extending the hotel, she would have told me, even if your grandfather hadn't mentioned it.. I go up to Fjærland quite often, you see.'

David felt his eyes closing. His neck muscles slackened and his head dropped until his chin touched his chest, then jerked up again uncontrollably.

'Yeah, yeah. I understand.'

'Look, my dear fellow, you're obviously exhausted. I think the best thing is for me to accompany you to Fjærland as soon as we've cleared up this police business. I need a few days off, anyway. Fjærland is quite spectacular, you know. A few days in the mountains would do me good.' He laughed and winked. 'Not to mention the opportunity to see Katrina again.'

'That would be great. I'd appreciate it.'

'In the meantime, I'll see what the Tourist Board have to say. Then, we had better contact the police.'

Having fed the dynamite story to the nationals in the early hours of the morning, Tor Falck had managed to snatch a few hours sleep but when he had strolled into the offices of the *Balestrand Posten* just after nine o'clock, the News Editor had greeted him with a face like an old lime and whispered: 'Editor wants to see you. There's going to be blood on the carpet. Yours.'

Falck knew what to expect and was not disappointed.

The Editor ranted at him for more than an hour, threatening to fire him for giving a local scoop to the opposition. He had read the Riot Act and told him that if he ever passed on a single line of copy to another newspaper, magazine, radio or television station, he'd be out. Finished. On the scrap heap.

With an eye to his future security, Falck had apologised and promised that in future he would abide by the rules, mentally adding "until the next time". Like a man who mentally strips a woman while at the same time assessing the value of her clothes, he reflected smugly that given the significant boost to his bank balance, a little blood on the Editor's carpet had been a small price to pay.

When the fuss had died down, he sat among the journalists and layout staff who had gathered round the Editor's desk for the mid-afternoon editorial meeting, his eyes smarting from the smoke of his cigarette.

A forty-a-day man, he exhaled twin plumes of smoke from his nose and reflected that the prime concern was how best to throw forward the dynamite story so that it would be fresh the following morning. Falck was not sure. The evening papers had boiled, broiled, braised and barbecued the immigration angle. There was not much meat left on the bone.

The Editor glared at him.

'Falck?'

He thought for a moment, again dragging on his cigarette.

'Look, so far the Dynamite Man - Larsen - hasn't shown up. That means all the morning papers will be saying it was a false alarm or that he's slipped through the net. If he's not turned up by nine o'clock tonight, it has to be the latter.'

The group listened attentively, some taking notes.

'Now, I have a different idea. First, there's no photograph of Larsen. We can castrate the police for that. We can ask how they could possibly put out a general alert when there's almost no hope of anyone being able to identify him. I mean six foot tall, blonde and blue-eyed? The police must have been inundated with calls. Half Norway answers to that description.'

The journalist shifted his weight, his thighs hanging over the edge of the hardback chair.

'Next, if he slipped through the net - how did he do it? That's a possible feature angle. Meanwhile, I 'phoned a detective agency in Minneapolis this morning. The people there weren't too pleased because it was two in the morning but they thought they could probably have a picture of Larsen on the wire by midnight.'

He looked round the group, then glared at the Editor.

'I also asked them to establish his whereabouts on the seventeenth, eighteenth and nineteenth of June. If Larsen was in the States on any of those days, we have another scoop because it would harpoon Chief Inspector Bloody Ingstad's entire theory.'

Chief Inspector Ingstad was in the shower when the operator at Kvikne's Hotel transferred the call from Bergen to Room 108. It was Nielsen.

'Tell them to hold him.' The Inspector grinned, unaware that he was dripping on the carpet. 'We'll drive down straight away.'

He dried himself and dressed quickly, wondering how, if Larsen had given himself up, he had managed to get through Immigration.'

Working the 'phone for nearly an hour, he dragged a succession of senior Immigration officers from their dinners. By the time he was through with them, it was nearly nine o'clock and his blood pressure was close to coronary level.

When the Inspector and Sergeant Nielsen arrived at Bergen police headquarters after a tortuous drive through the mountains, it was nearly midnight. Larsen was asleep.

A desk sergeant handed the Inspector a sheaf of messages, among them an urgent request to telephone Tor Falck, who had called several times in the last hour. Another was from the FBI in Washington.

'Oh, and Larsen's lawyer, Paul Stryn, is waiting to see you urgently, sir.'

Glancing at the FBI fax, Ingstad's heart sank. Short and typically terse, it read simply: "Several witnesses confirm Subject Larsen in Willmar, Minnesota, June 18. Regards."

Chapter Five

July 2, 9.15 a.m. - July 3, 5.30 p.m.

Unlike David Larsen, George Vito had slept well. Whereas Larsen was unshaven, Vito had showered, shaved, manicured his nails and doused himself liberally with an expensive French aftershave. And as Larsen wolfed a meagre breakfast at Bergen Police Headquarters, Vito was helping himself to a selection of sliced meats, cheeses and marinated herring from the lavish early morning spread at Oslo's Grand Hotel.

Similarly, while Larsen's mood was peevish, Vito was lighthearted. When the telephone in the sitting room of his suite rang, he told the Superintendent for Mines that he was delighted that the Minister had reconsidered his decision.

'Most far sighted, if I may say so, Superintendent.' Modulating his voice to its most unctuous, he reiterated that Schneider Barr would take every precaution to protect the fjord from pollution. 'We'll get our men and transport in right away. Then we can get started on that tunnel of yours, eh?'

Replacing the receiver, he pottered about the suite planning his day. His work in Oslo was done. Miami was seven hours behind Norwegian Summer Time, so he would report to Tripp in the afternoon, then have Delius fly him up to Fjærland.

Pulling on his jacket, he glanced at the front page of the morning newspaper. The hunt and subsequent detention of Larsen had taken him by surprise but there was nothing he could do about it. It was a complication but no more than that. He was unaware that at that precise moment David Larsen was standing at the front entrance to the Bergen Police Headquarters, a free man.

After lunch, he placed his call to Hans Tripp.

'Good morning, Hans. I hope life's as good with you as it is with me.' Vito smiled, waiting for the inevitable sour reply.

'Chill out, George. Update me.'

'Really Hans, you're so impatient.'

'Goddam right I am. This operation's costing megabucks.'

'It's going to make megabucks as well, Hans. Especially now we have the exploitation rights.'

'How d'you pull that off?'

Vito leaned back in his chair, folded one leg over the other and admired his new Italian shoes. 'I guess you could put it down to hard graft. I spent a lot of your money digging into the past business dealings of the Minister for Industry. Turned up quite a file.'

'Don't overdo the expenses, George.'

'Oh, given that the government had turned down our application, I'd say it was money well spent. The Minister reversed his refusal in less than forty-eight hours.'

'Okay, you'd better get the men and transport in as fast as you can.'

'That's already in hand but we do have some problems.' Vito could hear Tripp sucking on his cigar.

'I don't want to hear about your goddam problems, George. I want to know what you plan to do about them.'

'Hans, do I take it you're giving me carte blanche?'

'You consult me on all major decisions and all major expenditures. Okay?'

'Fine. That was precisely what I was trying to do, Hans. Now ...'

'Don't get smart with me, George. Else I'll put you right back on the garbage dump you came from.'

'Sure, Hans, I apologise.' Vito knew when to apply the lubricant, to give the man his head. One day, he'd trample him into his own excrement but for the moment it was better to concentrate strictly on the matter in hand.

'I'd like your advice. There's no road from Balestrand to Fjærland and it's not financially viable to build one. If we ship the men and materials in for the mining project, we'll have to build a new quay. That'll give us a high profile and cause huge problems from an environmental point of view.'

'Screw the environment.'

'Sure, Hans. My sentiments exactly. Nonetheless, we have to play it carefully. Don't forget, the government originally refused the exploitation licence because of our record in Greenland and, second, because the deposit is on the edge of a national park in a prime tourist area.' He leaned forward, inspecting his nails. 'If we are seen by the local or national press to be environmentally insensitive, there'll be a national outcry. That can only mean trouble. Real trouble. Given our record, it could bring the whole project to a permanent halt.'

'What are you saying?'

Vito rose from his chair and sat instead on the edge of the table.

'We're committed to building a tunnel under the glacier. That's part of the deal for granting the licence. My feeling is that we should first complete the tunnel, starting at Lunde at the far end, then bring the men and equipment for the mine in by road.'

'Are you crazy? That would delay the mining operation for five years.'

'Yes, but the copper isn't going to go away. And it means we could tuck away the equipment, accommodation huts and transport at the top of the valley. If we surround the complex with trees, we could keep a low profile.'

Vito sensed Tripp's anger rise. 'Trees? Are y' kiddin'? For Chrissakes, we have an operation here costing fuck knows how much a day and you want to plant fuckin' trees? What is this?'

'Believe me, Hans. We're on dangerous ground, here.'

'Chew my ass. If we build that tunnel, we're doing 'em a ten million dollar favour. You get the men and equipment in there and forget your goddam trees.'

Vito sighed and paced backwards and forwards. 'As you say, Hans.'

'I do say. Now here's what you do. First off, announce the tunnel project to the press. Win us some kudos.' Tripp rapped out his instructions without pause. 'Then you move in the men and tunnelling equipment. Those working at the Lunde end can drive in. Ship those needed for the Fjærland end in on the normal ferry service. High profile. That way, when the time comes to ship in the extra men and the heavy equipment for the mine, the locals will be used to a little activity.'

'I'll get right on to it.'

'You do that. Just remember, I want a fast return on this investment. Now the government have given us the exploitation rights, the rest is their problem.'

'As you wish, Hans. I'm flying up to Fjærland in an hour. If you need me, I'll be at the Glacier Hotel ...'

Tripp, however, had already cut short the conversation. Vito remained at the desk, thinking hard. Maybe Tripp was right. Still, when word of the mine got out, there would be instant protests. It had been a miracle no one had seen the backpack drilling unit or guessed that they were carrying out a geological survey during their months on the mountain.

Maybe, the local people would grow used to the idea of heavy transport and accommodation huts close to the village. They might even associate the idea of a new landing stage with equipment for the tunnel rather than for the mine.

An idea surfaced like a bubble from mud in his mind. He smiled. He'd have the Minister for Industry inaugurate the tunnel on the first day of drilling.

That would be a neat touch. The Minister would have to take the rap at some stage, anyway, because once they began processing the ore, the tailings from the mine would inevitably fill the fjord - a toxic cocktail that was likely to kill all marine life for miles around, just as the Minister had feared.

Smiling at the irony of it, Vito prepared a short press statement and telephoned *Norsk Telegrambyrå*, the national news agency.

David Larsen paused beneath the "POLITI" sign outside Bergen Police Headquarters, relishing the damp sea air. The cell bed had been cement hard and his bones ached. A surly Inspector had woken him well after midnight and interviewed him aggressively. He had not abandoned the interrogation until Stryn produced fax messages corroborating his story from Pete Henriksen and two musicians from the Kandi County Vanguard jazz group.

Despite Stryn's insistence that David be released immediately, the Inspector had refused on the grounds that he would first have to check the witnesses through his own sources. He had not been allowed to sleep until after three o'clock and they had woken him at seven o'clock for breakfast.

Afterwards, the Inspector had guided him to the front entrance and told him that he was free to go.

"I don't know by what devious means you got into the country, Larsen, but what I do know is that if you can slip into this country unnoticed you can slip out of it without being seen. I also know that whenever I'm near you, I smell guilt.'

'Inspector, you couldn't smell shit in a bottle. One day, your so-called sense of smell will get you into trouble."

'I decided to release you, Larsen, because I don't have the evidence I need. Not yet. But I'll get it. So don't think your freedom is permanent. Sooner or later, you'll make a mistake. When you do, I'll be right behind you.'

David ignored him. The man was a fool. He glanced up at the iron grey skies and skipped down the steps to the street below, reflecting that the land of his forefathers had not extended the most hospitable of welcomes.

Arriving back at the hotel, he slept, showered, arranged to drive to Fjærland with Stryn the following morning and lunched in the hotel restaurant. By mid-afternoon, a crowd of reporters and photographers had assembled outside the front entrance, presumably tipped off by Ingstad. Seeing them, David returned to his room, read two chapters of a novel and again slept fitfully, this time until six o'clock.

When he returned to the front desk, the news hounds were still there.

He retreated into the lounge, his thoughts focusing on the receptionist. If he was any judge of character, the twinkle in her eye was sending the kind of signals he could hardly refuse - and they reminded him that it had been a long time since he'd spent the night with Wendy, the redhead from the pizza parlour back in Willmar.

He ambled back to the front desk, waited for the right moment, then caught the receptionist's eye.

'You're having dinner with me tonight, okay? Have to be in the hotel, though. I'm under siege.' He nodded to the pressmen outside and smiled. 'They're at the back entrance as well.'

She hesitated, blushing, then laughed.

'You really are a Dynamite Man, aren't you?' Her limpid brown eyes sparkled like pools in Spring sunshine.

'Just a flash in the pan,' he quipped. 'I was cleared by the police this morning.'

'I know. I read about it. Your picture is on the front page of the paper. You can see it's you even though they've printed black squares over your eyes.'

He eyed her exquisitely small breasts. 'Yeah, I know. I'll tell you the sordid details over dinner.'

'I'd like that but the management don't allow us to mix with guests in the hotel.' She paused, then grinned. 'We'd have to eat out. Look, I'm off shift in half an hour.' She nodded toward the front entrance. 'I have an idea how to get rid of them. Meet me here at seven.'

Thirty minutes later, she handed David a portable radiophone and introduced herself as Isabelle. 'The porter will keep them out but make sure they don't see you. I'll go out of the back entrance, walk round and join them. Give me five minutes, then press this button and say loudly: "He's at the back entrance."'

Overhearing the message, the pack fell for the ruse, tripping over each other in a mad rush to the rear of the hotel. Isabelle seized the opportunity to bundle him into her ten-year-old Ford Fiesta.

Slamming the car into gear, she roared off, taking him on a tour of the city and quizzing him excitedly about his notoriety. Later, they had dined, then drifted into *Den Stundesløse*, a mecca of bars with a disco and nightclub where they danced until midnight.

Afterwards, she drove him up the hill to her neat, wooden-frame home high above the harbour and invited him in for coffee.

She hadn't needed seducing. A passionate woman, she had virtually torn off his clothes, burying her face in his chest, her hands feverishly exploring his body. They made love repeatedly, then drifted into a contented sleep.

In the morning, they drove back to the hotel together to find the press still there, forlornly enduring the drizzle that had settled on the city during the previous twenty-four hours.

Isabelle handed him an umbrella and kissed him on the cheek.

'We'll go in under this. They're expecting you to come out, not go in. And they're looking for a single man, not a couple.'

David smiled. 'You're a dream, Isabelle Sørensen.'

And you're dynamite, David Larsen.'

Laughing, they hurried inside, unnoticed by the media men whose sunken eyes reflected a long, miserable night of waiting for nothing.

The lovers parted then with mutual winks and blown kisses, Isabelle to the office behind the front desk, David to his room.

While packing, he wondered how he could avoid the press when the time came to leave the hotel. He concluded that indefinite evasion would serve only to reinforce the reporters' resolve to find him. If he faced them openly, eventually they would leave him alone. Another story would capture their interest. And, after all, why run? He had nothing to hide.

The doorstep conference lasted no more than ten minutes. He answered the stock questions and, eventually, the news hounds drifted away. Only one persisted, a tall, overweight reporter who introduced himself as Tor Falck from a provincial newspaper near Fjærland.

Strolling along the waterfront past the myriad of small yachts, the breeze slapping their rigging against the masts, they headed towards the coloured awnings of the fish market.

David assured the journalist that debts in Willmar, Minnesota, did not necessarily transform a man into a killer, especially when the victim was your only remaining close relative, someone who held a special place in your heart.

Stubbing out a cigarette butt with his heel, Falck paused at a stall to buy half a kilo of fresh prawns. David waited for him, watching a gaggle of boys dangle their fingers into a tank filled with live lobsters, their claws bound with strips of tape.

It was then that he again caught sight of the man with the moustache from the hotel, standing beneath a coloured umbrella next to a trayful of shellfish. He was still wearing his ridiculous yellow sunglasses. Inexplicably ill at ease, David moved on, recounting to Falck the details of his incarceration at Bergen police headquarters.

By ten o'clock, he had bid the journalist farewell and was chatting amiably with Paul Stryn as the lawyer drove northeast towards Voss and Sognefjord, leaving the drizzle behind them.

As they entered a long tunnel on the outskirts of town, David noticed a white Volvo in the offside rear mirror and reflected that it was strange how, even in fine weather, Norwegian law demanded that motorists drive with dipped headlights.

Later, as they wound along the edge of Veafjord on the main E16 route north, he again noticed the distinctive diagonal bar across the Volvo's radiator. There was something about the car that made him feel uneasy. He wondered whether it might be a police car.

When he mentioned it to Stryn, the lawyer merely laughed and told him not to let his imagination run rife.

Reassured, David relaxed. He opened his window allowing the fresh air, sweet and smelling of mountain pines, rush into the car, only half listening as Stryn discussed the possibilities of taking legal action against some of the newspapers.

'Sensationalist rubbish, most of it, dear boy. Incorrigible propensity to jump to conclusions. The question is whether your reputation has been damaged. We shall have to give that some thought.'

David wished he would not keep calling him "dear boy" and "old fellow". Stryn was good company but his English accent, or rather what he seemed to think was an English accent, was irritating. David shrugged his shoulders. 'Who cares?' he said. 'Let 'em have their day.'

When they reached Voss, Stryn cruised along a boulevard and pulled in behind Cafe Stationen, an old railway station that had been converted into a restaurant, for lunch.

Joining the queue at the self-service salad bar, David was about to take an open sandwich when a hand reached in front of him, the thumb and forefinger extracting smoked salmon salad from the cabinet.

Spellbound, he stared at the awkward, crablike movement and glanced up at the man standing next to him. The clown with the yellow sunglasses stared back at him, his face expressionless.

David waited for Stryn to pay, then quickly crossed the room and joined him at the table by the window. He cut Stryn short in mid-sentence. 'We're being followed and it's not by the police,' he muttered.

'My dear fellow, I really do believe you are beginning to develop a bit of a persecution mania.'

'Look, Stryn. I'm not your dear fellow and that fuckin' asshole over there is following us. Right?'

'Sorry old boy, didn't mean to be offensive. But really, this is quite ridiculous.' He glanced over his shoulder. 'But just as a matter of interest, which, ah, asshole are you talking about?'

David nodded across the room. 'Over there! The guy with the yellow shades. He has three fingers missing from his right hand. I noticed when he checked into the Bryggen Maria.'

'But that doesn't mean he's following you. Voss is a major tourist centre. People come here for all kinds of reasons.'

'Yeah, but don't you think it's strange he should be checking in at the hotel in Bergen at exactly the same moment I arrive?' David speared a prawn with his fork, unconvinced by Stryn's protestations. He watched the clown move to a seat in the far corner of the room. 'And that he just happened to be watching me when I stopped for a beer back in Bergen?'.

'It's just coincidence. Please. Don't get yourself worked up about it.'

Stryn laughed but David persisted. He knew he was right. Every time he saw the guy, he felt uneasy. It was the way he stared at him. Impassively, saying nothing. He'd met characters like that in the Delta Force. Utterly without feeling. They made very good killers.

'He was also in the fish market this morning - when I was talking to one of the journalists - watching us, pretending to buy prawns.'

Stryn seemed at a loss to know what to say. 'It's quite preposterous. That sort of thing simply doesn't happen in Norway. What possible reason could he have for following you?'

'If I knew that, I'd wire his ass to a pound of Semtex.' David reached into his pocket for a pencil and notebook.

'Unless, of course, he is a police officer,' Stryn said. 'Though I must admit he certainly doesn't look like one. Still you never know. Perhaps the police are keeping an eye on you after all, just as the Inspector said.'

David rapidly drew a sketch of the man. 'Do the police have white Volvo estate cars?'

'Absolutely no idea, dear boy. I shouldn't think so. Volvo's are a bit expensive for the police, aren't they? Why?'

David drained his glass and pushed his chair back over the tiled, chessboard floor.

'Because whoever he is, that's what he's driving.'

They sauntered back to the car. The white Volvo stood in a parking bay at the side of the café, its number plates and window sticker indicating that it was a hired car. David memorized, then wrote down, the number and eased himself into the seat beside Stryn.

Driving northwards out of the town, they climbed steadily, the road bordered by waterfalls and chaotic rivers fed by melting snow and ice. They were in the fells now, patches of snow stark against the dull green heathland.

Descending the other side of the mountain range, he glimpsed in the distance for the first time the glacier beneath which his grandfather had lived for most of his life, beyond a range of black hills in the foreground. Stryn rounded a bend and pulled into a layby, smiling.

'Well, my dear fellow, that's it. That's what you're inheriting. Or some of it, anyway.'

David gazed down the steep hillside at the fertile plain and the great Sognefjord below him, the surface of its green waters whitened by the reflections of the clouds. Its grandeur was breathtaking.

'Not bad, eh?' Stryn waved a hand. 'Norway in a nutshell. A hundred and twenty miles long. Longest fjord in the world. Deep, too. More than 4,200 feet at it's deepest point.'

David did not answer. He thought of his friends back in Willmar who were also of Norwegian extraction, who had never seen the country of their origin. Far below him, the small town of Vik fanned back from the fjord's southern edge, hemmed in on three sides by mountains brooding under a heavy sky.

Stryn moved back to the car.

Katrina … Fjærland is on the other side. We take the ferry from Vangsnes, at the end of the headland to the right.'

Driving along the narrow coast road, they arrived at the ferry point at one-thirty. They had just missed the ferry. It would be another thirty minutes before the next one. While they waited, Stryn pointed out the landmarks.

'The town to the northwest, under the high mountains, that's Balestrand. Used to be a favourite resort with the English salmon lords at the turn of the century. It's about fifteen minutes by ferry from here.'

'And Fjærland?'

'Another fifty minutes. Balestrand lies at the mouth of Fjærlandsfjord, opposite to Hella on its eastern bank. Fjærland itself is at the far end of the fjord.' Suddenly, David stiffened. He nudged Stryn and nodded towards the staging area.

'End of Lane Six,' he muttered. 'The white Volvo.'

Stryn turned to see for himself. 'Yes, I see. But you really shouldn't read too much into it, you know. The fellow could quite easily be a *bona fide* tourist or businessman.'

'I'll believe that when they prove the world is flat.'

The ferry approached the jetty, its propellers churning the water. Climbing onto the upper deck, Stryn pointed to a lifeboat and laughed.

'See, the ferry bears my name - *m/v Stryn* from Måløy.'

His words fell on deaf ears. David's attention was focused on the quayside where several members of the crew were remonstrating with a driver who had tried to jump the queue.

The shouting over, they motioned the last few vehicles on board and the ferry's engines rumbled. David stared across the widening gap of water. The man in the white Volvo had been left behind.

They changed ferries at Hella. David stood on the upper deck, staring at the mountains ahead, coal black peaks capped with snow and cloud. Despite the chill north wind blowing directly off the glacier, he preferred to be on deck. He shivered. It was as if the narrowness of the fjord and the steepness of its walls were acting as a funnel for the wind.

Soon, the fjord widened. Ahead, the sun broke briefly through the clouds to bathe a narrow strip of land in warm light, contrasting sharply with the ice-cold whiteness of Bøyabreen and Supphellebreen, the twin tongues of the glacier above the village.

The ship's siren echoed sonorously across the water, the unrippled surface mirroring a cluster of red and white houses on the shoreline.

David felt his heartbeat quicken. If anyone had asked him then to describe his thoughts and emotions, he would have been unable to answer them. For the emotions that stirred within him reached back through the centuries to Viking times and beyond. It was as if his very seed was as old as the massive, granite walls of the fjord itself.

This was where he was from, where his grandfather and great grandfather, and their fathers before them, had lived for centuries.

Fjærland. The name of the village rolled easily off his tongue. 'Fyairland,' he murmured, savouring each nuance of the word. He grinned, the neat houses, bright red in the sunlight, and the sands of dark green spruce evoking in him a sense of overwhelming belonging and joy. From some deep place within him emerged the recognition that he had come home.

Nosing up to the jetty on the western bank, the ferry shuddered to a halt, its black bow opening like the mouth of a humpback whale. David was filled with an excitement that he had not felt since his childhood. He grinned at Stryn and they returned to the car.

'The hotel is just up here on the left,' Stryn said, steering over the ramps and turning right onto the road leading to the village. 'No more than a couple of hundred yards.'

They swung past the sign announcing the Glacier Hotel into the car park. David eased himself out of the car, stretched and wandered round the hotel gardens. It was difficult to believe that the three-storey clapboard building belonged to him.

Hitherto, the idea of owning a 60-bed hotel with a restaurant seating 150 guests had merely amused him. Now that it was a reality, he began to calculate. If the place was fully booked and they charged seventy-five bucks a night, that would be $4,500 a day or $135,000 a month. Not including the restaurant potential. It made the most optimistic forecast for the demolition business back in Willmar look pallid.

He studied the front of the building. Two flights of wooden steps led to the front porch. On the righthand corner of the building, circular balconies in the form of a steepled rotunda reminded him of Hitchcock's *Psycho*, although there was no sinister aura here. Set against the fjord and its mountain backdrop, the building exuded warmth and old-world charm.

From the balcony of his second floor suite, he looked northwards up the valley towards a line of wooden buildings strung along the banks of the fjord, to Bøyabreen and Supphellebreen. Somewhere in the folds of those mountains, an unknown terrorist had killed his grandfather.

The water of the fjord was a pale pea green, cold and glacial. He gazed down at the garden directly below his room. A gardener was mowing a croquet lawn. The hotel receptionist, a woman of about twenty-five, had changed into shorts and a T-shirt, and was sunbathing by a flowering shrub at the water's edge. On one of several white-painted benches, two men were engrossed in conversation.

David caught his breath, his scalp tingling with apprehension One of the men was wearing mirrored sunglasses. The other was George Vito.

'Everything okay?'

'No problems.' Centaur stretched his legs and leaned back, looking up at Larsen standing by the hotel window. 'Guess, I wasn't expecting him to go to the police.'

'There was nothing we could do about that. Incidentally, how come you weren't on the ferry with him?' Vito sensed the man next to him stiffen. He was never at ease in Centaur's company. The man was dangerous and had an uncanny knack of generating fear and anxiety around him.

'Flat tyre.'

'No matter. He's here now.'

Centaur did not answer. His attention was focused on honing the four small blades of a device known as a broadhead, a deadly attachment for the bolt of a crossbow.

'I guess protection, acting as a bodyguard - it's not your scene, huh?'

'Right.'

'I'm grateful. I wouldn't have wanted anything to happen to him. He's worth a lot of money to us.'

Again, Centaur declined to answer. He held up the broadhead and admired his handiwork. Fitted to a bolt and fired from a semi-automatic crossbow with a draw weight of 130 pounds and a velocity of 250 feet per second, it would kill a man at seventy-five yards. The blades of the broadhead, or bleeder, were designed not just for penetration but for haemorrhage.

Once embedded, they could not be extracted from a wound, only pushed through it. Centaur grunted with satisfaction.

Vito took a sidelong glance at him. Centaur was a man who took orders and carried them out with ruthless efficiency. Conversation was not his strong point. When Vito had first met him on joining Schneider Barr, he had made the mistake of asking him his name. Centaur had quietly hooked a warped index finger into his waistcoat and with tremendous strength almost lifted him off the ground, breathing a warning never to enquire into his background again.

'Call me Centaur,' he had said. 'And don't ever make the mistake of thinking half of me is a horses' ass.'

He had laughed then, a chill grating noise from the bottom of his throat. In all the years he had known him, George Vito had never again heard Centaur attempt a joke or laugh. But then, Centaur was not prone to humour. He was, after all, a professional assassin.

Chapter Six

July 3, 5.30 p.m. - July 4, 10.15 a.m.

Each afternoon between five and five-thirty, Katrina Hagen took tea in the Piano Room. Of all the public rooms in the Glacier Hotel, this was her favourite. The light from the tall windows, the polished parquet floor, the furniture and the oil paintings gave it a lived-in elegance that spoke as much about her own character as that of the hotel. For Katrina was a homemaker, a generous and hospitable woman who enjoyed comfort and style. Sitting by the bay window, she was forced to confess that she felt no great liking for the two Americans she could see talking in the garden.

The smart one, Mr. Vito, was not too bad. An attractive man, he was courteous and always immaculately groomed, though strangely disconcerting. There was something about him that was unnatural. When he smiled, it was with the fixed grin of a politician in election year, his grey-green eyes humourless and as hard as marbles, as if he was looking through you.

The other man, Mr. Centaur, who rarely spoke, was completely soulless. Like a dead man in a living body.

Katrina walked back through the main lounge into the lobby. Framed photographs of nineteenth century mountaineers and colourful weavings adorned the walls. Paul Stryn was standing by the reception desk, choosing postcards.

'Paul, welcome back. How lovely to see you again. Is your room all right?' She took his arm and led him into the lounge. The words poured out in a torrent. 'I've put you in your old room, especially. When did you get here? How long can you stay?'

'As long as you'll have me, Katrina.'

'Come now, you know I never want you to leave.' She laughed, happy to see him again. He was a kind man. Handsome, too. It was a pity that he was so proper and pedantic because they had many common interests, not least mountain walking and sailing. She guided him to a leather sofa by the log fire.

'Sit down and let me look at you. It's been an age since you were last here.'

'An eternity. Each moment a lifetime.'

'Silly man.'

Stryn beamed, flushed with pleasure. 'I hope I shall see more of you this evening.'

'I'm not sure how to take that, Paul.' Her eyes twinkled mischievously. If he had lived in Fjærland or even Balestrand, they might have grown close, but living in Bergen he might as well have been in Australia. She was simply not prepared to live in a city.

'So Paul, Have you brought this Dynamite Man with you?'

'I have.'

'Judging by the newspapers, he sounds as if he's every woman's dream,' she teased. 'Is he as hunky as they say?'

Stryn laughed. 'Hunky, Katrina? What a dreadful word! No, he looked distinctly fragile this morning. Anyway, he's not for you. I have a suspicion you might disapprove of him.'

She leaned forward and ruffled the lawyer's hair playfully. 'Paul, you're jealous.'

'My dear Katrina, of course I am jealous.' He smoothed his hair. 'Will you dine with us this evening?'

Katrina cocked her head to one side. 'Of course, but I'm afraid Tor will be joining us. It's a long-standing arrangement.' She smiled, apologetically. 'Never mind, tomorrow we will go for a walk. Just the two of us.'

The moment David Larsen set eyes on Katrina Hagen, he knew she meant trouble. Bristling with efficiency, she was too self-assured for her own good, a career woman clearly sensitive to the merest hint of chauvinism. He also knew he would bed her at the earliest opportunity.

Taller than Isabelle in Bergen, she was slim and sensual, her dress and movements so elegant as to evoke in him a sense almost of cruelty. In the parlance of some Texas drillers he had known, what Katrina Hagen needed was a bit of rough. And he would be more than happy to provide it.

Katrina smiled, her eyes troubled and wary.

'I'm delighted to meet you, Mr. Larsen. I'm sorry you were not made more welcome on your arrival in Norway.'

David grinned, his gaze surveying her figure blatantly. 'These things happen, I guess.'

She was probably concerned about her future, he reasoned. Worried as to whether he would keep her on. Troubled about his plans for the hotel.

'I'd like to thank you for attending to my grandfather's funeral arrangements. I really appreciated that.'

'It was nothing. I was pleased to be able to do it. I was very fond of him.'

Abruptly, she turned on her heel, calling over her shoulder. 'Come, let me show you round the hotel.'

David nodded. Katrina Hagen had class. No doubt about that. She also had one helluva kissable neck and a figure that made his groin churn.

She guided him through the sumptuous lounges and showed him the Piano Room and the adjacent Billiard Room, its shelves crammed with books in several languages. Chatting amiably, she steered him back to the reception area through the Fireplace Lounge, so-called because of its antique tiled fireplace. She pointed out the family photographs hanging on the walls, then led him upstairs.

David followed, his eyes riveted to the contours of her legs and buttocks. When she had shown him the entire building, they retreated to the office. She tried to show him the accounts, but he waved her away.

'Leave that to Paul Stryn,' he said. 'He can have an accountant deal with them.' He smiled and eased himself into an armchair, his manner relaxed. 'You've done a good job here, Miss Hagen.'

'Thank you. I have - how do you say? - a vested interest. The hotel is a second home to me.'

'It shows. It's a second home to me, too, I guess.' David laughed. 'So, as we appear to be living together, what d'you say to dinner this evening?'

She smiled. When she spoke, her voice was polite but determined. 'There is no need to ask, Mr. Larsen. I have arranged for you to dine with Paul Stryn and another good friend of mine, Tor Falck. I believe you have already met.'

Given the rough treatment that David Larsen had received at the hands of the police and press, Katrina reasoned that he might not be best pleased to find himself dining with a local reporter, but the arrangement with Tor was long-standing and she was relieved that neither he nor Mr. Larsen showed any signs of animosity at the dinner table.

They sat overlooking the rear gardens, David recounting his experiences since his arrival. When he mentioned that someone had been following him to Fjærland, it was as if he instantly regretted it. Tor questioned him closely but David was evasive, muttering that it was probably just the police keeping an eye on him.

A waitress dressed in a simple white lace blouse and burgundy skirt brought individual dishes of smoked salmon, scrambled egg and caviar. Katrina seized on the interruption to steer the conversation towards David's plans. She apologised for raising the matter at the dinner table but added that she was naturally anxious about the future for both herself and the staff, and whether he intended to make changes in the running of the hotel.

Explaining that his financial circumstances left him no option but to place both his grandfather's land and the hotel on the market, he tried to reassure her. 'Believe me, you have no cause for concern. The jobs of the staff are safe. That will be part of a deal, a condition of sale.'

'I suppose it was to be expected,' Katrina said. 'There will be changes, of course. It is sad - but I think inevitable.'

Stryn reached for the bottle of Chevalier-Montrachet and refilled her glass. 'I shouldn't think so, old girl. They can hardly improve on what you've created here.'

For a moment, no one spoke, the buzz of general conversation in the dining room and the scraping of cutlery on plates accentuating their own silence. Katrina smiled. Paul was always so gallant. She turned back to David. 'Will you advertise?'

'No need,' he answered. 'I've already had an offer.' The waitress replaced his empty plate with a bowl of cauliflower soup.

Katrina looked at him, quizzically. 'Are you going to share the secret?'

David laughed. 'Sure. George Vito. You know, the natty dresser? He's made an offer I can hardly refuse. I'm seeing him in the morning.' He paused to sip his soup. 'He's from a company called Schneider Barr Incorporated. I thought you would have known, Miss Hagen.'

Katrina remained silent, her lips tight with disapproval.

Stryn coughed politely, concern creasing his brow. 'You haven't signed anything yet, I hope?'

'Not yet. Why? What's the problem?'

Falck pushed his bowl away, wiping his mouth with a napkin.

'The problem, Larsen, is that Schneider Barr is a multinational mining company…'

'Mining? Vito told me they specialised in overseas property development and tourism.'

'Maybe he did and maybe they do, but primarily Schneider Barr is a mining company. Ran into trouble a few years back after polluting the Greenland coast. Its environmental record leaves much to be desired.'

David sensed trouble. His entire future was riding on the sale to Vito. The last thing he wanted to hear was anything that would jeopardise it - and this sounded ominous.

'What happened exactly?'

'Oh, five, maybe six years ago, the company won a licence to extract lead and zinc near Melville Bay on the northwest coast of Greenland. They called it the Black Wilf Mine. Quite appropriate as it turned out.' Falck drained his beer glass. 'Unfortunately, the mine was located at the top of a fjord not unlike Fjærlandsfjord.'

'So what does this have to do with selling my land? They're not planning to set up a mine here, are they?'

'I doubt it, but it's not impossible,' Falck said. 'Certainly, they couldn't start without permission and, unless they've kept it very quiet, we'd probably know if the government had granted them a licence. But let me finish. When Black Wilf had been in operation for a year or so, the Fisheries Research Department discovered a marked increase in the lead and cadmium content in shrimps and seaweed, as well as in whole fish and fish livers. Not surprisingly, the Greenland government ordered the company to find alternative methods of disposing of its waste.'

Falck ordered another beer and attacked his main course.

'And the result?'

'Apparently, the company made a serious effort to cleanse the effluent, with some success. Even so, the amount of lead in mussels and shrimps was later found to be unacceptable and the government was forced to impose a twenty-mile ban on mussel harvesting.' He paused to shovel a mound of chicken curry and pineapple into his mouth, and to wash it down with a long draught of beer.

Again, silence fell on the table. Katrina gazed through the tall windows. Outside, it was still light, though the valley floor was in shadow. She pushed her meal away and turned to David, her voice laced with sarcasm.

'Schneider Barr sounds a very jolly company.'

David paused. 'It sounds grim, I agree, but there are always two sides to a story. We've only heard the one.'

'The company either polluted the fjord or it didn't.' Katrina's tone was adamant. 'I'm sure it's easy enough to prove.'

'Oh, there's no doubt about it,' Tor added. 'It's a matter of public record.'

Katrina pursued her theme relentlessly. 'Frankly, I cannot understand how you could even think of selling to a company like that.'

'Quite easily.' David said, his voice hardening. 'I don't know about you, but I'm not in a position to turn down the kind of offer Schneider Barr is making. If that meets with your disapproval, I apologise, but like it or not, that's the way it is.'

Katrina looked at him distastefully. Obviously, Fjærland meant nothing to him. He was a typically selfish American, interested only in sex and money. She could tell that by the way he looked at her and she despised him for it. What happened to Fjærland and people like herself was of no account. He would take what he could and then go back to America. Why should he care?

'I think it's despicable. Do you not realise what you are doing?'

'Doing? Come on, take it easy. There are other considerations here.'

'Take it easy? Is that all you can say? You come here and tell us you will sell half Fjærland to an unscrupulous mining company like Schneider Barr, then you dare tell me to take it easy?'

It was not often that she raised her voice in anger and she was aware that the other guests were watching, but she could not help herself. She leaned forward, her eyes fired with indignation and resentment.

'I don't know who these people are or what they are going to do, but a company like that is going to be interested in one thing only. Profits. They will not give a damn about Fjærland or the fjord. Or the people in it.'

Stryn moved to pacify her, but she shook him off, pushing her chair back from the table. 'You may own the hotel now but please do not think that gives you any rights here. This is one of the most beautiful parts of Norway. It is our heritage. It is your heritage, too, and it is your duty to protect it.'

David arched his eyebrows, taken aback by her onslaught. 'Hey, what is this?'

Incensed by what she considered his feigned innocence, Katrina glared at him witheringly, then pushed back her chair. 'Go ahead then - sell, you bastard. See what it does for you and your precious hotel.'

Katrina strode from the dining room with Stryn at her heels. Falck attempted to follow her, but by the time the journalist had managed to shift his bulk from the chair, she had long since disappeared. The dining room was humming with the comments and speculation of other guests as to the cause of the argument. Falck shrugged his shoulders apologetically and, twiddling his beard, questioned David more closely about his intentions.

When the gentle probing edged into an aggressive cross-examination, David called a halt, declined his after-dinner coffee. He retired to his suite nursing a distinct sense of injustice and wishing fervently that he had never left Minnesota.

Not surprisingly, he slept only intermittently, his mind chasing the events of the past three days. He had been genuinely surprised to learn that Vito was connected with mining and was aggrieved that the others should perceive him as uncaring, for he was as concerned about the environment as the next man.

Sure, he'd worked the oil rigs and demolition was not readily associated with an immaculate environment, but a guy had to earn a living. And back home in Willmar, he had expended considerable effort on behalf of the Nature Conservation Society, sweating blood in his attempts to clear Foot Lake of European water-milfoil.

So far as he was concerned, Katrina's attack on him was quite unjustified. It was time to assert his authority. After all, he owned the hotel now. She was his employee, not his mistress. Yet.

Exasperated, he tossed and turned on increasingly rumpled bedclothes, eventually climbing out of bed and walking to the open window. It was after three o'clock.

Outside, the early morning sky above the cliffs was light and cloudless, the air as crisp and cool as chilled lager. He drew a deep breath and looked down onto the gardens in which he had seen Vito talking to the man who had followed him from Bergen.

Aside from that nagging aspect, he had no reason to disbelieve Vito. When he had called in at the store at Willmar, he had been perfectly straightforward and friendly. Why should he believe the Norwegians? There was no evidence that Schneider Barr planned to extract ore from Fjærland.

Even if they did, it was no concern of his.

If these people could not treat him decently, he reasoned, why should he change his mind about the sale? It was all very well for them to pass judgement. They were not in debt. They didn't need the money as he did. He closed the window and straightened the bedclothes, determined to see Vito the following morning. The sooner he clinched the deal the better.

Having made his decision, he slept soundly.

In the morning, he breakfasted alone, aware that the other guests were staring at him. Not until he saw a copy of the *Balestrand Posten* in the lounge did he realise why. Again, the paper had devoted its entire front page to him.

In accordance with Norwegian press ethics, the layout staff had blacked out the eyes of his photograph to prevent positive identification, but he was still recognisable. The banner headline was incomprehensible to him, but he doubted that it was complimentary.

Catching sight of Katrina in the lobby, he spread the newspaper on the counter, pointed to the front page story and addressed her with a voice as searing as acid on copper.

'Maybe you could do me the courtesy of translating this, since your boyfriend wrote it?'

'I would be delighted,' she replied, her voice sweet with sarcasm. 'It says: "MURDER SUSPECT PLANS TO SELL OUT FJÆRLAND". Would you like me to read the text as well?'

'Go right ahead.'

She drew a deep breath, her mouth tight and unforgiving.

'The caption under the photograph says: "Debt-ridden American explosives expert quizzed by police about Fjærland bombing".'

'Brilliant! You've excelled yourselves.'

'The text reads: "The American explosives expert who slipped through a police net into Norway and was detained by police in connection with the Fjærland bombings three weeks ago is planning to sell the land he inherited to a multi-national mining corporation.

"It is not yet clear whether the company, Schneider Barr Incorporated, intends to begin mining on the land, which is part of a major tourist area bordering the Jostedal National Park.

"Six years ago, Schneider Barr was widely criticised and fined for polluting a fjord in Greenland. Yesterday, the corporation announced the imminent construction of a tunnel beneath the Jostedal glacier to link Fjærland with Lunde and the outside world."

Katrina tossed the newspaper onto the Reception desk. 'Do you want me to go on?'

'Don't exert yourself.' He pointed dismissively at the front page. 'I guess you feel real pleased about that, huh?'

'There's nothing here that is not true, I think.'

He smiled, bitterly. 'I don't expect to find a private dinner conversation plastered all over the front pages of the newspaper.'

'Then take it up with the newspaper. It is nothing to do with me.'

'I might do just that. They could find themselves facing a very expensive lawsuit.'

'I'm not interested in what you do. I'm just pleased to see you exposed for what you really are. A greedy, uncaring …'

'You wanna do battle with me, no sweat.'

'That is the trouble with you Americans. Always doing battle.'

She struggled to control her anger. 'If you insist on selling our land and heritage …'

'*My* land …'

'*Our* land. Norwegian land,' she contradicted in a tight voice, her eyes angry and defiant. 'You do not give a damn whether the fjord is ruined or not, do you? All you care about is money.'

She picked up the paper and threw it at him. 'I hope the press crucify you. You deserve all you get. Now, if you do not mind, I have a hotel to manage.' She turned on her heel and flounced towards the office.

'Not for long, Miss Hagen,' David called after her. 'Not for long.'

Katrina turned, slowly drawing herself to her full height, and stared directly into his eyes.

'If you wish to dismiss me, it is your privilege,' she said coldly, 'but it will do you no good. It will merely throw the hotel into chaos and give me the freedom to fight you. I shall relish every minute of that. By the time I have finished, Mr. Larsen, your name will be a national scandal.'

George Vito did not take his breakfast in the main dining room that morning, preferring to have coffee and toast brought to his first floor suite, together with the *Balestrand Posten*.

His knowledge of Norwegian, picked up from an advanced audio-visual course, was sufficient to enable him to read not only the morning newspaper, but also Ibsen in the original version. Nonetheless, he was aware that when it came to speaking the language, only the most patient victim could interpret the New York accent that he applied to its pronunciation.

When he emerged from his suite just after nine-thirty, it was with some concern. He was not best pleased to see the report labelling Schneider Barr as an international polluter and, like David Larsen, he was toying with the possibility of instigating a lawsuit against the newspaper.

From his point of view, he was obliged to drop the idea almost as soon as it occurred to him. The Greenland affair had been most unfortunate. They had done what they could but in the last resort, Hans Tripp had indisputably abandoned the Black Wilf Mine, arguing that the world was a big place and that people had short memories adding, in his words, "who the hell goes to Greenland, anyway?"

Wandering down the broad stairway to the lobby, Vito weighed the implications of the report in his mind, absent-mindedly flicking a speck of dust from his sleeve. His stream of thought came to an abrupt halt when Larsen, who had been leaping up the stairs two at a time, almost knocked him over. Similarly preoccupied, he was clearly upset. Vito turned and called to him.

'Good to see you again. David. He placed a hand under his elbow. 'So, you finally made it here. How about coffee in my suite?'

David nodded. Together they mounted the stairs to the first floor landing, Vito talking rapidly.

'This whole business ... it's not exactly been an easy time for you, has it?'

'I've had better welcomes, George.'

'Vito waved towards an armchair called Reception and ordered fresh coffee. 'Sit down, make yourself at home. I was real sorry about the police detaining you... all that nonsense.'

He eased himself into an armchair by the window. 'I guess it's not like the States here. The police are not quite as efficient.' He laughed. 'They sure got their asses burned on this one.'

David smiled and shook his head. 'It's not an experience I'd want to repeat.'

'I don't know what it is with these people. Maybe they just don't like foreigners. I'm glad you decided to sell, though. A good decision, if I may say so. And I wouldn't worry about press antagonism, David. Vitriol is the lubricant of journalism.'

David nodded. 'Maybe. Incidentally, there are a couple o' things I'd like to discuss …'

'Feel free any time. No hurry. We can go through the documentation any time you like.'

Vito rose to answer a knock on the door. A waiter placed a tray of coffee and biscuits on the table.

Signing the check, Vito was aware that David was troubled. He saw the waiter out and turned to him.

'You have to remember that people living in a place like this are unreal, completely isolated from the rest of the world. They have nothing else to think about except the fjord and what happens to it.'

He moved back to the window and looked out. A seagull called overhead, its cry strident in the still air.

'I guess they're a little uptight about more tourism and that's natural enough, but they'll come round to the idea once they realise they'll benefit from it.'

He swivelled back to face David. 'I can see you're wondering how I knew you'd decided to sell?'

David laughed. 'You understand Norwegian?'

'A little. Enough to get the gist of what the newspapers are saying. Sugar?'

'No thanks.' David stirred his coffee, thoughtfully. 'Tell me, who's the guy you were talking to in the gardens yesterday?'

Vito started, his brain transmitting warning signals. 'Centaur? He's just a colleague. Why do you ask?'

'I got the feeling he was following me.'

Vito laughed. 'Following you? What in hell gave you that idea?'

'I don't know George, but I saw him two or three times in Bergen and again at Voss. Then he tried to follow me onto the ferry.'

'Surely a coincidence. He was travelling up from Bergen with some documents about another business matter. Don't let this police business get to you, Dave. It's not worth it. Take my advice and forget it.'

David rose from his chair. 'By the way, you didn't tell me Schneider Barr was a mining corporation.'

'I wouldn't say it was a mining corporation, exactly. We deal mostly in property development, construction and tourism.'

Vito paused, his mind at high speed, exploring the best way to tackle the surprise question. Larsen must have seen the newspaper report, maybe had it translated for him. In that case, he would know about the Black Wilf mine. 'Mind you, we did dabble in mining some years ago. Rather unfortunate experience, I'm afraid.'

'What? Polluting part of the Greenland coast?'

Yeah. Nasty business. We went to extraordinary lengths to clean up. Cost us all our profits in the end. After that, we decided to get out of mining altogether. Couldn't afford to take any more risks. You have to maintain your integrity in business or you're finished, as I'm sure you know.'

'I guess so.' David moved towards the door, nervously. 'I have to be going. Thanks for explaining.'

'Sure, Dave. Anytime.'

Vito was uneasy. Larsen suddenly seemed desperate to leave, as if he was having second thoughts about the sale. What was it the detective agency in Minnesota had said? That Larsen was connected with some conservation group? Christ, that was all he needed, a goddam dome-headed liberal. Vito smiled and moved to intercept him by the door.

'By the way, I, ah ... I had the draft agreement drawn up so it's ready for signature whenever you like.' He pulled a pen from his waistcoat pocket.

'Great. Actually, if you don't mind George, I thought I'd take a quick look at the land first. It's what I came here for, y'know?'

'Fine, fine. No hurry. I'll be here whenever you want,' Vito said smoothly, replacing the pen and showing him out. He closed the door and swore quietly. That newspaper report could jeopardise everything. He would have to work on Larsen fast. Let him see his land, then start applying the pressure. His thoughts returned to mining.

With Tripp on his back on a daily basis, he needed to get the men and equipment in quickly, first for the tunnel, then for the mine. Aware that it was the middle of the night in New York, he nevertheless reached for the 'phone and called his New York headquarters, dictating a string of commands to the answerphone. He smiled. His orders to the Personnel and Transport divisions would galvanise the respective department heads and change the entire future of Fjærlandsfjord.

Now, the office bureaucrats would bring together the initial requirements for the two projects. Until they could build their own quayside, they would have to charter roll-on, roll-off ferries that could dock at the small Fjærland jetty. It would require careful organisation. Global had sub-contracted construction of the tunnel to the Norwegian Roads Directorate. In all, they would need about thirty men to drive the tunnel, working continuously two or three shifts a day. All being well, the men and their equipment would be in place by the end of the week.

Later, when they were ready to start work on the mine, he would ship in one hundred men together with the bunkhouses, canteen and food for their immediate requirements. The same ship would probably carry the hand-held diamond rock drills and high explosives.

After that, they would need bulldozers, heavy lorries, excavators and CAT 793 dump trucks - so gargantuan they were never seen on normal roads, each one capable of shifting two hundred and forty tons of spoil in a single trip.

Vito pushed open the door of his balcony and gazed towards the dark mountains and the glacier. It was undeniably a beautiful place. As soon as the word was out, they could expect vociferous protests. Not least because this would be a full-blown open cast operation.

First, they would shift the overburden, the trees and topsoil covering the mountain, then blast away the rock until they hit the ore-bearing strata.

Vito frowned and walked pensively back into his suite. He would handle those problems when the time came. With luck, the ship with the first consignment of mining personnel and equipment would arrive by the end of the month. By then, the operation would be too far advanced to cancel without a flurry of lawsuits and the loss of millions of dollars.

From his own standpoint, it was imperative that Larsen sign over the land - the sooner the better. It was time to put the frighteners on him. Vito smiled, grimly. Maybe he would call it the White David mine.

Less than ten minutes after David had left Vito's suite, he met Paul Stryn in the lobby and complained bitterly at the way the *Balestrand Posten* had treated him. Stryn massaged his hackles, underlining that the newspaper was a local publication with an insignificant circulation.

Gradually, David's resentment subsided and together they drove past the waterfront stores to Båyaøyri, the hamlet in which his grandfather had settled on his return from the States some forty years earlier.

The charred remains of the three houses had not been touched since the fire. David fell silent, his mind troubled. Idly, he kicked a piece of burned timber, vaguely aware that Stryn was standing a short distance away, respecting his need to be alone.

In the light of day, the blackened wreckage seemed macabre, dwarfed by the magnificence of the mountains. He looked around him. For the first time, he noticed the details of the landscape. Foxgloves burgeoning in the warm sunshine. Cylinders of silage carefully wrapped in black and white plastic covers stacked neatly in fields the colour of emeralds. Over to his right, a line of washing billowed in the glacial breeze and, in the distance, he could hear a dog barking and children squealing delightedly at play.

Above him, bastions of dark rock burst from thickly wooded slopes leading to the flat, snowcapped mantle of Marabreen, an access route to the icy Jostedal plateau five thousand feet above him.

Further round to his right, the chaotic blue-white tongues of ice that comprised the Bøyabreen and Supphellebreen glaciers broke away from the lip of the snowfield like frozen waves tumbling from the skies.

Such was the serenity of the place that he had no difficulty in sympathising with Katrina Hagen's desire to protect it, but to protect it from what? The vague possibility that Schneider Barr would start a mine here? The idea was appalling. Despite her remonstrations, he was keenly aware that it was his heritage. For he could feel in his bones an inexplicable sense of personal history, an affinity with the valley so deep and eternal that it was as if his very soul had been created here.

He turned slowly and walked back to Stryn.

'Y'know Paul, what I can't figure is why my grandfather decided to sell all this to Vito.'

Stryn caught his breath and snapped his fingers. 'He didn't. I meant to tell you, but after last night's episode with Katrina, I'm afraid I forgot. The National Tourist Board returned my call yesterday afternoon. They said they'd checked their records but knew nothing about a proposed agreement, either with Schneider Barr or George Vito.'

David whistled and shook his head, bewildered. 'There's somethin' strange goin' on here. I don't know what the hell it is, but first my grandfather is murdered. Then, I'm told he was about to do a deal and sell his land just before he died. Yet he never mentioned it in his letters either to you or to me. Now I hear there was no deal in the first place. So why would Vito say there was?'

'I don't know, It's a mystery, I agree.'

'And why would he have me followed?'

Stryn moved as if to protest but David stopped him. 'Hold on, I know you think I'm crazy, but I know I was followed and I saw Vito talking to the guy after we arrived at the hotel. Okay, he claims he's just a business colleague but I'm not so sure.'

'You really should take people at face value more, David.'

'Maybe, but this guy looks more like a circus clown than a businessman.'

David's mind moved into top gear.

Another thing - when I saw Vito after breakfast, he couldn't wait to have me sign that agreement on the sale. How come he's so keen?'

'I really don't know ...'

'What bugs me is that if there's no deal with the Tourist Board, what does he *really* need the land for?'

He fell silent, dismayed by his own questions. It was as if he was being torn apart. Three and a quarter million dollars was a lot of money, too much to turn down.

'I have to sell,' he muttered. 'There's no alternative.'

Stryn waved his hands in a gesture of despair.

'What can I say? It has to be your decision. All I can say is that in the circumstances - be careful! And don't sign anything without letting me see the documents first.'

David nodded. 'Right. Y'know, Paul. I have a sneaky feelin' that Vito's lying. Maybe it's time for a face-off.'

Chapter Seven

July 4, 11.30 a.m. - 1.00 p.m.

From the moment David Larsen had stepped from the eight-storey Bergen police headquarters into the welcome freedom of the city drizzle, Chief Inspector Odd Ingstad had been subjected to a campaign of whispered jibes and jokes, many of which centred on the Inspector's nose, once renowned for its unfailing ability to detect a criminal. Now, according to those who delighted in sniggering behind his back, it couldn't sniff out a bad egg in a bottle. The Dynamite Man and the Fjærland bombing, they chuckled gleefully, had blown up in his face.

'You're a mite testy today, sir,' Nielsen commented cheerily, when he bumped into the Inspector in the Kripos canteen.

'I've been a mite testy for thirty years, Nielsen, so why don't you try to find the place where your brain lives and come up with some answers instead of auditioning for vaudeville?'

Nielsen smiled. 'Always the funny man, aren't you, sir?'

The Inspector ignored him and pointed to a sheaf of papers in the Sergeant's hand. 'What's that?'

'It's a subsidiary report from Forensic. I was just bringing it up to you.'

'In the canteen?'

'Actually, I was going to grab a beer and a sandwich first ...'

'Forget your stomach, Nielsen. I haven't got all day.' The Inspector turned on his heel and clattered up the wide, stone steps leading to his second floor office. Nielsen followed, his face a portrait of resignation. Ingstad motioned him to a chair. 'Well, go on, what are you waiting for?'

Nielsen sighed. 'Seems as if we might be up against a professional terrorist organisation, sir.'

'Any other good news?'

'The lab's positively identified the residues of explosive. It's consistent with the use of high performance plastic explosive.'

'Very helpful.'

'Yes but wait. The timing device was the same type as one used by Ahmed Jebril's mob - the Popular Front for the Liberation of Palestine.' Nielsen licked his finger and flicked through the report. 'According to this, the bomb blew up a TWA plane in mid-air.' He searched the text with his finger and began reading:

"The Boeing 727 was on a flight from Athens to Rome. On detonation, the device blew a hole in the fuselage, through which four passengers were sucked to their deaths. Accident inspectors are of the opinion that the incident was a retaliation by Libyan backed terrorists. This follows American naval action against Libyan ships and aircraft in the Gulf of Sirte the previous week."

Ingstad groaned. 'Which gets us precisely nowhere. First, why would an international outfit like that blow up a group of houses in Fjærland, for God's sake? Second, the fact that whoever did it used a timing device similar or identical to that used by a terrorist group does not necessarily mean that the organisation in question is the guilty party.'

'No, but it means we're up against professional killers. I mean, whoever did the Fjærland bombing either had access to terrorist organisations or the kind of equipment used by terrorist organisations, so it's not exactly a domestic crime, is it?'

'You're thrashing about in the dark, Nielsen.'

The Sergeant shifted his position. 'I suppose we do tend to trample about a bit, don't we, sir?'

Ingstad did not miss the sarcasm but thought better of pursuing it. 'Frankly, I'm still not convinced about that fellow Larsen. I have an instinct about him.'

'Instinct or gut reaction, sir?'

'Very funny. If anybody knew where to get hold of explosives and timing devices, it was Larsen. Knew how to use them, too.'

Ingstad walked to the window and gazed down on the street below. 'Maybe we should just keep turning the proverbial screw until he squeaks.'

'Look, sir, do us all a favour and forget Larsen, will you? If we stay on that tack with the Chief Superintendent in his present mood, we'll both be police history and I've got a family and career to think about.'

'What do you suggest?'

The Sergeant stood up and paced across the room.

'The only link between the explosions and whoever was responsible for the bombing is the helicopter. We know from the military authorities that it wasn't one of theirs, so whose was it? Remember, we checked with all the hire companies and the only machine in the vicinity of Fjærland that day was one hired out by a company in Leikanger to the American pilot, Delius Greenwood.'

'Go on.'

The Inspector returned to his desk and sank into his chair.

'They - the company - said a condition for hiring out the machine without their own pilot was that Greenwood file a flight plan whenever he left the Sognefjord area.'

'What are you trying to say?'

Nielsen leaned across the desk. 'Just this, sir. On the eighteenth, the day of the explosions, Greenwood filed a flight plan to Fornebu Airport in Oslo.'

'Come on, Nielsen. We know that. '

'Yes, sir, but there's more. I checked with traffic control at Fornebu. They say no helicopter with the registration letters L-XRYA landed at the airport that day.'

Ingstad whistled through his teeth, quietly. 'I see. That *is* interesting. In fact, Nielsen, I think you might have made my day, as they say in the movies. We'd better pay this Greendale a visit.'

'Greenwood, sir.'

'Never mind, he's all we've got.'

Sergeant Nielsen moved towards the door. 'Thought you'd be interested in that.' He grinned, pleased by the Inspector's reaction. 'Fancy a sandwich, sir?'

'No, I don't, Nielsen,' the Inspector said, irascibly. 'I've just had one. Don't you ever stop thinking about your stomach?'

When David next saw George Vito, it was with a sense of foreboding. Whereas his instinct exhorted him to sign a contract for the sale of the land and return to Willmar as quickly as possible, leaving Katrina, Falck and Stryn to sort out their own problems, his intuition suggested that he would do no such thing.

His conscience told him that Katrina Hagen's comment about Fjærland being his heritage was legitimate and that if he wished to be true to his deepest beliefs he ought not to sell - not, at least, to Schneider Barr Incorporated.

Troubled by these thoughts and the prospect of losing three and a quarter million dollars for the sake of an environmental principle, he tapped nervously on the door of Vito's suite.

Vito waved him into the room with a stream of small talk. David settled into the armchair by the table. A lingering smell of burning drew his attention to an ashtray filled with charred matches. So far as he could remember Vito did not smoke. Nor was there any evidence of cigarettes.

There was something strange about that. When Vito had visited the store in Willmar, he had sat in the back room similarly burning matches for no apparent reason. He would have paid little attention to the idiosyncrasy had it not been for the curious expression in Vito's eyes. It had been an almost manic gleam. Had he not been drawing Vito's portrait at the time, he probably would not have noticed it.

David studied the man again. Even without his jacket, he was debonair. Yet the fancy, coloured waistcoat, the watch chain, starched cuffs and enormous gold cufflinks suggested a practised rather than natural sophistication.

'So, David, what do you think of your land now that you have seen it? Quite impressive, is it not?' Vito balanced on the edge of the desk.

'Sure is. I couldn't figure out where the Viking village you mentioned is supposed to be, though.'

'Ah. That's because right now it's no more than a few mounds of earth.' Vito curled his fingers into the palm of his hand and, almost effeminately, examined his nails. 'Obviously, we haven't started work on the project yet but Skarestad - that's the name of the site - is at the junction of the two valleys leading north out of Fjærlandsfjord.' He crossed the room and flipped open a slim, brown leather briefcase.

David did not answer. He leaned back, resting his cheek on his hand. Vito was talking continuously, as if worried that silence might provide a chance for second thoughts.

'So, how do you feel about our deal, now? Ready to go ahead? No point in stalling, I guess.' He retrieved the contract from the briefcase.

'David drew a deep breath, aware that if he wanted the answers to the questions that concerned him, this was the moment to ask.

'You know, one thing puzzles me. As I recall, you said you were about to do a deal with my grandfather when he died …'

'Right. He was to have signed a contract the next day.'

'And the Norwegian government and National Tourist Board were part of the deal?'

'Not exactly part of the deal. They're not putting money into the project but as you saw from the documents I showed you in Willmar, they sanctioned it. I guess they're as keen as anyone to see the benefits that the Viking project will bring.'

David leaned forward, sitting on the edge of the chair. 'That's what I don't understand, George. You see, when the Tourist Board talked to my lawyer, Paul Stryn, they said they'd never heard of you. They know nothing at all about a Viking project here.'

Vito stared at him. 'That sounds like a bureaucratic mixup to me. What can I say? I think that must be a case of Tom not knowing what Jack is doing.' Vito placed the contract on the table in front of David and took out his pen. 'I can assure you they are very much involved.' He smiled and pointed to a space at the end of the document. 'Now, if you could just sign here, we can get the boring paperwork out of the way…' He laughed, uneasily.

David leaned back in the armchair, ignoring him. 'You seem very anxious that I sign, George. I get the feeling you're pressuring me.'

'Not at all. I apologise. It certainly wasn't my intention to give that impression. There's no need for haste, I can assure you.' Vito placed the pen beside the document. 'Of course, we do have a great deal riding on the deal. I make no secret of that. We've had to pay many of the local contractors in advance and it's not exactly a small investment, as I'm sure you'll understand.'

David rose from his chair. 'Payment in advance? Before you even own the land? That sounds a little presumptuous, not to mention risky.'

Vito smiled and waved his arm as if to suggest that such methods were unavoidable.

'Business is full of risks. You know that as well as I do, David. Unfortunately, predicting the future is the biggest hazard of all …'

'No matter. Look, you offered me three and a quarter million dollars for the land and the hotel. That seems a fair price and I accept it…'

Vito moved quickly to shake David's hand. 'That's great. I'm really delighted. It's a pleasure to do business with you.'

David backed off, raising his hands to dampen the other man's enthusiasm.

'Not so fast. I said I accepted the price. Whether I want to sell is another matter. When I make up my mind, I'll let you know. Until then, I'm afraid you're just gonna have to wait. Okay?' David nodded curtly and moved towards the door.

'Sure, sure.' Vito watched him, shaking his head, his face souring with impatience and exasperation.

'But don't wait too long.' His voice hardened. 'You can walk out of this room a millionaire or you can be a dumb punk for the rest of your life, Larsen. It's your decision. But remember this. You're the one who has to face the bank manager.' Vito's eyes narrowed with menace. 'I'm not waiting around forever. It's an easy equation. I suggest you figure it out for yourself. Fast.'

David wheeled round angrily. Striding back across the room, he snapped Vito's chin back with his thumb and forefinger, almost lifting him from the ground.

'You ever talk to me like that again, deadbrain, you'll lose your voice for life. Understand? I can face my bank manager any time I choose.' Releasing him, he prodded Vito in the chest so forcefully that he fell backwards into the armchair. 'Not that it's any of your goddam business.'

David leaned over him, his mouth as tight and white as an old scar.

'You're not the hot suit you pretend to be, Vito. It may come as a surprise to you but I don't need your deal. Not half so much as you seem to need my land.' He backed off and opened the door. 'You want me to sign that contract? You sit around and wait, my friend. When I'm good and ready, I'll cable you.'

If George Vito had looked in the mirror immediately after David had left, he would have seen a face drained of colour, the combined result of fury and fear. Fury because in the old days, back in New York, anybody talking to him like that would have been an automatic contender for a concrete collar; fear because he knew that he had underestimated Larsen.

It had never occurred to him that he might respond as he did, or that he might have inherited money as well as the land and hotel, and would therefore be in a sound financial position. Clearly, he could no longer regard him as a pushover, prepared to sign anything so as to write off his debts. That in itself was a serious setback. The only alternative was to tighten the screw. If he could not induce Larsen to sell willingly, he would have to adopt more forceful tactics.

Standing by the window, he heard the rotors of a helicopter chopping the motionless air, the sound reverberating between the steep sides of the fjord. Probably it was Delius returning from another survey. His thoughts returned first to Larsen, then to the Hagen woman. Maybe he could persuade her to exert a little pressure on Larsen? The promise of increased tourism and an extension to the hotel would surely be in her interest.

Turning away from the window, he sat absent-mindedly in the armchair, toying with the box of matches on the table. If that ploy failed, he would have no option but to take a tougher line. Striking a match, he gazed into the flame and set himself a mental target to force through the deal within the next twenty-four hours.

His decision reached, he pocketed the matches, returned to the lobby in search of Katrina and found her huddled behind the Reception desk poring over a pile of hotel invoices.

Smiling broadly, she showed him into her office as if he was a friend from the other side of the world rather than a rather obnoxious guest asking for ten minutes of her time. They chatted amiably about the capriciousness of the weather, the success of the season and future plans for the hotel.

'Tourism, of course, is a staple of many national economies', Vito said, blithely. 'I believe that when the income from North Sea oil ultimately begins to dwindle, as it undoubtedly must, tourism will assume the same importance for the Norwegian economy. As you know, work on the tunnel is about to begin and we - that is to say my company, Schneider Barr - are planning to reconstruct the Viking settlement that was discovered here some years ago.'

Warming to his subject, he repeated the story he had told David. 'You know, build a Viking farm with houses, equipment, tools and boats. Show people the way it used to be. In short, capitalise on Viking traditions so as to exploit the tourist potential. Put money back into the local economy.'

Katrina sat at her desk, smiling politely. 'I see. And you think I can help in some way?'

'Maybe you can, Miss Hagen.' Vito said, exuding charm. 'You see, our first objective is to enhance Fjærland's tourist potential. The tunnel and a reconstructed Viking village will be excellent ways of achieving that goal.'

Katrina studied him, her face set in a professional smile. 'A museum dedicated to the glacier might be a better way but that's just a personal ambition.'

'Quite so. And, if I may say so, one deserving of serious thought. Indeed, perhaps I might recommend it to my superiors. We are, of course, hoping to buy David Larsen's land so that we can accomplish this task.'

'Really?' Katrina pushed aside a bundle of papers and leaned forward, her elbows on her desk.

'Yes, ma'am, and as you know we're bidding for your excellent hotel, although let me say right away, that will not involve any staff changes. Absolutely not. No, our aim is to attract more visitors to Fjærland, to extend the hotel to accommodate them and in that way plough some money back into the local economy.'

Katrina smiled sweetly. 'Yours is a very benevolent company, Mr. Vito. Profits, I suppose, do not enter into it?'

Vito laughed. 'You're a shrewd businesswoman, Miss Hagen. Naturally, Schneider Barr would hope to make a small profit, as well.'

'Or even a big one. Please, don't patronise me, Mr. Vito. I wasn't born yesterday.' Katrina glanced demonstratively at her watch. 'How exactly do you think I can help?'

Vito crossed one leg over the other, cupping his knee in his hands. 'As you may imagine, we have invested a good deal of time and money into these projects. Unfortunately, their success depends first on being able to buy David Larsen's land and, secondly, the hotel. However, for some reason, he seems undecided and frankly our time is running out. I wondered whether you might help to persuade him? It would be to our joint benefit, I assure you.'

Katrina did not answer immediately. When she did, her initial friendliness had dissipated. Her voice was as cold as tempered steel.

'I was under the impression that Schneider Barr was a mining company, not a public benefactor?'

Vito started, surprised by her animosity. 'Really, you are too hard on us. It is true, we were once involved with mining but nowadays …'

'You think only of the people of Fjærland and how you can help them. Very worthy. Incidentally, why do you have a helicopter here?'

Vito gazed at her. She had a brain and a tongue like a razor.

'A mere convenience. Happily, we are a large international company and executives above a certain level receive certain privileges … I'm sure you understand.'

He ran his eyes over her body. She was an attractive woman, too thin, but she had a good figure and he wouldn't throw her out of bed if she happened to be there. Not that there was much chance of that. He imagined her as a frustrated she-cat, a woman who needed taming.

'Perhaps you would care to have dinner with me this evening?'

'Thank you, but I think not, Mr. Vito.' Katrina shuffled the bundle of papers and signalled that the interview was at an end. 'As for persuading David Larsen to sell the hotel and his land to you, I regret to say that I have no influence over him.' She pushed back her chair and moved to the door, holding it open. 'Even if I had, I could not possibly consent to such a request. It would be quite unethical …'

Vito stood up but remained by her desk. When he spoke, his voice was tight and threatening.

'I'm sorry you should feel that way.'

'I am sorry, too, but I confess to being suspicious of your company's intentions. We are a small village and a simple people here. There is no interest for us in an organisation like yours. I have a most unpleasant premonition that you will bring us only trouble.'

Vito stared at her, anger rising inside him like steam in a kettle.

'A pity. I had hoped that you would cooperate.'

Instinctively, he reached inside his pocket for the box of matches. He thought for a moment, then striking one held it to a piece of paper. As the flame caught and raced to his finger tips, he sneered at her.

'Just a piece of paper, Miss Hagen. Wood burns just as well.' His eyes, hard and cruel, bored into hers.

'The hotel *is* made of wood, is it not?'

Shocked by the menace behind Vito's threat, Katrina sat at her desk for several minutes, shaking. Never before had she experienced such evil. She thought of calling the police but abandoned the idea, aware that apart from the remnants of burned paper on her desk, she had no evidence of what had taken place.

Vito would merely deny everything and she would be made to look foolish. Instead, she picked up the telephone and asked the restaurant staff to bring her a pot of strong coffee, her thoughts racing off at tangents. She would tell Tor, of course. He would know what to do. Perhaps, he could also find out whether Schneider Barr had really stopped mining as Vito had suggested. Not that she believed anything Vito said any more.

Hanna, the new waitress, brought her coffee. When she had gone, Katrina stood by the window gazing across the fjord. In the sunlight, the water was a cold, translucent green, discoloured by natural glacial deposits. She forced herself to think more rationally.

Taking Vito's threat to burn down the hotel as her starting point, she reasoned that if he needed her to help persuade David Larsen sell his land, it could only be because he had failed to do so himself.

Why then, she wondered, was the acquisition of the land, or the hotel, so important to him? It was certainly not because he wanted to reconstruct a Viking village and help the people of Fjærland. No, George Vito was clearly desperate to buy the land and she suspected that his motive sprang from greed rather than benevolence.

Sipping her coffee, she called the *Balestrand Posten* and learned that Tor was out and would not be back before evening. The news left her with a sense of isolation and helplessness. She pushed the coffee away half-finished and wandered into the hall, absent-mindedly rearranging the forest of walking sticks, ice axes and climbing ropes in the container by the stairs.

When David Larsen emerged from the lounge, her first inclination was to avoid his gaze, but on seeing him she felt a degree of remorse. She hated the unpleasantness that had arisen between them.

'Mr. Larsen, I want to apologise to you. I should not have spoken to you as I did. I hope you will forgive me.' The words gushed out in a stream of embarrassment. David seemed as taken aback by her apology as by her initial tirade.

She smiled, awkwardly. 'Perhaps you would care to have lunch with me?'

David hesitated, torn between simmering anger and the chance to lay the foundation for her seduction.

She placed a hand on his arm. 'Please do. All this unpleasantness, it … it is horrid. And please, call me Katrina.'

'Okay, though I have to say I'm a little confused.' He gazed down at her. 'Y'know, not two hours ago, you were saying you wanted to see me crucified by the press - as if I haven't been already from what I can gather.'

'I know, I am sorry. I have not been myself lately.' She led him back into the lounge, her eyes routinely swivelling from the hand-painted frieze to the antique cabinets and chairs, checking for dust. There was none. 'Let us have a drink. I think I need one.'

'Need one? This early in the day?' David flopped casually onto the light brown leather sofa. 'That sounds like a crisis.'

Katrina laughed, half-heartedly. 'It is.'

She straightened a flower arrangement and walked round the group of armchairs to poke the log fire. 'You are not the only one with whom I seem to have arguments. I have just walked away from a most unpleasant encounter with Mr. Vito.' She called for a waitress. 'I shall have a sherry. And you?'

David ordered a whisky and ginger.

'Good idea.' She turned to the girl. 'Bring two whiskies with ginger and forget the sherry, would you Hanna? We will lunch in about twenty minutes.'

Slipping elegantly into an armchair, she again grew conscious of his muscular build. It gave him an air of strength and dependability. With his fair hair and sunburned face, he was an attractive man. She caught him glancing at her legs and fought off the faint stirring of excitement, pulling her skirt over her knees.

David smiled, amused that she had noticed. 'So, what have you been arguing about with George Vito?'

'You, I'm afraid.'

'Oh? And what have I done now?'

She waved a hand, dismissively. 'It's not so much what you have done as what you haven't. Vito tried to use me to persuade you to sell your land to him.'

The waitress placed their drinks on the table.

'Is that right? He seems pretty darned keen to get his hands on it. What did you say?'

'I told him that I had no influence over you. And that even if I had it would not be ethical.'

She raised her glass and looked into his eyes, surprised by the intensity of their blueness.

'*Skål*' ... David.'

'*Skål*. I guess Vito wouldn't have been too happy about that.'

Katrina hesitated. 'That is when he threatened me. It was horrible. He struck a match and set fire to a piece of paper, and then he stared at me in the most menacing way and said that a hotel built from wood would burn just as easily.'

David whistled through his teeth shook his head. 'Wow. That guy's something else.' For a moment, he remained deep in thought. 'I guess I've brought you nothing but pain, huh?'

'Shall we just say that life has not been its normal, peaceful self since you arrived?'

David frowned. 'Y'know, he must be real desperate to get that land because he also threatened me this morning. Told me that if I sold, I'd be a millionaire and if I didn't, I'd be a dumb punk for the rest of my life.'

'And how did you respond?'

'I told him that talking like that to me was an excellent way to achieve a permanent voice loss. That if I decided to sell, I'd send him a cable.'

Katrina laughed. 'Does that mean you're *not* going to sell?'

'I don't know. I really don't.' David paused and sighed heavily. 'See, I have a real problem. Back home in Minnesota, I run my own company.' He laughed. 'I specialise in demolition. With the right explosive charges, I can collapse a 30-storey building into its own basement, but thanks to a general economic downturn, business has been pretty poor. In other words, the company's going broke and I'm being hassled by the bank.'

He reached for his glass, stirred the ice cubes with a swizzle stick and sipped his whisky.

'I am sorry.'

'Until my grandfather died - or was killed - I was facing financial ruin, but he left me some money as well as the land and the hotel, so that danger's over now. There'll be enough money to stop the bank closing the business and foreclosing on a personal loan, but there won't be enough to guarantee my financial security forever.'

'I see.' Katrina nodded, thoughtfully. 'And selling the land and the hotel would provide that security?'

'Right. It would set me up for life. Vito was right. I'll be a multi-millionaire. I guess I ought to be over the moon about that but it's not that easy. I'd like to have the money, that's for sure, but I don't like Vito, I don't like being put under pressure. And I do like Fjærland.' He looked at her sheepishly, and smiled.

'I also thought a lot about what you said last night. Y'know, I'm a hard man. I worked the oil rigs down in Texas. Then construction sites up in Minneapolis and St. Paul. Now, I blow things up. But this morning, something happened to me, deep inside. I stood by my grandfather's house and just stared at the mountains and the valley and the fjord.' He sighed, deeply.

'It's a beautiful place and I felt a deep sense of belonging here. So I hope you'll believe me when I say I really don't want to be a trigger that ruins the valley.'

'I believe you - and I cannot tell you how happy it makes me to hear you say that.'

Katrina's eyes softened. She placed a hand on his sleeve.

'I have spent all my life in Fjærland. To see it destroyed would be to lose the desire to live. Perhaps I understand your feeling of belonging more than anyone. You must feel as if you are being torn in half.'

David nodded. 'Yep. That's exactly how I feel. I can't promise that I won't sell to Vito. I don't know what to do. All I know is that I need time to think.'

'I understand. Do you think we should call the police? About the threats, I mean?'

David thought for a moment but rejected the idea. 'No. You can't prove threats and so far as we know Vito has done nothing criminal. The police wouldn't be interested.'

'Why do you think he is so anxious to buy the land? I can't help thinking that he represents Schneider Barr and that they are a mining and construction company.'

'Whatever their plans, you can bet conservation won't be top of their list.'

Katrina nodded. 'You know, the environment is like a wheel. If you break a spoke, the wheel is weakened. If you break two, it is finished.'

'I suppose it's always possible that Schneider Barr really does want to reconstruct the Viking settlement,' David said thoughtfully. 'Y'know, build a Viking museum, attract tourists and extend the hotel, as Vito claims. It's not a bad idea at that.'

Katrina sat on the edge of her chair. 'And burning down my hotel would help them to extend it?'

'No, I guess it wouldn't.' David grinned at her. 'And, by the way, it's *my* hotel, now.'

She laughed and apologised. 'Now that we do not have to fight any more, would it not be better if you called me Katrina?'

David laughed. 'Only if you call me David, okay?'

'All right, David Okay,' she mimicked, rising from her chair. 'Let us have lunch.'

Chapter Eight

July 4, 4.30 p.m. - 8.30 p.m.

Lunch was most enjoyable. David had been charming, and the smoked salmon and new potatoes were delicious. Katrina thought she detected a lingering tension between them, but she had learned a great deal more about him and his background and, as a result, better understood his dilemma.

Unable to influence his decision about selling the land, she had at least made him aware of her strong feelings about Fjærland and he had appeared sympathetic to her views.

If he needed time to think, she reasoned, that was an immense improvement on his stance the previous evening.

Together, they had examined the possible reasons for Vito's interest but their discussion had been limited to pure speculation. This inability to provide an answer to the puzzle irritated her but just after four-thirty, as she watched Vito and Centaur leave the hotel from her office window, an idea began to form in her mind.

When she saw them climb into the white Volvo and drive off in the direction of the glacier, she hurried into the reception area.

Removing the hotel pass key from its hook, she mounted the stairs as nonchalantly as her pumping heart would allow and slipped into Vito's suite, the sound of blood rushing in her ears.

The room was so immaculate that she could have been forgiven for believing that it was unoccupied. Not a chair or cushion was out of place. There were no clothes strewn about, nor books, nor papers. The only hint of occupancy was a faint smell of burning.

She moved first to the writing desk and flipped open the briefcase, surprised that the combination lock had not been set.

Inside, she found the contract that Vito had prepared for David to sign and beneath it, a slender box containing a dozen or so old coins, some gold, the remainder silver. Judging by the ancient inscriptions on them, she presumed them to be Arabic.

Replacing the box, she riffled through a sheaf of papers but, finding nothing more of interest, crossed the room to the chest of drawers next to the window.

Glancing through it, she noticed David pushing out the hotel's blue and white rowing boat from the jetty. But she paid little heed to him, instead concentrating on the contents of the drawers. A bundle of letters hidden beneath a pile of clothes justified her intrusion into the room. The instant she saw them she knew that George Vito was in some way connected with the Fjærland bombings.

The envelopes were written in a hand she recognised clearly as being that of Ragnar Larsen. They were addressed to David Larsen at Number Fourteen, Quincy Avenue, Willmar, Minnesota.

Quickly, she retrieved the letter. It was several pages long. Skimming through it, she noted that it described the old man's concern at being badgered into selling his property by a smooth-talking businessman whose description could only refer to Vito. Her hands shaking from the shock of the discovery, Katrina hurriedly cast an eye over the rest of the contents.

Another letter, from a Professor Berg at the University of Oslo, was about Viking runestones. For a moment, she was relieved, half persuaded that Vito really did want the land so as to reconstruct the Viking village. But the fleeting hope, for it was no more than that, remained short-lived.

Another document, clearly a geological report, left her in no doubt that Schneider Barr was planning to open a copper and zinc mine in the valley. Pausing fractionally before deciding on her course of action, she gathered up the papers and retreated down the stairs to her office.

Here, constantly peering through the window for fear that Vito might return, she duplicated the report and the letter from Professor Berg, together with one of the letters addressed to David. That done, she dropped the copies into a large envelope, sealed it and placed it in the hotel safe, then hastened back to Vito's suite to replace the originals. Heading straight for the desk, she again glanced out of the window. David was drifting in the centre of the fjord. She slid the documents back into the desk drawer.

Almost simultaneously, she sensed a movement behind her. A chill crept up her spine and her neck stiffened with fear. Uncannily, she knew even without looking that Centaur had returned.

She pirouetted round to confront him. He was standing by the closed door, his massive arms hanging slackly by his sides, his face impassive and his eyes unseen behind the mirrored lenses of his glasses.

Rank terror struck at Katrina's mind, leaving her weak and for several moments unable to utter a word. She reached behind her for support, the palm of her hand moist and clammy.

'I am sorry, I was just …'

'Cleaning. Sure.'

At first, Centaur made no move. Not for thirty seconds or more did he advance slowly across the room.

Katrina gasped. 'What are you going to do?'

He did not answer but stood two feet in front of her, breathing heavily. Crossing her hands over her breasts, she turned her head away from him and tried to move sideways but he intercepted the move and wordlessly blocked her escape.

'Stop it. Please ... let me go.'

She placed her hands on his chest and struggled to push him away, terrified now that he would harm her. Filled with dread, she was conscious only of his dispassionate leering and his forefinger hooked into her blouse.

She felt him pull her body into his, his other hand groping for her buttocks. He tried to kiss her then, a gust of fetid breath floating over her. In desperation, she dropped the papers on the floor, and jerked her knee into his groin, straining with both hands to force back his chin as she had once seen in a television movie, but to no avail.

With a wave of revulsion, she felt his left hand fondling her breast. Her knees weakened and she was aware of a sharp pain as his deformed thumb and forefinger gripped her arm in a crablike grip, swinging her round so that she fell backwards onto the sofa.

Throwing himself onto her, his hands fumbling between her legs, he laughed - a hollow, grating, humourless laugh. She tried to scream but the warped hand that now lay clamped across her mouth prevented the sound escaping.

And reflected in his yellow mirrored sunglasses, she saw the fear written across her face.

Returning to his suite, George Vito heard both the scuffling inside the room and her muffled shout. He frowned and threw open the door. Centaur was lying full length on the sofa, struggling like a warthog on heat with the Hagen woman, who was in a state of considerable distress not to mention disarray. Appalled, he ordered Centaur to leave her alone, then closed and locked the door behind him.

'You goddam idiot,' he barked. 'What in hell d'you think you're doing?' He stepped forward and turned to Katrina. 'What's going on?'

Katrina moaned. 'He ... he tried to rape me.'

She sat up, shaking uncontrollably, pulling her unbuttoned blouse across her chest.

Vito glared at Centaur. 'That true?'

'A little fun, that's all.' He stood by the window, unconcerned.

Vito poured a glass of water and passed it to Katrina. 'Here, drink this.'

He moved toward Centaur.

'I want to know exactly what happened. And I mean exactly.'

'She was searching through your desk.' Centaur nodded to the papers on the floor. 'I thought I'd help her explain why.'

'By trying to rape her? Are you insane?'

Vito fought back his anger. This could wreck the whole operation. He cursed the man. He was an ape. And he cursed Tripp, who, despite his protests, had overruled him, insisting on bringing in Centaur.

Vito bent down to pick up the papers, his mind moving into overdrive. Even if the Hagen woman had not read them properly, she would have seen too much.

The geological report didn't matter. That would be common knowledge soon enough, but the Larsen letters and the letter from Berg were a different ball game. Goddamit, why in hell hadn't he burned them? The letters linked him directly with the bombing and the runes were a secret he had no plans to share with anybody. He stood up, walked over to Katrina and shook her shoulder.

'What were you doing in my room, Miss Hagen?'

'I ... was checking to see if the room had been cleaned properly,' she lied.

'Yeah, with a bundle of papers in her hand,' Centaur interjected. 'The bitch was snooping.'

'Shut up.' Vito turned back to her. 'Well?'

'I didn't read them ...'

Vito rounded on her. 'But you were going to, weren't you? That was your intention. Unfortunately, we'll never know. That presents me with a problem, Miss Hagen.'

'I'm sorry. I ...'

'I'm afraid it's too late for apologies.'

The situation allowed for only one decision. She had to be silenced. But disposing of her could create more problems than it would solve. He turned to Centaur.

'Put her on ice for a while. I'll decide what to do with her in the morning. When I've slept on it.'

Centaur sneered, opened the desk drawer and moved silently behind Katrina. Vito walked to the window. He had no wish to watch. What he did not see, he could not know. He heard a hefty slap and guessed that Centaur had immobilised her with a single blow.

When he next saw her, Katrina was oblivious to her surroundings, her hands, feet and mouth bound firmly with vinyl packaging tape.

'I want her out of my suite as fast as possible. Put her where she can't be found and make sure no one sees you.'

Centaur nodded, his face contorted into a sadistic grin. Vito opened the door, peeped out and turned back to Centaur.

'And when you've done that, soften up Larsen. I want him on his knees. I want him in here tomorrow morning begging me to buy his goddam land.'

After lunching with Katrina, David had read and dozed for a couple of hours in his room, then decided on some fishing. Katrina had excited his interest by telling him that the fjord was alive with cod, whiting, flounder and sea trout. 'You might even equal the record for a one hundred and eighty pound halibut,' she had told him, adding that, if he wished, he could borrow tackle from reception and use the hotel's rowing boat. The middle of the fjord, he reasoned, might also be a better place in which to think.

His first catch was a whiting of such minute proportions that it scarcely warranted being used as bait. He returned it to the water and gazed contentedly along the fjord. The great pinnacle of rock that separated the twin ice tongues of Bøyabreen and Supphellebreen reached into the clouds, its dark walls and snowy crags mirrored in the water.

David drew a deep breath, savouring the warm, clean air. Apart from the occasional slapping of water against the boat and the sound of someone hammering among the cluster of shops and houses on the shore, the fjord was silent. With the warmth of the afternoon sun on his face, he relaxed, mulling idly over his predicament and reflecting on the beauty of the fjord.

He had been drifting for ten minutes or so when the distant whine of a high speed engine intruded into his thoughts.

Not for some moments did he pinpoint its source, a white motorboat powering inconsiderately up the fjord from the south. He watched it, idly, mildly surprised when the hunched figure at the wheel failed to throttle back and nose into the jetty where Vito's pilot had parked the red-and-white helicopter.

Instead, the launch maintained its course and sped along the centre of the fjord, the stern its only contact with the surface, the wasplike whine of its twin engines reverberating between the steep walls of the fjord.

David watched the boat power past him at a distance of no more than ten yards, shattering his peace. Its wake rolled towards the rowing boat, rocking it so violently so that he was forced to cling to its gunwhales, his gaze riveted on the craft as the pilot slewed round in a tight turn.

When David saw the motorboat heading back to within a few feet of him, he shouted a warning but his words were lost to its yowling engines.

Almost simultaneously, he recognised the figure at the controls as Vito's accomplice, the man who had followed him from Bergen.

Fully aware now that the launch's presence was no accident, David stared mesmerised as it wheeled round and bore down on him for the third time, this time missing him by less than a yard.

He watched helplessly as Centaur swung the wheel round so that the launch's wake would have the maximum effect. By the time David had steadied the rowing boat, the clownlike figure had turned in a wide arc and was lining up for a fourth run.

David decided on his course of action, all his senses heightened. Crouching on the flat seat, he tensed, gauging the difference in height between the gunwhales of the two boats.

When the powerboat drew level, he jumped, crashing into the fibreglass well that housed the twin outboards.

Centaur, intent on steering the craft, had scarcely realised that he was on board when David lunged forward, his right arm raised above his head, the muscles locked, his hand as rigid as a board.

Centaur turned full face towards him, startled. Timing his moment precisely as he had been taught while training with Delta in the Florida Everglades, David was upon him before he could react.

Slamming the hardened edge of his palm into the sensitive muscles linking the man's neck and shoulder, he immediately threw himself to his left, at the same time bringing his right elbow hard into Centaur's face.

Then, with his left hand grasping his right wrist, he swung his arm back so that the knuckles of both fists crunched into his right cheek, sending the clown's sunglasses spinning into the well of the boat.

A split second later, David rammed his knee into Centaur's groin and instinctively brought back both arms, his fists clenched ready for steps five to eight. He did not need them.

It was all over in four seconds. Centaur was groaning at his feet, barely conscious. He was lucky. Had it not been for his size and David's precise judgement, he might have been lying there with a broken neck.

David grabbed the wheel, straightened the boat's course and throttled back, steering towards the upturned rowing boat.

He smiled, grimly. If Vito wanted to play games, maybe it was time to give him an expensive lesson.

Bringing the motorboat to a standstill five yards on the Fjærland side of the rowing boat, he pointed the launch's nose at the sheer wall of granite opposite and eased the throttle forward to full, grinning mercilessly. Then, as the power boat picked up speed, he leapt into the water.

Gasping as the glacial water knocked the breath out of him, he struck out for the rowing boat. Despite his efforts he was unable to right it.

Instead, he abandoned it and settled into a fast crawl, aware that no human could survive more than a few minutes in water so cold.

He did not hear the motorboat hurtle into the rocks on the other side of the fjord. Nor, when he climbed ashore, was it anywhere to be seen. Centaur's journey home, he imagined, would be long, cold and painful. If, indeed, he had survived.

Shivering uncontrollably, he ran across the road into the hotel leaving a trail of wet footprints behind him, gratified that the key to his suite was still in his pocket.

Sprinting up the stairs, he unlocked the door and peeled off his clothes, heading straight for the bathroom. Even immersed to his chin in steaming hot water, he was unable to control his shivering for several minutes and not for some time after that did he detect the acrid smell of burnt cloth.

Clambering reluctantly out of the bath to investigate, he wrapped a towel round his waist and walked into the bedroom. A pile of his clothes had been burned and dumped the floor. There was a large package on the bed.

Tearing off the wrapping, he saw that it was fire extinguisher. A typed note attached to it read, simply: 'A warm welcome to Fjærland.'

Tor Falck returned to the cramped newsroom at the *Balestrand Posten* shortly after six-thirty, tired and disgruntled. He had left Balestrand at first light to drive to Oslo. Apart from short visits to Kripos headquarters and the Ministry of Industry, and a late lunch on the ferry, he had spent the entire day in his car.

He would not have minded if his trip south had been more fruitful but it had raised more questions than it had answered. Ingstad had been about as forthcoming as a cat with a stolen chicken and, at the Ministry, he had been unable to talk his way past a low level bureaucrat, who had clearly been briefed to be as unhelpful and evasive as possible.

All Ingstad had been able to tell him was that Delius Greenwood, the helicopter pilot working for Schneider Barr had filed a flight plan to Fornebu airport but had not landed there. It was an interesting snippet of information but it proved nothing. The helicopter was equipped with floats and could have landed in the fjord immediately adjacent to Fornebu airport or at a hundred and one other waterside landing sites nearby.

Falck lit a cigarette and gazed blankly across the fjord, trying to make sense of the lack of information. Ingstad was blundering about like a rampant bull in a cowshed. That was clear. The answer, he suspected, lay with the Ministry. When Ministry underlings were deliberately obstructive, it was usually because they were following the instructions of their masters. That meant that senior civil servants, perhaps even the Minister, had something to hide. And if so, what was it?

Falck's mind revolved endlessly around the four principal components of the puzzle - David Larsen, the police, Schneider Barr and the Ministry. It was as if he were trying to unlock a safe when he knew the numbers of the combination but not their correct order. He forced himself to think logically.

First, Larsen wanted to sell land he had inherited from his grandfather. Second, his grandfather had been murdered, almost certainly by professional assassins. Third, Schneider Barr wanted to buy the land, ostensibly so that they could reconstruct a Viking village. That, he thought, seemed about as likely as finding life on the Sun.

The crucial question was why an international mining company with a turnover of billions of dollars a year would be remotely interested in providing a minor tourist attraction in a village of two hundred people? Answer: they weren't.

Questions tumbled through his mind like beans in a blender. Why then was Vito - and by definition, Schneider Barr - so keen to buy Larsen's land? Had they discovered metal or oil in the mountains? Or perhaps uranium? If so, that might explain why the Ministry was so tight-lipped. Fjærland was, after all, a prime tourist attraction. If they'd granted exploration or exploitation licences, they would want to keep it quiet for as long as possible so as to prepare their case for the inevitable protests.

The more Falck thought about it, the more he was convinced that Schneider Barr was planning to start up a mining operation. A sense of excitement coursed through his veins. Maybe he was on to something big here.

Cupping the flame from his lighter, he lit another cigarette and gazed round the newsroom.

Could there be a link between the death of Larsen's grandfather and Schneider Barr? Was it possible that the company executives were so desperate to get hold of the land that they were prepared to kill for it?

Again, he found himself tormented by the question: "If so, why?" He sensed that he was sitting on a powder keg of a story that did not quite add up and in which every lead was blocked.

Nevertheless, one thought nagged him, taking him back to the events of June the eighteenth. If Schneider Barr could afford to hire a helicopter indefinitely for general transportation purposes, there was no reason why they could not have access to another, the one with the military markings that he'd seen immediately before the bombing.

Yet, if Schneider Barr *was* responsible for the killings, what was the motive? Surely not the mere discovery of oil or metal ore. Nor even of uranium. That was only part of the story. There had to be something else.

If he was any judge, it was probably rooted in corporate greed or personal gain and that, unless he was completely mistaken, pointed either to George Vito or David Larsen.

Unquestionably, Larsen was the better story but instinctively, his mind focused on Vito. He reached for the 'phone, called the Glacier Hotel and asked for Katrina. The receptionist said she had not seen her since she had lunched with Larsen. Falck thanked her and replaced the receiver, a seed of jealousy firmly implanted in his mind.

While Tor Falck mulled over the story in the Balestrand newsroom, David was changing, cleaning his room and disposing of his burned clothes, similarly reviewing the events of the past few days.

His personal mental agony was not so much who was responsible for what, but whether he should take Vito's money and run. Despite Vito's threats, a part of him wanted to do just that.

Another part of him swore that one day, he would ram a stick of dynamite up Vito's ass, detonate it and implode him into his own anus.

Vito, Katrina and Stryn did not belong in his life. Although his origins might have been in Fjærland, his roots were in Willmar with people like Pete Henriksen - good, sane Americans who lived ordinary, undramatic lives.

Wandering downstairs, he asked for Katrina. The girl at Reception said she had not seen her for a couple of hours and suggested that she might have gone home for the evening.

Thanking her, he called Stryn and asked if he would like to join him for a drink. Five minutes later, David was sipping a much-needed beer, urgently bringing the lawyer up to date. Stryn was clearly shocked.

'We had better call the police, old boy.'

'The last time you did that, I ended up in jail for the night.'

'Yes, but that won't happen again. I can assure you of that.' Stryn sipped an orange juice. 'By the way, where is Katrina?'

'No idea. Haven't seen her since lunch. The receptionist said she might have gone home.'

'You lunched with her?'

David shrugged. 'Sure, she apologised for last night. We made up.' He reached in his pocket for a pencil and began to draw. 'Why? Do you object?'

'Of course not. It's just that we had planned to climb up to the glacier this morning. We both enjoy mountain walking, you know. But she seemed so preoccupied that I cancelled it. I was a little surprised, that's all.'

'She had a tough day. First, I laid into her about this morning's newspaper. Then Vito threatened her.' He glanced up from the portrait, checking the angles between Stryn's mouth, eyes and ears. 'She knew he'd threatened me, too. Hardly the stuff for a tranquil mind.'

Stryn nodded, thoughtfully. 'Strange that she should go home, though. Without leaving a message or anything.' He looked at his watch. It was ten minutes after seven. 'We were supposed to meet at seven. We had a date for dinner. I know I'm not the most important person in her life but she would never, how do you say, stand me up on a date. It's most unusual.'

'Maybe she's beautifying herself for you, Paul.' David yawned, exhausted by the day's exertions.

'She doesn't need to do that. She's quite acceptable as she is, dear boy.' Stryn grinned, then rose from his chair. 'I'm going to see if I can find her.'

David drew a line through Stryn's portrait in disgust and ordered another drink. The drawing was terrible. Instead, he began to sketch a bunch of flowers on an antique side table, blooms that were beginning to wilt from the warmth of the fire.

David stared at them with sudden curiosity, and a hint of concern. Hadn't Katrina said all the hotel flowers were either cut from the gardens each day or delivered fresh on the mid-afternoon ferry? That arranging them was one of her favourite pastimes?

Yet the flowers by the fireplace were the same ones he had seen the previous day, when he had first arrived.

Paul returned, flopping into the leather armchair. 'Absolutely no sign of her. Not answering her home 'phone, either.' He toyed with his drink. 'Apparently, she retreated into her office at two o'clock and nobody's seen her since. Most unusual, by all accounts. Girl at Reception says she always lets them know where she is.'

It doesn't figure.'

'What's that, old boy?'

'The flowers.'

Stryn wrinkled his brow. 'Why, what's the matter with them?'

'They've not been changed, Paul. Every day, without fail, Katrina changes the flowers. She told me so herself. Today, she didn't.'

'I say, that's pretty astute of you.' Stryn drained the orange juice. 'I wonder why?'

'I don't know, but something inside me says we should be worried.'

'It's a most unfortunate situation but I can't see what else we can do.

I telephoned the police, incidentally. A Chief Inspector Ingstad left Oslo for Balestrand this afternoon. The sheriff's assistant said he would recommend that he comes to Fjærland on the morning ferry.'

George Vito, renowned for his ice cold temperament, was burning the Larsen letters, struggling to dampen a growing panic.

Katrina's curiosity and Centaur's stupidity had forced him into a line of action fraught with danger. He wouldn't give a snip of cotton for Katrina and her welfare but he was extremely sensitive about his own skin.

Not that kidnapping held any fears for him, providing he was suitably distanced from the action. Personal involvement was a different matter. He bit his lip and stared into the flames, his concerns temporarily receding as a strange sexual impetus took hold of him.

Fire had always intrigued him, even as a boy. He remembered vividly the first blaze he had ever seen, a New York tenement building torched by its landlord in an insurance fraud.

The combination of flames, heat and screaming had excited him rather than horrified him and, to his horror, he had wet himself. He recalled his mother beating him. And the taunts of his elder brother, Danny, still rang in his ears. He was only four years old at the time but the incident marked the beginning of a lifelong fascination with fire.

At the age of eight, he had attempted, with a degree of success, to burn down his school. It was an act directed as much against his teachers as the school itself, for he resented their patronising attitude to the Italian kids, who were in a minority.

The only benefit he had derived from school was a passion for Viking culture. He admired the Vikings for their courage and audacity, and their ability to amass vast amounts of money from foreign raids. In them, he saw himself. Like them, he knew that he would strike out into the world to make his own fortune, by fair means or foul.

Young Giorgio was also intrigued by the Vikings' effective use of fire as a weapon but it was not until he was fourteen years old that he discovered the link between fire and sexual arousal. From that moment onwards, he had dabbled in arson, always willing to do the bidding of Don Antonio's boys. Sadly, Danny and Giorgio's links with the Mafia had so distressed their father, Joseph, that he suffered a nervous breakdown from which he never fully recovered.

Despite Joseph's warnings about the intrinsic evil in the Mafia, Danny and Giorgio paid no heed. Danny had joined one of the lesser New York Mafia families. Giorgio, who was intellectually brighter than his brother, was keen to shed his Italian background.

Insistent that his friends call him George, he drifted towards the business world. Here, his cunning and shrewd eye for a bargain had propelled him towards the markets. His flair and willingness to enter shady deals soon boosted his bank account.

Breathing heavily, he struck another match and stirred the charred leaves of paper with his pen.

An alien sense of frustration and desperation overwhelmed him. Centaur was a fool. Not that his attempted rape of the Hagen woman mattered any more. The essential point was that she had seen Larsen's letters. It was difficult to know exactly what she had and had not seen but he could not afford to take any chances. The stakes were too high. He had to assume that she knew that he had frightened the hell out of the old man and intercepted his letters. And that could provoke a lot of questions.

As to the letter from Professor Berg, it was unlikely that she would have had time to figure out its implications. The difficulty was that he did not know how long she had been in the room before Centaur discovered her. If she had rifled through the other drawers, she might well have seen the Viking coins and put two and two together. That, too, could be dangerous.

Grinding the last of the letters into tiny flakes, he tipped them into a porcelain bowl and was walking to the balcony when Centaur crashed into the room, his clothes soaking wet. Vito wheeled round, furiously.

'What in hell's name d'you think you're doing?'

Centaur halted, momentarily, then sank into the sofa.

'That bastard, Larsen …'

'Jesus, what's happened now?'

'I was softening him up, like you said. On the lake …'

'Fjord,' Vito corrected.

'He got into the boat.' Centaur winced with pain. 'Got me from behind, then totalled the boat.'

Vito stared at him in disbelief. 'Smashed up … Jesus. You're supposed to be a professional, you braindead schmuck.'

Centaur struggled to get up. 'Say that again and you're a dead man.'

Vito stared at him. There was no doubting Centaur's sincerity. His eyes were unflinching, as cold and penetrating as diamond drills. It was as if he were viewing him as a target rather than a human being.

'Okay, I apologise. But get this. I am running this operation and, frankly, I wouldn't spit in your mouth if your teeth were on fire. You're not indispensable. Remember that.'

Centaur sank back into the sofa, nursing his head.

'What's the matter?'

'He gave me a hard time, that's all.'

'He should have broken your neck.' Vito opened the door. 'Now get out of here.'

Centaur obeyed, his eyes mean slits. 'That sleazeball Larsen, he's mine, okay?'

'Sure, but right now I want you to go to your room and stay there.'

Vito closed the door, his head spinning. He wandered into the bathroom and took two headache tablets. It had been one helluva day. His thoughts returned to Katrina. He was left with no option. Centaur would have to dispose of her in the morning.

That evening, Vito dined in his room and watched television. The programmes on the Norwegian State Broadcasting channel, NRK, that evening were excruciatingly boring. Shortly after ten o'clock, his mind numbed by an asinine quiz show, he called New York and spoke to Dick Longman, the head of the Human Resources Division.

Vito was reassured to learn that the young executive had not only received his previous message but had already acted on it.

'We've placed ads for semi-skilled labour in Scotland, England and Wales. My bet is we'll get a healthy response.'

'What's wrong with Norway?'

Longman laughed. 'In my experience, Norwegians are kinda choosy about the type of work they do.'

'It would save the cost of transporting men from the UK.'

'Believe me, George, you'll find it difficult raising a hundred men in Norway.'

'How about Sweden?'

Again, Longman's laugh echoed down the telephone. 'They're worse than the Norwegians. I've been in Swedish hotels there where they're so averse to service jobs they won't even make your bed. No, the UK's the best bet. The government has laid off thirty thousand miners over the last few years and the construction industry is in a helluva mess. They're hungry.'

'What are you offering?'

'British Coal rates plus a twenty per cent bonus for working overseas. They'll work four weeks on, two off.'

'Make it ten days off. We have to cut costs. What about work permits?'

'That's all in hand. We're fixing temporary work permits with the Norwegian immigration authorities. Seems the Industry Ministry put in a request to speed up the procedure. For some reason, they're being unusually cooperative.'

Vito smiled to himself and reached for his nail clippers. 'Excellent. Any idea how long before we can get started?'

There was a pause. 'The ads are scheduled for tomorrow morning's newspapers. Assuming we get the response I anticipate, we'll have the men signed on in two days - by the sixth. We'll start assembling the equipment tomorrow.'

'What about shipping the men?' Vito clipped a nail and drew out a small emery board with which to file it.

'The Transport Division have provisionally chartered a Ro-Ro ferry from the Sørensen Line for the ninth. We have an option to bring that forward by a couple of days if necessary.'

'That means we could have the men in here in, what, a week?'

'Right. Maybe less.'

'Good man. Keep me posted. And have a beer on me.'

Vito replaced the receiver. Longman had done well. Not yet thirty, he was living up to his reputation for being a whizz kid with high ambitions. On the basis of the work he had done in the past twenty-four hours, there was little doubt that his rise to the highest echelons of management would be rapid. Vito opened the door to the balcony and looked out over the fjord.

Lights from the apartments and houses along the shore glowed against the dark shadows of the mountains. The peaks of the mountains and the glacier were bathed in a suffused yellow light. Soon, the scene would be very different. The head of the valley would be bathed in arc lights. Excavators and dump trucks would be trundling back and forth, noisily shifting gears as they picked up loads of spoil.

In the morning, he'd have Centaur dispose of the Hagen woman, or maybe take care of her himself. His breathing quickened at the thought of it. By mid-morning, the ferry would have brought in the men and equipment for the tunnel project.

By then, with luck, he would have forced Larsen to sign the contract.

He moved back indoors. If Larsen still persisted in wavering, he could always forge his signature. As for the Hagen woman's body, once the tunnel engineers started blasting, he'd have Centaur fake an accident or use the rock spoil for a concrete collar.

Chapter Nine

July 5, 7.00 a.m. - 11.05 a.m.

David awoke as he had fallen asleep, his thoughts spinning as if in a maelstrom. Vito had threatened to burn down the hotel. His accomplice had burned his clothes and attempted to drown him. Now, it seemed that Katrina was missing. From all accounts, it was unlikely that she would leave without telling anybody, which led him to wonder whether Vito might have had a hand in her disappearance. In view of the previous day's events, it was not impossible.

Yet, even if Vito was desperate to get hold of his land, for whatever reason, he would be mad to run the risks associated with kidnapping. Trying to use Katrina as a lever to make him sell simply didn't make sense. Beyond their relationship of manager to owner, she had no influence over him. Vito must have known that. If he was involved in her disappearance, it had to be for another reason.

After breakfast, he ambled back to the Reception desk and again asked for Katrina. Once more, the receptionist told him that nobody had seen her since the previous afternoon.

'She didn't sleep in the hotel and she's not at home because I've just 'phoned,' the woman behind the desk told him. 'Perhaps she's on the way in. If she is, she'll be here in the next ten minutes.'

David waited, then returned to the desk. 'She wouldn't have gone hiking in the mountains, would she?'

'Not on her own and not without telling us,' the woman replied. 'She's much too experienced. I suppose she could have gone to Balestrand to stay with a friend. She does that sometimes. She normally lets us know, though.'

David thanked her and strolled into the gardens. The fjord was damp and silent. The ice of Jostedal tumbled blue-white from the lip of the snowfield, ribbons of meltwater cascading headlong down deep gullies carved into sheer cliffs.

From the corner of his eye, he noticed Vito hurrying from a cluster of wooden fishermen's huts off to his right, heading towards the jetty where the helicopter was moored. Without hesitating, David moved to confront him, grabbing his waistcoat and almost lifting him off the ground.

'I don't know what in hell you think you're doing, Vito, but if you think you're going to get my land with threats, you'd better think real hard about it. I don't take kindly to people burning my clothes.' He released his grip. Vito began to protest but David was not about to let him interrupt. 'Or, for that matter, to that clown of yours trying to run me down in the middle of the fjord.'

Vito hesitated, momentarily, smoothing his rumpled clothes. Backing off, he abandoned all pretence at innocence.

'We shall see, Larsen. Perhaps, Fjærland will become, shall we say, a little too hot for you.' He smiled, thinly. 'Life in Minnesota is so much simpler. In my experience, most men bow to a little heavy persuasion sooner or later.'

'Is that so? Well, maybe you're about to have a new experience.'

Vito sneered. 'Look, slaphead, I've put a lot of time and effort into this Viking project. I'm not going to let a comatose little jerk like you stop it. You want war? Fine. Don't be surprised if it gets nasty.'

David's fist had crunched into the man's face almost before he knew it himself. Vito fell backwards, collapsing on the grass. David knelt down, one knee on his throat. 'You ever threaten me again, asshole, I'll break your fuckin' neck. You understand?'

He rose, dragging Vito to his feet with one hand. 'Now get the fuck outa here.'

Vito clutched his throat. 'As you wish,' he croaked, turning on his heel and heading for the hotel.

David walked on. Nothing would induce him to sign over the land and hotel to Vito now. He would just have to find another buyer. Stryn could take care of it. He would take his time - have the land and property valued properly. For all he knew, he might even get a higher price for them. After all, as soon as the probate on his grandfather's estate was completed, he would inherit more than six hundred thousand dollars. There was no need for a quick sale. The days of financial panic and pleading with bank managers were over.

He stood by the jetty watching the helicopter drifting gently in a breath of wind. Further along the shore, a wisp of smoke rose from one of the deserted fishermen's huts.

Somewhere behind him, a curlew cried, the sound triggering an alarm bell in his mind. Suddenly, he found himself racing along the shore, all his senses screaming danger, alerted by the smell of burning and the realisation that Vito had passed, or left, the fisherman's hut only minutes before.

At the base of the building, a pile of rags soaked in gasoline was burning fiercely. The flames were beginning to lick the wooden planking and blister its red paint. Snatching an abandoned bailer from the rocks, he repeatedly scooped ice cold water from the fjord and cast it onto the fire.

Not until he had completely doused it did he hear Katrina's stifled groan. The door to the hut was shut tightly but not locked. It gave easily under the weight of his shoulder.

Katrina was struggling frantically in the dirt less than a yard from the burning timbers, her dark eyes filled with fear. Her wrists and ankles were bound together with the same two-inch packaging tape that had been wrapped around her mouth.

David slipped one hand beneath her knees and the other under her waist, and carried her outside. Laying her on the grass, he gently peeled the tape from her mouth as the impact of her ordeal surfaced in a spate of sobbing.

'Relax. Take it easy. Everything's okay, now.' He turned her over, his fingers picking at the tape that bound her wrists.

'Vito ... that awful man, Centaur. They ... '

'I said relax. Tell me later.' He unravelled the tape, simultaneously noting the shapeliness of her legs.

'There is no time,' she sobbed. 'Vito had your grandfather's letters.'

David paused. 'He what?'

'He ... stole them.'

She burst into tears again. David waited patiently, massaging her wrists until she composed herself.

'Ragnar, your grandfather ... he used to bring his letters to the hotel to be posted. Vito must have taken them. I found them in his room.' She struggled to sit up. 'That was when ...'

She burst into tears again and he put an arm round her shoulder. 'Come on, it's okay now.' He fished in his pocket for a handkerchief. 'Here, make yourself look pretty again, huh?'

She wiped her face. 'I am sorry. I ...'

'I guess that's why my grandfather never mentioned the government and the National Tourist Board. Never could figure that out, but if Vito stole the letters ... '

'I do not understand.'

'Vito claimed my grandfather was about to sign a contract with him and that the government and tourist people were backing the deal.'

He rubbed her ankles and wrists to restore the circulation.

'That can't be true,' she said. 'He would have mentioned it. Everyone would have known about it.'

'Yeah, that's what Paul Stryn said.'

'David, we must call the sheriff's office straight away.'

'Don't worry. Paul Stryn called them last night. They'll be here this morning.'

She smiled, weakly. 'Good. We are thinking alike again.'

'I guess I owe you an apology. We didn't pay too much attention when we first noticed that you weren't around …' He stood up. 'Then I noticed the flowers in the lounge hadn't been changed. That really had me worried because I knew you always did change them.'

'So you telephoned the police?'

'Paul had already called by then because of Vito's threat to burn down the hotel. Also, Centaur tried to run me down with a powerboat. Trying to scare me, I guess. Except I don't scare that easy.'

He helped her up and she stood there, shakily, explaining between bursts of fresh tears how she had secretly entered Vito's suite, copied the documents and been caught redhanded while replacing the originals.

The words spilled out, accentuating her fear and vulnerability, as if by talking she could purge the events from her system. She dipped the handkerchief into the water and wiped her face.

'I must look terrible.'

'I guess you could use a shower. You okay?'

She nodded and drew a deep breath, as if drawing on a secret source of courage and determination.

'Come, we must hurry,' she said. 'Once Vito knows I have escaped, he will stop at nothing, I think'.

Clutching his arm, she began walking unsteadily back to the hotel. It was as if she had thrown off an old coat, intent only on her future course of action.

'The letters prove that he was responsible for the bombing. I'm certain of it. And now that I've seen them, I am a danger to him.'

David shook his head and whistled.

'Jesus, what a mess, huh? Where are the letters?'

In the hotel safe. I only took one, but there are other documents. We must get them quickly.'

She pulled his arm urgently and crossed the road into the hotel car park. 'We will go in the back way. With luck, Vito will not see us.'

As David and Katrina slipped into the hotel, Tor Falck was emerging from a troubled sleep in his one-bedroom apartment at Balestrand, still wearing his clothes. He had managed to take off his jacket but his trousers and shirt were crumpled and reeked of stale beer. Resting his head on his hand, he gazed bleary-eyed around the room.

The ashtray on his bedroom table was overflowing with half-smoked cigarettes. Another cigarette butt had burned into the parquet flooring. Beneath the window, a crumpled beer can lay on the floor where he had dropped, or thrown, it.

He squinted, his eyes hurting from the brightness of the sunlight streaming through the curtains. Climbing gingerly out of bed, he recalled the previous night's binge, the consequence of a furious argument with his News Editor.

The man was an idiot, universally disliked by the editorial staff. Nicknamed Handjob, he not only had the news sense of a dead cabbage but he had earned the contempt of his fellow journalists by consorting with management, thus weaseling himself into a position of influence beyond his capability.

Obsessed with the Fjærland bombing story, Falck had refused flatly to cover a lecture on "The Wildlife of Sognefjord" at Leikanger. Instead, he had written a speculative piece suggesting that the Ministry of Industry was about to grant mining concessions in Fjærland to a multinational company guilty of pollution. Unable to provide a shred of evidence to support the story, he had argued that it was designed to flush out the truth and was therefore valid.

Handjob had disagreed and they had argued, then fought, pushing each other around the newsroom like children in a playground.

When the Editor learned of it, he had first called in the News Editor, who was nursing a bruised eye. Handjob had emerged sore but smug, muttering with a twisted smile: "You're for it now, Falck."

The assessment proved correct. Although the Editor had accepted Falck's apologies for causing the rumpus, he had castigated him for his lack of interest in the wildlife of Sogneford, then summarily dismissed him on the grounds that his irresponsible style of journalism was not for the *Balestrand Posten*.

Peering through the curtains, Falck blinked. The sun glared back at him. Lighting a cigarette, he committed himself to chasing the story anyway, job or no job. When he'd cracked it, which he was certain he would, the Editor would be desperate to avoid the ridicule of missing the biggest story in Norway on his own patch. Then, Falck argued to himself, he would ask him to return and he would be able to dictate his own terms of employment. It would be a gamble, but a gamble worth taking.

In the meantime, he would have to survive on whatever money he could get from the nationals.

Reaching for the bottle of aspirin in the kitchen cupboard, he realised that the time had come for him to share his thoughts on the story with Inspector Ingstad. He picked up the telephone and learned that the Inspector would be in Balestrand briefly that morning, before taking the police launch to Fjærland.

Falck glanced at his watch. He would join him there.

As was his custom, Centaur had also risen early. Glancing out of the window, he routinely scanned the car park and gardens and the neat little graveyard surrounding the steepled church. As usual, there was no one to be seen. He sometimes wondered if anyone lived in the village. Even at mid-day there were never more than a handful of people in the streets.

Drawing a chair up to the window, he polished the bolts and broadheads for his crossbow. Honing the razor sharp blades was a ritual that he followed each morning before breakfast, an act as essential to his life as his constant security precautions, for Centaur was a man with many enemies.

His ability to spot the unusual had enabled him to survive far longer than most in his profession. It was the little things that caught his attention, tiny differences .that not infrequently had saved his life; a strange car in a car park or perhaps someone wearing an overcoat during summer - a coat that could hide a folding rifle.

When he saw Vito torching the hut in which he had dumped the Hagen woman the previous evening, the action did not shock him. Centaur merely stored it in his memory for possible future use.

Watching Larsen hurry across the lawn to confront Vito, he opened the sash window and reached for the crossbow, impassively aiming it at Larsen's torso.

He calculated the distance to target at about seventy yards.

Had he released the bolt, Larsen would have died instantly, but when the tall American grabbed Vito's waistcoat and with one hand nearly lifted the smaller man off the ground, Centaur had lowered the weapon, his eyes glinting with professional approval.

The way Larsen had subsequently floored Vito showed that he had clearly been trained. Probably ex-Army. Soon, Centaur reflected, he would kill him. In the meantime, he was a man to observe and respect.

Dispassionately, Centaur watched Vito return to the hotel. The boss was clearly angry. No doubt, he would vent his feelings on him when they next met but one day he would take Vito out, too.

Centaur's eyes tracked Larsen as he walked off in the direction of the ferry terminal, then he carefully packed the crossbow in its case and showered. Ten minutes later, he returned to the window, his eyes again checking each detail. This time, something was wrong.

Rapidly, he re-examined each aspect of the scene before him, all his animal instincts alerted. There were no new cars in the car park. Nobody was lurking in the graveyard. The gardens were empty. Standing motionless behind the curtain, he peered beneath and then above the window.

No one was there, either. Nothing moved, except a red and yellow painted rowing boat in the fjord. He recognised the oarsman as a resident who lived nearby.

Again, his eyes ran over each tiny detail. Then it came to him. The fisherman's hut was still there. It should have burned to the ground. Vito had fired the hut with gasoline, so somebody must have doused the flames. That somebody must have been Larsen. If so, it signalled trouble.

Silently, Centaur slipped out of his room and hurried out of the hotel. Even before he reached the hut, he could see that the door had been smashed in. A glance inside confirmed that the Hagen woman had disappeared.

Instantly realising the implications, he ran back to the hotel. The woman had seen both the Larsen letters and the geological report. That linked Vito to the bombing - and Vito was the link to him.

Bounding up the wide stairway, he crashed through the swing doors and hammered on the door to Vito's suite. Vito answered, his mood ugly.

'I told you to stay in your room ...'

'Forget it. The Hagen woman's gone.' Centaur pushed past him, striding across the room to the window.

'What in hell do you mean, she's gone.'

'Just that. Larsen got to her. She's gone.'

Vito stared at him in amazement. 'But, I saw her ...'

'Yeah, yeah. You tried to waste her. You torched the hut. Big deal.' Centaur turned from the window, massaging his neck and shoulder. 'Unfortunately, you're one lousy arsonist.'

Vito swore, then reached for his mobile 'phone and punched a number. 'Delius?'

Centaur could just hear the pilot's voice answering in the affirmative.

'I want the Bolkow ready for immediate takeoff,' Vito snapped.

He turned to Centaur, cupping a hand over the receiver.

'Have your henchmen meet you by the chopper. I want Larsen and the woman found. Fast.'

Again, he spoke into the 'phone.

'I don't give a damn if you are low on fuel. When I say I want you to fly immediately, I mean immediately. Now move it.'

Centaur moved to the door. Vito called after him.

'When you've picked them up, take them onto the mountain and lose them. And make it permanent.'

Half running, half hopping, Katrina hobbled into her office across the corridor from the reception desk, her legs and ankles still hurting from the lack of circulation during the night. Spinning the dial of the safe urgently, she retrieved the bundle of papers that she had copied the previous day and closed the safe door. Her handbag and car keys were on the desk where she had left them the day before. Scooping them up, she rushed out, nearly knocking over the stand of postcards by the door.

David was waiting by the Reception desk, which was temporarily unmanned.

'We'll go to my house,' she panted, hurrying out to the car park. 'We'll go through the papers there.'

Opening the door of the Mitsubishi, she slipped behind the wheel, kicking off her shoes, and leaned over to let David in. She was in first gear and moving even before he had closed the door.

Sweeping down the short hill, she slammed the gear into second and turned sharp left into the road, the tyres screeching on the tarmac. Out of the corner of her eye, she observed three men running through the hotel gardens towards the jetty where the helicopter was moored.

One of them was Centaur. Instinctively, she glanced up at the hotel and noticed George Vito watching from his balcony.

Katrina moved into third gear, pushing the gas pedal to the floor. The needle crept over seventy miles an hour and the Colt's engine screamed. David gripped the armrest in alarm.

'Change gear for Chrissakes,' he muttered.

'Do not tell me how to drive,' she snapped, changing into fourth. 'I may be fast but I am very careful.'

'Yeah, I noticed,' he said, his voice heavy with sarcasm. They sped along the road running along the western side of the fjord, Katrina overtaking a German camper on a right hand bend, narrowly missing an oncoming pickup truck. David clapped a hand to his eyes in exaggerated horror.

'Fast, real careful and terrifying,' he added.

Ignoring him, she headed north along the new road towards the Bøyabreen glacier. A river, bubbling and milky green, rushed down the valley to the head of the fjord behind them.

Katrina pointed to a cluster of wooden buildings strung neatly along the hillside to their left. They looked unreal in the sunlight. Like dolls' houses, painted red and white as if to accentuate the lush green of the surrounding fields.

'My house is over there,' she said. 'It's the highest. With the best view of the valley.'

She swerved onto a dirt road edged with arctic poppies, foxgloves and fences fashioned from birch twigs. David clutched his seat as she crashed back into second gear, a cloud of dust rising behind them. Above them, stands of silver birch and dark green spruce climbed steeply to the icefields five thousand feet above them.

Katrina swung off the road and steered the car along a rutted track up the hill, eventually pulling up in front of a double-storey home bordered by endless acres of forest. A red and blue Norwegian flag hung limply from a flagstaff in the garden.

David climbed out of the car and glanced over his shoulder, alarm spreading across his face. The sound of rotors chopping the still, warm air was unmistakable. He listened intently.

'Bolkow one-oh-five. Five hundred yards,' he muttered. 'Vito must have seen us.'

'What?'

'The helicopter,' he shouted. 'We're being followed.'

'Then we must hurry.'

She reached for her keys, opened the door and watched him step inside, his eyes absorbing each detail. This was her home and she was aware that it was the most revealing statement of her personality.

Hand-woven rugs covered the parquet flooring. The furniture was deep and comfortable; the atmosphere cosy, freshened with vases of roses and lilies. Like the hotel, the house was filled with antiques and memorabilia. One wall was lined with books, another with fading pictures of her father and his mountaineering friends, mustachioed men clutching ice axes and with great hanks of rope coiled round their chests.

Rushing straight into the bedroom, Katrina changed, discarding the navy blue suit she used for the office in favour of a bright green woollen jumper and a pair of navy blue slacks.

'We must move up the mountain quickly,' she said, craning her neck and peering through the picture window. The helicopter had parked beyond the trees in a field five hundred yards below the house, its rotors idling. Darting into the kitchen, she retrieved a packet of ham, some cheese, dark chocolate and a bottle of mineral water from the refrigerator. David stood by the door, awkwardly.

'They've landed,' she called to him. 'Three of them. Not counting the pilot. Look under the stairs, you will find a small backpack. There are some boots there, too, I think.'

David urgently pulled on the boots. They were too large, but they were the only pair. He rejoined her in the kitchen and handed over the backpack.

'They will recognise my car. It is only a matter of time before they find it.' She spoke tersely, a woman in command. This was her territory and she knew every inch of it.

Dogged by tiredness and longing for a hot bath, she forced herself to concentrate, wolfing a bar of chocolate and placing the emergency provisions in the backpack as she planned her next move. The three men were running towards the trees below them, armed with what appeared to be crossbows.

'We must leave immediately,' she said, moving into the hallway. She struggled into an anorak, unhooking another for David.

'Take this. It was my father's. It will be cold above the treeline.'

Slipping into her hiking boots, she took the stolen documents from the hall table, guided him to the back door and cut across the garden to a narrow path that led into the darkness of the forest.

Settling into a fast but steady rhythm, they climbed constantly, heading north along the left flank of Bøya valley, their feet silent on the carpet of pine needles.

Gradually, the shouts of the three men below them faded. For two hours, they pounded relentlessly up the path, not speaking, conserving their breath. Soon, the forest thinned.

Katrina paused in a clearing and listened intently, her breathing heavy from exertion. Apart from the whisper of the breeze and the occasional chatter of small, fast-moving birds, there was no sound. They stood together admiring the panorama of trees and gazing up at the bastions of rock and the ice gleaming in the sun. Katrina looked at her watch. It was after eleven o'clock. Two thousand feet below them, Fjærland was just coming to life.

'We will rest here,' she said, sinking to the ground. 'Then we will cross Marabreen.' David looked at her, quizzically.

'*Bre* means glacier,' she explained. 'Marabreen is one of the flatter parts of the main Jostedalsbre. There are fewer crevasses there.' David sat down beside her.

'Sounds a great way to spend a day.'

'Don't worry,' she laughed. 'It is not a difficult route. Just long. In the old days, the farmers used to take cattle and horses over it.'

'You make it sound real simple.'

She glanced up at the thin line of clouds banked against the glacier, frowning. The air was chill against her hands and face. 'It is not always so. My father once rescued a farmer who had been caught in a snowstorm up there.' She rummaged in the pack for the documents. 'He only survived by killing his horse and cutting it open. When my father found him, he was huddled up inside it, barely alive. He owed his life to that horse.' She grimaced. 'Do you have gloves in your pocket, by the way?'

David felt in his pocket. 'No, why?'

'It is no matter. We shall just have to hope you do not get frostbite.'

'Thanks a bundle.'

'It will be cold up there. Wet, too. If the wind is strong, your fingers will freeze.'

'That what happened to your heart?' David asked, scornfully. 'Jeez, you're as cold as ice. The blue ice - that's the coldest, isn't it? In fact, that's not a bad name for you. Blue. I'm gonna call you Blue.'

Within a few minutes of David and Katrina sitting down to study the stolen documents, the Sheriff's Assistant from Balestrand lowered the fenders on the police launch and docked neatly alongside the quay at Fjærland. Inspector Ingstad thanked him and strode off towards the Glacier Hotel, followed closely by Sergeant Nielsen.

Five minutes later, Ingstad wondered whether the Gods were plotting against him. The two men he had come to interview were both unavailable, the journalist Tor Falck was badgering him for an interview and the lawyer, Stryn, who had been instrumental in forcing him to free Larsen in Bergen, was demanding that he take action about an alleged kidnapping.

'Let's not jump to conclusions, Mr. Stryn,' he said, curtly. 'The fact that Katrina Hagen hasn't been seen since yesterday afternoon doesn't necessarily mean that she's been kidnapped.'

They moved into the lounge and Stryn ordered coffee.

'All I can tell you, Inspector, is that Katrina, that is to say, Miss Hagen, always informs the staff of her whereabouts if she is going to be away for more than a couple of hours. She has not done so.'

The Inspector sighed and sank into an armchair. 'I repeat. That does not constitute kidnapping ... '

'And George Vito, the American businessman who is staying here, had previously threatened to burn down the hotel.'

Ingstad groaned, then laughed in disbelief. 'Any other dramas?'

'Too many for my liking, Inspector. Yesterday afternoon, a deliberate attempt was made on my client's life.'

'Your client being David Larsen, I suppose.'

'Quite so. He was nearly drowned while fishing. I understand that a colleague of Vito tried to run him down with a speedboat.'

Ingstad turned. 'You getting all this down, Nielsen?'

'Yes, sir. Turning out to be quite a farce, isn't it?'

'A nightmare might be a better description,' the Inspector muttered. 'You'd better start at the beginning.'

They talked for nearly an hour, Stryn describing in detail the events since his arrival in Fjærland two days earlier. When he had finished,

Ingstad thanked him and conferred with Nielsen, who was sitting on the arm of a sofa.

'Hearsay, most of it,' he said, darkly.

Nielsen studied his notebook. 'Yes, sir. Still, if this Vito chap is desperate to get his hands on Larsen's land so they can start mining ... '

'Mm. There's not a shred of evidence for it, though. And I can't believe the government would give them a licence to mine here. It's a national park for God's sake.'

Nielsen chewed his pen, thoughtfully. 'That's true. Still, I'll check it out. Y'know, just to make certain.'

'We'd better have a word with this George Vito. If Delius Greenway works for him, as Stryn claims, it could put a different complexion on things.'

'Greenwood, sir.' Nielsen corrected. 'Not that Vito is likely to tell us if he's been threatening to burn down the hotel or having people run down by motorboats.'

Together, they walked back to the reception desk. The woman behind the desk confirmed that no one had seen Katrina since the previous day and verified Stryn's contenton that she always let the staff know her whereabouts. At the Inspector's bidding, she telephoned Vito and directed them to his suite.

Vito opened the door and glanced at the Inspector's identification, a puzzled frown on his face.

'Come in, Inspector. How can I help?'

'Just a quick word, sir, if you wouldn't mind. Just a routine enquiry.' He introduced Nielsen, who remained standing by the door as he moved further into the room, at the same time making a rapid and superficial judgement of the man before him.

'Sit down, Inspector,' Vito said, sinking into the armchair by the coffee table.

'That's all right, sir. I shan't be here long. Tell me, does one Delius Greendale work for you?'

'Delius Greenwood. Yes, he's my pilot.' Vito smiled, exuding charm. 'As a senior executive, I'm very fortunate to have a helicopter at my disposal.'

'So I understand. Were you in Fjærland on June the eighteenth?'

Vito shifted uneasily in his chair. 'No, as a matter of fact I was in Oslo attending to some private business. A very sad day, if I may say so.'

'It certainly was. And you'll no doubt appreciate that I'm investigating multiple murder. You can verify your presence in Oslo, I take it?'

'Certainly. I purchased some coins at *Oslomynthandel* and stayed at the Grand Hotel.'

'You flew there in the helicopter?'

'I did.'

'You see, I'm concerned because when we checked at Fornebu airport, air traffic control said they had no record of your helicopter landing there.'

Vito laughed. 'That's probably because we didn't land there, Inspector. We landed in the fjord about a mile from the airport so as to keep clear of the main air traffic lanes.'

'I see. Where is Greenwood, now ...'

Vito stood up and walked to the balcony. 'Do you know, I'm not exactly sure.' He peered out of the window. 'The helicopter is not here, so he has probably taken it for a spin. He does that sometimes. Gives the local children a ride. Good public relations, you know.'

The Inspector joined him by the balcony window. 'I'd like to turn to another matter, if I may. I understand you wish to buy some land and the hotel here?'

'You're well informed, Inspector. As you know, the company I represent, Schneider Barr, is building a tunnel under the glacier. That's just part of an overall project to boost the tourist potential here.' He smiled, urbanely. 'There'll be a Viking farm with houses, tools, even Viking ships. Bringing history to life, as it were.'

Ingstad looked at him hard. 'It has been suggested that Schneider Barr is planning to start mining here?'

Vito hesitated. 'I can't imagine who might suggest that, Inspector, but whoever it is, they've been reading too many newspapers. We haven't mined for years. Not since a rather unfortunate experience in Greenland.' He sat down again and adjusted his cuffs, adopting a confidential tone. 'Unfortunately, we polluted a fjord. Cost us a great deal of money to clean it up, too.'

'Speaking of fjords, sir, I don't suppose you know anything about a gentlemen in a rowing boat being run down by a motorboat yesterday evening, do you?'

Vito looked at him, surprised. 'I'm afraid not. I did hear at breakfast that a boat had crashed on the far shore but that's all. I did not see it myself.'

Ingstad nodded and fell silent for a moment.

'Would you both like some coffee?' Vito asked. 'I can have the girl bring some up in no time at all.'

Nielsen responded immediately. 'Thanks. I could just use ...'

'No, thank you,' the Inspector replied, simultaneously. He stared at Nielsen disapprovingly and turned back to the American. 'Just one more thing, Mr. Vito. It seems the manager of the hotel, Katrina Hagen, has been missing since yesterday afternoon. The staff seem a little concerned. I don't suppose you've seen her, have you?'

Vito hesitated. 'As a matter of fact, Inspector, I saw her earlier this morning. She was with the new owner of the hotel. What's his name? David Larsen.'

'What time was that, sir?'

'Oh, just after breakfast. About eight, eight-thirty, I guess. Strange, it was almost as if he was forcing her into the car. She seemed quite stressed.'

'Where did they go? Can you describe the vehicle?' Ingstad asked.

'Sure. A red compact model. A Mitsubishi, I think. She drove off at a hell of a rate, wheels screeching, the whole works. Just like the movies. They were headed up towards the glacier.'

Ingstad thanked him and, nodding to Nielsen, indicated that they should leave. They did not speak until they reached the hotel lobby.

'Enjoyed the coffee, sir. Thanks,' Nielsen chided him.

'We're not here on a picnic, Nielsen. We've got work to do.'

'Yes, sir. Unfortunately, some of us still haven't had any breakfast. Incidentally, why didn't you ask him about his threat to burn down the hotel? Not to mention Larsen's burned clothes?'

The Inspector paused by the front door. 'Use your head, sergeant. A man who's about to buy a hotel isn't going to burn it down, is he?.'

They walked down the wooden steps into the gardens. 'No, I suppose not. But what about the clothes, sir?'

'As you so rightly said, if Vito did burn Larsen's clothes he's hardly going to tell us. I agree, there's something about the man that doesn't add up, but if Stryn's story is right, what's Vito's motive? There's nothing, not a trace of evidence to support it.'

'You still think Larsen's the guilty party, don't you, sir?'

'I don't know what to think, sergeant. I'm not ruling anything out.' He paused as they reached the road. 'Larsen was in the States on the day of the bombing, so that seems to be that. On the other hand, he didn't have to be here. He could have paid for someone else to do his dirty work.'

They crossed into the lower gardens and sat on a bench overlooking the fjord. 'Except that he was in debt,' Nielsen added.

'True, but if he did pay someone they might have done it on account, knowing that he would inherit a lot of money as a result.'

'I suppose it's possible,' Nielsen said, dubiously.

'Trouble is, we're no closer to the truth than we were three weeks ago. But I can't get it out of my head that Larsen had the knowledge, the information, the expertise - and the motive. He was desperate to get his hands on that land and the hotel because they were the answer to all his problems. Once he had them, he could sell them off and pay his debts.'

'So why would he kidnap Katrina Hagen?'

'Because she was trying to stop him. She didn't want Larsen selling his land to Schneider Barr, not if it meant they could start mining here.'

'I see what you mean …'

'And what better way to avoid suspicion, Nielsen, than by setting fire to his own clothes? To pretend that he's the injured party? You heard what Vito said. He forced her into a car and drove off with her against her will. And that, sergeant, is kidnapping.'

Chapter Ten

July 5, 11.05 a.m. - 11.40 a.m.

High on the mountain, David and Katrina sat on the ground and, leaning against the trunk of adjacent ageing pines, examined the documents that she had taken from Vito's suite. David was appalled by the letter from his grandfather. It was as if the old man was speaking to him from the grave. Not that the letter was much different from a thousand others he had written.

It described mundane events in Fjærland, his joy at seeing the Spring flowers again and his concern that he might not survive another harsh winter. He was, after all, eighty-three years old. David smiled. His grandfather had expressed the same sentiment for at least ten consecutive years. What disturbed him about this letter, though, was the section in which the old man spoke of meeting an American businessman, whose name he could not remember.

David nudged Katrina. 'Listen to this,' he said, reading a passage from the spidery handwriting:

"He is a suave young man, always very dapper with fancy gold cufflinks and soft hands that have not seen a day's hard work in ten years. I can tell you one thing, David, he is not a farmer! He seems well brought up and can be quite charming but for all that there is an unpleasantness about him. On each occasion that he has come here, I have always felt that he was trying to push me and make me agree to something against my wishes.

"The last time he came, he told me quite plainly that if I would not sell him the land and the hotel, he could arrange to have me certified and put in an institution. What an extraordinary thing to say! I know my nerves are not what they used to be and it is not easy looking after myself now that I am confined to a wheelchair, but the Oskarsens are very kind and Ingvild Nygaard from next door comes in from time to time to make sure that I am taking my pills and eating properly.

"Anyway, I told the fellow that my land and the hotel would be passed on to you when I die, and that I would shoot him down rather let him buy it. He did not like that at all. Ha! We had quite an argument. I gave him the full benefit of my tongue, as you might imagine, but I don't have the stamina I once did. These days, I get upset too easily. My heart isn't what it was ..."

David shivered. Despite the anorak, the cool mountain air and lack of motion was beginning to chill his body. 'There's more in the same vein,' he said, thoughtfully. 'You're right. The letter proves nothing in itself but it definitely links Vito to the bombings. It gives him a motive.'

'I thought so, too,' Katrina said. 'I wish I'd been able to copy the other letters. There must have been half a dozen of them.'

David sighed. 'I guess Ragnar sealed his own death warrant when he stood up to Vito.'

'I'm sorry.' She put a hand on his arm. 'He was such a lovely man. Full of humour and fun. He thought the world of you, you know. He was always talking about you.'

David nodded, but remained silent. The pines rustled in the breeze. Through a clearing in the trees, his eyes followed the bowl of mountains to Bøyabreen, the mass of ice piling up chaotically between dark slabs of granite.

Again, Katrina cocked her head to one side, listening for sounds of the men below them. Satisfied that they had gone, she turned and watched him, quietly.

'You know, for me this is the most beautiful place in the world. That's what makes it so hard.' She sighed, flicking the pages of the geological survey. 'This report confirms what we suspected. They are going to start a mine. Apparently, there are huge deposits of copper and zinc here.'

She pointed to the steep slopes on the opposite side of the valley.

'That mountain over there. It is called Skeisnipa. It's like a wedge separating the Bøya valley below us and the Supphelle valley on the other side of the mountain.' She passed the report to him. 'According to this, there are ore deposits under the entire mountain, from the glacier right down to the edge of fjord. That's six kilometres - more than three miles.'

David took the report and leafed through it. He whistled in surprise.

'Forty million tons of the stuff. They'd have to tear out half the mountain to get that out. It won't be so bad if it's a deep mine but if they're going to start an open cast mine, the valley will be ruined. It'll just be a giant scar.'

She groaned. 'I suppose there will be heavy trucks driving about all day and men getting drunk in the village at night. It will be terrible.'

David did not answer her. He gazed across the valley, trying to focus his mind. Something was bothering him but for the moment he could not pinpoint it. It was as if he were trying to catch an elusive fish that he knew was just beneath the surface, but could not quite see.

'You know, all that stuff about reconstructing a Viking village and attracting tourists - it never did add up.' He sat forward pensively, hunching his knees under his chin. 'If Vito *was* behind the bombing that killed my grandfather, he must have been really desperate to get hold of the land. But why? Why?'

Katrina glanced at him, an expression of surprise on her face. 'I should have thought forty million tons of copper and zinc were reason enough. Men would kill for that, I think.'

'Maybe they would,' he answered, thoughtfully, the trapped thought for which he had been searching slowly bubbling to the surface. It hit him, then, with devastating impact.

'But Katrina, that's not my land. Only the southern tip of Skeisnipa belonged to my grandfather. Apart from Skarestad, where they discovered the Viking settlement, most of my grandfather's land is on the far side of the mountain, in the Supphelle valley.'

Katrina handed him the other letter. 'I don't understand …'

David took it from her but was lost in his own thoughts. 'Vito didn't want to buy my land because of the ore deposits. A landowner doesn't necessarily own the mineral rights to his land, so there has to be another reason …'

Katrina was deep in her own reverie, only half listening to him.

'I cannot believe the government would let them mine here, in what is virtually a national park. It's incredible…'

'… Vito must have killed Ragnar because there was something else on his land - something unconnected with copper and zinc.'

He flipped through the letter she had given him. It was from a Professor Berg in Oslo, something about a Viking runestone. At first, it made little sense but as he read it, the full extent of Vito's deviousness dawned on him. And only then did he understand fully the imminent danger of their own position.

If the shoulder of the mountain had not blocked David and Katrina's view of the fjord, they might have seen the mid-morning ferry dock at Fjærland, its open bow disgorging articulated trucks, loaders, crates of explosives, and hydraulic and pneumatic rigs for drilling and bolting the tunnel.

George Vito stood by the little kiosk next to the ferry terminal in the midst of a knot of villagers, a slightly odd figure in his dark suit and stiff collar, a man estranged from his natural city environment.

Although preoccupied with the Hagen woman's escape, he watched the unloading operation with satisfaction. Stage One was going exactly according to plan.

The first explosive charges would be fired the following morning after the men and their equipment had assembled at Bøyabreen, three and a half miles north of the village.

By the time they had finished, they would have used 650 tons of specialised explosives. They would have blasted 450,000 cubic yards of bedrock from the mountain and secured a steel lining to the tunnel with 40,000 steel bolts.

And that would be only half the story, for they would then have to surface the road and install sodium lighting, emergency stations equipped with fire extinguishers and telephones, and VHF communications for the Police, Fire Brigade and Health Authority.

Vito reasoned that the people of Fjærland had good reason to be grateful to Schneider Barr. Having lobbied for years for an end to their isolation, they had finally persuaded the Norwegian parliament, or *Storting*, that the village should be served by a road of national standard.

Now, Schneider Barr would pick up the tab for the Fjærland Tunnel, which would be nearly four miles long.

Vito reflected that the estimated fifteen million dollar construction costs were a relatively inexpensive price to pay for the exclusive, tax-free mineral rights to the massive Skeisnipa ore deposits.

For more than an hour, drivers and passengers in three parallel lines of cars waited patiently for the tunnellers to unload their dump trucks and heavy equipment. Eventually, the convoy trundled up the narrow road towards the village.

Vito strolled back to the hotel, his face creased with lines of worry.

Two hours had passed since he had seen the Hagen woman driving off with Larsen. In those two hours he had heard nothing from Delius or Centaur, although he had heard the helicopter criss-crossing the valley in search of them.

Vito wondered what would happen if they failed to recapture the couple. When the police inspector had interviewed him earlier that morning, he had shown an unhealthy interest in Delius. More seriously, he had also known, or guessed, about the mining project.

That information would not have come from the Ministry for Industry. Of that he was certain. So it was either guesswork or the Inspector had an unknown source of information. That worried him. He liked to control events. Right now he felt as if he were being pushed inexorably by some unseen force towards disaster.

Striding into the hotel, he forced himself to be rational, to deal only with the facts. The lack of contact with Delius and Centaur might just as well mean that they had accomplished their mission. In any event, there was nothing he could do until they called him.

Meanwhile, the tunnelling operation was under way and when he called Hans Tripp in the evening, he would be able to concentrate on the good news rather than Katrina Hagen and David Larsen.

If Tripp asked, he could always say that Larsen had concluded the sale, then forge the signatures. Clearly, though, the sale would not now go through and he would just have to take his chances. Lie as low as possible. Do what he had to do in secrecy.

He had been a fool to threaten the woman, but that was history now. Of infinitely greater concern was the fact that Larsen had found her and extinguished the fire. That left him with no choice but to assume that they were both fully conversant with his movements and plans - his contacts with the old man prior to the bombing, the mining operation and most disturbing of all his approach to Professor Berg in Oslo.

That they knew about the mining operation was neither here nor there; it would be public knowledge in the near future, anyway. The link between old Ragnar Larsen, himself and the professor was a different matter altogether.

While it had been necessary to provide an instant alibi to the Inspector, the mere mention of his presence at *Oslomynthandel* that day was dangerous if linked to the professor. Vito sat in the armchair by the coffee table and reached instinctively for the box of matches in his pocket. It was imperative that Delius and Centaur dispose of Larsen and the Hagen woman. The alternative did not bear thinking about.

If they did escape, at least he had managed to finger Larsen successfully. He was sure the Inspector now believed Larsen had kidnapped the Hagen woman. He struck a match and gazed into its flame. This time, though, he gained no satisfaction from the process. He was aware only that his hands were shaking.

'Vito couldn't have killed my grandfather,' David said, suddenly. He grasped Professor Berg's letter tightly so as to prevent the wind snatching at its pages and began to read:

"Dear Mr. Vito. Further to our conversation at the Grand Hotel on June 18, I have translated the runes that you gave me and commend you on the extent of your knowledge about the Vikings …"

He looked up at Katrina. 'That means Vito was in Oslo when Ragnar died. And it's confirmed by independent evidence.' He turned back to the professor's neat but tiny handwriting. 'I'm not too sure I understand all this,' he added, reading aloud again:

"Although, as I explained when we met, the Vikings simplified their alphabet and in so doing made exact translations more difficult to decipher, I believe the following is the closest interpretation of your fictitious runestone:

Ejulf Deathsword brought from Serklandi
five ships of silver and gold, buried
by Vetle at Moa.

"I note that you have researched your project well because there was indeed a Viking settlement known as Indre Moa, close to the hamlet of Skarestad in Sogn …"

Katrina craned her neck to read over David's shoulder. 'But that is not far from here.'

'What I'm trying to figure out is whether it's real or fantasy.'

'Knowing Vito, it is probably lies.' Katrina said, her thoughts racing. 'But if this Deathsword man buried five ships of silver and gold at Skarestad - on your grandfather's land - it would be worth a fortune.'

'Exactly. A fortune big enough to have my grandfather killed.' David read on:

"I was also surprised to see that you were aware of the word *Serklandi*, which was used by the Vikings to described 'the land of the dark-skinned people in the Arab Dominions.' *Vetle*, I am afraid, is a word unknown to me. Is this a real place or from your imagination?

"Incidentally, if Ejulf Deathsword had really brought back five shiploads of silver, he and his men may have been obliged to make long and treacherous journeys along Russian rivers. If so, either they or their captives would have been required to haul their boats across country, rolling them over the trunks of felled trees from one river to another until they reached the silver mines east of Lake Aral and the trading centres nearby. As I am sure you know, the mines were situated on the borders of Kazakhstan and Ukbekhistan (now CIS) in the Eastern Caliphate of the Arab Empire.

"This would have been the only source of such enormous quantities of silver. Such a treasure would probably be in the form of coins, although the Vikings would have transformed much of the silver into ingots and finely crafted jewellery. Therefore, if Ejulf Deathsword had truly returned with five ships of silver, there would be several tons of it, perhaps more than one ton per ship.

"Unfortunately, those Vikings who travelled eastward to Asia would most likely have lived along the east coast of Sweden, whereas the Vikings living along the west coast of Norway would have been more likely to travel south, down the Swedish west coast to Denmark and on to Europe.

"This does not necessarily destroy the basic idea for your novel because the Swedish Vikings may well have brought silver and gold back to the island of Gotland, off the Swedish east coast, which was also frequented by Norwegian Vikings.

"Deathsword, fully provisioned and far fresher than the Swedes, could have visited Gotland and made off with the silver. When the Swedes realised they had been duped, they would have been unlikely to publicise the fact and would have set off in pursuit. In your novel, you would have to arrange for them to perish at sea, for there clearly could be no Swedish attack if, in your plot, Deathsword is able to bury his hoard at Indre Moa.

"Such a hoard, of course, would be priceless. Even if the silver was melted down, it would be worth several million dollars. The acquisition of such a treasure is certainly not beyond the realms of possibility. At least 85,000 silver coins from that area have been found in Scandinavia. It is, therefore, a great pity that your cache of silver is mere fiction. However, perhaps the writing of your novel will bring you similar riches and to that end I wish you great success."

David folded the letter and carefully pushed it deep into the backpack. 'That's some story. I find it hard to believe that Vito's writing a novel, though.'

'It explains everything,' Katrina replied. She stood up and stretched her limbs. In the far distance, she could hear the helicopter. 'Vito must have found a runestone, then pretended to be a novelist so that he could persuade Professor Berg to translate it for him.'

David nodded. 'If he met the professor in Oslo on June eighteenth, he must have known about the silver before that.'

'Or suspected it.'

'Yeah.' David bit his lip, thinking hard. 'When he came to Willmar, he told me that Viking culture was a hobby. In fact, he said he was obsessed by it and I seem to recall him saying he could speak Old Norse.'

Then perhaps he was able to translate enough of the runestone to make him suspect that there was silver here. That would explain why he went to the professor posing as a novelist. He wanted confirmation.'

David rose to his feet, slowly. 'And if he suspected there was that much silver, he would want to make sure that he owned the land, so that if he couldn't smuggle it out secretly, he could at least claim it officially.'

'That could be why he put so much pressure onto your grandfather.'

'You bet. And when Ragnar wouldn't sell, Vito had him killed. Then he came to me, in Willmar. He probably knew all along that I was in debt, that I'd jump at the chance to sell …'

Katrina clutched his arm, urgently.

'The point is David, we are the only people alive who know all this. Apart from Vito, only we know the silver really exists. And if he killed your grandfather for it, he will kill us, too, I think. He has no choice. It is us - or him.'

Tor Falck exhaled a lungful of smoke and gazed up at the high ceiling of the Glacier Hotel's dining room, replete and relatively content. He had arrived in Fjærland just in time for a late breakfast and was the only guest remaining in the dining room. He had been amazed to see the army of men and machinery bound for Bøyabreen. Although the local people had agitated for a tunnel under the glacier for many years, there had been no hint that such a tunnel would be built until two days ago, when the nationals had carried a brief announcement.

Thanks to the incompetence of Handjob, the *Balestrand Posten* had failed to pick up the item and enlarge upon it. Falck shrugged. Let the little hotshot write his own story, he thought. He had bigger plans. And he had not wasted his time.

Fjærland was buzzing with rumours about strange people and stranger events. Unaware that work on the tunnel was about to begin, local residents had been unsettled by the sudden appearance of engineers and labourers, of drills, trucks and high explosives. As is the nature of those who are kept uninformed, they were suspicious and spoke excitedly of cars driving at reckless speeds towards the glacier and of a motorboat that had tried to mow down a man fishing in the fjord.

Gesticulating and all talking at once, they showed Falck where the motorboat had subsequently exploded on impact with the cliffs and complained bitterly of the noise caused by the incessant flights of the red and white helicopter.

A Mrs. Tystad volubly condemned the "helicopter people", as she called them, for taking children for rides without their parents' permission.

'Fancy taking a young lad off in a thing that's only just been painted. No insurance or anything. Came back home with his hands covered in red paint, did young Jan. All over the house, it was.'

At first, Falck did not react to what she had told him. Not until he was midway through breakfast did her plump, wind-freshened face and strident voice again intrude into his thoughts. When they did so, it was with the force and speed of lightning.

The helicopter had been painted to hide military markings. He would lay a year's salary on it.

Chain smoking, he pushed back his chair and lumbered into the lounge, looking for Chief Inspector Ingstad. He caught up with him in the village, on the quayside by the general store. Sergeant Nielsen glanced at him, his eyes rolling skywards in despair. Ingstad's mood was positively rancid.

'What's your problem, then?'

Falck sighed, patiently. 'Inspector, I really do wish you'd stop suggesting that I have a problem. I don't have a problem. The problem is all yours and if you'd do me the courtesy of listening for a moment, maybe I can solve it for you.'

'God save me, the helpful journalist.'

'Please yourself, Inspector,' Falck said, preparing to leave. 'But I have information that's likely to change the entire course of your investigation. Whether you listen or not is up to you. I suggest you buy me a beer and then we can sit at a table outside here and talk like civilised human beings.'

Ingstad looked as if he might explode with fury or arrest him on the spot, but slowly his temper subsided.

'Get the man a beer, Nielsen.'

'Yes sir. I wouldn't mind one myself, as it happens. Instead of breakfast. How about you, sir.'

'Yes, all right,' the Inspector snapped, ungraciously. 'But out of your own pocket, Nielsen. I don't want to see items of alcohol on your expenses.'

Again, the Sergeant glanced at Falck. 'It's being so miserable that keeps him happy,' he commented, turning on his heel and walking into the shop.

The Inspector grunted. They sat around the wooden table looking out over the fjord, the police launch bobbing gently at the quayside.

'All right, talk.'

Falck hesitated, stroking his beard, uncertain for a moment whether it was in his best interests to share his thoughts with Ingstad. The man seemed utterly disinterested in anything other than his own line of enquiry. On the other hand, he needed information and Ingstad and his sidekick, Nielsen, were in the best position to provide it. He explained how he had been stonewalled at the Ministry for Industry and how this had led him to the conclusion that Schneider Barr were planning to open a mine in Fjærland. As he spoke, he could see that Ingstad was about to erupt.

'*Herre Gud*, man. That's the most unadulterated speculation I've ever heard. To suggest that a multi-national corporation would murder seven people just so they can start a mine ... You've been seeing too many movies.'

Ingstad huffed and puffed, his face contorted with exasperation.

'No company in their right mind would do that. Why would the Ministry for Industry want to hush it up? If it were true, it would have to come out sometime. They wouldn't risk a political cover-up just because a few environmentalists might stage a protest.'

'Inspector, I'm just trying to put across a few thoughts ...'

'Thoughts? It's evidence we need, man, not thoughts.'

Falck eyeballed him, then relaxed. The man was a fool.

'You want evidence, Inspector? Try this. This morning a Mrs. Tystad, who lives in the valley behind the hotel, told me that her son, Jan, came home on June the eighteenth with his hands covered in red paint ...'

'Lord save me,' the Inspector exploded. 'You call that evidence ...?'

Falck looked at him with contempt. He turned to Nielsen, who was placing three beers on the table. 'Doesn't want to know, does he?" he said, shaking his head in exasperation. He turned back to Ingstad.

'The fact is, the boy had just been given a ride in the helicopter and the helicopter had obviously been repainted. Very recently. Because the boy had wet paint on his hands. My guess is that if you scrape the surface of that helicopter, you'll find military markings underneath.'

Nielsen nodded, the realisation of what Falck was saying evident on his face.

'So, that was the helicopter you saw on the day of the bombing ...'

Again, the Inspector interrupted. 'Sergeant. The helicopter was in Oslo. We have independent evidence of it.'

'No sir, we have George Vito's word for it. That's not quite the same thing.'

'Vito was in Oslo. He went to a coin shop. He said so himself. Would you drive if you had your own personal helicopter?'

'No sir, but ...'

'We'll have another word with him, if that'll put your mind at rest.'

Falck drained his beer and lit a cigarette.

'With respect, Inspector, wouldn't it be better to wait? Examine the helicopter when there's no one around?'

'He's right, sir.' Nielsen added. 'Otherwise, we'll only alert this Vito fellow. No point in that.'

The Inspector concurred, reluctantly. 'All right, we'll take a look as soon as it comes back, but I'm not convinced we're on the right track.'

'Why's that, sir?' Nielsen asked.

The Inspector sighed. 'Well, I know you both think I'm a complete idiot, but let's look at the facts, calmly and dispassionately. First, only two people saw the military helicopter, Falck here and Katrina Hagen. Second, they both claim it crashed, but it didn't because there's no wreckage. The assumption then is that the pilot must have seen the explosions, or even caused them. There's no evidence for that. We also know there were no military helicopters in the area at that time.' Ingstad paused, toying with his beer.

'Now, I'm not saying you're wrong, Falck. Only an examination of the helicopter will prove that. Meanwhile, we know a flight plan to Oslo was filed that day. Vito says they landed a mile from Fornebu and there's no reason so far to disbelieve him.'

Nielsen groaned. 'So we're back to Larsen again, sir? Is that it?'

'Yes, it is, Nielsen. Incidentally,' he said, turning to Falck, 'did you know that Larsen's abducted that girlfriend of yours, Katrina Hagen?'

'Abducted her?' Falck shifted his bulk and leaned forward in surprise.

'That's what I said. She'd been missing since yesterday afternoon. Vito saw him bundling her into her car a couple of hours ago and driving off like a bat out of hell towards the mountains.'

'What on earth for?'

'You tell me. You're the one with all the answers.' Ingstad smirked malevolently. 'Maybe he's eloping with her.'

'He's welcome,' Falck answered.

The Inspector finished his beer. 'I've said it a thousand times before and I'll say it again. Larsen had the knowledge, the expertise and the motive for these bombings. Now he's seen forcing her into a car and driving off with her. She seemed quite stressed, apparently.'

'I thought Vito said she was driving, sir.'

'For heaven's sake, Nielsen,' the Inspector said, testily, 'does it matter?'

'Well, if she was driving, he could hardly have forced her into the car, could he? And if he did, he'd have had to walk round the car to get in himself. If she'd wanted to, she could have got away from him then.'

Falck blew a succession of smoke rings. 'Sounds as if she went voluntarily. She seems to be spending quite a lot of time with David Bloody Larsen.'

'Don't worry, we'll get them,' the Inspector said. 'If they're going up to the glacier, they'll want to be up there for as short a time as possible. Then there's only one place they can go and that's down. That means either Lunde or Stardalen.' His face creased into a rare smile. 'I've already contacted the police at Skei. They'll be waiting for them as soon as they come off the other side of the mountain.'

Chapter Eleven

July 5, 11.40 a.m. - 3. 30 p.m.

Katrina crouched on the banks of a mountain stream just below the treeline, washing her face and arms as best she could. She was grateful for each scooped handful of the breathtakingly cold meltwater. The narrow torrent rushed beneath patches of frozen snow, then creamed out again moments later, bubbling and frothing round iceworn boulders. Above, a line of puffy white clouds gathered in a sky the colour of gentians.

Refreshed, Katrina dried herself vigorously with the small tea towel in which she had wrapped their provisions, listening intently to the helicopter's rotors further down the valley. She called to David, sitting against a tree re-reading his grandfather's letter.

'They are still searching but we must take a chance and move. We have a long walk ahead of us if we are to cross Marabreen. We will go to the police at Skei.'

'You feeling better?'

'Like a million dollars, as you Americans say.'

He groaned. 'Those are forbidden words, Blue.'

She looked at him disapprovingly, but said nothing. David pulled himself to his feet and shouldered the backpack. They set off then, Katrina leading. When they broke cover above the treeline, she pointed to a great buttress of rock that seemed to be holding back the entire glacier, the exposed strata streaked with snow and tumbling water.

'*Kvitevardane*,' she said. 'It means "White Cairns". Not that there are any but that's the route we must take.'

'Looks pretty steep.' His voice was edged with concern.

'It is not so bad. The last bit is a hard climb but nothing to worry about. Then we will be above the snowline and on the cone.'

'The cone? What's that?'

She smiled briefly, a tight, worried little smile that belied her true feelings. 'It is the route across the snow up to the glacier. It is like walking up the outside of an ice-cream cone. We will be on it for about an hour and a half, so that is when we'll be most exposed.'

David hesitated. 'Shit, I hope it's not *too* steep.'

'Why, are you afraid of heights?'

'Not afraid. I'm not afraid of anything. Just get dizzy, that's all.'

'You mean you suffer from Vertigo?'

'Acrophobia. Vertigo is the dizziness and nausea that results from it.

Doctors says it's an inner ear and balance problem. Just kinda crept up on me - but that's partly why I quit the Army. And working the oil rigs. Same with the construction industry. Couldn't take walking along steel girders thirty storeys above the ground any more.'

'Well, you will just have to control it. We have no other options.'

She spun round and pushed on, setting a relentless pace, the soft carpet of pine needles gradually giving way to a coarse, tufted grass strewn with rocks and boulders. This was all she needed, a man who was scared of mountains. She was both surprised and disappointed. He had not struck her as a man with a weakness. He had always seemed so self-assured, a tough man used to taking decisions and acting on them.

Much would depend on the severity of his phobia, but the real danger would come if he slipped on the cone. She pushed the thought to one side. It was a problem she would have to deal with when it arose, and not before.

Glancing over her shoulder, she was gratified to see that David was no more than three yards behind her, his head down and his fair hair blowing in the wind. At least, he was fit. Handsome, too, she thought.

Working their way across a succession of tumbling streams towards the right hand edge of the rock basin, they began the steep climb to the ice cone. If David was fearful, he kept his thoughts to himself and for that she was grateful.

Climbing steadily to four thousand feet, they skirted the base of *Kvitevardane*, moving quickly across patches of rock and frozen snow until they reached the cone itself.

For nearly an hour, they drove themselves onwards, their boots crunching on the ice crystals. From time to time, she paused briefly to regain her breath. Each time she heard him mutter: 'Keep going, goddam it, keep *going*.'

A quick glance told her that he was concentrating only on his next step, his hands shielding the edge of his eyes so as to shut out all extraneous vision.

Katrina knew from others plagued by acrophobia that peripheral vision could bring even the toughest to their knees. She did not argue or stop to ask him if he was all right. Instead, she drove herself onwards, aware that once they were over the cone, they would dip down onto the glacier itself.

It was not until they were almost at the summit of the cone that she again heard the helicopter. This time, it was close.

'Run,' she shouted. 'We must get to the top before they see us.'

Even as she uttered the words, the red and white Bolkow swung round the shoulder of a mountain to the south of them, its rotors noisily chopping the cold air.

'Too late,' she yelled, making for the summit fifty yards ahead of her.

It was then that she heard David's cry. Even before she turned round to look, she knew that he had fallen. Wheeling round, she saw him hurtling down the cone, scrabbling at the ice with his hands and jamming his boots into the ice until, eventually, he slithered to a halt.

For a moment, he lay there prostrate and unmoving. Then, as the helicopter headed straight towards them, he slowly raised himself on all fours, kicking his toes into the ice to gain a more secure foothold.

Katrina hurried back to help him, scarcely conscious that she was screaming. The strangulated sound echoed across the valley, a desperate, high-pitched cry that warned not of the danger of falling, but of the helicopter turning broadside on to him not a hundred feet away, hovering with its doors removed.

And helplessly, she watched the dark, clown-like figure lean out and slowly and deliberately take aim at him with a crossbow.

Five hundred and fifty miles to the southwest, at Peterlee new town on the north east coast of England, Jimmie Hargreaves was walking home from the Job Centre, distraught with worry. A brawny man with a shock of red hair, he was among thirteen hundred miners and administrative staff who had been sacked when the government and British Coal announced the closure of thirty pits.

Among them was Easington Colliery, a couple of miles to the north of Peterlee. Jimmie had worked there all his adult life and the closure had been a devastating blow, not only for him but for many towns and villages in the north-east.

In Peterlee alone, seven hundred and fifty Easington miners had joined the ranks of the unemployed. That morning, the girl at the Job Shop had again told him to keep trying. Something would surely turn up sooner or later, she'd said. But she said that every week and in their hearts everybody knew that it was only a remote possibility.

Jimmie unlocked the front door of the terraced house that he had bought seven years earlier, bitter at the apparent insanity of closing down profitable pits. He sighed, the burden of life weighing heavily on him. It wasn't just the stupidity of it all, it was the frustration, the boredom of a life that was suddenly empty and devoid of meaning.

Just thirty-two years old, he was a man who liked to work, who enjoyed the comradeship of other miners. He had first gone underground at the age of sixteen. In the years that followed, he had graduated to become a power loader operating the huge coal cutting machines that burrowed five and a half miles off the coast one thousand feet beneath the North Sea.

It was a dirty, dangerous job of which he was proud. Yet, his only reward had been forty-eight weeks' pay and a ten thousand pound redundancy payment, a total of twenty-four thousand pounds. Jimmie was one of the luckier ones. Some of the lads got as little as seventeen thousand pounds. It was peanuts, when the likelihood of getting another job was about as likely as winning the lottery.

Sinking into the sofa in his small front room, he stared into the irony of an empty fireplace. It was imperative that he find a job. He'd spent most of the pay-off already, just trying to survive. The two boys, ten and eight years old now, were growing fast, constantly in need of new shoes and clothes. And there was no way they could survive on the money Doris brought home. Her wage helped, of course, but part-time shop assistants are not well paid in the north east of England. After taxes and bus fares to Sunderland, ten miles up the road, there was almost nothing left.

As with so many of his fellow miners, he was at a loss to know what to do with his time. He had finished the housework, tended the patch of garden and done the shopping by mid-day. Doris would not be back until six o'clock and the boys would be at school until four o'clock. He sighed and eased himself out of the sofa. The Miner's Social Club was his only relief from despair. There, at least, he could share his concerns over a pint of ale with other miners in the same boat.

The club was as busy as it had ever been in the good times. Miners crowded round the bar in the corner of the room, vying for the barman's attention, shouting to make themselves heard over the buzz of conversation. Clouds of cigarette smoke spiralled up to the high ceiling.

In another corner, some of the lads were playing snooker. Elsewhere, groups of men played cards at small tables or read newspapers. Others complained about the government and discussed endlessly the hard times that had befallen them, and what they would do with the Chairman of British Coal if they could lay their hands on him. A voice shouted to him from across the room.

'Hey, Jimmie, 'ave you seen this, man?'

Jimmie glanced up at him. It was Jack Lambert, another coal face operator, a burly man dressed in jeans and a blue sweat shirt. He was sitting with Bill Ackhurst, who lived three doors away in the same street.

'Hang on, Jack. Let's get a pint first. What'll y'ave?'

'Pint o' best, mate. An' 'urry up. I'm dyin' o' thirst over 'ere.' The former miner roared with laugher.

'Bill?'

'Ay, I'll 'ave the same agin, man.'

Jimmie bought the beers and pushed his way through the crowd.

'Will y'look a' that,' he said, planting the glasses on the table in disgust. 'Gorra head on it like a vicar's collar. Don't know what the world's comin' to.'

'Ne'er mind about that. Sit down and 'ave a look at this.'

Lambert handed him a well-thumbed copy of the *Sunderand Echo*.

'There. Top o' the page.'

'What's this, then?' Jimmie read the advertisement quickly, his heart beating faster.

'Bloody lifesaver, that's what it is, man.'

The advertisement solicited applications from semi-skilled workers prepared to work shifts of four weeks on and ten days off on a mining project in Norway, all transport costs paid. Jimmie looked up.

'Bloody 'ell. Tha's a bit of all reet. Three 'undred quid a week?'

'Ay. Better'n slap in t' face with wet 'addock,' Jack answered. 'An' they're looking for 'undred men. Tha's to ring that number and go for interview at County Thistle 'otel in Newcastle.'

'Where's that?'

'Opposite central station. Me and Bill's going up 's afternoon. Will y' join us?'

Jimmie thought rapidly. 'Ay, I'll go. I dunno 'ow our Doris'll take it. But I'd be a reet plonker t' miss that kind o' chance. Nae doubt about tha'.'

David was not aware of the helicopter until he felt the powerful down draught from its rotors pinning him to the ice. Glancing round, he looked up at the impassive figure of Centaur sitting half in, half out of the machine. One of his feet was dangling above the float. He watched mesmerised as the clownlike figure raised the telescopic sight of a crossbow to his eye.

Despite the distance, David identified the weapon instantly. It was a semi-automatic Demon Safari. With quicksilver smooth control, it could launch half dozen bolts at one hundred and seventy miles an hour, maintaining deadly accuracy at seventy-five yards.

Instinctively, he hurled himself sideways, kicking his feet into the ice and zig-zagging back up the cone, all trace of his acrophobia gone.

A bolt fitted with a razor-sharp broadhead slammed into the ice beside him and disappeared, its velocity carrying it deep beneath the surface.

From the corner of his eye, David noticed Katrina above and to the left of him running down the cone, screaming. He shouted at her to turn back and again lunged to one side. Another bolt thumped into the ice, not a foot away from him.

Katrina turned on her heel and climbed desperately towards the outcrop of rock that was the summit of *Kvitvardane*.

The helicopter was circling around now, weaving in front of them, the pilot skilfully using the downdraft from his rotors in an attempt to prevent them climbing up to the rock face. He was nearly successful. David raced to the shelter of the rock, spurred on by the thud of crossbow bolts.

Katrina squeezed herself next to him in a narrow gully. Whitefaced, she shouted in his ear, her chest heaving.

'We must climb up to the glacier,' she cried. 'The clouds. They are our only chance.'

'How's that?' He peered round the small buttress of rock that was their only protection. The pilot was turning again, behind them now, lining up for another attack. David was the crack Delta Force Master Sergeant again, his mind racing ahead, exploring possibilities, assessing risks.

'The clouds. It is not possible to fly in clouds.'

'If we move, we're dead,' he yelled.

'We are dead if we stay,' she argued. 'He will just sit and wait for us. Do you not understand, you stupid, impossible man? It is a phenomenon peculiar to ice. The clouds are too low for him to fly up there …'

David looked up at her, puzzled. 'They're not that low.'

Katrina groaned with exasperation.

'They are low enough to create a white out. They will reflect the light from the ice so there will be no horizon. He will be completely disoriented. It is like being suspended in a milk bottle'.

The Bolkow's pilot edged round to give Centaur and the other offside passenger a clear line of vision.

Another bolt from the crossbow settled the issue, pinging on the rock beside them. Simultaneously, they lurched from their hiding place, grateful that turbulence and wind were affecting the accuracy of their assailants.

'Whatever you do, keep moving,' David shouted, the wind snatching at his words, but Katrina was already ahead of him, darting round the rock and climbing fast along the right hand edge of the buttress.

When they reached the top, they again huddled in a fold of rock, this time looking northwest over Marabreen, the cone behind them. Now, the ice fell away into a depression, slushy and pocked with lakes and pools. David sighed heavily, relieved to be off the cone. Next to him, Katrina was shaking.

He placed an arm round her shoulders. 'Come on, get a hold of yourself,' he ordered. 'You're doin' just fine.'

'Don't I have the right to be frightened?' she snapped back. '*Gud i himmel*. These people are trying to *kill* us.'

David poked his head round the rockface. The Bolkow was hovering behind and to the right of them now, the pilot clearly cautious of flying too close to the rock. The edge of the cloud bank was no more than a hundred yards away, a cold, wet drizzle wrapping itself over the ice.

Katrina pointed to an overhanging stand of rock about seventy-five yards off to their right.

'We must go to the *helle*,' she panted.

'The what?'

'That rock over there. It is called a *helle*. In the old days, Viking farmers stored provisions under them.'

He shook his head in amazement. 'Now's the time for a lecture on Vikings? You're unbelievable.'

But she was right. The *helle* offered the only protection between themselves and the edge of the clouds. Reaching it would be a calculated risk. They would have to cross directly in front of and beneath the helicopter.

'Okay, let's go,' he said, grabbing her hand and running down the slope.

It was a mistake. The pilot saw them instantly and the egg-shaped machine moved forwards. By the time they had covered twenty yards, it was powering towards them on full throttle, climbing rapidly.

David glanced up to his right and saw it stand almost vertically on its tail, hanging in the sky like a manic pendulum before diving and swinging round in a smooth, wide arc, banking so steeply that it seemed to be flying on its side.

The machine headed straight for them, it's thirty-three foot rotors nearly ninety degrees to the ground and screaming.

'Get down,' David yelled. But there was no need. Katrina had already instinctively thrown herself to the ground. David followed, landing headfirst in a pool of slushy ice.

Curving away, the Bolkow straightened, then banked left to repeat the manoeuvre.

They scrambled to their feet and raced towards the *helle*. Again, the helicopter sliced through the air as if trying to chop them down with its rotors. As it roared overhead, David dived full length onto the wet ice, half burying himself in the coarse surface crystals and light snow thirty yards from the *helle*.

Clambering to his feet again, he was aware that the pilot's tactics were sapping his strength. Katrina was ten yards behind to his left, crouched like an Olympic sprinter on the starting blocks, fear written all over her face.

Once more, the Bolkow swung round, this time more acutely. David ran down the slope. The pilot pivoted the machine round sharply.

It was then that David saw the tiny figure in the rear seat loose his balance and tumble out, his hands desperately seeking a hold on the float. For an instant, it looked as if he might retain his grasp but the Bolkow reared up temporarily from the loss of weight and the man fell headlong, his black clad body spinning as if in slow motion until it smashed onto the serrated rock like a child's doll.

There was no scream. Or if there was, it was lost to the sound of the helicopter. The pilot abandoned the manoeuvre and instead spiralled in apparent confusion. David raced towards the rock, his eyes homing in on the crossbow that lay in the snow.

Snatching it from the ground, he hurled himself against the cold rock, rolled over and in a single fluid movement expertly slotted one of the four remaining bolts into the groove. Pulling back the drawstring, he raised the front sight to the circling helicopter and squeezed the trigger.

Unhindered by a broadhead, the slender bolt sped unerringly to its target. David was scarcely aware that it had left the forestock when he saw the dark figure in the rear seat crumple, then fall forward.

The Bolkow retreated then, leaning away from the mountain and disappearing over the cone. Katrina watched as if transfixed, both shocked and relieved. David sank down, squatting, the crossbow loose in his hands.

Neither of them spoke. Drifts of damp, ice cold cloud swirled around them. As the din of the helicopter's rotors receded, there remained only the sound of a moaning wind, an eerie, wraithlike ululation which served only to accentuate their sense of isolation.

In the helicopter, Centaur twisted his body round to peer into the rear compartment, his shoulder throbbing with pain, but he was in better shape than the man behind him. Slumped forward, his head was wedged up against the seat, a crossbow bolt standing erect and bloody from the back of his neck. Centaur knew instantly that he was dead. He glanced out of the door. Delius was descending rapidly, hugging the sides of the mountain.

'Maintain your height,' Centaur ordered. 'Head for that mountain. We got a stiff to lose.'

'We're low on fuel, we have to get to Leikanger.'

'You'll be low on life if you don't do what I say, dickbrain. And cut out the fancy flyin' tricks. You done enough damage for one day.'

'You know a better pilot?'

'Don't argue. Just do it.'

Delius changed course. Centaur leaned out of the open door, scanning the horizon, searching for a suitable place to land. They would have to bury the body and clean up the back seat before they could refuel in Leikanger. They'd also have to try to locate the other stiff and lose it. If Vito learned that Larsen and the Hagen woman had escaped, and that he'd lost two men, there would be all hell to pay. Best keep out of Vito's way until he'd located and wasted them.

Freezing now from the cold air rushing constantly through the open doors, he rubbed his gloved hands against his legs, wincing from the arthritic pain caused by his severed nerves and fingers.

Below them, the terrain rose and fell steeply, icebound mountains and barren valleys meandering and slotting into each other like the pieces of a jigsaw. Centaur leaned out, absorbing the detail, then motioned Delius to land.

'Over there, by the lake.'

'We have fuel for thirty-six minutes.'

'How long to Leikanger?'

'About thirty.'

'Should be enough. When we land, shut down the engine and clean up the back. I'll take care of the stiff.'

Delius nodded, circled and feathered the machine onto the banks of a small mountain lake covered with ice floes. Centaur leapt out, swung his arms vigorously to restore his circulation, then dragged the crumped body from the back seat.

The sight of a crossbow bolt piercing a human being's neck did not disturb him. The man was a fool. He should have realised that Larsen would use the dropped crossbow against him and kept his eyes skinned. Larsen was an expert, highly trained and deadly. He'd figured that out in the boat. He'd told them what to expect, but the kid hadn't listened and he'd paid the price. Centaur signalled to Delius, who was shutting down the engine.

'No stains, okay?' he commanded.

Delius nodded, jumped down and pulled an old sheet from the rear locker. Tearing a large piece from it, he soaked it in the ice cold water and set to work. Fortunately, the pencil-clean entry and velocity of the bolt through the man's neck had effectively cauterised the wound. Most of the bloodstains were on the floor of the rear compartment, conveniently making his task easier.

Dragging the body a few feet from the helicopter, Centaur scouted round for rocks of a suitable size and weight for his purpose. He would lower the corpse into the lake rather than carry it on the float, reducing the danger of damaging the float or smearing blood onto the helicopter again.

When he had collected enough rocks, he rummaged in the locker and retrieved a coiled rope and roll of sisal hemp. Using the twine to attach the rocks securely to the dead man's arms and legs, he placed a foot on his shoulder and pulled out the bolt, wiping it clean on the grass. Centaur did not believe in wasting bolts. Nor did he intend to leave more evidence behind than necessary.

Finally, he secured the last of the rocks to the man's neck and wrapped the sisal round his body, leaving a large loop through which he could pass the rope.

Wincing and holding his shoulder, he glanced up at Delius. 'Finished?'
'Just about.'

Centaur inspected his work, his eyes methodically covering each square inch of the interior. He reached for the cloth and rubbed a speck of blood from the base of the seat, then nodded approval.

'Okay, let's go. Here's what you do. Take off real easy, then fly to the centre of the lake. When I hit the door, hover as close to the surface as you can get. When I hit it twice, come back here and land. And no foolin' - if I go in that water, you're a dead man.'

Delius switched on the ignition and flicked a sequence of switches. Slowly, the rotors turned and the whine of the engine heightened in pitch. Centaur passed the rope through the loop, wrapped the ends around his right wrist for a better grip and positioned himself on the float behind Delius.

As the helicopter lifted, banking to port to counteract the weight of Centaur's body, the corpse began to swing, twisting the tautened rope. Centaur countered the motion as best he could, leaning back against the fuselage, but the body was heavy and his shoulder painful. It was all he could to maintain his balance.

When they reached the centre of the lake, Centaur slammed the door with his left fist and they descended to within a few feet of the surface, the downdraft pushing away the ice floes. With infinite care, Centaur lowered the body into the water, at the same time releasing one end of the rope. For a moment, the rope caught in the loop but then the weight of the rocks dragged the body to the bottom and all that remained were a few bubbles.

By the time they reached the shore, the lake was again covered with floes. It was as if they had never been there. Centaur nodded with satisfaction.

'Okay, let's go refuel. Then we'll check the maps and waste Larsen and the broad.'

Katrina shivered and glanced across at David squatting motionlessly against the rock of the *helle*, the wind cutting through her wet clothes.

'We had better eat something, I think. Then we must move.'

David stirred, gazing out at the expanse of ice.

'You know what I'd like, Blue? I'd like to be back in good old ordinary Willmar, Minnesota, doin' what I do best, blowin' up buildings. I'd like to be sitting in a deep sofa in my centrally heated home drinking gallons of fresh, hot coffee listening to Charlie Mingus or Miles Davis with Septimus, my ginger cat, sitting on my knee. That's what I'd like.'

She looked at him and smiled. 'And I would like to get to the other side of the glacier as quickly as we can, because if we do not move we will both be as stiff as boards in two hours.'

He struggled to his feet. 'Blue! It's a good name for you. Cold an' hard as ice.'

'And it is good for you that I am. Give me the backpack. We can eat as we walk.'

She took the backpack and handed him a slab of cheese and some ham, then turned on her heel and strode off towards the northwest. It would be a long and difficult walk. The surface of the ice was soft, indented with meltwater. Katrina knew the route well.

As a child, she had come here many times, her father pointing out the landmarks. He had died sixteen years earlier, just after her sixteenth birthday, trying to rescue a woman who stupidly had ventured onto the Supphelle glacier without crampons.

Setting a steady pace, she retreated into her own thoughts. Her father was only fifty when he had fallen into the crevasse and her mother had also died young. Her father's greatest wish had been for her to qualify as a glaciologist in Oslo or Bergen.

To that end he had taught her everything he knew about the movement of the ice and its properties. He had talked about Bergen when they were together on *Kvitvardane*. That was the first time she really accepted that there was a world beyond Fjærland. For apart from the odd trip to Balestrand she had remained firmly and happily entrenched in the village until she was eighteen.

A two-year business studies' course in Bergen had cured her of any desire to travel. She had detested city life. Her only relief from the traffic and the crowds had been at weekends when she sailed off the west coast with friends. Studying navigation in her free time, she had become an expert yachtswoman. But the weekdays had been torture. From the very first moment she arrived at the college, she had longed to return to the fjord and the mountains.

She trudged on, swinging her arms to keep warm for what seemed like an eternity, climbing gently out of the depression towards the plateau on the far side of the glacier, the sound of David's boots crunching on the ice behind her.

Stamping her feet, she turned to him and saw that his wet clothes, like hers, had frozen solid. Despite his sunburn, his nose and cheeks were blue with cold. She checked for any sign of whiteness that might signal frostbite.

'Let me see your hands,' she ordered.

'Hands, what hands? I don't have no hands no more.'

His humour was wasted on her. Without gloves, his hands were white and frozen. She took them and squeezed them gently. 'You must keep them moving, exercise them, move the fingers all the time. If you don't you will have frostbite in another ten minutes.'

'Sure, Blue, anything you say.'

'Now look at my face. Do you see any white spots?'

'You look just beautiful to me.'

She stamped a foot and sighed with exasperation. 'This is no time for foolishness. We are exposed and in danger here.' She examined his skin, talking continuously. 'Don't be fooled by the air temperature. It doesn't have to be freezing for us to get frostbite. The wind and the ice are enough. Last year, a man had three fingers amputated after being up here. That was in the middle of summer, too. Now, look carefully.'

'No white spots, Blue.'

'Good. Now gently rub your hands and face, and especially your nose and chin. Constantly. Don't stop for one minute. And do not forget the tips of your ears.'

She turned on her heel without waiting for an answer and set off again. They were both shivering uncontrollably and that worried her. This was the body's way of retaining warmth but it was using up their energy - and fatigue was a deadly enemy. Combined with altitude, wind and cold it could affect their judgement, causing them to disregard the bodily discomforts that precede the onset of frostbite. David's laconic humour, she reasoned, was an early sign of that.

Climbing up to the plateau, she calculated that the entrance to *Lundeskaret*, the narrow gulley through which they would drop down to the Skei road, was another two miles, at least an hour's walking. She glanced at her watch. It was three-thirty; it would be five o'clock before they reached the road and the wind showed no signs of dissipating.

Chapter Twelve

July 5, 3.30 p.m. - 6.30 p.m.

In Fjærland, the afternoon sun shone gloriously from a sky brushed with scattered clouds of cotton. A two-stroke engine was the only sound to break the deep silence of the fjord, a small boat putt-putting gently beneath the steep cliffs. The water was still, the air clean and dust-free, the temperature in the eighties.

Five miles north of the village, at the base of Bøyabreen, it was so warm that the tunnellers erecting portable offices and stores for the crates of dynamite had stripped to the waist and parked their vehicles in the shade of the mountain. Indeed, there was nothing on this soporific summer afternoon to suggest that life in Fjærland and the Bøya Valley was anything other than idyllic.

For George Vito, life was anything but idyllic. He, too, was feeling the heat but in his case, it was heat of a different nature. Closeted in his suite, he waited for Centaur and Delius to contact him, thrashing out in his mind the implications of his conversation that morning with Inspector Ingstad. No matter how he viewed it, he was filled with foreboding, overwhelmed by an unnerving premonition that his world was closing in on him.

Soon after lunch, he thought he heard the helicopter higher in the valley but by mid-afternoon there was still no sign of it. Increasingly concerned, his thoughts focused on Larsen and Katrina Hagen. If Centaur and his men disposed of them, his problems would be solved. The police would simply believe that Larsen had kidnapped her and had then disappeared. He could then continue his search for the Viking silver without hindrance.

The flip side of the coin was that if Larsen and the woman escaped, details of the Viking silver would be public knowledge, destroying months of planning and hard work. Every fortune hunter in the country would want a piece of the action. They would be swarming all over the place with metal detectors and God knows what, hoping to stumble on what could be the greatest collection of Arab coins and Viking jewellery that the world had ever seen.

Apart from that, the police would know that he had stolen Ragnar Larsen's letters and conclude from them that he had a strong motive for having the old man killed.

If they matched these deductions with the evidence Larsen and Katrina Hagen were likely to give, and discovered the truth about the helicopter, they'd flush his future down the pan faster than a laxative purging a ghost.

Certainly, he would have to change his base, move out of Fjærland, if not out of the country for a while. He would have to concoct an imaginative explanation for Hans Tripp but he could handle that if and when the time came. Pacing backwards and forwards across the room, he knew that if he was based elsewhere his real dilemma would be how to pinpoint the burial site, then surreptitiously remove several tons of silver and gold.

There was no doubt in his mind that such a hoard existed or that it had been buried near the old Viking settlement at Skarestad. The piece of bone that he had found all those months ago and the translation of the runes had convinced him of that.

On his calculations, the five Viking ships mentioned on the fragment of bone could have brought back coins worth between fifty and eighty million dollars on the current grey market. The question was where had Deathsword and his men buried them? Poring over geological maps and scouring the area personally had thus far led nowhere.

There was a knock at the door. Answering it, he instantly recognised the heavy, bearded figure standing in the corridor as Katrina Hagen's boyfriend.

'George Vito? My name's Tor Falck,' he said, ponderously. 'We haven't met, though we've seen each other often enough in the hotel. I wonder if I might have a word?'

Without waiting for an answer, Falck pushed the door open wider and walked into the room, giving Vito no chance to refuse.

'I'm a reporter for the *Balestrand Posten,* the local rag. Just a village busybody, really.' He laughed and sat unasked in the sofa, flipping open his notebook. 'I, ah, need a bit of help ...'

Vito thought rapidly. There was no point in remonstrating with the man. Better to find out what he wanted and, more importantly, what he knew.

'I'm not sure how I can help, but fire away.'

'I understand from the police that you saw the hotel manager, Katrina Hagen, being forced into a car this morning. What happened, exactly?'

Vito smiled, aware now that he could turn the interview to his own advantage.

'News obviously travels fast in Fjærland,' he said, describing what he had seen. He sank into the armchair and embellished the story suitably.

'There's no doubt in my mind that Larsen was forcing her into the car. He had a quite vicious grip on her arm. Practically threw the poor women into the seat.'

'She was driving?' Falck asked, holding his lighter to a cigarette.

'She was. And the way she drove indicated to me that she was under a great deal of stress.'

'Let me get this straight. He forced her into the driving seat and she was driving?'

'That's right.'

'So if she was under threat, why didn't she run away or drive off when he walked round to the passenger seat?'

Vito thought quickly. This guy was sharp as a needle.

'Oh, she wouldn't have had time,' he answered. 'He was in the passenger seat before she'd had a chance to pick herself up. She was sprawled all over the seat, shaking like a leaf. When she drove off, my God, it was like a Hollywood movie - crashing gears, screeching tyres. The poor woman was obviously terrified ...'

'Perhaps they were just having an argument?'

'No, no. There was somethin' much more sinister than that going on, no doubt about that.'

Vito watched the journalist closely. He seemed to be accepting his version of the story. Maybe he wasn't so smart, after all.

Certainly, he was certainly no flag-flyer for the journalistic profession. His sense of dress was appalling, scruffy and crumpled as were many obese men in his experience. But what made this man so disgusting was the cigarette ash that he rubbed into his trousers. Vito returned to his theme.

'No, for what it's worth, Tor, I had the distinct impression that he was abducting her.'

'What did you do about it?'

Vito hesitated. 'I, ah, informed the receptionist. Asked her to contact the police immediately. I saw them soon afterwards. An Inspector Ingstad, I believe.'

Falck drew long and hard on his cigarette and exhaled a plume of blue smoke.

'Right. The world's most miserable policeman. He could win prizes for stupidity.'

'I rather had that impression myself ...'

'If it wasn't for that Sergeant Nielsen, he'd have been fired years ago.' Falck smiled. 'Incidentally, he was chuntering on about someone called Delius Greenwood. Who's he?'

'My pilot?' Vito thought quickly, then explained Ingstad's interest in the pilot's movements. It would be a mistake to write Falck off as incompetent because of his slovenly appearance and dangerous to underestimate him. He was no fool.

Falck spread his hands apologetically.

'As I said, I'm just the village busybody around here but what I can't quite figure out is why Greenwood had the helicopter painted? It was hired, wasn't it?'

Vito's heart flipped. For all his slothful ways, this guy was something else. He rose from his chair and stood by the balcony window. 'I, ah, I'm not too sure what you mean …'

'Well, nothing really,' Falck said. 'It's just that one of the women in the village complained that when Greenwood took her little boy for a ride in the chopper, the lad's hands and trousers were covered in red and white paint.'

'I'm afraid I don't …'

'Well, you see, Mr. Vito, it means the helicopter had been repainted. I was just wondering why.'

'I've no idea.' Vito stared at him, his mind racing. 'Maybe it needed another coat?'

'Maybe.' Falck ground his cigarette butt into the ashtray. 'Except that on June the eighteenth a helicopter with military markings flew up the fjord within minutes, if not seconds, of a series of explosions that killed seven people.' He paused. 'It was never seen again. But you know what makes that so extraordinary? The military say they had no helicopters anywhere near this area on that day.'

'I don't see how …'

'Obviously, a helicopter that has been repainted would be of some interest.'

'I see …'

Falck held up his hand. 'No matter, I'll figure it out eventually. He laughed. 'By the way, what's all this about you opening up a mine in Fjærland?'

Vito gulped. This man was not only devious, he was dangerous. 'My, my, Tor what on earth gives you that idea?'

'Ministry of Industry. Plus a little speculation on my part. It's a common failing amongst us journalists.'

'Well, I hope you'll forgive me, but I really can't comment on that.'

'Are you denying it?'

'Neither denying nor confirming.' Vito apologised, smiling. 'Look, I hope you won't think I'm being evasive. It's just that I'm not in a position to give you an answer right now.'

He crossed the room and opened the door. The sooner this interview was over the better. He needed time to think.

'I also have a lot of work to do but if I can be of further assistance, please feel welcome to call any time. You have a business card?'

Falck answered in the negative but scribbled his name and telephone number on a piece of paper.

'I'll be in the hotel all day but if there are any developments about the mine, you can call me day or night.' He struggled out of the sofa and handed him the note. 'I wouldn't necessarily have to quote you. It could be off the record if you wish.'

'I'll remember that.'

Vito closed the door, his mind in overdrive. He would have to announce plans for the mine immediately. There was no alternative. Clearly, Falck knew, or thought he knew, about the helicopter. If his enquiries brought him any closer, everything he had worked for would be ruined. An exclusive story might divert his attention.

With luck, the mine would attract far more publicity than the paltry coverage given to the tunnel and there would be instant protests. He reflected grimly that a week earlier he would have shied at the very thought of such a prospect. Now, he needed plenty of red meat for the prying reporter to gnaw on.

It would be infinitely preferable to have the media scrutinise Schneider Barr rather than himself. He could deflect any flak directed at the company simply by shrugging his shoulders and pointing to company policy, pleading helplessness in the face of his superiors. Prying into his personal affairs would be more difficult to handle.

The clock on the mantlepiece showed four on the nose. Ten a.m. in Miami. He sat on the desk nervously filing his nails, planning his next move. He reached for the 'phone and asked the operator to put him through. For once, the President of Schneider Barr was in a buoyant mood, merely caustic rather than vitriolic.

'That you, George?' the voice from the States rasped. 'How ya doin' in the frozen north?'

Vito waited while Tripp laughed at his own joke, an obscene cackling caused partially by smoking too many cigars. 'Just fine, Hans. You're obviously in a good mood today.'

'Sure as hell am. Y'read what happened on the currency markets yesterday?'

'Ah, no. The newspapers here are somewhat inadequate.'

'Y'missed out on a bonanza, George. Banks and pension funds speculatin' like crazy against the British pound. Figured it was gonna be devalued against the Deutschmark again. Bank of England piles in to support sterling, buying like there's no tomorrow. Sold 'em one billion pounds.' Vito listened to him chuckling. 'Then they're forced to devalue and we buy the whole goddam lot back at a differential of point three-two-three-oh Deutschmarks.' Tripp cackled again. 'Made a hundred and fifty-five million sterling in twelve hours. Never seen anything like it.'

Vito sighed. It was typical of his current luck, trapped in a hick Norwegian village unaware even that there had been a crisis.

'Congratulations, Hans …'

'Ain't never been so scared in my life. Real brown trousers time. What d'ya want?'

'With your kind of luck, how about a raise?'

Tripp did not pause even to think about it. 'Horseshit. I pay you more'n enough already. Now like I said, what d'ya want?'

Vito shook his head. The man was unbelievable, an odious, rat-brained toad. A boil on the butt of humanity.

'What do I want? Ten million bucks and Madonna for a night.' He clicked his tongue in exasperation and shrugged. 'I was calling to let you know that we've successfully completed Phase One of the tunnel project. The men and their equipment are all in place.' He waited for Tripp to comment but he declined. 'Blasting starts tomorrow morning,' he added. There was a silence while Tripp spoke to someone else. When he had finished, he made no reference to the tunnel project.

'You ain't been buyin' no trees, huh?'

'No, Hans. I have not bought any trees. And, sadly, I haven't made a hundred and fifty-five million sterling, either.' Vito replaced his nailfile in its case.

'Don't get funny with me, George. Y'know I don't have a sense o' humour. How about the mine?'

'Everything is in order. Dick Longman's doing a great job. We're bringing in a hundred unemployed British miners.'

'What in hell for? What's wrong with Norwegians?'

'Cost. We'd have to pay twice as much for Norwegians.'

'Now you're talkin' sense. What else?'

'I think we should announce the mining project to the media. The men and heavy equipment will be here in a week. No point in delaying.' Vito held his breath, prepared to argue his case but it was not necessary.

'No sweat,' Tripp said. 'Never could figure out why you wanted to be so goddam secretive about it.'

'Our record is not the best.'

'So who cares? If you can't handle a few pointy-headed liberal protesters, you're no use to me.'

'Quite so, Hans. I just wanted your approval.'

'You got it. Sooner we start shippin' ore outa that mine the better.'

The 'phone clicked and Vito sighed. Tripp didn't change. Other men would be ecstatic at pulling off a multi-million dollar coup. Hans was merely arrogant and rude. Still, that at least, was an improvement on being poisonous.

Vito walked downstairs to the lobby. Inspector Ingstad was standing by the reception desk, idly looking at postcards.

Apologising profusely, Vito explained that when they had met that morning he had been unable to reveal his company's plans because he had been ordered specifically not to do so by his superiors. He smiled unctuously. Lying came naturally to him.

Immediately after he and the Inspector had spoken, he added, he had remonstrated with the President of Schneider Barr himself, insisting that his position was untenable. He had certainly not wished to mislead the police and he hoped that the Inspector would understand the impossibility of his position at the time.

Meanwhile, he could now confirm that the group did indeed plan to begin mining copper and zinc, probably within the next ten days.

Ingstad gruffly accepted his explanation and said that on this occasion he would overlook his economic approach to the *actualité*. Had he perjured himself, the Inspector warned, he would not have been so lenient.

The lecture over, Ingstad mellowed and they talked amiably for some minutes, then parted.

Vito wandered into the lounge and buttonholed Tor Falck, who was ordering a beer.

Asking for an iced tea for himself, he again apologised for his reticence that morning, explained that he was no longer constrained by his masters and gave the journalist the exclusive details of Schneider Barr's plan to mine copper and zinc in the Bøya valley, assuring him that there would be no repetition of the Greenland fiasco.

Far from the warmth and elegant comfort of the Glacier Hotel, David and Katrina trudged along the western perimeter of Marabreen up to the plateau, constantly swinging their arms, and rubbing their hands and faces to ward off the cold. Fortunately, the wind had dropped and the clouds had dissipated. Now, the sun beat down on them again, helping to warm their frozen limbs.

It was fortunate that they were both fit or they would long since have succumbed to the twin dangers of ice and exhaustion. Instead, they skirted an icebound lake, tired and freezing cold in their wet clothes but otherwise unscathed.

Rounding shallow tarns and hopping across a myriad of streams, they pushed on silently, reaching the *Lundeskardet* gap at four-twenty, almost exactly as Katrina had predicted.

David glanced down the gulley. The entrance to the narrow gully fell away sharply, packed with snow.

One downward glance was enough to set the landscape spinning.

Nausea and dizziness engulfed him, sweeping up from the pit of his stomach. Trembling, he sank to his knees.

'Jeesus H. Keriiist,' he mumbled. He swallowed, his breath coming in short gasps. 'We have to find another way.'

Katrina stopped and turned back to him.

'It is not possible. The only other route is miles away and just as steep.' She gripped his arm. 'Force yourself to look down. The more you do that, the easier it will be. It is not so bad as it looks, I promise.'

David's breathing was fast and shallow, his arms and legs quivering with apprehension. 'I can't …'

'Please, do not be so stupid and impossible,' she snapped impatiently. 'Of course, you can! As long as you dig your heels in, it is not possible to fall.'

'You don't understand …'

'Look, if you think I am spending the night with you up here, you are mistaken. Take hold of yourself.'

Consumed with embarrassment, David jammed his toes into the frozen snow and crawled crablike towards the cement-coloured rocks at the mouth of the gulley.

Katrina followed, her hand clamped on his arm.

'Promise me you will never sell your land to Vito or I will push you,' she joked, her teeth chattering.

I promise.' He smiled weakly. 'Guess I'm a real pain, eh, Blue?'

'You are nothing but trouble.' She pointed to the valley below. 'Go on, the rest is easy.'

David edged down the gulley, clinging to the rock sides, his knees trembling, his knuckles taut and ice-white. He could no longer feel his finger tips and his feet were so numb that he was scarcely conscious of the narrow stream of meltwater rushing from beneath the snow's edge over his boots.

Stumbling over stones and boulders, they reached a narrow path leading down to a sloping carpet of blueberries and dwarf willow. Ahead of her now, he stopped and waited.

'Sorry about that,' he said, when she caught up with him. 'Heights didn't used to bother me, but now I get dizzy even when I see someone else near the edge. The blood just seems to rush out of my legs and leaves me like a jelly. It's weird …'

'It is no matter. We are all different. Let us have some chocolate.'

He unshouldered the pack and they sat together on a boulder, hemmed in by sheer granite cliffs scarred with vertical striations left by centuries of falling ice and waterfalls.

Everywhere, ribbons of white water cascaded down the slabs of iceworn rock and moraine, converging into a central torrent of water that rushed and gurgled round sculptured rocks, each one coated with orange-yellow lichen and moss.

David rummaged inside the pack, extracted the crossbow that he had taken at *Kvitevardane* and handed her half a bar of chocolate. As they ate, he tried to explain further about his acrophobia, but she was not listening.

She cocked her head and motioned him to be quiet.

Above the sound of turbulent water, she could again hear the faint thwacking of a helicopter's rotors.

'It's coming back,' she breathed. 'The helicopter.'

As one, they rose to their feet and scrambled noisily over the damp boulders down the track. The Bolkow appeared over the skyline as they reached a collection of portable wooden huts and vehicles by the roadside, the Lunde end of the Fjærland tunnel. Katrina paused, uncertain which direction to take.

At the far end of the layby, someone had parked a Ford Transit motor home bearing Swedish registration plates. She ran towards it.

'Over here,' she yelled, peering inside. The keys dangled fortuitously from the ignition. Scrambling into the driving seat, she grinned widely as David heaved himself onto the seat beside her, clutching the crossbow and backpack.

'I will drive,' she said. 'I know the way.'

Fifty yards away, a family of Swedes returning from the river's edge watched uncomprehendingly. Katrina kicked the engine, slammed the gear into first and released the handbrake. The vehicle lurched forward and she spun the wheel, the Swedes shouting in protest behind her.

Accelerating down the long, winding gradient to the edge of the Kjösnes fjord, she turned the heater full on, alternately shivering and laughing.

'Wonderful, stupid Swedes,' she shouted above the din of the engine. 'Do you realise what this is? It is a camper. A home on wheels.'

David shook his head disbelievingly, as if unable to appreciate the monumental impudence of their actions. Life in Willmar was tame after a day with this woman.

'Look behind you,' Katrina yelled. 'Stove, food, hot water. There is even a *shower*.'

'For Chrissakes, slow down,' David shouted. 'You're driving like a goddam maniac.'

Katrina swung the wheel to negotiate a goat grazing on a bend. Swaying alarmingly, the vehicle careered along the narrow road. In the wing mirror, David glimpsed the familiar red and white markings of the helicopter sweeping across the fjord to his left. It was losing height and approaching rapidly.

'They've seen us,' he cried. 'Can't you go any faster?'

'You just told me to slow down,' she shouted back at him, accelerating again. 'Make your mind up.'

They entered a tunnel, the helicopter less than one hundred yards behind them. Sodium roof lamps snaked into the distance, curving first to the right, then to the left, bathing the tarmac and dripping rock walls in yellow-orange light.

Half way through the tunnel, Katrina slammed on the brakes without warning. The vehicle shuddered to a halt. David turned to her, astonished.

'Keep going. Holy shit, woman, what are you doing?'

'Do not blaspheme,' she snapped, cutting the engine. 'And do not swear. And do *not* call me "woman". What do you think I am doing? We are safe here.'

'Safe? You gotta be out o' your brain. If they drop a guy with an Uzi at each end, we're gonna be history.' He waved a hand impatiently. 'Now, move it, woman. Let's get outa here.'

She stared at him, eyes blazing, then gunned the engine again as the realisation of what he had said dawned slowly, then overwhelmed her. Again, she crashed through the gears, rushing towards the semi-circle of daylight that signalled the end of the tunnel.

When they emerged into the sunlight, the helicopter was hovering fifty yards ahead of them, one hundred and fifty feet above the ground, waiting with deathlike patience. Instinctively, David glanced in the mirror. There was no other traffic.

'Back up into the tunnel,' he commanded.

'I said it was safer there,' Katrina muttered, braking sharply and reversing. 'You always have to argue.'

David ignored her. Once inside the tunnel, he ordered her to stop, then jumped out and raced back to the exit. Leaning with his back against the wall, he peered out gingerly. The Bolkow was skimming over the water back to the tunnel entrance, as he had hoped. He motioned to Katrina and she drove towards him uncertainly. Grasping the door handle, he swung in beside her, his face set and determined.

'Okay, now go, go, *go*.'

David leaned out of the window. The Bolkow was far behind, hovering at the far end of the tunnel. He turned back to Katrina.

'We have to get off the road. We've fooled 'em for now, but they'll be back.'

She nodded. David knew that she was angry, simmering at the way he had spoken to her.

Two minutes later, on his instructions and still fuming, she spun the wheel and swung onto a stony track, the motor home pitching and swaying as it lurched into the shade of the spruce and birch woodland.

She braked and jerked the handbrake, simultaneously peering into the rear view mirror. Her hair looked as if it had been washed in goose fat. She turned to him disdainfully.

'Satisfied?'

'Not yet. We have to cover the vehicle. So let's move it.'

He jumped onto the ground.

'Collect as much brushwood as you can,' he commanded, breaking into a smile. His teeth flashed Hollywood-white against his tan.

'Then I'll apologise and you can have first shot in the shower.'

As the sun dipped into the west and the shadow of the mountains crept across the Sheriff's office at Balestrand, Inspector Ingstad gazed across Sognejord appreciatively, his mood as melancholy as the birch leaves prematurely yellowing in preparation for autumn.

He was tired and disillusioned. The responsibilities and disappointments of police work weighed on him heavily. This had been a particularly trying day with little more to show for his efforts than yet more frustration and embarrassment. He was just fifty-five and he longed for retirement.

First, he had pooh-poohed the idea of Schneider Barr starting a mining operation in Fjærland. Only to hear George Vito and the radio news confirm it that very afternoon. Next, Vito's helicopter had not returned and, despite hanging around for hours, he had been unable to discover whether it had been repainted - and by inference whether it was the machine seen immediately prior to the bombings.

Ingstad's only success that day had been to locate Katrina Hagen's car, abandoned outside her home. He could only assume that Larsen had forced her to accompany him into the mountains. Short of manpower, Ingstad was now reliant on the police at Skei to detain Larsen but ten minutes earlier they had telephoned to say that they had found no trace of the couple and that they had been obliged to call off the search.

The Inspector was pondering his next move when the telephone rang again. Picking up the receiver, he was surprised to hear that it was the Skei police.

'Just had a report in from a Swedish family at Lunde,' the Sheriff's assistant said. 'They say a man and a woman stole their motor home and drove off at high speed. We're looking for them now.'

'*Ja*, that's them,' Ingstad replied. 'Heading right into your patch. Any details?'

'Seems the Swedes parked the motor home at the entrance to the new Fjærland tunnel and walked down to the river bank for a few minutes,' the Skei policeman continued. 'They were walking back to the vehicle when they saw this fellow armed with a crossbow. Said he looked desperate.'

The Inspector drummed his fingers on the desk, shouted through the open door for Nielsen, then spoke again into the receiver. 'A crossbow, eh? Any idea where they are now?'

'No, but wherever they're going, they've got to come here first. We're manning a roadblock until seven o'clock. With only two men available, that's the best I can do.'

'Should be enough. It's only six miles from Lunde to Skei.' Nielsen put his head round the door and Ingstad motioned him in. 'They should be with you any minute. Call me again in half an hour.' He thanked the Sheriff's assistant and replaced the receiver.

'They're heading for Skei,' he told the Sergeant. 'I was right, he's abducted her. Stolen a motor home. What's more he's armed.'

The interview at the County Thistle Hotel had been quick and straightforward. Jimmie Hargreaves had been nervous when he lined up with the scores of other miners waiting outside the hotel conference room but his anxiety was ill-founded.

The fat cat in the natty suit had asked only for his name, address, date of birth and occupation, then pushed the contract in front of him and told him to sign. With a couple of exceptions, the first 100 men were given contracts, the rest an apology. Jimmie, Jack Lambert and Bill Ackhurst had been among the first to arrive.

Afterwards, the three friends had travelled back to Peterlee on the bus, stopping off at the social club to celebrate with a few beers before going home to their respective families.

Doris was in the kitchen making tea when Jimmie stumbled through the front door, the effects of the last beer pleasantly numbing his brain.

'Tha's got t' stop all this drinkin', Jimmie.' She kissed him on the cheek and led him into the kitchen clutching a bread knife. 'Else tha'll end up like auld Jimmy up road.'

He sank into a chair by the table.

'Ay, lass, but today's kind o' special, like. I got a job.'

She looked at him, her liquid brown eyes widening, her face creasing happily into a grin. 'Tha's *what*?'

'Got a job,' he said proudly. 'Open cast mine, an' all. Only one catch.' He paused nervously and belched. 'It's abroad.'

Her smile faded but he gave her no chance to reply, describing the details of the contract in a torrent of words.

'Three 'undred quid a week, Doris. No way can I shake me 'ead to brass like that. Redundancy money isn't goin' to last forever.' He leaned forward and pulled her towards him, sitting her on his knee. She placed the knife on the table and prodded him in the stomach.

'I'm reet proud o'you, Jimmy 'Argreaves. But tha'll be off with some Norwegian girl at blink of a gnat's eye.'

'There won't be none. It's in the middle of nowhere.'

He shifted his legs so that he could more easily feel her soft buttocks. 'It's right at the end of a fiord, underneath a glacier.' He grinned and put a hand on her breast but she pushed him away.

'Geroff, Jimmie! Tha thinks o' nothin' but sex. When 'av you got to go?'

He sighed. 'Day after tomorrow, luv. Ship's leavin' at eight-thirty in the mornin' from North Shields.' He brushed his lips across her cheek and neck, sniffing her cheap perfume. They kissed passionately then and their breathing quickened as he stroked the inside of her leg, his hand creeping up her cotton skirt.

'Jimmie, doan't.' She giggled. 'We 'aven't even 'ad tea, yet.'

Chapter Thirteen

July 5, 6.30 p.m. - July 6, 9.15 a.m.

Katrina stood in the mobile home's tiny washroom awkwardly holding the dual purpose tap and shower head, revelling in the hot water streaming over her body. In her entire life she had never had such a wonderful shower. She had washed her hair and soaped every inch of her body several times and was now luxuriating blissfully in the steam heat; clean, warm and content, glowing from every pore. When she had finished, she poked her head round the door, her slim body sheathed in a thick cotton towel.

David was sitting on the sofa by the curtained rear window nursing a bottle of whisky with one hand and clutching a foot with the other. His wet clothes and boots were strewn across the floor. He had changed into a pair of baggy trousers and a shirt with a loud Hawaiian motif that he had found in a cupboard.

Twisting a hand towel round her hair, Katrina knelt down and took one of his feet in her hand. It was glacial to the touch, the skin deathly white from an excess of icy water. His toes and heels were pocked with skinless patches, blisters rubbed raw by ill-fitting boots.

Instantly recognising the early stages of frostbite, she drew on the knowledge that her father had passed on to her. It was vital to rewarm his feet rapidly, but if the tissue was to be preserved it was equally imperative that this should be achieved without friction, for it was a common myth that rubbing the affected area was the best way to deal with the condition.

Unwinding the towel round her hair, she wrapped it around his toes and placed his feet between her thighs, sensing as she did so the early stirring of a sexual pleasure. Although this faint awakening revived the memory of Centaur forcing himself on her the previous afternoon, the sensation took her by surprise and, not for the first time, she looked at David as a potential lover. Instinctively, she rejected the thought and briskly thrust his feet aside, addressing him in the efficient manner of a professional nurse.

'It is not serious,' she observed, 'but you are lucky. One hour more on the glacier and you would have needed hospital treatment.' She peeled off the towel and again inspected his feet.

'You had better shower sitting down so that you can keep your feet out of water. Whatever you do, do not rub them afterwards. Wrap them in a towel and exercise them very gently. Keep them elevated and do not walk until the circulation is moving again.'

'Sure, Blue.' He held the whisky bottle to his lips and drank, holding the fiery liquid in his mouth for a moment before swallowing, then hobbled to the washroom. 'Hey, I'm sorry I yelled at you.'

'And blasphemed and swore.'

'Yeah, I do that sometimes.'

He disappeared into the shower and she heard him turn on the water. 'Extenuating circumstances, though,' he shouted. He peered through the door and nodded towards the top bunk. 'There are some clothes up there if you want them.'

Desperately tired from the previous night's ordeal and the trek across the mountain, Katrina wanted only to sleep, but she was also conscious of the urgent need to seek help from the Skei police. She selected a cotton blouse, a sweater hand-knitted with bright red wool and a pair of green corduroy trousers too voluminous and too short for her long legs, then dressed quickly and turned on the radio.

'Skei is just up the road,' she said. 'We must see the police as soon as we can.'

A radio news item announced that within the next ten days, the American multi-national corporation, Schneider Barr, planned to begin open cast mining for copper and zinc in the Bøya valley. The environmental group, Planet Watch, had mounted a twenty-four hour vigil outside the Norwegian parliament in protest.

Meanwhile, Kripos police again wanted to question the American citizen dubbed by the press as the Dynamite Man.

Police believed that the American, whom they had quizzed in connection with the Fjærland bombings, had abducted the manageress of the Glacier Hotel at Fjærland, a woman in her earlier thirties named as Katrina Hagen.

The *Dynamitt-mann* was believed to be driving a motor home stolen from a Swedish family near Skei. Police were advising the public not to approach the wanted man, who was said to be armed, professionally trained in hand to hand combat and extremely dangerous.

'*Himmel*' Katrina muttered. 'How can they be so stupid?' She reached into the refrigerator beneath the sink unit, helping herself to some ham, cheese, a packet of smoked salmon and a carton of coleslaw with prawns.

'Did you hear that?' she shouted. 'You are supposed to have kidnapped me.'

She buttered several slices of bread and made coffee.

David crawled crablike from the shower, one towel wrapped around his waist, another round his feet, shuffling across the floor on his backside.

'How's that?'

'The radio. They said you have abducted me and that you are armed, trained to kill people and dangerous.'

'You bet. With you in those sexy corduroys, I could do anything.'

'Oh, do be serious. How are your feet?'

'They hurt like hell.'

'Let me look.' She examined them again and noted with satisfaction that the colour was returning. 'Good. Do not rub them. They will be painful for a while, but it will not last long. Keep them raised and keep moving your toes.'

She moved back to the kitchen unit and placed the sandwiches and coffee on the table, studying him. He had a strong face and a torso that reminded her of Michelangelo's David. Almost hairless. Strong and quite beautiful.

'What do you think we should we do?' she asked. 'We cannot go to the police. Not if they will arrest you, which they will, I think.'

He gestured to the sandwiches and coffee. 'First off, we'll finish these. Then we'll go to the police. They're not going to arrest me for kidnapping if you tell them it's not true.' He winced, then grinned, his eyes alight with amusement. 'Or maybe I'll seduce you, first.'

'Ha. Pigs will fly. I would rather take a troll from Hell.' She turned away, her cheeks burning, secretly pleased but embarrassed, too.

'Thanks,' he said. 'I like a challenge.'

'I have friends at Sandane,' she continued, changing the subject. 'We could go there. It is a small town. About an hour's drive from here, north of Skei.'

He poured a small Scotch into his coffee and drank it black, clutching the towel round his waist. He glanced at her and raised an eyebrow. 'What are you smirking at?'

She pointed to his borrowed clothes in a heap by the washroom. 'I was wondering when your feet would allow you to make the great American leap into your trousers.'

'Not while you're around, Katrina Hagen, so go sit in the front while I change. We'll hit the road as soon as I'm through.'

Taking some bandage and a packet of waterproof dressings from the first aid kit, he applied them to his blisters. She left him then, ducking through the door into the driving cab. Moments later, David joined her, wearing jeans, a thick sweater and a pair of sneakers, clutching the backpack containing his grandfather's letters and other documents.

He waved a hand at the wheel. 'You want me to drive?'

'No, thank you.'

'Okay, let's go.' He grinned at her. 'But, Blue, nice and gentle this time, huh?'

She eased out of the clearing and headed slowly down the track to rejoin the road, pulling down the sun visor as she turned right into the early evening sun. The way ahead twisted and turned, a narrow band of tarmac scarcely wider than the motor home itself.

She neither saw nor heard the helicopter approaching from behind. Neither did David. Only when she heard the turbines immediately above them did she see the dark shape of its underbelly.

Swooping down, the pilot was clearly trying to pace himself to their speed, holding the machine fifty feet above them, the clatter of its rotors drowning out all sound.

Mesmerised, she watched a dark figure lean out of the open door and toss out what she thought was a bottle. A split second later, there was a thunderous bang and the motor home ran into a curtain of fire.

Unaware that she was screaming, she braked hard as the side of the vehicle scraped along the knee-high metal crash barrier separating the edge of the road from the deep waters of the fjord. As if caught in a confused, turbulent dream, she heard David shouting at her, his voice dim and distant.

'Fire bombs. Keep goin', keep goin'.'

Automatically, she wrenched the wheel round and pushed the accelerator to the floor. The Bolkow swung back for another run, this time approaching them head on. David leaned forward, craning his neck.

'Do exactly as I say,' he barked. 'Keep your speed. Stand by to brake.'

Again the figure leaned out, the arm poised, timing the precise moment to release the next fire bomb. Slowly, he drew his arm backwards. David turned to her, shouting.

'Now brake. Brake!'

Katrina jammed her foot onto the brake pedal. The motor home slewed to a halt. She watched the bottle arc down and explode on impact thirty yards ahead of them, harmlessly scattering broken glass over the roadway and into the fjord. David opened the door and swung his body outwards, facing the rear of the vehicle.

'Now go,' he yelled. 'Go, go, go.'

'*Herre Gud*, I don't believe this,' she muttered, accelerating again, David hanging half in and half out of the vehicle as she swerved to avoid the burning petrol on the road.

'Okay, they're comin' in again.' He poked his head inside. 'Slow right down. Then when I tell you, give her everything you've got.'

She realised what he was trying to do now, her nerves taut and vibrant. Glancing in the wing mirror, she saw the helicopter swooping down and held her speed at thirty miles an hour, ready for David's command. It came a millisecond later.

'Now!'

She gunned the engine and shifted into third gear but this was no sports car. The motor home lumbered forward ponderously. Mentally, she urged it on, willing it to pick up speed. 'Come on, come *on*,' she cried, but the vehicle did not have the necessary power.

Out of the corner of her eye, she saw David hurl himself into the cab as her wing mirror filled with flame. The missile must have landed right under their exhaust because she could feel the blast pushing them forward. The helicopter roared overhead, then peeled off in a great circle, flying low over the fjord.

David picked himself up and opened the door to the rear compartment. Shards of charred glass were strewn over the table and sofa, the bottle of Scotch rolling across the floor. The place was a mess.

He crept in and rescued the Scotch, then crawled back to the front seat, shutting the door behind him.

'They've gone,' Katrina said, simply.

David did not answer. He nodded, unscrewing the cap from the bottle. He swallowed long and deep. Katrina threw a sidelong glance at him.

'You might offer me some.'

David looked at her in surprise and handed her the bottle.

'Sorry, I didn't ...'

'... think a woman would drink from a bottle? This is the trouble with you men, you do not think.'

Steering with her left hand, she raised the bottle to her mouth and savoured the golden liquid as it seared the back of her throat. She no longer felt frightened. She had kept her head and shown that she was no simpering female. When necessary, she too could be tough.

Rounding a small bay, she skirted the eastern side of a headland and glimpsed the helicopter climbing over the wide expanse of water. Emerging from the shade of the mountain back into the sunlight, she realised why the pilot had abandoned his attack, and groaned.

'Uh-uh! Do you see what I see?'

Ahead, two policemen stood by a roadblock, talking.

'No problem,' David answered. 'Just pull up and tell 'em what happened. We got nothin' to hide.'

Katrina slowed down, wondering what she would say if they started asking questions. Twenty yards from the road block, she saw one of the policemen pointing out the number plates to his colleague and speak into his personal radio.

Obviously, he had recognised the registration number.

Katrina did not hesitate. Moving swiftly through the gears, she increased speed and crashed through the barrier, splintering the single wooden boom.

'What in hell …'

'They will never believe us,' she said, shifting into fourth gear. 'Not now …'

'Holy shit, woman …'

'Don't swear and *do not* call me woman. We are in a stolen vehicle. They would arrest us in two seconds.' She swerved violently to avoid a car, the motor home swaying disturbingly on its small chassis. David grabbed the armrest.

'Jeez-*us*. Are you crazy or what? Don't you realise that was the only chance we had to explain everything? How can there be a kidnap charge if you tell them I didn't kidnap you?'

He shook his head in bewilderment, then looked up at her. 'We've only gotta show 'em the back of this thing and drive two miles back along the road and they gotta believe Vito's tryin' to have us killed.'

'You are armed and dangerous, remember? They think you kidnapped me. They would say you caused the damage while I tried to escape. Or that I had fallen for you. There was a woman who did just that in a bank siege in Stockholm. Hostages often fall for their kidnappers.' As an afterthought, she added: 'Not that there's any chance of that in your case.'

She sounded the horn and swerved as a car pulled out of a side road.

'Anyway, now it is too late. We are also wanted for evading the arrest and smashing up a police road block.'

Thundering through the scattered community of Skei, she turned north onto the road to Sandane and sped past a series of lakes, their banks swathed with purple wild flowers. David groaned.

'Why me? Why in hell did I ever come to Norway?'

'Because in your bones you are as Norwegian as I am - and what is more, you know it,' she snapped.

They fell silent then and she drove on through a more gentle landscape, the road running north beside the swift waters of the wide but shallow river.

The clock on the dashboard showed eight-fifteen, but the sun was still high and it would be light for at least another two hours. Sandane and the comfort of her friends' home were less than fifteen miles away, another twenty minutes' driving.

The Bolkow returned without warning.

It swept down from a 4,000 foot hump of a mountain slightly off to their left and before either of them had seen it, a firebomb exploded beneath the rear nearside wheel, engulfing the side of the vehicle in flame, heat and noise.

The explosion ripped the wheel apart. Desperately, Katrina tried to hold her course but the heavy vehicle slewed left uncontrollably. David was shouting at her but in the tumult his words were lost to her.

The helicopter pivoted round and a second firebomb slammed home.

Sounds of splintering glass combined with the screech of metal on metal, tore at her nerves. From the corner of her eye, she saw David crashing onto the floor beside her.

Inexorably, the motor home ripped through the metal barrier at the side of the road, lurching and bouncing across a narrow field towards the river.

'Now look what you've made me do,' she yelled.

They were the last words she was to speak for some time. As if in slow motion, the motor home tipped forward and sideways into the water, flowing faster and deeper now, the full weight of a thousand glacial streams behind it.

Katrina remembered only hitting her head on the windscreen and the icy, green water pouring through the open windows as the vehicle somersaulted first onto its roof, then toppled onto its side as the full force of the current swept it away.

Moments later, she lost consciousness.

As the stricken motor home tumbled downstream, David was engulfed by the coldest water he had ever known, a heavy, foaming torrent so cold that it sucked away his breath.

Katrina was slumped face down in what was now the bottom of the half-filled cab. Reaching for her arm, he dragged her towards him with his right hand, groping with his left for the door handle.

The vehicle shuddered, then pivoted slowly round, crashing against the rocks.

He opened the door - a hatch now, opening upwards - and struggled out, pulling her limp body after him. He lost his balance then and, unable to retain his grip, was torn away from her by the ferocity of the current.

For a moment, the sheer weight and volume of water forced him beneath the surface. Then he saw her, surrounded by swirling debris and the backpack containing Vito's documents. Again the current sucked him under.

Surfacing, he gulped for air. He kicked his body away from a cluster of rocks that divided the river into narrow channels of roaring water. It was impossible to swim. The torrent carried him 400 yards downstream in less than a minute, transporting him as if on a liquid roller coaster.

His body slammed against the broken branch of a tree, but again the racing current snatched him from it, hurling him down a three-foot waterfall like a broken twig.

As the current again sucked him underwater, his chest tightened and he kicked out in panic, his lungs bursting. Swallowing large amounts of water, he was soon disoriented, coughing and spluttering, events flashing past him like a video on fast forward.

A mile downstream, the water shallowed and he was able to wade unsteadily across a bed of rounded pebbles to the bank. There was no sign of Katrina. His watery descent had been so tumultuous that he had not spared her a single thought.

It was not that he was uncaring, simply that survival had been paramount, all else obliterated from his mind. Exhausted, he stood thigh deep in the water clutching a handful of young birch shoots growing at the water's edge. It was then that he heard a shout and saw Katrina floating towards him.

Aware that if he did not reach her in time, she would be carried out into the open waters of a large lake, he launched himself back into the water, arms flailing. He judged his timing carefully, lunging for her arm.

The current, still swift, swivelled her body round and for a brief moment she slipped away from him. Instinctively, he dived after her, catching hold of her corduroys and dragging her to him, struggling to improve his grip.

Slowly, he manoeuvred her over his shoulder and inched back to the bank, crawling onto an uneven bed of rocks and stones. They lay there then, gasping and spluttering, their chests heaving, both recovering in their own time.

Eventually, David raised himself on all fours and glanced at her.

'You okay?' She nodded pathetically. He could see that she was dead beat. He leaned over her and she sighed, closing her eyes.

'Nothing but trouble,' she whispered.

'I told you - you should have let me drive,' he answered. He began to laugh. Uncontrollably. Scarcely knowing whether to be amused, shocked or relieved.

'This is insane. I don't believe I'm here,' he said, wiping the tears from his eyes and suddenly shivering. He looked down at her. Strands of hair were plastered to her bruised forehead, her cheeks white with exhaustion and exposure.

She was still one hell of a good looking woman, though. He stood up, his sodden clothes clinging to his body uncomfortably, and looked around.

Less than 100 yards away, behind a clump of trees, a few dozen caravans and motor homes were parked in neat rows, a camping ground on a spit of land between the river and another fjord.

He knelt down beside her and placed a hand on her arm.

'I'm gonna take a look around, okay. I think we may have struck lucky.'

'Say I am dead,' she groaned.

'Sure, Blue. Don't go away, huh?'

When he returned a few minutes later, she was sitting up, shivering. He jangled a set of keys in her face.

'Guess what? I got us a place to stay the night,' he told her. 'Come on, you can't stay here. You'll get pneumonia.'

She moaned, protesting, but he pulled her to her feet and wrapped her arm round his neck, then walked her up the path, his arm round her waist, his feet cold and numb again.

'Got a real cosy log cabin. You'll be dry and tucked up in bed in no time.'

She smiled weakly as he helped her inside. A table and four chairs were grouped by the window and there were two double-tiered bunk beds against the right hand wall. In the centre of the room, opposite the door, a fireplace was flanked on one side by a basket of kindling and on the other by a pile of birch logs.

Over in the far left hand corner, there was a small but fully equipped kitchen area and immediately to their left, a tiny bathroom. David led her to a chair and she sat, shivering, a pool of water forming round her bare feet.

'I'll get a fire lit. Then you'd better get those clothes off.' He hobbled over to the bunk and handed her a blanket. 'Here, hide yourself in this, but don't complain if I take a sneaky look, okay?'

Within a few minutes, the little fire was crackling brightly, the reflection of the flames dancing on the walls, mingling with the yellow-gold rays of the evening sun.

'I got some food from the store. Hope you like Italian cookin',' he said, opening a packet of spaghetti.

She disappeared into the bathroom.

'Woman in the camp store could hardly believe it when I handed her the money,' he called after her. 'The notes were soaking wet but I said: "What the hell, you can always iron them". Guess she thought I was nuts. Can I turn around now?'

'Yes, you can turn round now,' she said quietly.

Huddled in the blanket with the fire reflected on her high cheekbones and legs, she looked up at him and smiled, her dark eyes soft and limpid.

'I should have stopped at the road block, I think.'

'I dunno, Blue. Lookin' at you right now, I'm not so sure.'

He turned back to his cooking. 'What I do know, though, is that if we weren't both so goddam bushed, I'd give that troll from Hell you were talking about a run for his money.'

He glanced round, his mouth spread in a wide grin, but Katrina had fallen asleep.

In the cluttered offices that were the Norwegian branch of Planet Watch in the centre of Oslo, Sigrid Monk, a committed Marxist, was busily stacking new campaign posters on a trestle table. She brushed aside a strand of frizzy hair with her arm. It had been a tedious night, standing vigil outside parliament and collecting names for the new petition, and she had been working flat out in the office since six-thirty that morning.

The moment Johan Michelsen, their group leader, had heard that a multi-national company was about to embark on a mining project in the Jostedalsbre region, he had called for a twenty-four hour demonstration outside parliament. The mine would not actually be *in* a national park, but that hardly mattered. The proposed site was near enough.

Johan was in the other room planning the details of a wider campaign that would include demonstrations and mass marches in Oslo, Fjærland and other towns.

For the moment, though, she was fully occupied drawing up shifts for volunteer demonstrators. There were forms for the new petition to be duplicated and more coffee and sandwiches to be prepared for the handful of early volunteers still outside parliament.

This was the best opportunity to organise a full-blown campaign for some time. People had tired of acid rain as an issue now and trying to run an anti-whaling campaign in a whaling nation was an impossibility - like trying to be natural. Apart from that, most Norwegians rebelled against being told how to think by an environmental group they perceived as being run by foreigners.

Sigrid shifted another batch of posters and sighed. Part of the trouble, she reckoned, was that whales didn't have big brown eyes. Not like seals - and that was what you needed; big brown eyes and preferably a white furry coat to bring in the subscriptions.

When Johan emerged from the other room, his long, dark hair fastened at the neck with an elastic band, his face was bright with suppressed anger.

'You can forget the whole campaign, Sigrid,' he blurted out. 'We've been told to keep our heads down.'

Surprised, she peered at him through owlish spectacles. 'What do you mean, forget it? Who says?'

'Bloody New York, that's who says. They've been bought off, the corrupt bastards. They're as bad as everyone else. It's just big business to them.'

'But Johan, don't they understand …?'

'Of course, they don't. They said the campaign had been brought to their notice by an important contributor and, after a high level meeting, they'd decided it wasn't in Planet Watch's best interests - that we should keep as low a profile as possible.'

'Why? What right have they to order us about like that?' She, too, was angry now.

'Because Schneider Barr gives them a million dollars a year, that's why. God, they're rotten, the whole bloody lot of them.'

'Schneider Barr don't give us anything. Their only interest is in raping and polluting the country.'

'I know, but what can we do...'

She thought for a moment, then looked searchingly into his eyes. 'New York doesn't own us. We make our own decisions. It's nothing to do with them. I say we take no notice.'

Her eyes blazed with determination. She could see that he was uncertain, trying to assess New York's likely reaction.

'We can do anything we want to do, Johan,' she said quietly. 'You can't give in to them.' She took his hand. 'We *have* to fight. We can involve the whole country, run a really big anti-American campaign and increase our membership at the same time. Its the best chance we've ever had.'

Johan nodded, his forehead puckered with a frown.

'Maybe you're right,' he said, thoughtfully. For a moment he was silent. Then he grinned broadly.

'Okay, we'll go ahead as planned. We'll have a committee meeting at two o'clock this afternoon.'

When Katrina awoke, she had no idea where she was or how she had arrived there. It was some minutes before she remembered the events of the previous twenty-four hours and longer still before she recalled that she had fallen asleep in front of the fire.

She realised then that David must have carried her to her bunk.

Triggered by the pungent smell of burned birch logs from the previous evening's fire, her eyes veered automatically towards the fireplace. David had spread her borrowed clothes neatly over a chair to dry.

Raising herself onto one arm, she was filled with a deep sense of warmth and well-being. Thoroughly rested now, she dressed quickly and prepared breakfast, thankful that David had shown the foresight to buy provisions.

They ate as soon as he woke and again discussed their predicament. David repeated his view that they need have no fear of the police if she told them the truth, that she had not been kidnapped.

'That is nonsense,' she argued. 'For a start, if the police have made up their minds about something it is notoriously difficult to change their thinking. They believe you kidnapped me. That is obvious from the radio bulletin.

They also know that we stole a motor home and they actually *saw* us evading arrest by driving through the barrier.' She buttered a piece of toast.

'Add to that the press reports about your background - all that stuff about hand to hand combat and being armed and dangerous.' She shook her head. 'They would never have believed us.'

David stroked his chin, now covered with a blonde stubble as soft as down.

'Secondly, what are we going to tell them?' she asked, her voice was laced with sarcasm. 'That a helicopter full of men armed with crossbows and fire bombs tried to kill us? Because an American businessman is trying to find hidden Viking silver in Fjærland? They will think we are mad.'

David scooped up a forkful of mushrooms and spread them on his toast. 'I dunno, Katrina. You can't deny the truth …'

'It would not be so bad if we still had your grandfather's letter and that geological report,' she continued. 'Or the letter from the professor - but they are at the bottom of the river now.'

David sighed. 'Yeah, an' we don't have the motor home as evidence any more, either. With our luck, someone's probably swept up the glass from the fire bombs, as well.'

'Our best hope of convincing the police is to find the silver ourselves. They must believe us then because it will prove Vito's motive.'

'Sure, so we just go find it, huh? Get us a metal detector and wham! Go buy a yacht and a tropical island.'

Katrina poured the coffee. 'It may not be so difficult as you think. We know that if the silver exists, it will be buried somewhere near Skarestad. We can also be certain that if there were several tons of it, Ejulf Deathsword would not wish to carry it very far.'

'You mean we can narrow the area to search?'

'That's right. To begin with, the head of the fjord would have been much further inland in those days.'

'How come?'

'Because the meltwater under the ice contains tiny particles of clay and silt. That is what makes the water in the fjord green or milky-white, depending on how much there is. When the meltwater reaches the fjord, the sediment settles and gradually the shoreline is pushed further and further out.' She took another piece of toast and spread it with butter and marmalade.

'That's why a Viking ship was discovered in Skarestad - or Indre Moa - which is now at least a mile inland.

'So, if Skarestad was on the shoreline in Viking times, the silver couldn't be buried south of it because that would have been part of the fjord?'

'Exactly, but we can get even closer than that. You see, the edge of the glacier moves at about six feet a day. In Viking times, when the climate was relatively warm, the ice was probably quite far back - but in seventeen fifty-two, during the Little Ice Age, it would have been at least one thousand yards further down the valley than it is today.' She smiled. 'In fact, the farmers went to the King to try to get compensation because they said the glacier was claiming their farms. Not that he gave them anything. Anyway, that was the maximum extent of the glacier.'

'I don't get it ...'

'Let me explain.' She pushed her plate away from her, gesticulating. 'When the glacier moves, meltwater under the ice often spins small stones and pieces of rock as if they had been caught in a whirlpool, scouring out potholes from the earthen bed of the glacier.'

'Some of these potholes - they are called *moulins* - are about six feet wide and maybe three feet deep. They would be a perfect hiding place.'

'So if it's that easy, how come no one has found the silver before?'

'Two reasons. First, they were not looking. Second, even if they had known about the silver, they did not know where to look. Thirdly, Ejulf Deathsword would have covered them with earth. '

'That makes it easy?'

'Yes, you see, if Deathsword did bury the silver in a pothole, it would have to be somewhere near the edge of the ice today because after that the climate cooled and the ice moved down the valley. Only after seventeen-fifty two did it begin to recede again.' She grinned. 'I happen to know that there are two potholes at Skarestad and several more in the Supphelle valley, not far from the ice.' She grinned broadly. 'I also know where they are.'

David whistled through his teeth. 'Maybe you have something at that.' He gazed through the window, then pushed back his chair, startled.

'Jeezus. Get down,' he whispered, urgently.

Katrina looked at him, alarmed and perplexed. 'What's the matter?'

'Centaur and the pilot,' he croaked. 'They're right outside.'

Chapter Fourteen

July 6, 9.10 a.m. - July 6, 10.25 a.m.

For the Norwegian media, the morning of July the sixth marked a frenzied eruption of speculation and wild exaggeration. Tabloid newspapers splashed the alleged kidnapping of Katrina Hagen over as many as a dozen pages, combining the story with the theft of the motor home and what was assumed to be David's desperate bid to evade arrest.

Reflecting a Norwegian paranoia about the country's "big brother" neighbour, Sweden, some writers ridiculed the unfortunate family who, in the words of one tabloid, "stupidly left the ignition keys in their motor home".

Others, having calculated the driving time between the lay-by at Lunde and the police barrier, deduced that the Dynamite Man must have stopped en route and speculated as to whether he had attacked Katrina sexually.

Tor Falck's by-line was prominent in several competing publications. By selling a personal photograph of Katrina to a picture agency, the reporter had ensured that her portrait was splashed next to that of David's on most front pages.

The only difference was that layout staff had not blacked out her eyes as the law required in the case of a suspect criminal.

Inspector Ingstad had been interviewed extensively by the media representatives and was quoted at length in the newspapers as well as on radio and television. While this nurtured his ego and sense of personal importance, it also increased the pressure on him for a solution.

Was there any connection, the interviewers wanted to know, between the kidnapping and the Fjærland bombings three weeks earlier? How was that enquiry progressing? Had there been a breakthrough yet? And was there any connection between the two Americans, Larsen and George Vito? Or between Larsen and the open cast mine?

The Inspector fielded the questions as best he could but he was rattled by the experience. He longed for a week's fishing away from it all.

George Vito, on the other hand, was delighted by the media coverage. It diverted attention away from more pertinent and potentially incriminating matters. Just as importantly, it enabled him to use the media to his own advantage. He, too, had been interviewed extensively and was everybody's favourite eyewitness to the kidnapping.

The newspapers quoted him as saying that Larsen had "shoved and kicked the poor woman onto the floor of her car ... she had been stricken with terror … her appearance was dirty and dishevelled. "Small wonder," Vito added in an interview for the television cameras, "that she had driven off so erratically".

Although stating that he could not be certain, he told the reporters he thought he had seen Larsen waving a gun. The tabloid scribes needed no prompting and adhered faithfully to the journalistic maxim "Never let facts get in the way of a good story".

By the time they had keyed Vito's suggestion into their word processors, the lie had matured into a variety of weapons ranging from a "snub-nosed Beretta" to a "small but deadly Walther PPK". Only one newspaper correctly identified the weapon that David was carrying as a crossbow.

Vito knew that, if this were true, he had almost certainly taken it from Centaur or one of his men. That signalled trouble, as did Centaur's failure to contact him. What worried Vito most was that he had no way of knowing whether Centaur and Delius were dead, injured or still searching for the couple.

In any event, each moment Larsen and the Hagen woman were free threatened his own position. If the police saw the letters from Larsen's grandfather and the professor, they would doubtless want to interview him urgently. The only encouraging news was that Larsen had driven through the police barrier apparently in an attempt to avoid arrest, a development that Vito found difficult to comprehend.

He also sensed that it would not be long before the reporter, Tor Falck, began to ask more awkward questions about the helicopter. Briefly, Vito considered diverting Falck's attention by publicising Dick Longman's announcement that the ship bringing the miners and equipment to Norway would be leaving Newcastle the following evening.

After some reflection, he rejected the idea. Falck was about as trustworthy as a fox in a chicken pen. A single question on the subject of the helicopter in the company of other's of his ilk would provoke a barrage of similar enquiries, leading only to disaster.

Instead, Vito opted to lie low in his suite for the day. Calling Reception, he asked for a picnic hamper to sustain him for a long day's travelling and told the telephone operator that he would be leaving the hotel at ten o'clock that morning, and would not be returning until the following day.

If Hans Tripp called, it was too bad. He would have to learn a little patience for once. The thought brought a thin smile to his lips. He waited until the hamper had been delivered to his suite, then unfolded a local map and spent the morning trying to deduce where Ejulf Deathsword might have hidden his silver.

The Room Service waiter delivered Vito's hamper at nine-fifteen. At that precise moment, the first blast of the tunnelling project to Lunde rocked the valley. It was the first of many hundreds of such explosions. In the months and years ahead, each one would remind those who lived in Fjærland and its surrounding hamlets of the Oskarsens and Nygaards, and old Ragnar Larsen who had been blown apart in his wheelchair.

A group of British and Norwegian hikers who had left the Glacier Hotel to cross Marabreen soon after six o'clock that morning also heard the blast far below them. They paid little heed to it, however, for they had stumbled upon the crumpled body of a man hanging grotesquely over a *helle* not far from *Kvitevardane*.

Clad in a black overall, gloves and balaclava, his frozen corpse was wedged in a gulley, the neck and spine broken.

After the initial shock of the discovery, Peer Diesen, the group's leader, groped inside his backpack for the portable telephone he had brought for emergencies. A meticulous planner, he had written down a list of useful telephone numbers the previous evening. It was a precaution that paid off handsomely, for among them was the number for the Sheriff's Office at Skei.

Speaking to the Sheriff's Assistant, Peer described the man and assured the policeman that the body had not been touched. He added that he had taken a series of photographs of the corpse from different angles and gave the policeman a precise map reference for the body's location.

Confirming that the group would remain at the Glacier Hotel for another week, he promised to report immediately to the Sheriff's office on their arrival at Skei. In the meantime, the Sheriff would arrange for a helicopter to pick up the body within the hour.

During those eventful few moments, David opened the cabin door a crack and watched Centaur and Delius searching between the caravans. Waiting until they had disappeared behind a motor home parked by the water's edge, he turned to Katrina urgently.

'You got the food?'

She nodded and his eyes again scanned the camping ground.

'Okay, now!'

He grabbed her hand and they tiptoed round to the back of the cabin. Half running, half walking, they slipped past the camp store, bidding *God dag* to a group of vacationers breakfasting by the water's edge, and headed for the dirt road that led through wide fields to the village of Reed.

With luck, David reasoned, they would be able to lose themselves there - perhaps catch a bus to Sandane - but they had scarcely reached the camp exit when he heard a shout. Two hundred yards behind them, Delius was pointing in their direction and yelling to Centaur.

Breaking into a run, David realised that if they continued along the path, there was a fair chance that Centaur and Delius would catch up with them. Moreover, they were probably armed, whereas he had lost his crossbow when the motor home had fallen into the river.

Katrina was beside him, panting, one arm clutching the plastic bag of food, the other swinging awkwardly. David glanced across the fields. Vito's red and white helicopter was tethered to a wooden jetty 200 yards off to his left, next to a couple of seaplanes.

Instinctively, David deviated from the main path, cutting across a tussocky field towards a footpath that led to the aircraft, not yet sure what he would do when he reached them. In the event, he was left with little choice. The path was a dead end.

Centaur and Delius were still 200 yards behind them. David jumped onto the floating jetty, passing the helicopter, then hesitated momentarily. A young man was tinkering with one of the two seaplanes moored at the far end of the pontoon, one on each side of it.

He had no alternative now. The hunched figure turned in surprise and David slammed a fist into his face, noting that he was probably still in his early twenties.

'Sorry, old buddy.' he said, bending over him urgently, his hands rifling the pockets of his leather jacket. A Swiss army knife, nuts, bolts and screws, a box of matches, a handkerchief and two sets of key rings spilled out onto the pontoon.

Attached to each of the key rings was an identification tab with the registration lettering of the two aircraft.

'Come on, Blue, inside,' he ordered, bundling her into the passenger seat.

A loud clang on a metal bollard told him that Centaur was armed with a powerful handgun. Judging by the sound and the damage to the bollard, it was a large gun, probably a heavy service revolver with high velocity bullets.

He glanced over his shoulder and assessed the shortening distance between them at 150 yards, the range far too great for accuracy.

David bent over the young man stretched out groggily on the pontoon and grabbed the collar of his jacket.

'You know how to fly that thing?'

The mechanic shook his head. 'No, I ...'

'Okay, swim for it or they'll kill you.'

He rolled him into the water with a soft splash and he swam off, still in shock. It was then that David saw the bottle of cleaning fluid. Quickly, he sprinkled the clear blue liquid over the handkerchief.

Centaur was down on one knee taking aim a little more than 100 yards away. Delius fanned out to the right behind him, also armed.

The sound of splintering wood marked Centaur's improved accuracy, but he was still wide. For a handgun that size, he'd have to be no more than twenty-five yards distant for any degree of accuracy and the recoil would be so great that rapid firing was out of the question. That gave David the time he needed.

Zigzagging towards the helicopter, he lunged forward and lobbed the bottle through the helicopter's side window. Another bullet ripped into the pontoon.

Pausing on the helicopter's float, he struck a match, shielding the flame from the stiff breeze, and held the flame to the cloth. It caught immediately. Tossing the burning handkerchief after the bottle, he turned and raced back to the Cessna, a fourth shot smashing into the pontoon behind him.

In a single fluid motion, he cast off and climbed into the pilot's seat. Turning the ignition, he flicked the key back to both magnetos. As the engine roared to life, he set the fuel mix to rich. There was no time for pre-flight checks. He released the brakes and eased the throttle forward, his hands clammy with apprehension.

Only when the Cessna was moving out into the lake, out of Centaur's range, did he trim for take-off and scan the instruments. Starter light off. Fuel primer in and locked. Oil pressure and temperature normal. Battery re-charging. To his right, Katrina was shouting at him.

'You did not say to me you could fly.'

'Dunno if I can yet,' he shouted back at her.

Her face was frozen in shock. 'You crazy bastard. You will kill us.'

'If I don't, they will,' he answered. 'Don't worry. I've flown a thousand times on my PC back home. Got a software simulator. Same machine as this.'

Katrina shut her eyes, her face white and grim. David turned into the wind, smoothly applying full power and extending the flaps for maximum lift.

Heading into a stiffening nor'westerly sea breeze, the little seaplane bucked and jolted against the wavelets. He fought to keep the Cessna straight, toggling the rudder with his feet to counteract yawing.

For a moment, it seemed as if the aircraft would not lift off, but gradually it gathered speed, the water creaming beneath the floats. When the needle on the air speed indicator passed eighty knots, he eased the control column towards him and felt the nose lift.

Centaur cursed. The Smith and Wesson .44 Magnum was useless for this kind of work. One of the most powerful handguns in the world, it was too heavy, too slow and too inaccurate. He regretted leaving his crossbow in the helicopter.

With the Demon Safari, he could easily have put a bolt through the back of Larsen's head at that range, but he could hardly go tramping around public camping grounds carrying a seven pound crossbow.

Delius was peeling off to his left and raising his arm to fire, but Centaur could see from his stance that he would do no damage. He was as likely to hit the helicopter as Larsen.

Centaur knelt down on one knee and fired, steadying his left wrist with the thumb and forefinger of his right hand.

Again, he missed, the recoil power of the Magnum forcing his arm to the sky. He shrugged. No way could you hit a moving target at that range. The revolver was truly accurate only at twenty yards. Its advantage was the wound.

With the gun's enormous power, high velocity and thumb-sized bullets, it could blast a man's arm off. A body shot would turn his guts into soup.

As the seaplane's engines revved, Centaur rose to his feet and sprinted towards the jetty, then paused again for another shot.

It was then that he saw the flames licking through the Bolkow's windows thirty yards ahead of him. Stopping in his tracks, he yelled to Delius over to his left, approaching warily now, fearful that the helicopter would explode.

The Cessna began to move out into the lake, out of range. Centaur quickly assessed the options. The flames in the helicopter were not yet out of control. Delius was crouching behind a clump of young birch shoots on the shoreline. Centaur yelled across at him.

'Get that other seaplane started.'

Delius leapt onto the pontoon, followed seconds later by Centaur who wrenched open the rear door of the helicopter. A wall of flame rushed out, caught by the breeze. He shielded his face with his arm and reached in, grabbing his treasured Demon Safari, then hurled himself back onto the pontoon.

Delius, a competent fixed-wing pilot, had found the keys abandoned by the mechanic on the pontoon, and was already at the controls of the second seaplane, gunning the engine. Centaur cast off and climbed in beside him.

'Okay, let's go get the mothers. This time, I want that sonofabitch Larsen in his grave.'

At two hundred feet, David raised the take-off flaps, his eyes scanning the skies above and to either side of him, his adrenalin flowing and his heart thumping. Katrina sat silently and frightened beside him.

Craning his neck, David glanced through the side window to the rear of the aircraft and was gratified to see the Bolkow engulfed in orange flame. At any moment now, the fuel tanks would blow. He was less gratified to see the second seaplane moving out into the lake for a take-off run.

Holding the Cessna on a straight and steady climb, steering three-zero-zero degrees for Sandane, he turned to Katrina and told her to strap herself in, then did so himself.

'We got a problem,' he shouted. 'Correction. We got two problems. First, they're following us in the other 'plane. Second ... well, I guess taking off and flying is fairly easy. Landing's a different ball game.' He grinned at her sheepishly. 'Still, you create your own luck in life, huh?'

Katrina groaned and shook her head, her dark brown eyes wide and disbelieving.

They were at seven hundred feet now, climbing steadily. David trimmed the aircraft and set the fuel mixture back to lean, then gently tested the control column and rudder pedals. The Cessna banked and yawed wildly. Katrina remained silent, clutching her harness, her knuckles shining like white beacons from her sunburned skin.

'No panic,' he cried. 'Controls are a little more sensitive than I thought, that's all.'

She rolled her eyes to the heavens. Five minutes after take-off they flew over Sandane heading seawards over the dark and choppy waters of the *Gloppenfjord*. To their left, a range of snow-capped mountains was partially shrouded in banks of cloud, their base heavy and grey.

David reduced throttle and pushed the control column forward to drop the nose so that he could see to his right. Below them, a windsock at Sandane airfield was stretched parallel to the ground. Katrina leaned towards him, shouting above the noise of the engine.

'Why are you heading out to sea?'

He shrugged. 'Because without coordinates, I don't know how to navigate. I don't even know where we are.'

'Then we must turn right, over there,' she said, pointing to the mountains.

He grinned. 'Have faith. We'll be okay.'

'I will believe that when I am on the ground again,' she shouted. 'Preferably in one piece.'

'In that case, you'd better put a parachute on. There'll be one under the seat.'

Katrina glanced at him, the import of what he had said bringing a new fear to her face.

'Dear God, are you insane?'

She groped under the seat and David banked into a twenty degree right turn. Maintaining his climbing speed with the elevator, he followed a new heading of three-two-four degrees, a course which, although he was unaware of it, was taking him directly towards Stadt, possibly the most exposed and dangerous section of the entire Norwegian coast.

Levelling off at two thousand feet, David showed Katrina how to don her 'chute, then reached for his own. 'Hold her steady while I sort mine out,' he said.

Katrina leaned towards him, holding the column with her left hand, but she was unable to retain control. The 'plane dipped and yawed.

'I said steady,' he yelled.

'I am holding it steady, damn you.'

'It's like being in an airborne rodeo.'

'Yes, well I am not such an experienced pilot as you,' she said, sarcastically. 'Anyway, you're going the wrong way. At this rate, we will soon be over the Atlantic.'

He looked at her in alarm and banked right until the compass showed sixty degrees. Climbing to avoid the mountains ahead, he watched the altimeter creep to four thousand, then five thousand feet. Katrina gazed out of the window.

'I think that must be *Horninsdalsvatn*,' she said. 'It is the deepest inland lake in the world.' She pulled out a map tucked between the seats and with her finger traced their route since take-off. 'We can fly to Åndalsnes. I have friends there.'

'Wherever you say. Where's that other 'plane?' David asked, skirting another peak.

She peered out of the window. 'Over there, behind us.'

'Yeah, but where behind us.'

Katrina looked at him, puzzled. 'Up there,' she shouted, pointing. 'You see it? It is just a dot in the sky.'

'Jeez, you stupid bitch, *where?* Two o'clock, four o'clock? *Where?*'

Katrina turned to him angrily. 'If you ever again call me a "stupid bitch", I shall hit you.'

'If you don't like it, you have my permission to leave. Now where in hell is that 'plane.' He leaned across her, inadvertently pushing the control column. The Cessna lurched to the right, losing height rapidly. Katrina screamed.

David regained control quickly. 'Four o'clock high, six miles away and closing,' he said. 'You take the nose of the aircraft as twelve o'clock and the tail as six, then estimate the rest. Simple.'

'Thank you for the lesson.'

'Okay, okay. Sorry.'

Delius checked his instruments. Heading zero-four-eight. Ten-hundred hours. If Larsen kept his present course and speed, he'd be with him in about ten minutes, then he could choose his moment. The other aircraft's attitude told him that Larsen was an inexperienced pilot. It was a miracle he hadn't stalled, the way he'd set the flaps on take-off.

Since then, the aircraft had flipped into several uncontrolled manoeuvres, notably skidding turns with too much rudder pressure. Delius hummed tunelessly, smiling to himself. He had already calculated a plan of action. All he needed now was a sheer mountain rockface dropping down from a plateau.

Ahead, a group of mountains known as The Chessmen - King, Queen and Bishop - were four miles distant at one o'clock low. He checked the map on his knee and selected his point of contact, *Trollveggen*, The Troll's Wall. It was exactly what he needed, the highest vertical mountain wall in Europe. Five thousand five hundred feet high, of which three thousand feet were sheer with a one hundred and fifty foot overhang. If he could force Larsen over that, the rest would be simple.

Banking left, Delius eased the control column forward. The nose dipped and the needle on the air speed indicator crept to one-forty knots. Levelling off at six thousand feet, slightly above, behind and to the left of Larsen, he gradually drew parallel with the other 'plane.

Deftly, he edged closer, so that the wing tips were nearly touching. Centaur slid back the small half-window, grinning as Larsen peered at him from the other Cessna, his mouth tight and thin.

Ice cold air rushed into the cabin as Centaur rested the barrel of the Magnum on the window ledge. Suddenly, Larsen peeled off to the right. Centaur simultaneously drew back the trigger and fired.

The sound of the blast filled the interior of the plane and the recoil was so forceful that the barrel slammed into the top of the window nearly breaking Centaur's wrist. But the bullet did more damage, ripping through the Cessna's float and tearing a hole the size of a football in its skin.

Delius banked and followed the other aircraft, first climbing, then descending. As Larsen straightened out of his roll, heading directly for *Trollveggen*, Delius lined up with the little 'plane and with infinite care positioned himself directly above and slightly behind it.

Inspector Ingstad rose that morning dreading the thought of having to go to the office. He had slept atrociously, waking from a nightmare in which he had been locked inside a room filled with ping pong balls. His superiors had ordered him to catch them, but the balls had been bouncing off the walls at high speed and he had failed miserably.

This sense of inadequacy continued to permeate his thoughts as he gazed out of the breakfast room window at the Kvikne's Hotel at Balestrand. No matter how beautiful the fjord, he would gave given much to be back in Oslo with his wife, Janice, and leave the case to Nielsen, who was breakfasting alone at a separate table.

A waiter interrupted his daydreams to inform him that the Sheriff's Office in Skei was on the telephone. He pushed his cereal to one side and walked through to the lobby. The Sheriff sounded buoyant.

'*God morgen*, Inspector. I hope you're ready for this.' He chuckled. 'Quite the most exciting morning I've had in forty-five years of police work.'

'I really need some excitement in my life,' Ingstad said sarcastically. 'What's happened?'

'Everything!' The Sheriff's voice was tight with exhilaration. 'Gun battles, a helicopter on fire, two seaplanes stolen, bodies turning up on Marabreen. It's like Hollywood over here.'

'*Jøsses. Hva siger De*?'

'First of all, we had a report at nine-fifteen this morning from a group of hikers up on Marabreen. Said they'd found a body. Male, aged about thirty. From the description, it sounds as if he might have a broken neck and spine. I've arranged for a chopper to pick up the corpse.'

The Sheriff babbled on. 'Don't know if it has anything to do with your case but as your man, Larsen, was up there yesterday, I thought you'd like to know.'

Ingstad whistled. 'I certainly would. *Fy Satan*! What a bastard!'

'Well, you said he'd been trained in hand to hand combat. From the first reports, the injuries suggest that the victim might have been attacked.'

'I'll get Sergeant Nielsen. We'll come over right away. We'll be with you in two or three hours. What's all this about gun battles?'

The Sheriff chuckled again. 'We had another report half an hour ago from an aircraft mechanic at Reed. All hell's let loose there. Seems a man and a woman - no doubt Larsen and Katrina Hagen - were involved in a shoot-out near a camping ground …'

'I told you, this man's dangerous …'

'Insane, too, probably. According to the mechanic, who was on a pontoon, Larsen knocked him out, emptied his pockets and dumped him in the water. Then he set fire to the helicopter, bundled the woman into the seaplane and took off. Cool as you like.'

'We have to catch this man. He's a menace. Any idea where they are now?'

'No. They flew northwest. That's all we know.'

'We'll put out a national alert immediately.' Ingstad thought for a moment. 'Why would he want to set fire to a helicopter?'

'Presumably because it belonged to the two men who were shooting at him.'

Ingstad paused, conscious of a sinking feeling in the pit of his stomach.

'Two men? What two men?'

'That's just it. We don't know. Eye witnesses at a camping ground nearby say they arrived in a helicopter last night, then turned up again this morning claiming they were private detectives. Asked if anyone had seen a man and a woman answering to the description of Larsen and Hagen.'

A cold chill crept up Ingstad's spine. When he spoke, his voice was tight. 'And the two men started shooting at Larsen and the girl? Not the other way round?'

'That's right. The mechanic was quite specific. He said the two men were firing at Larsen and the woman. Larsen was desperate. Asked the mechanic if he could fly the seaplane. When he told him that he couldn't, he knocked the lad out and stole the keys.'

'So these men were trying to kill Larsen?'

'That's right.' The Sheriff's words poured out, excitedly. 'Bullet's flying round all over the place. When Larsen saw the mechanic coming round, he told him to swim for it or the two men would kill him. That's when he pushed him into the water. The lad swam off and said he then saw Larsen - if it was Larsen, of course - set fire to the helicopter, jump into the seaplane and take off.'

The Inspector's mind was reeling. He no longer knew what to think. If someone was trying to kill Larsen, who was it - and why? Could it be for the same reason that Ragnar Larsen had been killed? And if the gunmen had arrived in a helicopter, whose was it?

His mind was alert now. Could this be the helicopter that Falck and Katrina Hagen had seen immediately before the Fjærland bombing? The breakthrough that he needed so desperately? The Sheriff's voice cut across his thoughts.

'You still there, Inspector?'

'Yes. Tell me, what colour was the helicopter?'

'Red and white, I believe. Why?'

Ingstad spoke urgently now, his voice impatient. 'Any idea of the registration letters?'

'Yes, I have them here somewhere. Hang on a second.' The line went dead. Ingstad drummed his fingers on the 'phone book.

'Yes, here we are,' the Sheriff said. 'L-XRYA. Why? Is that significant?'

It was Vito's helicopter.

'Significant? *Jøsses i helvete*. It's the most significant thing that's happened for three weeks.'

His voice took on a commanding tone now, the voice of a man who knew what he wanted and how to get it.

'I want that helicopter or what's left of it sealed off immediately. No one - and I mean no one including you - is to touch it. I want a twenty-four hour guard put on it.'

'I'm not sure I'll be able to do that.'

'You'll find a way. I don't care if you have to bring someone in on overtime or drag 'em out of a sick bed, but I want that helicopter under guard immediately. In the meantime, I want to know if it has been repainted recently. I leave that to you. Find out if there are military markings beneath the red and white paint.'

'Right, straight away, Inspector.'

Ingstad thought rapidly. 'Before you go - what happened to the two men?'

'The two men? I thought I told you ... They took the other seaplane. Took-off in the same direction about five minutes after Larsen.'

'*Helvete*!' Ingstad's mind raced through the options. 'The helicopter that's collecting the body on Marabreen,' he demanded, 'where's that?'

'Should be here in ten minutes or so, Inspector.'

'Good. Have the pilot pick us up first. We'll be waiting on the jetty opposite the Glacier Hotel. I'll be with you as soon as I can.'

He replaced the receiver, then picked it up again. He knew now that he'd been a fool, obsessed with the idea that Larsen was to blame for the Fjærland bombings. He owed Larsen - and Nielsen - an apology.

Dialling Kripos headquarters in Oslo, he requested that all air controllers in western Norway be alerted to look out for the two aircraft. Then he walked back to the breakfast room.

'Nielsen,' he bellowed.

Chapter Fifteen

June 6, 10.25 a.m. - 11.45 a.m.

Straightening out from his right hand turn, David searched the skies for the other Cessna but, unable to see it, could only assume that it was somewhere behind him. He had intended to drop down from the mountains into a wide valley to his left, then attempt a landing at Åndalsnes, a small town clustered on a peninsula that jutted into the Romsdalsfjord. That plan was now redundant; the other pilot had forced him to change course to starboard and instead he was now heading directly towards the plateau leading to *Trollveggen*.

Levelling off at five thousand eight hundred feet, he heard a thud on the roof of the aircraft and simultaneously experienced a sharp loss of height. Katrina gasped, her arms rising involuntarily as she sought wildly for support.

'David, they are on top of us,' she shouted. 'They're trying to force us down.'

Grimly, David pulled back the control column, but the aircraft failed to respond. He increased power for extra lift, but to no avail. Ahead, the lip of *Trollveggen* was less than half a mile away. A scraping of metal on metal above him preceded a further loss of height, but this time his enforced descent was steady and relentless. Katrina moaned despairingly.

Craning his neck, David could see the wings of the other plane directly above him. It was if the Cessna had suddenly grown into a biplane.

'Jeezus,' he shouted. 'The bastards are sitting on us.'

The altimeter showed five thousand seven hundred feet - less than two hundred feet clearance between them and the rough, snow-covered rock below.

Pushing the control column forward, he nosed the plane into a shallow, diving bank to port, then starboard. If he could make it to the edge of *Trollveggen*, he would have room to manoeuvre. Flying at no more than seventy feet above the ground, he glimpsed the needle sharp pinnacles of rock directly ahead of him and again tried to climb, but the other pilot followed. Another sharp "clunk" on the roof of the cockpit signalled that he had failed to shake him off.

David's hands were sweating. Beside him, Katrina was mute, her body frozen with fear. They were fewer than two hundred yards from *Trollveggen* now and he was being pushed inexorably into a descent - with nowhere to go.

It was as if he was flying in a room in which the ceiling was gradually being lowered onto him, his only escape through a tiny, narrowing window. Unable to climb, turn or land, he glanced at Katrina.

'If you've got any prayers, Blue,' he yelled, 'for God's sake - say 'em now.'

In the breakfast room at the Glacier Hotel, Tor Falck had chosen a corner table by the tall windows. Here, he reflected that freelancing was proving more lucrative than he could have imagined, although he appreciated that success at this level was likely to be short-lived.

When Ingstad had burst through the double doors demanding Nielsen's immediate attention, the scrape of cutlery and muted conversation had died instantly.

Nielsen and Falck rose from their chairs as one man, both wondering what momentous event could have galvanised the Inspector into making such a spectacle of himself.

Nielsen abandoned his coffee and toast and joined the Inspector in the lounge. Falck followed them out. Ingstad paused briefly at Reception and asked for George Vito, but the woman on duty informed him that Mr. Vito had gone out for the day and would not be back until late evening.

'Lucky for him,' Ingstad chuckled.

Nielsen looked at him sharply. The Inspector had changed. He'd hadn't seen him this cheerful for years.

'What's up, sir? Won the national lottery? Or are you just feeling a bit off colour?'

'Nielsen, when you've heard what I've got to tell you, you'll be a happy man, as well.' He turned to the journalist. 'What are you waiting for, Falck? Turn of the century?'

'I know the smell of a good story, Inspector. And you've got one.'

'All right, you put us on to it,' he said, relenting. He clattered down the hotel's front steps. 'Seems you might be right about that helicopter. They've found it over at Skei.'

He hurried down the path to the gate and strode across the gardens to the jetty.

'Sheriff's checking the paintwork now. We're going over there as soon as his chopper can pick us up.'

'Any chance of a lift?'

'If there's room, but we've a body to collect as well.'

Nielsen started. 'A body? Whose body is that, sir?'

'That'll be for you to find out, Sergeant.'

The Inspector grinned. Pacing up and down the jetty, he brought the two men up to date. Tor Falck couldn't remember ever having seeing the Inspector smile before.

Jimmie Hargreaves was not the kind of man to lie around in bed in the mornings, but when he had awoken at seven-thirty to see the sun streaming through the curtains, he had decided that this day would be different. When Doris had stirred beside him, he had told her that she was on no account to go to work.

Today would be a day off, he whispered. She had sighed contentedly and they had both slept on. When he next woke, Jimmie was surprised to see the digital display on his bedside radio clock glowing ten-thirty.

Stretching, he turned over and snuggled up to Doris, kissing the back of her neck and running his lips along her bare shoulder. She stirred, happily, and looked up at him, her grey-green eyes soft and sleepy.

'I love you, Jimmie,' she whispered.

'Ay, an' I love thee an' all, our Doris.' He stroked her hair, tousled from the night, and kissed her, his hand resting gently on her cheek before moving down to her breast. 'I doan't know what it is, but tha's always 'ad this strange effect on us.'

'I know. I can feel it, Jimmie 'argreaves, but I'm 'ungry an' it's breakfast time.' She giggled, struggling to escape his embrace.

He massaged her breast and felt her nipple rise to his touch.

'Aw, come on, Doris love. Tha canna leave us like this.'

She smiled then and relaxed, her eyes alight with mischievousness. 'You're a devil, you are. A big, lovely, cuddly devil.' She clutched him to her, her tongue seeking his, her hands parading up and down his strong, broad back and over his lean buttocks.

Joyously and with passion they loved each other then until, exhausted, they lay warm and content in each other's arms.

'We'll go t' Durham for t' day,' Jimmie said. 'I'll buy thee lunch and we'll take the bus out to 'amsterley Forest. 'Ave a day in t' country together.'

'Ay, but not just yet, our Jimmie.'

She propped herself on one arm and grinned at him, running a hand down the flat of his stomach.

'If tha's goin' t' be away for four weeks, I want a bit more of t' same.'

Jimmie laughed. 'You're a reet little trollop, you are, Doris 'argreaves.'

For a full ninety seconds, David Larsen held his breath. Flying little more than ten metres above the undulating surface, he no longer had any height to lose. The other pilot remained directly above him, leaving him no room to turn. Instead, he steered the Cessna through the jagged pinnacles that marked the lip of *Trollveggen*.

The rockface fell away, sheer and terrifying, so steep that apart from isolated ledges, there was no place even for the snow to rest.

'Hold tight,' he yelled, nosing the aircraft into a tight dive. Levelling off at three thousand five hundred feet, he gave the engine full throttle and climbed steeply to starboard.

The other pilot followed. David maintained his climbing turn. A plan began to form in his mind. If he could gain enough height, he could play the same game - sit on top of them and force them into the Troll's Wall.

On full climbing power, he dragged the control column back, setting the aircraft to its maximum climb angle. But in his anxiety, he forgot to re-set the mixture to fully rich. Nor did he notice the engine temperature creeping rapidly upwards as the engine produced greater heat energy and his lower airspeed reduced the air cooling.

Inevitably, the engine overheated and stalled. The nose of the 'plane dropped sharply. *Trollveggen* was directly ahead, the altimeter reading five thousand feet. David struggled with the controls, then turned desperately to Katrina.

'I've lost it,' he yelled. 'We'll have to jump.'

Katrina looked at him, her face tight and drawn. David leaned over and unsnapped her harness.

'Count to three, then pull this handle real hard, okay? Now go!'

Katrina leaned against the door with all her strength, forcing it open against the wind. Then she was gone.

David tried to steady the Cessna, but the seaplane was in the first downward arc of a spin. He reached for his own door and wrenched it open. The needle on the altimeter spun past four thousand one hundred feet.

He jumped then, spreading his arms and legs wide as he dropped into free fall. He had jumped many times before with the Delta Force and felt the same exhilaration now. It was one of the few times he could enjoy heights, his acrophobia inactive because he was not in contact with the ground. But this time the joy of flying free was tainted with concern.

His anxiety was relieved only when he saw Katrina's 'chute open, the canopy billowing yellow and scarlet against the damp blue-grey scree far below him. Streaked with water channels and edged with birch trees, it fanned out like a ballerina's skirt to the valley floor.

His own 'chute snapped open with a crack at about three thousand feet, wrapping him abruptly in a deep, pervasive silence. Checking the blue and white canopy, he tugged a guy line and steered away from the rock face, helped by a gentle three knot breeze.

Below him, the Cessna spun out of control, then hit a rock ledge.

Surprisingly, it did not burst into flames, breaking instead into several sections, the tailplane, wings and fuselage bouncing soundlessly down the mountainside.

Katrina was drifting towards the open fields that bordered the wide river snaking along the centre of the valley. He wished he had been able to give her rudimentary landing instructions. With no experience or instruction, she did not know how to steer the 'chute and her landing was likely to be heavy. Toggling his canopy, David steered towards her and, moments later, turned into the wind for a stand-up landing.

'What now?' Delius asked Centaur.

'They jumped. We gotta get down.'

'I can put down on the fjord or on a lake.'

Exasperated, Centaur slammed the butt of the Magnum into his thigh. 'I don't give a shit. Just get down.'

'Okay, keep your hair on ...'

Delius had scarcely uttered the words than he felt the barrel of the Magnum jammed into his neck, just below his right ear.

'You ever make a crack like that again, dickbrain, an' your head's gonna be a nasty smell on the ceilin'. Now get this crate down. We got some catchin' up to do.'

'We'll go for the lake,' Delius answered tersely. 'It's closer than the fjord and there's a road leading to the next valley - where they landed.'

He headed back the way they had come, sweat breaking out on his forehead.

The lake was about half a mile from *Trollstigen*, a mountain road comprising eleven hairpin bends and a tortuous gradient of one in twelve. Delius pointed to a group of log cabins at the top.

'That's the tourist information centre. We'll get a vehicle there.'

Delius executed a perfect landing and switched off the ignition. Jumping onto the float, he pulled two large paddles from the rear locker and handed one to Centaur. Slowly, the two men sculled the seaplane to the shore and moored it to a rock, then hopped across snow-covered tussocks and gurgling bogs to the cluster of log cabins. On reaching them, Centaur wasted no time.

'You know how to drive an auto with a gear shift?'

'Sure, why?'

'Not everyone can.' He nodded towards the parking lot. 'Over there.'

Striding towards a bright yellow Citröen, he shoved the Magnum through the window and menacingly demanded the keys from a French tourist and his wife.

'If you wanna live, out!.'

Eyes bulging, the couple relinquished the car without a word. Delius slipped into the driving seat. Centaur nuzzled the Magnum into the Frenchman's neck.

'Stay where you are. Count to one thousand. One murmur and I'll be back to take your legs off.'

Delius released the handbrake and gunned the engine. Centaur slipped into the passenger seat.

'Okay, we got transport. How long before we get to Larsen and the broad?'

Delius accelerated, then braked hard to negotiate the first hairpin. 'Fifteen, twenty minutes, maybe.'

'Make it ten. I'm in a hurry.'

Delius glanced in the rear view mirror. The French couple were rooted to the spot.

Katrina was ecstatic, all fear of the flight dissipated. The parachute jump had been an incredible experience; quite indescribable - exhilarating, beautiful, tranquil and exciting all rolled into one. She couldn't think of enough words to describe it.

Landing had been a jolt, but somehow - perhaps due to a lifetime coping with the hazards of skiing - she had rolled over and spread the shock over her whole body.

Once she had untangled herself from all the guy ropes and realised that she was not hurt, she was unable to resist whooping with joy.

A gust of wind caught the canopy, carrying it flapping across the field towards the river until its scarlet and yellow panels caught in a birch tree. Elated, she watched David drift to the ground and ran towards him as he folded his 'chute into a tight bundle.

'It was fantastic,' she cried, grabbing his hands and gaily swinging him round.

'Hey, hold on. What is this? You okay?'

'Brilliant. It was wonderful. The silence. I never knew it could be so beautiful.' Her words gushed forth excitedly. 'It was so *quiet*. At first, I was scared. You know, when the ground started to sway. I had not expected that. I thought *I* would be the one to sway - and the ground came up much faster than I thought when I landed, but I did not hurt myself and …'

'Okay, okay. Calm down.'

'Oh, David, it was wonderful.' She leaned forward and kissed his cheek, surprised at the softness of his stubble. 'I am so *happy*.'

'Happy? You're crazy. Two maniacs are trying to kill us, we get shot at and steal a seaplane we can't fly, then nearly kill ourselves destroying it - and you're happy? It's been a hell of a morning.'

He pointed to the sheer, granite cliff that was *Trollveggen*, slate grey and gloomy, a pillar of cloud spilling over its edge.

'Look at that thing. It's unreal.'

She laughed, tossing limp curls off her forehead. 'It is real, all right. It is called "The Troll's Wall". People said it could not be climbed. Then, in the mid-sixties, some English and Norwegian climbers proved that it could. It took them fourteen days, climbing different routes.'

'They're as crazy as you are.'

'People have jumped off it, too - parachutists, I mean. That is forbidden now. But *we* have done it, David.'

Her shook his head, disbelievingly.

'You are one crazy woman. Come on, let's stow these 'chutes and go find civilisation.'

'Well, what's the answer?'

Inspector Ingstad stepped onto the pontoon and shook the Sheriff's hand, followed by Sergeant Nielsen and Falck. Moored in the shallows, the scorched remains of the helicopter had been sealed off with white tape. The Sheriff's men had assembled other pieces of metal on the pontoon.

You were right. Look.'

The sheriff pointed to a section of the door. The paintwork had curled and flaked with the heat of the fire, revealing two distinct layers of paint.

'Hm. Doesn't show the colouring, though,' Ingstad muttered.

'No, but this does.' The Sheriff picked up a piece of twisted metal. 'Part of the window panel. The paint's brittle enough to peel off. See?'

He picked at the edge with his fingernail. 'It's like a blister. Top skin is clearly red, with a small white border. Underneath its dark green - and, here, this wavy area is sand-coloured paint.'

'Camouflage, sir. No doubt about it,' Nielsen said.

'I can see that, Sergeant. I'm not blind.' He turned back to the Sheriff.

'We'll get Forensic up here immediately. In the meantime, I want the entire area sealed off. If, as you say, there's been shooting here, I want any evidence I can get of it. Right Nielsen, get on with it.'

'Yes, sir.'

Nielsen strode off across the field towards the camping ground. The Inspector yelled after him.

'And pass the word to whoever's running that camping ground; all ghouls will be arrested immediately for obstruction.' He winked genially at the Sheriff. 'Well done. You've done a good job. Intriguing case to retire on, eh?'

'Another six weeks, Inspector. That's all. Then it's sailing, skiing and slippers for me.'

'Lucky devil,' Ingstad replied. He was a different man now, with renewed confidence and direction. He clapped the journalist on the back. 'Well, Falck, where does this leave us?'

Falck grinned, revealing a set of teeth stained by nicotine. 'It leaves you with the helicopter that was directly involved in the Fjærland bombings, Inspector ...'

'Right. A helicopter that belongs to, or was hired by, George Vito ...'

'... who's been trying every trick in the book to buy old Ragnar Larsen's land.'

The journalist flipped over the cover of his notebook and pushed it into the pocket of his anorak.

'My guess is that both Ragnar and David Larsen told him where to get off. If Vito subsequently arranged Ragnar Larsen's death, killing six other people in the process, then he's about as ruthless as you can get.' He lit a Prince Light cigarette. 'And if that assessment is right, there's no reason why he wouldn't try to have David Larsen killed, as well.'

Falck waddled back to the shoreline, Ingstad at his side.

'You know, Vito was very quick to push his version of the so-called kidnapping, but he was the only witness. Suppose there *was* no kidnapping. It's not impossible that Vito invented that story for his own convenience.'

'Yes, but why, Falck. Why?'

The reporter frowned. 'I don't know. At first I thought it was something to do with that copper mine, but that doesn't seem logical now. I reckon there's something else that we don't know about.'

'You mean, Larsen and Katrina Hagen might have stumbled on something?'

'That's right. Something Vito is desperate to stop them revealing. I think they were just desperate to get the hell out of the place and avoid him.'

They fell silent for a moment, then paused on the grass bank at the end of the jetty.

'So he sent Greenwood and that other wierdo, Centaur, after them in his helicopter?'

'That's exactly what I mean, Inspector.' He gestured to the wrecked helicopter. 'The remains of the chopper, eye witness accounts of the shooting and the descriptions from the people in the camping ground -

they all fit. And Greenwood is an experienced pilot. He'd certainly have known how to fly a Cessna.'

The Inspector nodded, turning back to the Sheriff, who was scraping more paint from the twisted metal door.

'Mind if we borrow your helicopter again, Sheriff?'

'Anything you say, Inspector.' The Sheriff chuckled. 'Best day's policing in forty-five years. Couldn't have wished for a better way to end my career.'

Falck flicked his cigarette butt into the water and tapped the inspector on the arm. 'Any chance of a lift, Inspector? So I can make the evening papers?'

'I'm hungry,' Katrina said, taking David's arm. She steered him through the parking lot at the foot of *Trollveggen*, weaving neatly through rows of automobiles, motor homes and coaches towards the cafeteria. Ordering coffee and rolls filled with slices of Norwegian goat cheese, they sat by the window next to a party of musicians jovially discussing their next gig.

Their leader, a trumpet player with a hairline moustache and hair drawn back into a pigtail said they were scheduled to play that afternoon at the annual Jazz Festival at Molde.

Amused, Katrina studied David's face as he slipped naturally into their conversation, oblivious both to her and his surroundings.

'How long have you been playing tenor sax?' one of the bandsmen asked him politely.

'Since I was shoulder high to Coleman Hawkins,' David replied, laughing. 'Back home in Willmar, in the U.S., I have my own group, the Kandi County Vanguard. Play rhythm and blues mostly.' He finished his roll and wiped his mouth. 'Mind you, I'm not averse to somethin' a little more avant garde. A little Mingus, maybe.'

'Hey, now you're talkin', man,' said the drummer. 'You should come join us - be an East Street Jammer for a while.

Katrina smiled, mentally tracing the line of David's face. Even in repose, it was strong and resolute, the square jaw and deepening lines of his forehead reflecting the character of a man who had experienced life to the full, yet remained undaunted by it. She gazed out of the window strangely excited, the babble of jazz talk receding as her inmost thoughts drifted back to Tor, Paul Stryn and her barren life in Fjærland.

Only vaguely aware of the scraping of chairs that signalled the impending departure of the East Street Jammers, she knew that she wanted David more than ever now. It had been inevitable since that first dawning moment in the motor home the previous day. Again, as if unwilling to admit the obvious, she deliberately ejected the thought from her mind.

The sound of brakes squealing outside rocketed her back into the real world.

Alarmed by her sharp intake of breath, David noticed her staring mesmerized through the picture window, her gaze drawn to a yellow Citroën and the bulky figure of Centaur coolly surveying the parking lot, Delius at his side.

'How in hell did they get here?' David asked.

'I don't know. They must have found a car and driven down *Trollstigen*. From the top of the mountain.'

David glanced round. The remaining Jammers were gathered by the door, pulling on their anoraks, bantering with each other noisily.

'Quick,' David said, grabbing her hand. He pulled her round the table. 'Mingle with them. Safety in numbers.'

'Can we ride with you to Molde?' she asked the bassist, sweetly. 'We would love to hear your concert.'

'If you don't mind sitting on a box,' he said, looping an arm round her shoulder. 'The coach is over there.'

He pointed to a line of vehicles thirty yards from the Citroën and escorted her to a dilapidated nineteen-forty-nine Leyland, its flanks covered with dust and mud. Centaur and Delius were searching frantically further along the line.

'It's a miracle she's still going,' the bassist said. 'She'd seen better days quarter of a century ago, but she's home to us.'

'And a haven for us,' David muttered.

They climbed on board, the jazzmen laughing raucously amongst themselves at some private joke.

'Welcome to the kennel,' the bassist said, hurriedly clearing seats for them. The driver started the engine and the old bus shuddered in protest, then swung out into the clearway that separated the lines of vehicles, slowly gathering speed.

David glanced out of the window and, startled, found himself staring directly into Centaur's eyes.

Both men were equally stunned. Centaur immediately turned on his heel and began to run. The coach swung round the corner onto the main road. David craned his neck and watched him motioning to Delius to join him. Swivelling round, he peered through the opposite window in time to see them clambering into a yellow Citroën. His eyes sought Katrina's.

'They've seen us,' he mouthed.

Beyond the odd comment, Tor Falck and Inspector Ingstad slipped into an amiable silence as the Sheriff's helicopter transported them directly to Fjærland, its rotors drowning out any sensible conversation. Ingstad had left Nielsen at Reed to help the Sheriff. If Vito was out for the day, he shouted into the journalist's ear, there was not much he could do until he returned. At this stage, he was reluctant to issue a general alert for him. It seemed more logical to take him by surprise.

The thirty-minute flight from Reed was uneventful. Immediately on landing, Falck moved into a single room at the Glacier Hotel, pausing only for a brief word with Paul Stryn, who was preparing to take Hanna, the new waitress, for a walk on her morning off.

'To be honest, I've been at a bit of a loose end, old boy. All this business with that Vito fellow. Dashed nuisance. Any news of my client, by the way?'

'Only what's in the papers,' Falck replied.

'Ha. One can't believe half of what you journalist chappies write. Oh well, must dash. Let me know if something turns up, won't you?'

He took Hanna by the arm and escorted her to the front steps, the ultimate gentleman, infinitely more British in his outlook and manner than the British themselves.

Falck watched them go and speculated that within twenty-four hours Stryn would have forgotten that he was besotted with Katrina Hagen. Instead, he would have fallen head over heels in love with the girl on his arm. And why not, he reasoned. They made a better couple.

Lumbering up the stairs to the second floor, he unlocked the door to his room. The telephone was ringing.

'The *Balestrand Posten* for you, sir,' the hotel operator informed him.

Falck smiled. He had wondered how long it would be before he heard from them.

'Hello, Tor?' It was Handjob.

'Handjob, you unpleasant little turd, how's life at the factory?'

He could picture the weasel-like face and weak chin. He'd be squirming with embarrassment. Ordered by the Editor to contact him. Unable to disobey, yet unwilling to speak to him.

'Come off it, Tor. No need to be like that.'

'Of course not. Not now we're on first name terms. It was always Falck before, wasn't it? Now, all of a sudden, it's Tor.'

He peered out of the window. Stryn was strolling round the gardens at the edge of the fjord, Hanna clutching his arm.

'Just trying to be friendly,' the News Editor said.

'You don't have friends, Handjob. People either detest you or hate your guts. There's nothing in between. By the way, how's that black eye I gave you?'

'Healing. Thanks for the concern.'

'Taken up diving, yet?'

'No, why?'

'Because I have a very good scuba kit for you. It's made of concrete.'

Falck listened cruelly to the silence, revelling in the News Editor's discomfort. In their world, no quarter was asked for, or given.

'The Editor asked me to call. He says you can have your job back.'

'Is that so? How very kind of him. What makes him think that I want it back?'

Falck sank onto the bed and lit a cigarette, his mood unforgiving. He would accept the offer that was bound to come, of course, but he'd give Handjob a hard time first - and he would set his own conditions. The fruits of freedom were as sweet as an arctic summer. If they wanted him back, they would have to be prepared to unshackle him and that meant a hard time for Handjob.

Lying full length on his bed, he blew smoke rings at the ceiling and waited for the answer. When it came, it took him by surprise.

'Because when you've finished prostituting yourself on the Fjærland bombings, Falck, you'll be a nobody again, a provincial hack like the rest of us. Your trouble is that you think you're God's answer to journalism. You're not.'

'Is that so?'

'Yes, it is. What's more you never will be. Not until you realise that you're working for a provincial paper ...'

'Correction. Worked ...'

'... and may again, *if* you can live with a few essential facts. Like the fact that most of our readers are actually *interested* in the wildlife of Sognefjord. When you come to terms with that and learn to take names at the local regatta and ski races, then - and only then - can you call yourself a journalist.'

Stung by the truth of what he said, Falck furiously heaved himself up and sat on the edge of the bed.

'You know what you are, Handjob? You're a nasty little haemorrhoid.'

There was a pause. The line crackled.

'It's up to you, Falck. The Editor's offering you double salary to come back.'

'To get me to work with you, he'd have to quadruple it.'

Falck paced back and forth, then slumped into the wicker chair by the window, filled with foreboding, aware now that his hatred of Handjob could ruin his future. The News Editor continued, his voice persistently and deliberately needling him.

'It's your decision, Falck. Personally, I've always thought you were a prat of cosmological proportions, and pompous with it.' He laughed, a tinny sound over the telephone.

'Incidentally, the Editor also said he'd appoint you special investigative correspondent, answerable only to him - in other words, cutting me out. But between you and me, Falck, if you do come back, I'll make your life a fucking misery. That's a promise.'

The reporter took a deep breath, conscious that his loathing of the man had so warped his mind that he could no longer stop himself, that despite himself he was deliberately bent on wrecking his career.

'Handjob,' he said after the briefest of pauses. 'I'd rather work with something that crawled out of the cheese than with you. So go stuff yourself.'

Chapter Sixteen

July 6, 1.35 p.m. - 3.45 p.m.

The East Street Jammers' coach rattled into Molde shortly after one-thirty that afternoon and nosed through the crowds spilling into the streets to celebrate the annual jazz festival. Inside, the musicians perched on the edges of the aisle seats, cigarette smoke swirling around them, oblivious to the carnival atmosphere outside.

They had produced plastic cups, bottles of whisky and Spanish brandy, and then launched into a medium-tempo piece called *Hallo Lola*. From then on, their music had become wilder and more intense as they swung joyously from the music of Coleman Hawkins into a frenzied session of improvisation.

David borrowed a tenor sax and no sooner had he put the horn to his lips than the entire band realised that he was a musician of talent. His musical agility was enviable, his tone deep and pure and sonorous.

Driving home each musical phrase, his style was both provocative and reflective, harmonising zestfully with the pulse and beat of the rhythm section, which on this occasion consisted of a pair of spoons and a rolled-up newspaper.

Katrina sang along, too, improvising in the style of Ella Fitzgerald, her light soprano voice as clear and sparkling as water from a fountain. Edging the yellow Citröen out of her mind, she allowed the music to consume her utterly, so that she became a mirror to its soul. As David had said, there was safety in numbers and as long as they were surrounded by the Jammers, Centaur and Delius could do them little harm.

Inching down Storgata, Molde's main street, the coach drew in to the central square and was immediately engulfed by enthusiastic fans. This was Molde's most prestigious annual event, known in jazz circles throughout the world. As the Jammers stepped onto the pavement, they were applauded eagerly.

David paused anxiously by the doorway, one hand signalling Katrina to wait, his eyes seeking out the Citröen. The little car was a hundred yards behind them, its horn harsh and discordant against the strains of a distant rhythm and blues group. Hurriedly, David and Katrina bade farewell to the musicians, promising to stay cool and in touch, then slipped into the anonymity of the crowd.

'We have to get to a 'phone,' David said. 'To call Stryn.'

Katrina nodded, her hand grasping his tightly. They pushed and squeezed through waves of milling revellers, past quartets and quintets, and Dixielanders in striped blazers and bowler hats.

Everywhere there were the sounds of shouting, laughter, shuffling feet and jazz of all schools. Above them, bunting fluttered in a light nor'easterly breeze, framing the fjord and the Romsdal mountains capped with snow beyond.

David elbowed his way along the main street, his eyes scanning the crowds for Centaur and Delius, pausing only to dart briefly into a doorway and seize a morning newspaper from a news stand.

'Looks as if we made the front pages again,' he muttered, flicking a finger at Tor Falck's by-line. 'I see your boyfriend's been busy.'

Katrina gasped, shocked to see their portraits on the front page. Hers was a picture she had taken years ago, setting the camera to the self-timer while she and Tor had posed outside her father's house.

'He must have given it to them,' she muttered angrily. 'And cut off the half with him on it.'

David took another newspaper from the stand. 'Same picture,' he said simply, handing it to her.

'The rotten bastard!' she exclaimed. Her eyes swept over the headlines. 'There's nothing that we don't know about,' she added. 'It just that it all seems so much worse in print.'

'What does?'

'All this.'

She translated the main headline: DYNAMITE MAN IN KIDNAP DRAMA?' Their portraits stared back at them beneath the triple-decker banner headline. Separate sub-headings proclaimed: FJÆRLAND WOMAN MISSING MOTOR HOME STOLEN. POLICE BARRIER WRECKED. Katrina shook her head in dismay. It was difficult to believe that it related to her.

In all, the newspaper had devoted fourteen pages to the story, including six double-page spreads illustrated with pictures of the Swedish family, maps showing David and Katrina's route, and photographs of the two policemen and the smashed barrier. Subsidiary articles dealt with Schneider Barr, the proposed copper mine and the hint of strange goings-on in Fjærland. A photograph of Jan Tystad and his mother accompanied a half-page article warning parents not to allow their children accept rides with strange men in helicopters. David whistled.

'Jeezus. If they think this is a good story, they'll be putting out special editions when they get to hear about this morning's caper.'

Katrina took his arm. 'Come, let's find that 'phone.'

They pushed back into the crowd. A street vendor careered into them drunkenly, clutching a truss of balloons. Crossing into the market place, they waited impatiently while a group of Dixielanders in white overalls paraded past, their leader dancing and singing beneath a giant-sized umbrella. They found a call box next to a beer tent crammed with noisy youths, ecstatic because a Danish brewery was giving away free beer.

Katrina dialled the number for the Glacier Hotel and waited, her fingers drumming on the shelf. The hotel operator was delighted and relieved to hear from her, bubbling over with questions. Was she alright? Should she call the police? Was what she read in the newspaper correct?

'The whole village is talking about you,' she gushed.

Calmly, Katrina explained that all was well and asked to speak to Mr. Stryn. The operator babbled on. Unfortunately, Mr. Stryn was out at the moment and had left no message. She had no idea when he would be back. He had taken Hanna out for a walk.

'Hanna? The new waitress?' Katrina asked, surprised.

'Yes, quite taken with each other, they are. They make a lovely couple - but what about you and that Mr. Larsen?' the operator wanted to know. 'Are you sure you don't want me to 'phone the police? I could have a word with that Inspector Ingstad.'

Katrina assured her that there was no need and thanked her, promising to return to the hotel shortly.

'What do we do now?' she asked, replacing the receiver.

David peered out of the call box window. Silently he pointed to the driver of a police patrol car, who was staring at them as if transfixed, a copy of the morning newspaper in his hand.

'We get the hell out of here,' David said. 'That's what we do, Blue. Now.'

Hastily, they slipped out of the call box and again melted into the crowd, David periodically glancing over his shoulder. The police driver was speaking into a handset. Holding hands to avoid being separated, they squeezed through the mass of people congregating in the main square for the East Street Jammers' two o'clock concert. Their leader, the trumpet player, was announcing the first number.

A canvas shelter bearing the legend "Norway's biggest jazz tent" offered a collection of records, cassettes and compact discs as well as a temporary haven, but as soon as they had joined the browsers inside, David realised that the move had been a mistake.

Police sirens wailed, then died, and he sensed that within minutes the area would be swarming with police. He ran his eyes round the tent. The entrance was the only exit. And standing right in the centre of it was Delius.

'It's fixed grin time, Blue,' David whispered. Katrina stood as if rooted to the spot, her mouth open, her eyes bulging with horror.

'Don't worry,' he added, putting an arm round her waist. 'I'll take him out. But whatever happens, stay real close to me.'

Edging towards the entrance, David moved mentally into an attack mode, concentrating exclusively on the dual moves that he knew he must make at precisely the right moment. A split second too early or too late and Delius would have an opportunity to retaliate.

Delius reached tentatively inside his leather jacket. David anticipated the move, recalling that the pilot was armed. Moving in front of Katrina, he drew back his right elbow, his forearm and fingers as rigid as steel bolts.

Smiling, his gaze never left Delius' eyes. For the briefest moment, the pilot wavered, unsure of his next move. If he ever thought of it, he was too late, for David seized the moment and jammed his fingers into the soft flesh just below the rib cage.

Delius doubled over in pain, his breath expelled forcibly by the power and depth of the blow. David swung round and expertly sought out the pilot's right ear and twisted it forwards, at the same time placing his right hand on the back of his victim's head, pushing it downwards so that the pilot toppled head first to the floor.

'Goddam drunk,' David said loudly to no one in particular. Stepping sideways, he motioned to Katrina. 'Come on, honey. Leave him be.'

Katrina followed, the look on her face suggesting that she was still not sure what had happened. It was all over so quickly. Nor had anyone else noticed anything untoward. Those who witnessed the incident merely assumed that a drunk had fallen over.

David paused for a moment, his eyes taking in the scene before him. To his left, on the temporary stage, the Jammers were exploding into a Benny Goodman number, ironically entitled *Watch What Happens*.

Beneath the stage, the first few rows of fans sat on coats and anoraks laid out on the hard paving stones, using the rest of the audience as a shelter from the breeze blowing gently in from the fjord.

Behind them, off to David's right, police officers were fanning out into the crowd from three patrol cars parked at the edge of the square.

It was then that David saw Centaur not thirty yards away, the mirrored lenses of his sunglasses flashing like beacons, his dome-like head turning slowly as he systematically searched the mass of bobbing heads.

David snapped into action.

Grabbing Katrina's arm, he propelled her towards the musicians. The movement, combined with the rumpus now emanating from the jazz tent behind him, clearly attracted Centaur's attention, for he sprang forward then, heading directly for them.

Bounding up the steps that led along the side of the stage to the City

Hall, David hoped to find an escape route from the square, but there was none and the plate glass doors to the building were locked. A security guard at the back of the stage eyed them curiously as the Jammers ended their piece with a flourish. Katrina's fingers tightened, digging into David's arm.

'David!' she shouted, her voice tight with panic.

His eyes followed the direction of her gaze. Centaur was moving slowly up the steps, his arms dangling loosely and his lips drawn back over yellowed teeth. David did not hesitate.

He strode onto the platform, stepping over the tangle of cables past the pianist and a bank of amplifiers, dragging Katrina after him. The trumpet player, who was about to announce the next number, beamed, delighted to see them again.

'Hey man, put it there,' he cried, slapping his hand against David's outstretched palm.

They consulted hurriedly with the saxophonist, who enthusiastically handed his tenor sax to David and reached for an alto sax for himself. The band leader nursed the microphone, his voice rasping in the manner he thought audiences expected of him.

'And now folks, direct from the U. S. of A. - David and Blue from the Kandi County Vanguard.'

The audience applauded enthusiastically, although it was doubtful that any of the Norwegian jazz fans had heard of the Kandi County Vanguard, much less David and Blue. Nonetheless, a buzz of eager conversation suggested that they sensed a musical happening was in the offing.

David clipped the sax to his neck cord and took the microphone, his eyes sweeping over the crowd. Beyond the market place and quayside, a bank of scattered clouds scudded across the mountains. Two policemen stood in the front ranks of the audience studying the morning newspaper, its pages flapping in the breeze, and glanced up at them.

Behind him, Centaur spoke urgently with the security guard in the wings.

David shrugged helplessly, his eyes signalling to Katrina that this time there was no escape, that the police were the better option. Then he smiled at her, murmured 'What the hell' and, squeezing her hand comfortingly, turned to the audience.

'A Charlie Mingus number, ladies and gentlemen,' he announced, tersely. 'That great, shoutin' spriritual blues immortalised by Eric Dolphy - *Fables of Faubus.*'

He took a deep breath, put the mouthpiece to his lips and closed his eyes as his opening notes slid plaintively into the main theme. His playing was both rich in melody and harmonically adventurous, authoritative yet unpredictable.

Playing from the heart, he immersed himself in the music, plunging into long cadenzas with an inherent sense of improvisation so deep and precise that it seemed as if the piece might have been written specifically for him. It was as if he no longer existed - a mere medium between the musical extremities of his mind and the reality of the horn.

Listening intently, Katrina followed each phrase until she saw an opportunity to break in, her voice probing the spaces with pristine clarity, then harmonising perfectly both with David and the alto sax. Gradually, their confidence grew and the three became one, extemporising within the parameters of the Mingus composition.

Striking off at tangents, often discordantly, they ranged across the fringes of musical space, then sought each other out again with haunting, calling notes until they found each other and merged once more into harmonic union.

In the wings, next to the gathering policemen, a stagehand beat time with a rolled up newspaper. So compelling was his beat that it affected all the musicians. The Jammers played crisply and with inventiveness and the number began to boil. Six minutes into it, fans at the front of the crowd had risen to their feet and were pushing forward to the edge of the platform. And still David drove them on.

The bassist, enthused both by David and the stage hand with the newspaper, attempted to break in but neither of the two saxophonists were willing to give way. Only when Katrina finally gave ground did they concede, enabling the bassist to launch into a solo of constantly shifting cross-accents.

Not once did David open his eyes or lose the thread. He stood poised, his foot tapping, waiting for the slightest chance of re-entry. When it came, it was with the explosive scream of a banshee, a long, sliding, wailing note that dived like an aircraft onto its target, delving into the deeps of his soul.

It was as if he had tapped the very source of creation, for from it emerged a second cadenza, stunning in its complexity. Gradually and reluctantly, he veered back to the main theme and retreated into the comfort and safety of numbers for the finále.

When he was done, the fans roared their approval, shouting for more. The East Street Jammers, too, were on their feet, applauding a solo which they knew would still be a talking point amongst those who had heard it decades hence.

David acknowledged them and hugged the band leader, then waved to the spectators. He unclipped the tenor sax and handed it back to its owner. Bowing once more to the audience, he took Katrina's hand and walked with her to the wings.

'Good afternoon, sergeant,' he said, smiling at the police officer who was waiting there. 'My name is David Larsen - the Dynamite Man. And this is Katrina Hagen.'

Johan Michelsen sat at the head of the trestle table fidgeting impatiently. One member had still not arrived and the committee meeting should have started fifteen minutes earlier, at two o'clock. Surveying the assembled gathering, he noted that Sigrid, shuffling owlishly through a pile of papers to his left, looked pale and tired.

The three other members were discussing the early success of the parliamentary vigil. Had they worn suits instead of jeans and open-necked shirts, had they styled their hair rather than wearing headbands, pigtails and designer stubble, they might easily have been the board of a company corporation. Only the uniform was different.

Johan glanced at his watch and decided to proceed. More effective than many corporate chairman, he was determined to keep the meeting on track, for there was no time to lose.

'Right, we have a quorum so let's get on with it,' he said decisively. 'The situation is this. New York have told us to keep a low profile on the Fjærland issue because Schneider Barr finances them to the tune of a million dollars a year. Not,' he added bitterly, 'that we get any of it.'

The others murmured in surprise.

'In my view, that's utterly corrupt,' he continued. 'Sigrid makes the point that we are autonomous and suggests that we ignore them', Johan said. 'I agree, but I propose to take a vote on it.' He paused briefly. 'Anyone against?' he asked, intimidatingly.

'Seconded,' said the young man slouched at the end of the table.

The committee noisily condemned New York's arrogance, proclaimed it typical of foreign interference and voted unanimously to steer a separate course.

'Right, now we have to decide what to do,' Johan said. 'As Sigrid says, this is a great opportunity. The bonus is that Schneider Barr is an American multi-national, so if we play our cards right we can orchestrate a major anti-American campaign and boost subscriptions to the cause at the same time.' He swivelled round to the woman on his left. 'Sigrid?'

Sigrid blinked and continued the theme. 'Johan is right. All the signs are that we're onto a winner. The parliamentary vigil is proof. Since yesterday evening, nearly four thousand people have signed the petition and we've signed up sixteen new members.'

'That's a record,' Johan added. 'And in less than twenty-four hours, too. So if we're going to ignore New York - lets do it in a big way. Any ideas?'

'We could stage twenty-four hour vigils in all the main towns,' a woman in denim overalls said. 'And organise a co-ordinated national march.'

'And burn the American flag and effigies of the President,' added the man with the headband. 'He's supposed to be an environmentalist. Show him up for the Establishment puppet that he is.'

The door opened and the missing committee member slipped through the doorway, apologising. She discarded a hand-knitted coat, shapeless through over-use, and sat next to the woman in overalls, who quickly brought her up to date.

'Right, good idea, but we must have standardised placards throughout the country. That way, the television fat cats will see the same reports coming in from all over the country. Then, they'll have to take us seriously.'

For the sake of uniformity, Sigrid suggested that there should be no more than six different placards and called for a separate meeting later to decide their wording. There was plenty of material to work on - not least Schneider Barr's previous record of pollution, she added.

The woman in the overalls proposed that volunteers chain themselves to the Ministry for Industry in Oslo and to as many civic halls as possible throughout the country.

'It's very important to keep the police busy,' she explained. 'They're under-manned already, so when they have to divert forces to deal with us, it will cost the Establishment money. That, more than anything, will make the politicians sit up and take notice. I suggest we also find volunteers for a hunger strike outside parliament.'

The committee members murmured their agreement. The man with the headband coughed.

'Wouldn't it be better if we had a national chain-in?' he asked. 'Like we did with the Alta dam in Lapland? We'd get international TV coverage then.'

'I was coming to that,' Johan interrupted. 'And, yes, it's a great idea. However, I propose that we have our chain-in at Fjærland.'

There was a chorus of disapproval.

That was ridiculous, the committee members protested. Whoever would take notice of a chain-in in a remote fjord? They'd be completely reliant on the presence of TV crews.

If something else happened that day, it would be the first story they'd drop. Surely, it would be better to have a chain-in outside parliament, where everybody could see them.

Johan waited for the protests to die down.

'A hunger strike outside parliament - yes. But when I said a chain-in at Fjærland, I meant Fjærlandsfjord. And I didn't mean a people chain-in. I meant a boat chain-in. We'll blockade the fjord with boats and chains.'

'Oh, wow!' exclaimed the latecomer.

Johan ignored her. 'I had a message from a friend at Planet Watch in London at lunchtime. Apparently, Schneider Barr have been advertising for British miners to work on an open cast mining project in Norway. That can only mean the Fjærland project.'

He paused to let the importance of what he was saying sink in. No-one spoke. He had their full attention now, hungry for every word.

'Apparently, they're hiring one hundred miners and they've chartered a Ro-Ro ferry, the *m/v Arctic Constellation* from the Sörensen Line. According to the latest information, they're loading her with heavy equipment now. She's scheduled to leave Newcastle in England tomorrow evening. The North Sea crossing to Bergen takes about twenty-four hours. That means she'll arrive at Fjærland early on the morning of the ninth.'

He smiled and reached for a regional map.

'If we move quickly, that's just about enough time for every boat from Bergen to Kristiansund to sail there.' He unfolded the map, spreading it across the table. 'Fjærlandsfjord is perfect for our purposes. It's not much more than a twenty-mile crevasse in the mountains, but the important thing is that its only two thousand metres wide.'

He paused for effect, aware that they still did not yet fully comprehend the significance of what he was saying.

'If each boat is an average of three metres wide and linked up with ten metres of chain, you'd only need a hundred and fifty odd boats to seal off the fjord - even to the ferries. That in itself will guarantee television coverage.'

'And the *Arctic Constellatio* would never dare try to force a way through,' the man with the headband interjected, 'because it would automatically mean sinking boats and probably killing people.'

The committee members looked at Johan in amazement. It was a brilliant idea. No television company could ignore it. The man with the headband shuffled his feet and leaned forward, looking up the table.

'Trouble is, to get to Fjærland from Kristiansund, you'd have to sail within the next three or four hours. How will people know about the plan in time?'

John smiled. 'I've already thought of that. First, not everybody will be sailing from Kristiansund or Bergen. There are hundreds of suitable boats within an hour's sailing. But just to make sure, I propose a tactical public relations exercise.' He grinned. 'If we light a large fire in front of the *Storting* and burn an effigy of the Minister for Industry, an anonymous 'phone call will have the media there in hordes. We can use the effigies already made up in the storeroom.'

'Why don't we burn the Prime Minister?' the woman in overalls asked.

Johan beamed at her. 'Because we'll save him for when the media actually arrive. Then, I'll make myself available to give separate interviews to radio and television, and announce a major campaign. In other words, we'll use the interviews to get the word of the blockade out.'

He leaned back in his chair, content with his planning.

'By six o' clock tonight the whole country will know of our plans,' he predicted.

Sigrid twirled a strand of frizzy hair round her finger. 'Brilliant, absolutely bloody brilliant, Johan.'

'I've also provisionally chartered a fishing boat,' Johan continued. 'With your approval, she'll sail tomorrow evening with six ocean-going dinghies to intercept *Arctic Constellation* the following morning.' He laughed cynically. 'Naturally, we'll provide berths for a TV crew and pool photographer. We'll harry her all the way up Sognefjord.'

The police sergeant ushered David into an interview room at the back of Molde police station and interrogated him aggressively while Katrina drank tea in an adjacent room. She assured the station Inspector that David had not kidnapped her. Each told the same story - how George Vito's men had abducted her and attempted to burn the fisherman's hut while she was bound hand and foot inside it, and how David had rescued her.

In the one room, Katrina described how they had fled the hotel in fear of their lives and later been attacked by a helicopter and men with crossbows on Marabreen. They had stolen the motor home in desperation, she said, describing vividly the attempt to kill them with petrol bombs.

Next door, David explained about his grandfather's letters, the Viking silver and Vito's attempts to purchase his land and subsequently kill them. But, as he had anticipated, the sergeant did not believe him.

Neither they nor the police had yet seen the afternoon newspapers, which covered the gunfight and destruction of the helicopter at Reed in some depth. Editors had allocated an average six to eight double page spreads to the story, in which the comments of Inspector Odd Ingstad of Kripos were quoted extensively.

That none of the Molde police was aware that Ingstad had publicly declared the Dynamite Man innocent was unfortunate.

'Nasty little man, aren't you, Larsen?' the sergeant taunted. 'Theft, destruction of private property, evading arrest, kidnap. Possibly murder? You're going to be inside for a long time.'

'That's a matter of opinion, sergeant,' David replied. 'As I said before, I'd like to speak to my lawyer.'

Also unaware of Ingstad's changed viewpoint, David was increasingly aware that, given the sergeant's attitude, the only chance of proving his innocence was to find the Viking silver.

He cursed the loss of his grandfather's letter and the other documents in the rapids. At least they would have gone some way to confirming his story. Without them, he had nothing with which to prove Vito's interest in his land.

Finding the silver, on the other hand, called for a rapid departure from Molde police station.

'There'll be plenty of time to speak to your lawyer later,' the sergeant said. 'After you've answered a few questions.'

'No deal, sergeant. I'll say no more until I've spoken first to my lawyer, then to the American Embassy in Oslo.'

'You talk to your lawyer when I say so, Larsen. Not before.'

'Fine. Go ahead and deny me my rights. That's probably an offence in this country. So is wrongful arrest.' David leaned across the table, his voice tight and determined, 'What's more, if I don't get to a 'phone in sixty seconds from now, it's also gonna be an international incident.'

'The only time you'll be an international incident, Larsen, is when you're expelled from Norway. In about ten years' time.' The sergeant laughed harshly. 'I do not think you are in a position to dictate to us.'

He leaned forward, his eyes venomous, his breath hot on David's face. 'Bloody Yank,' he said, the words heavy with loathing.

The sergeant moved to turn away, his lips curled disdainfully, but David gave him no time.

Erupting from his chair, he slammed both fists simultaneously into the sergeant's temples, then grasped his right shoulder with his left hand and brought down the edge of his right palm - outstretched and rigid now - with such force that he thought the interviewer next door would hear the collar bone snapping.

With the slightest of sighs, the sergeant crumpled silently to a heap.

David surveyed him grimly. If they were going to indict him for a string of crimes he had not committed, he might as well go down for one that he had. The guy was a boil on the butt of humanity. He had it coming.

Pausing by the steel door, he listened carefully and poked his head round the door. At the end of the corridor to his right, an officer with his back to him was speaking into the telephone. Next door, he could hear Katrina answering questions. All he had to do now was to take out the officer interrogating Katrina.

Incredibly, the police had not placed a guard outside the rooms. Probably understaffed, he thought. Or lazy. Maybe their lack of security was due to the station being small - in a two-bit town where nothing ever happened. He wondered if the police in Willmar were as casual in their approach to security.

Peering along the corridor, his eyes took in a heavy steel door marked with an illuminated sign reading "Utgang". He imagined it meant "Exit". Next to it, several bunches of keys hung from a row of four-inch nails that someone had hammered into the white-washed wall. If the keys were what he hoped they were, he was in luck.

A chair scraped in the main office. Pulling back, he crouched motionless by the door, his hand clamped across the mouth of the sergeant, who was beginning to come round. David listened to the approaching footsteps on the linoleum, his heart pumping.

Pausing outside the adjacent interview room, the owner of the heavy boots spoke briefly in Norwegian. The interrogator muttered '*Jaha*' and followed him back to the main office. Speaking loudly to himself, David again protested his innocence and demanded to see a lawyer.

As the footsteps receded, David cradled the sergeant's head in his left hand, smiled at him, then again slammed his right fist into the man's temple. That done, he slipped into the next room. Katrina's eyes widened.

'David, what on earth …'

'We're leaving . Get your shoes off,' he ordered.

'David, we can't …'

'You walk or I carry you,' he whispered urgently.

She hesitated, then slipped off her shoes obediently. They tiptoed rapidly down the corridor and tucked themselves into an alcove by the back door. David caught her eye and nodded to the bunches of keys.

Beneath them, small labels indicated the registration numbers of the police cars to which they belonged, precisely as he had hoped. Gently lifting off the nearest bunch, he tried the door. It was locked.

Katrina nudged him, her eyes directing his gaze to the ledge across the top of the door. David ran his finger along it, groping hopefully. He found the key, astonished that the police could be so stupid as to choose the most obvious hiding place imaginable.

Unlocking the door, he slipped out into the parking lot, taking care to lock the door again. Katrina stood beside him, breathing heavily.

The police car was parked round the corner beneath the barred windows of the interview rooms. Incredibly, it was not locked. David eased into the driving seat and switched on the ignition, Katrina collapsing into the seat beside him.

'David, this is crazy ...'

'This time I drive,' he said, ignoring her. He slammed the car into reverse, then sped through the gates heading out of town along the western coast road.

'Any idea where we're headin'?' he asked, negotiating a corner.

'I have no idea. Hell and back, I should think.' She gazed fixedly out of the window.

'Look, Blue, do me a favour. Don't sulk, huh? That sergeant in there - no way was he going to believe anything I told him.'

'The policeman I talked to was perfectly charming,' she answered haughtily.

'Did you tell him I didn't kidnap you?'

'Of course, I did.'

'And he believed you?'

'Well, he said he could make no sense of it, but ...'

'You bet your sweet ass he couldn't. He had his mind made up, already, that's why.'

They fell silent as the traffic thinned, and headed west on Route six-six-two.

'What will we do?' Katrina asked.

'I don't know, Blue. All I know is we gotta get back to Fjærland and find that silver. If we don't, those bastards are going to put me away for a ten-year stretch.'

Chapter Seventeen

July 6, 3.45 p.m. - 9.45 p.m.

Checking out of the Glacier Hotel, Tor Falck trudged to the ferry point with his overnight bag, cursing his stupidity. As far as the *Balestrand Posten* was concerned, he was history. Another hack who'd allowed his independent spirit and sense of self importance get the better of him. An unemployed hack, he thought ruefully, who might have been a special investigative correspondent on a highly lucrative salary.

Despite the drop in temperature, he was hot and uncomfortable. Beads of sweat trickled into his beard. Red-faced, he struggled through the line of cars waiting to board the afternoon ferry. His only option now was to sell his apartment in Balestrand, move to Oslo and find employment, capitalising on his success with the Fjærland bombing story.

Having burned his bridges with Handjob and the *Balestrand Posten*, he had quickly written up the morning's events and 'phoned them through to his newspaper, radio and television contacts. The story would be splashed in the late editions of the afternooners, providing another profitable boost to his bank balance.

His satisfaction with this brief gain was tempered by the knowledge that the Fjærland story was nearing its end, that within a week it would probably all be over.

There was money to be earned from magazine articles, of course, and there would be trials and enquiries but after that the future looked bleak.

What made it so much worse was the recent closure of an Oslo newspaper, *Kveldsbladet*, a financial catastrophe that had thrust more than fifty other journalists onto the open market.

The ferry bumped gently against the jetty. A stream of vehicles rumbled across the ramps onto the quayside, some occupied by reporters, photographers and television crews flooding into Fjærland from the capital.

Falck waved to them, but as he boarded the ferry for the fifty-minute voyage to Balestrand, he was filled with a sense of foreboding. The Fjærland bombing story was common property now; he had lost the advantage over his competitors.

Ingstad's disclosure that Larsen was no longer wanted for questioning in connection with the bombings was his last exclusive. The rat pack had finally caught up with him. He'd taken the flesh; they were picking the bones. It was time to move on.

Slumped at a table in the cafeteria, chain smoking and drinking canned beers, his mood grew increasingly morose. Even with his recent success, the chances of finding a staff job in Oslo or Bergen were remote.

According to some of his colleagues, the managements of most newspapers, radio and television stations had already committed themselves to taking on the redundant journalists from *Kveldsbladet*.

On docking at Balestrand, Falck manoeuvred his bulk into his Saab and drove up the hill to his apartment. His life suddenly seemed bereft of all that was meaningful. He had lost his job. He had no family. Katrina had lost interest in him and he suspected that she would revile and despise him for selling her photograph to the picture agency. By now, she would probably have fallen for Larsen anyway.

Unlocking the door to his apartment, he dumped his bag in the hallway, kicked off his shoes and sank into the sofa.

The apartment, as usual, was a mess, drab and devoid of warmth or colour.

Lighting a cigarette, he reflected on his predicament, then heaved himself up to fetch a bottle of Johnnie Walker from the kitchen. Unscrewing the cap, he drank long and deep, so that his stomach tingled with the whisky's warmth.

For some minutes he sat there gazing into space, periodically lifting the bottle to his mouth, masochistically driving himself into the depression and bitterness of self pity.

He drank with the slovenly action of a man rapidly losing his faculties and coordination, wiping his lips with the back of his hand, nursing the whisky bottle in the crook of his arm. Eventually, he stirred and reached for the telephone.

His stubby fingers sought out the number of *Aftenposten*, Norway's biggest afternoon newspaper. Screwing up his eyes to avoid the smoke from the cigarette clamped between his lips, he asked the switchboard operator to transfer his call to the News Editor, only vaguely aware that he was slurring his words.

The voice on the other end of the 'phone echoed as if its owner was speaking from the bottom of the sea. Hollow, distant and curt, it had the ring of a man imminently facing a deadline. Falck drew a deep breath and felt his throat constrict.

'Rolf? It's me. Tor Falck,' he stammered. 'I ... I was just calling to ask what the job situation is?'

'Jobs? You've got to be joking, mate.' The News Editor laughed, instantly cutting short the conversation. 'Look, Tor, I'm really tied up now. Call me in a couple of hours, okay?'

'Yes, but ...'

'By the way, this latest stuff of yours is sensational. We're putting out a sixteen page extra. Talk to you later.'

The 'phone clicked and he lowered the receiver to his knee, the dialling tone and his own laboured breathing the only sounds in the room.

Despairingly, he drank another long draught from the whisky bottle, ruminating on his self-inflicted misfortune. Almost imperceptively, tears trickled over his cheeks into his beard.

In his maudlin despondency, he leaned forward to replace the receiver but in his drunkenness fell off the sofa. Rolling over, he crawled towards the bathroom, the folds of his buttocks and thighs trembling with the reverberations of his uncontrollable blubbering.

Clutching the edge of the bath and the wash basin, he hauled himself upright and unsteadily spilled the rest of the whisky into a tooth mug. For a moment, he stared uncomprehendingly at his reflection in the mirror. His flesh was pink and pasty, his blonde beard only partially hiding the jowls and double chins.

Journalism had been his entire life. It was a tough business, cynical and uncaring. What did people's feelings or futures matter so long as the next edition, the next news bulletin was better than that of the opposition?

He rubbed his eyes, blearily. He'd been as ruthless and determined as the best of them in the quest for what supposedly was the truth. Many was the time when he would have swapped his own mother for an exclusive - if she'd been alive, of course.

Smug and uncompromising, that was the only way to describe the world of journalism. No quarter asked, none given.

Stubbing out his cigarette in the wash basin, he reached inside the wall cabinet. He was tired and needed to sleep. Swaying drunkenly, he took out a small, brown bottle and shook a couple of sleeping tablets into the whisky, slowly grinding them to powder with his toothbrush.

Raising the mug to his lips, he tipped back his head and quaffed the solution in a single draught. The action threw him temporarily off balance and the window and ceiling swayed alarmingly.

'No quarter,' he murmured, drifting into unconsciousness.

With infinite slowness, his knees sagged. His huge body toppled grotesquely into the bath and his head smashed onto the taps, splitting open his skull.

The police car sped along the coast road, its siren silent. Katrina stared out of the window at the yachts and small craft plying the *Moldefjord*, anxiety etched across her face. Everything that had happened until their arrest could be justified by their fear of Centaur and Delius; breaking out of the relative safety of a police station and stealing a police car was a different matter.

Now, she wanted nothing more than to abandon the vehicle, no matter what the alternative. David, clearly, was thinking along the same lines.

'Blue, I don't know where we are or where we're headin',' he said decisively, 'but we have to dump this patrol car. We have to get to Fjærland fast. Any ideas?'

'All this stealing,' she said, unhappily, ignoring his question. 'We cannot continue like this.'

'We got no option, Blue. Not yet.' He glanced in the mirror and decelerated at the approach to a bend. 'We either have to locate that silver or find the rest of my grandfather's letters - the ones you said you saw in Vito's suite. If we don't, we're finished. It's the only way we can prove Vito killed all those people and then tried to kill us.'

David changed gear and accelerated out of the turn. Katrina nodded, resigned to her fate. He was probably right. She'd noticed the police inspector's eyes clouding over when she was recounting the events since leaving Fjærland. Not that she blamed him; the whole story defied belief. She reached into the glove compartment and retrieved a map, unfolding it on her knee.

'Matter of fact, we do have an option,' David said, braking without warning. He reversed quickly, then swerved off the main road and bumped down a track, pointing to a deserted bay.

'The police are going to be looking for us on land, in a police vehicle,' he said, glancing at her. 'Maybe it's time for us to go to sea.'

Katrina followed his gaze and stared at the two-masted yacht tethered to a stone jetty, her sails wrapped loosely along the boom, the jib furled. The crew of *Ulrika* had clearly not intended staying long.

'No, David, please. We can't ...'

'Sure we can, Blue. We can do anything.' His eyes sought hers earnestly. 'We have to,' he said, laying a hand on her arm. 'It'll be okay, I promise. Now here's what I want you to do.'

After poring over large scale maps for most of the day, George Vito was enthused, confident that he had come closer to pinpointing the whereabouts of Ejulf Deathsword's silver.

The name *Vetle* appeared on the map twice, firstly marking a glacier next to Bøyabreen and secondly, in minute print, a peak close to Supphellebreen, not much more than two miles from the old Viking settlement of Skarestad. He was convinced that this was the *Vetle* mentioned in Deathsword's runes.

Fishing the gold Half-Hunter from his waistcoat pocket, he checked the time and switched on the radio above his bed, turning the volume low so that his presence in the suite would not be detected. Centaur and Delius had still not contacted him.

To some extent, the four o'clock news bulletin explained why. Although he could not understand everything the announcer said, he gathered that there had been a shooting and that someone had blown up the helicopter.

When the announcer reported that police believed the helicopter was identical to the one described by witnesses immediately following the Fjærland bombing, he made an instant decision and reached for the small overnight bag in the wardrobe.

With Centaur and Delius apparently out of action, it was only a matter of time before the police caught up with Larsen - and then came looking for him. Vito had other plans and they did not include making himself available for further police questioning.

Taking the spare clothes he had packed in the bag for just such an emergency, he spread them out on the bed and stepped into the bathroom. He washed his hair, doused it carefully with talcum powder and spent the next ten minutes in front of the mirror.

Satisfied, he changed into the clothes on the bed, hanging up those he was wearing in the wardrobe. He was emptying the drawers of his desk, tossing his coins and bundles of letters and documents into the bag, when the telephone shrilled.

Agonised by the dilemma of whether to answer it, he peered quickly out of the window.

There was no sign of police activity, nor of anything untoward. He decided to take the risk and picked up the receiver. The voice on the other end was brusque.

'Vito? Centaur.'

'Where in hell are you?' Vito breathed venomously.

'Some place called Molde. We got trouble.'

'You're damned right we got trouble. You heard the news?'

'We are the news,' Centaur snapped. 'You want an update or not?'

Vito sighed, prepared for the worst. 'Go ahead,' he said simply.

'We lost two men up on the glacier. Gave one a concrete collar, dumped him in a lake. Had to leave the other to find Larsen. Meantime, the cops found him.'

'And then got yourself into a shootin' match, you cretinous schmuck.'

'So what d'ya expect? You wanted him marmalised, remember?'

'Not in public. Not in broad daylight for Chrissakes.'

Centaur's tone rose argumentatively. 'What d'ya expect me to do? Sit around while the guy totals the chopper and takes off in a goddam seaplane?'

'Yeah, I heard about that. What happened?' He tucked the receiver into his shoulder.

'We followed in another 'plane. Delius forced him to crash. Larsen and the Hagen woman bailed out and hitailed it. Long story.'

'So cut it short. Where are they now?'

'Here in Molde. With the fuzz.'

Vito swore, sweat breaking out on his brow. 'Jesus, do you have any idea what that means? I thought you were supposed to be a professional.'

'You wanna find better?'

'You've haven't got a goddam thing right from Day One,' Vito muttered through clenched teeth.

'What are you gonna do? Take away my pension?'

Vito fought against his rising temper. If he was to find Deathsword's silver, he needed all the help he could get. He had already prepared contingency plans for moving out of Fjærland. He needed Delius and Centaur more than ever, but they'd have to move fast - find the silver and get the hell out of Norway before the police got to him. He rose from the bed, his mind in overdrive.

'Can you get more men?'

'Sure I can get more men,' Centaur answered confidently.

'How soon?'

'Next flight outa London if the pay's good.'

'The pay's good,' Vito snapped. 'Get 'em.'

Centaur hesitated. 'How many?'

'At least a half dozen. And Centaur? Dip it in chilli, huh?'

'If we charter a 'plane outa London, they'll be here tonight.'

'Do it.'

Vito relaxed, more confident now that he was again taking positive action. 'One more thing. Things are gettin' kinda hot around here so I'm re-basing. You'll find me in a little place called Hafslo. It's off the main road just north of Sogndal.' Vito smiled to himself. 'I'll be at the Hillestrand Hotel, registered under the name of Robert Marito - and, ah, I may look a little different.'

'I'll recognise you. I saw the picture in your fake passport.'

Vito started. He thought he'd kept the document well hidden. Maybe Centaur wasn't so amateurish, after all. The thought boosted his spirits and he let it pass.

'Fine. Meanwhile, have Delius find another chopper.'

Katrina stood at the helm steering west-sou'west along Moldefjord, the mountains on the island of Otrøy rising high above her to starboard, dwarfing the hamlets strung along its southern coast road. *Ulrika* was pitching gently a third of a mile offshore, flouncing her stern before a light to moderate east-nor'easterly that was the tail end of a depression moving across northern Denmark and the Skagerrak.

Almost as soon as they had cast off, David had agreed that she should be the skipper, for he was familiar with neither the boat nor the coast. She had tuned the VHF radio to the latest weather report and, initially, the news was comforting.

The depression was tracking eastwards into the Baltic and due to be followed by a shallow ridge of high pressure moving eastwards across the Norwegian Sea. In the next few hours, the wind would back round from the east to the northwest giving them a following wind all the way to the outer skerries.

For the first hour, they familiarised themselves with the boat and its equipment, Katrina explaining the emergency procedures and showing David how to use the safety harnesses.

That done, she began to relax, filled with a sense of freedom and abandon. It was as if the demands of navigation and handling the yawl had purged her earlier concerns.

She had been distressed when David had removed the washboards and forced the hatch, and even unhappier when he had pushed the police car into deep water to delay its discovery. That had been unnecessary and she had protested vigorously. Yet, once she had found the keys to the engine on a rack above the chart table and they had reversed away from the jetty, responsibility for the boat and their own safety took precedence.

Shivering, she stood before the mizzen mast, her hands light on the wheel, debating in her mind whether turning about and raising the sails would give them more speed than the eight knots provided by the Volvo Penta diesel. So far as she was concerned, the greater the distance between them and Molde the better.

If their luck and the winds held, she calculated that they would be able to round the Stadt coast, a treacherous confluence of cross currents and Atlantic rollers, at around midnight. It was the one part of the coast that she feared more than any other. Still, she thought, the forty-two foot Hallberg-Rassy yawl was fast, safe and elegant with a wide, teak deck and all the latest navigational aids.

Below decks, she was furnished luxuriously. David had been popping up and down the companionway like a schoolboy with a new toy ever since casting off, showing little outward concern over their actions.

· 'Only ever sailed on Foot Lake in Willmar before,' he shouted from the galley. 'I was on a motor cruiser one time off Miami but I've never been on an ocean-goer like this. She's a dream.'

'She should be. With all the extras, she probably cost more than a quarter of a million dollars,' Katrina laughed.

A gust of wind whipped the hair off the back of her neck and she shivered again, glad of the woollen sweater and corduroy trousers she had taken from the motor home. Breathing in the sea air, she savoured its invigorating saltiness. David joined her in the cockpit clutching two mugs of hot, sweet coffee.

'Here - to you, me and the future,' he said.

Taking a mug from him, she sensed the blood rush to her face.

'If you want me at the helm while you run around like a little boy with a new train set, you must find me a windproof jacket or I might not have a future,' she said primly.

He disappeared again and she smiled at her secret thoughts, her embarrassment superseded by a sense of anticipation and excitement so intense that it set her heart racing.

Ahead, the sun shone between light clouds of cotton, burning their faces. In these waters, the sun was scarcely below the spreaders by late afternoon and it would not disappear below the horizon until an hour before midnight. David clambered back on deck with an armful of oilskins, his face bronzed in the late afternoon light.

'I need your help,' she said, the ten-knot breeze snatching at her words. 'I shall come about and raise the sails. Then, once we are through the skerries, we will put her on auto-pilot and take a rest. God knows we need it.'

'Sure, Blue, anything you say. What do I have to do?'

'Exactly as you're told,' she laughed.

Reducing the engine speed, she checked that the sheets were slack, then brought *Ulrika* round into the wind, pitching and rolling in protest.

Releasing the sail ties, David led the halyard round the winch drum as Katrina had shown him, mildly alarmed when the mainsail flapped noisily and the sheets whipped dangerously around him. Taking up the slack, he belayed the main sheet and raised the genoa, hauling it in until it stopped flapping.

Katrina bore away then, steering due west on a broad reach, the north-easterly breeze gentle to moderate and the waves lengthening, white horses occasionally creaming along their crests. Ahead, the sun was sinking into a bank of cloud, its rays casting beams of copper-gold light across a deepening sky. Astern, gulls wheeled raucously hoping for scraps.

Handing the wheel to him, she went below, sipping her coffee and poring over the charts. Later, they chatted about Fjærland, the events of the day, music and Ejulf Deathsword's silver.

By eight-thirty, she had taken command again, navigating a fine course through the maze of offshore islands and low-lying skerries. Rounding the island of Godøy, with the port of Ålesund off the port quarter, she quietly engaged the auto-pilot, switched on the navigation lights, and beckoned to David.

'We have a free run ahead into Brei Sound now,' she said. 'There is nothing but open sea ahead of us. We will take an hour's rest - get something to eat.'

She knew she was taking a risk, that one of them should stand watch, but her mind was set. They would stand watches after they had eaten.

Pausing at the chart table, she glanced at her watch, checked their position on the Decca Navigator and entered it in the log. Twenty forty-five hours, 62.27N. by 6.02E.

They were making six to eight knots. Another hour would see them just north off the occulting Grasøyane Light. After that, they would need to keep their wits about them, but now it was time to relax.

'I will shower now, I think,' she said.

'Okay, I'll get supper. You want wine with your meal? There's a Chateau Batailley here. Grand Cru Classé. Very expensive, though I'd prefer a beer, myself.'

'No drink, David,' she remonstrated. 'Rules of the sea.'

'Okay, so we drink seawater.'

Ignoring him, she kicked off her boots and peeled off her oilskin jacket and sweater. David busied himself in the galley pretending not to look as she bared her midriff, his potatoes peeled but uncooked, cans of chilli and vegetables lined up neatly ready for heating.

Katrina went aft and closed the shower room door, quickly shedding the rest of her clothes. Turning her face to the jet, she revelled in the hot water, soaping and massaging her body sensually, glorying in the delicious warmth that surged through her bloodstream.

With her heart thumping, she rinsed and dried herself carefully, then slipped into her pants and borrowed blouse, taking care to leave it unbuttoned.

She tossed her sweater and corduroy trousers onto the floor, and eased past the table to the galley. David turned, his face alternatively showing surprise, pleasure and confusion.

'The captain invites you to kiss her,' she said, wrapping her arms round his neck and pressing herself hard against him.

Her mouth sought his, her pelvis gyrating almost imperceptively. Closing her eyes, she held him tightly, her tongue reaching for his throat. She was aware of his hand feeling for her breast, pushing the blouse off her shoulders and returning to hold her, his forefinger and thumb gently manipulating her nipple. His other hand moved down her back and pressed her to him, slipping inside her pants.

Pausing only to draw breath, she pushed his sweater over his head and drew him back to the bunk, pulling him on top of her, her breathing heavy with expectation.

'I want you, David. Dear God, I want you so much.' She caressed the back of his head, her lips pecking at his nose, mouth, eyes and neck, her hands grappling with the buttons of his shirt.

'Ssssh,' he whispered.

Holding her breath, she clamped her eyes tightly, each nerve sensing the soft beginnings of his beard as he brushed his lips down her neck to her breasts. She drew his head back so that she could kiss him again, her hands travelling alternately up and down his back.

Mumbling endearments, she writhed round and buried her face in his chest, impulsively kissing the flat of his stomach, her hands impatiently groping for his belt and dragging his jeans over his hips, as if driven by a deep, animal stimulus that she could no longer control.

Clutching his buttocks, she slid her face along the golden down of his thighs and legs, and nuzzled into the back of his knees, then worked her way back up again, casting herself upon him.

Joyously, she smothered his face with more kisses, tears of happiness rolling like jewels down her cheeks.

He struggled up onto his side and gently pushed her down, wiping her cheek with his little finger, smiling at her, his eyes filled with wonder.

She lay back then and guided him to her, listening to the slap of waves under the hull and rejoicing in the way that he slowly and sensitively brought her to the fruition for which she had yearned for so long.

Wearing gabardine slacks, a plain blue shirt and bow tie, George Vito pulled on a jersey and bright red anorak, and tied the laces of his sneakers. Surveying the suite, he was satisfied that everything was as it should be.

Being forced to leave behind his expensive suits and shirts, not to mention his new Italian shoes and the Louis Vuitton briefcase, was unfortunate but infinitely preferable to failure. If he was to change identities, it was important to do it properly.

He stopped short at leaving his solid gold Lapponia cufflinks, however, tossing them into the overnight bag with his coins, maps and other papers.

Picking up the telephone, he advised the hotel operator that he was back, but informed her that he expected to be travelling to Oslo and Copenhagen shortly and may well stay there for a couple of days. He would be grateful, he said, if she could keep his suite for him.

Again, he glanced round the room checking details, content that anyone entering would be convinced that he fully intended to return.

Pausing briefly in front of the full length mirror, he pushed his fingers through his hair and smoothed the pencil-thin moustache to ensure that the gum had set.

Gone was the urbane image of the successful business executive. His hair, normally slicked back and held in place with hair gel, now flopped loosely across his forehead. Combined with the heavy spectacles, it gave him the appearance of a university lecturer.

Ensuring that he had not forgotten the forged passport and driving licence, he closed the door and tiptoed along the corridor to the head of the stairs. The receptionist was busy in the small office at the back. He slipped out of the rear door, tossed his bag into the white Volvo and drove to the jetty to catch the evening ferry.

The two-hour journey to Hafslo was tedious, the road along the banks of the Sognefjord twisting endlessly round damp granite walls. He did not reach the Hillestrand Hotel until nearly nine o'clock.

The two-storey building was perfect for his purposes; small, comfortable, off the main road and on the banks of an inland lake. In the lobby, plush burgundy sofas satisfied his need for luxury. A plethora of notices advising tourists of local attractions and a lobby bar illuminated with Japanese paper lanterns ensured that while the hotel was perfect for Robert Marito, George Vito would not have been seen dead in it.

His room, by normal standards, was both comfortable and functional, but it was a room not a suite and it lacked the character, style and elegance of the Glacier Hotel. Vito found it depressing. On settling in, he telephoned Hans Tripp in Miami, as much out of a need for communication with another American as a desire to impart information.

The moment he heard Tripp's voice, he knew he had made a mistake. Holding the receiver at arm's length until the string of expletives came to an end, he sighed, loudly and demonstratively.

'Always good to hear you in good form, Hans,' he said, his voice dripping with sarcasm. Tripp ignored him.

'How come you don't call earlier? Yesterday, you call me at ten a.m. Today, it's three-thirty. What's the matter, ain't you never heard of consistency? I been waitin' for your call and I don't like being kept waitin'.'

Vito listened patiently. Moan, moan, moan. The man never stopped complaining.

'In future, you call me ten on the nose, Miami time, y'hear? Every day. Now give.'

Vito stretched out on the bed. 'Not much to report, Hans. We started work on the tunnel this morning and the miners will be leaving Newcastle tomorrow …'

'Cut the crap, George. I wanna hear about Larsen.'

Vito froze. 'Larsen,' he stammered, swinging his legs onto the floor. 'Why?'

'Whad'ya mean "why"? You drivin' a hearse or somethin'? Liven up, George. I wanna know the full story, startin' with the kidnap.'

Vito thought rapidly, fencing, buying time. How in hell had Tripp found out about that? He wiped the palm of his hand against his slacks.

'Nothing to worry about, Hans, I can assure you. Everything's under control. I'm just surprised that you've heard.' The question was what - and how much had he heard. Tripp chuckled, briefly.

'I got my contacts. Talkin' to an old buddy at the state-owned Norwegian oil company, Statoil, about this Russian plan to build an oil base under the polar ice. Goddam Ruskies obviously think there's oil up there, but all he could talk about was Larsen. So talk.'

Vito sat on the edge of his bed, fighting a rising panic. If Tripp had contacts at Statoil, he might have heard everything. It depended on precisely when he had spoken to this friend.

Racking his brains, he tried to remember which elements of the story had been published when. The morning papers would contain news only of the kidnap, the stolen motor home and Larsen crashing through the police barrier, but if Tripp knew the contents of the afternoon papers, he would be aware of the shooting and the wrecked helicopter.

'Larsen flipped, I guess. According to the hotel staff, he fell for the woman running the hotel and kidnapped her. Seems he raped her in a stolen motor home, then tried to evade arrest by driving through a police barrier.'

'You holdin' out on me, George?'

Vito swore, exasperated by Tripp's badgering. 'Have I ever held out on you, Hans? Of course, I'm not.'

'So when I say I wanna hear the full story, I mean just that. I wanna hear about the chopper. That's my money you're screwing around with over there. Don't forget it.'

Vito sighed, wiping a film of perspiration from his forehead.

'Hans,' he said, patiently. 'I was not there. From what I hear Larsen set fire to the helicopter, then stole a seaplane and took off someplace up the coast. That's all I know.'

'And got himself arrested, then calmly walked out of the police station, stole a cop car and disappeared off the face of the earth.'

Vito started. Tripp obviously knew more than he did.

'I, ah ... I hadn't heard that, Hans.'

I suppose you didn't hear about Planet Watch blockading the fjord, either, huh? Jeezus, I pay those assholes a million bucks a year and they do this to me. You got that sorted, yet?'

'I'm working on them right, now,' he lied. His mind was in a whirl. Tripp must have spoken to the man at Statoil within the last hour. He cursed himself for not listening to the latest news bulletins.

'Good. Incidentally, did Larsen sign over that land?'

'Sure. No problem,' Vito sucked in a deep breath, glad of the opportunity to change the subject. 'The British miners and the heavy equipment will be leaving Newcastle tomorrow.' He waited while Tripp spat cigar tobacco and whispering to somebody close by. When he spoke again, the President's voice was rasping and full of menace.

'You'd better be levelling with me, George.'

'Hans, of course ...'

'You're not indispensable. You get my point?'

'Perfectly, Hans. You have nothing to worry about, I assure you.' He laughed nervously.

There was a pause. Tripp coughed, a strange gurgling noise contaminated with the phlegm of innumerable cigars.

'There's a helluva lot o' deep water here in Miami, George. You fuck with me, you'd better learn to swim in a heavy suit. Now, keep your goddam nose clean and get that mine operating. Call me tomorrow. Ten on the nose.'

The 'phone clicked. Vito replaced the receiver and reached for the pack of matches lying on the bedside table, his hands shaking. Clearly, the days of George Vito were numbered. Thank God, he'd changed identities. He supposed Robert Marito would suffice for a while, but he had no wish to live the life of a university lecturer. He would have to establish another alias more suited to his lifestyle.

But first he would find Deathsword's silver.

Chapter Eighteen

July 6, 9.45 p.m. - July 8, 11.50 a.m.

After checking their position on the Decca Navigator, Katrina confirmed the identity of the Grasöyane light one nautical mile off the port beam. The wind had backed round to the north and was gusting twenty-five knots, flecking the waves with spray. *Ulrika* pitched and rolled happily, swishing her stern. David had moved for'ard to batten hatches and trim the sails, his movements cumbersome in oilskins and safety harness.

Katrina had insisted that he familiarise himself with the harness, not least because the latest VHF weather report suggested worsening weather. Unusually for the time of year, another depression was moving in from the Atlantic north of the British Isles, promising gale force winds from the southwest within the next six hours.

She had intended to take a more southerly course seeking the shelter of Runde Island, three nautical miles off the port bow, but their love-making had denied them that. Not that she minded. She grinned to herself at the memory of it. David had been a wonderful lover; thoughtful, tender and playful.

When they had risen reluctantly from the bunk to snatch a quick meal and make sandwiches and hot soup for the thermos flasks, she had toasted him in mineral water, echoing his own words: "To you, me and the future". She had laughed and pressed herself hard against him, adding: "The future meaning again please. Very soon."

Watching him struggle as he winched the genoa, she knew they were in for a long and arduous night. With the weather deteriorating, she had thought seriously about spending the night on Runde, but she was impatient to round the Stadt headland. If they delayed, it could be for twelve hours or more.

They were both exhausted by the events of the past forty-eight hours and had agreed to keep two-hour watches to conserve energy. David would take first watch; she would take *Ulrika* round Stadt. She had shown him how to hold a course, keeping an eye constantly on the compass and the wind direction arrow at the top of the mast, and she had explained the dangers of allowing the boat to stray off course.

Happily, he had learned quickly, proving himself to be a natural helmsman with an enviable grasp of navigation.

David joined her in the cockpit, his voice half whipped away by the wind.

'You want me to take the helm now?' he shouted.

She nodded. 'I have programmed the waypoints into the Decca. Are you sure you will be all right?'

'No problem,' he yelled back. 'The auto-pilot takes us due west for fifty minutes, then I disengage and steer for 62.26N by 5.30E. After that, I reset it on two-two-five degrees. Then we head sou'west until it's time to wake you at midnight. Right?'

'Right. I will find you some seasick pills. We may need them before the night is out.'

She slipped down the companionway, exhausted and troubled by his inexperience. The course would take them approximately ten miles off the mainland, but at least it ensured they would avoid the sunken rocks and reefs to the north and northwest of Runde.

Handing him the fast-acting seasickness pills, she kissed him and went below. The barometer had fallen to one thousand and seven millibars, but she was too tired now to care. Still wearing her safety harness, she lay flat out on the bunk by the chart table, thought briefly of David, and drifted into a deep sleep.

In the cockpit, David peered into the pale light of the summer night, his eyes flicking constantly from the compass binnacle to the masthead. A ceiling of sullen cloud thickened in the west. *Ulrika* surged ahead, three hundred feet of water under her keel, the auto-pilot holding her steady.

Shivering, he turned his face away from the wind. The wind was whistling in from the starboard quarter now and he was cold despite the extra sweater, gloves and woolly hat that he had found in the locker below.

He wished he were below decks with Katrina. She was one helluva woman, full of surprises. He grinned to himself. When she had come out of the shower more steamed up than when she was in it, he'd nearly keeled over with surprise. She wasn't exactly short on passion, either.

For an hour his thoughts ranged from Katrina to Willmar and back to Katrina. To Septimus, his cat, and Pete Henriksen, and back again to Katrina. Always back to Katrina. He thought of the girl in the hotel at Bergen. What was her name? Isabelle something. Fun, but lacking Katrina's style and elegance. Katrina was beginning to get to him and the hell of it was that he didn't mind.

Checking his watch and the Decca, he noted it was ten of eleven, time to change course. After setting the next waypoint, he disengaged the auto-pilot and swung the wheel to port until the compass read two-two-five. *Ulrika* rolled unsteadily, her sails flapping, the sheets whipping dangerously.

Suddenly nervous and uncertain, he found it difficult to hold course. *Ulrika's* bow was yawing wickedly, her tail switching like a cat on heat. The waves, driven by the wind and cresting now, were racing under her hull, tossing her about like a toy boat in a bath.

Without warning, the boom swung over, ripping apart the night air with a resounding crack. David spun the wheel, struggling to keep the boat on course.

The yawl shuddered and heeled over, rocking uncomfortably. Again, he spun the wheel, cursing, afraid that she would tip over.

Poised on a wavetop, *Ulrika* plunged sickeningly into a trough, then gradually righted herself, her bow slowly climbing the next crest like a carriage on a roller-coaster.

Alarmed by the noise and the crash of the boom, Katrina scrambled up the companionway, snapping her harness to the guardrail. Expertly, she cast her eyes over the boat.

'We are carrying too much canvas,' she cried. 'We must shorten the sails and gullwing.'

David nodded and struggled for'ard, grateful for the safety harness.

From sailing on Foot Lake, he knew the principles of gullwinging - setting the genoa, or jib, to port and the mainsail to starboard when the wind was astern - but Foot Lake was one thing, he thought grimly. Sailing a forty-two foot ocean-goer in the middle of the Atlantic in a Force Five to Six was a different ball game.

Releasing the main halyard from its cleat, he braced himself against the waves and dragged the sail down to the next reefing point. Gratefully, *Ulrika* began to heel less acutely. David tightened the reefing line, stretching the sail taut along the boom.

Once the sails were reefed, Katrina again retired below, leaving David at the helm for another hour, his hands numb and his arms aching, grappling all the while with the wheel to keep the yawl on course. In the twilight, the waves foamed like ghosts, creaming in from astern.

Curtains of spray veiled the port and starboard lights, each droplet a needle waiting to pierce the exposed skin of his face when he turned into the wind. Increasingly he realised that there was no purpose in fighting the wind and sea, that the wisest and easiest course was to yield to them.

Ulrika rode the sea like a broncho-buster. Perching on the crests, her rudder high of the water, she would surge nauseously into the dark troughs, then pause and shudder before once more reluctantly raising her bow to the next wave.

By one o'clock, the barometer had dropped to nine-ninety-nine millibars, the wind backed to the west, shrieking through the rigging at more than thirty knots. The waves steepened, their foaming crests lashed by random squalls.

Drenched in spray, David was confident and at ease with himself now, no longer intimidated by the elements. Instead, he was at one with them, aware of their devastating potential, treating them warily and with respect.

Singing an improvised jazz solo at the top of his voice, he tensioned the mainsail and genoa, and brought the yawl back on course, locking the wheel on a course of two-three five degrees. As if enchanted, *Ulrika* raced, close-hauled, straight for Stadt.

Soon after one o'clock, Katrina emerged from the companionway, her face pale and her eyes sunken. Clipping on her harness, she clung to the grab rail by the wheel and again surveyed the boat's trim. She cupped a hand to her mouth to shelter her words from the elements.

'Still too much canvas.' she yelled, glancing over the side.

A plume of spray sheeted across the deck and ran down their oilskins.

'It is gusting Force Seven to Eight - a yachtsman's gale. We must put in an extra reef on the mains'l and reduce the genoa immediately.'

David grinned at her. 'Ay, ay, skipper,' he shouted back. 'This is fantastic, huh?'

'A warm bed would be better,' she yelled.

'Sure would.' He glanced at her, laughing. 'Here, take the helm. I'll go put that reef in.'

She nodded, her features strained and worried. The gale was at its peak now and would not abate for several hours, but at least now they were working as a team. He edged past her and began to move for'ard, staring into her eyes.

'You okay? You look worried.'

She grabbed his arm.

'David, wait. This is crazy. It's not worth the risk.'

He turned, rolling with the motion of the boat. 'How's that?'

'It is madness. We must run for shelter. It is not possible to sail round Stadt in this.'

He studied her face, wet and shining in the dim light.

'Sure we can. We can do anything.'

Katrina shook her head violently. *Ulrika* careered down a fifteen-foot wave into a patch of boiling sea. 'No. The wind is from the west. It'll drive us straight onto the rocks.'

She turned away as another squall ripped across them, then beckoned him closer, shouting into his ear. 'We must find a lee shore. We'll drop down into the fjord east of Stadtlandet.'

'You're the skipper.'

He moved for'ard to double-reef the mains'l, surprised that she had given in so easily. Exhilarated by the power of the storm and his own ability to cope with it, he was charged with excitement, adrenalin coursing through his body.

Reducing the genoa from the cockpit, he wondered if Katrina was turning about on his behalf, because of his inexperience, but discarded the idea. From the haunted look on her face, he knew that, like him, she was close to exhaustion - the worst of all enemies because that was when you made mistakes.

They ran hard before the storm then, driven by heavy Atlantic rollers maddened by the wind until they picked up the white, occulting flash of the Haugsl light. Katrina steered down the Vanylvs Gap, sheltered on the starboard side by cliffs rising steeply to twelve-hundred feet.

Rounding the light, David lowered the sails and they headed for a lonely stretch of coast, finally nosing close into the lee shore under power.

They anchored with twelve feet of water under the keel, *Ulrika* bucking in the wind. Shedding their oils and heavy clothing, they sat briefly at the little table in the cabin munching sandwiches and sipping hot soup from the thermos, listening to the wind in the shrouds and the sound of the halyards slapping against the masts. David smiled, his face gaunt with tiredness.

'Blue,' he said. 'I don't know about you, but I'm bushed.' He dragged a pillow and duvet from the locker, and kissed her goodnight. Stripping down to his underwear, he flopped onto the bunk, his mind wanting her but his eyes closing involuntarily.

I will come to visit you in the morning,' she said.

'It's two-thirty,' he mumbled. 'It *is* morning.'

On Tyneside in northeast England, a siren hooted and an overhead crane inched along the tracks set into the quayside at North Shields. Small knots of people, Jimmie and Doris Hargreaves among them, gathered in the terminal building on Ro-Ro Three Wharf, taking leave of each other as the crew of *Arctic Constellation* prepared to sail.

'Come on, Doris, turn the taps off. I'll be back in four weeks ...'

'I know,' she said, dabbing a handkerchief to her eyes. 'It's just that it seems such a long time - y'know, wi' the kids an' you never bein' away before, like ...'

'Ay, but when I come back, I'll 'ave twelve 'undred quid in my pocket.'

Jimmie placed his hands on her shoulders, his eyes earnestly seeking hers. 'As soon as I get back, I'll tek you dancin' again - just like last night.' He pulled her to him. 'Or we could 'ave a week in Spain. But only if you stop blubberin' and give us a goodbye kiss, like.'

She looked up at him, her eyes brown and damp, her cheeks stained. 'No Norwegian girls, mind,' she sniffed.

'No chance,' he said, pulling her to him, his hands groping beneath her coat for her backside. 'When I get back, I'll be reet rampant, lass.'

'Jimmie, stop it, you daft bugger. They'll see me coat twitchin'.'

Three blasts of a whistle signalled the ship's imminent departure. Jimmie hugged his wife once more, then grabbed his bag and strode on board, his throat tight with emotion.

As the crew cast off and the ship's propellers churned the Tyneside waters to a frenzy, he leaned over the side of the ship and waved. She was a good wife was Doris. There was no way he was going to play around with some Norwegian woman while he still had her.

Shivering in the early morning breeze, he waved until he could see her no more, then wandered down to the ship's bar to join Jack Lambert and Bill Ackhurst. By the time the ship had nosed out of the Tyne estuary and swung to the northeast, her course set for Norway, it was nine o'clock and he was supping his second glass of ale.

As the depression headed north and *Arctic Constellation* butted the tail end of the storm that had raged around Stadt, sailing conditions off the west coast of Norway improved markedly.

Among the myriad of coastal islands and skerries strung between Stadt and Bergen nearly a hundred and fifty miles to the south, both amateur and professional sailors alike took one sniff at the Force Five nor'westerly and weighed anchor, heading out to sea beneath an artist's sky.

For most of them, boats and the sea were as much a part of their lives as blood and tissue. In the case of Svein and Inge Solbakken, the boat was an O'Day 22, a basic but safe trailer-sailer that offered four berths and a fair turn of speed despite being twenty years old.

Wherever they looked, there seemed to be another boat. Svein could only presume that their skippers, too, had heard the news the previous evening and, like them, were heading for Sognefjord.

When he and Inge had heard the announcement that Planet Watch intended to blockade Fjærlandsfjord, it had stirred in them the same deep passions common to most Norwegians. "Why should an American multi-national company be allowed to spoil our countryside - our heritage - for sordid financial gain?" they had asked themselves.

It was a question that touched the hearts of all Norwegians. They had discussed the issue of Schneider Barr and Fjærlandsfjord in their homes and in bars, restaurants and dance halls long into the night.

By nine-thirty Norwegian time that morning, hundreds of small craft were plying the archipelagos, their owners intent on preventing *Arctic Constellation* reaching Fjærland. It was the biggest "sail-in" in Norwegian history.

At the Glacier Hotel at Fjærland, most of the guests were preparing to tour the glaciers or spend a blustery day in the mountains. Only Inspector Ingstad and Sergeant Nielsen remained in the breakfast room. Normally, they both preferred to eat alone, but this morning they had joined forces to discuss strategy.

'*Fy fan*, Nielsen. This case shifts about like a sandbank,' the Inspector complained. 'One minute we're trying to find Larsen, then we realise he's innocent and what happens? He escapes from a police station, dumps a patrol car in the sea and steals a bloody yacht.'

'I know, sir. It's as if he *wants* to go to prison. I've alerted the coastguards to keep an eye open for her. She's called *Ulrika*.'

'It'll be like looking for a flea in a market. Half the yachts in the country have put to sea thanks to this Planet Watch lunacy.' The Inspector clicked his tongue and sighed. 'That's the Sheriff's problem, thank God. Better contact headquarters. We're going to need reinforcements. If these people are going to string boats across the fjord, it could be ugly.'

'Right, sir. I'll get onto that right away,' Nielsen replied dutifully. 'Incidentally, what shall we do about Vito?'

'Find him, Nielsen. Find him.'

'Yes sir, but the hotel says he's still in Oslo or Copenhagen and it might be a couple of days before he's back.'

'We'd better take a look at his suite. Should have done it when he didn't turn up last night,' the Inspector said gruffly, pushing back his chair.

The two policemen wandered into the lobby and accompanied by the acting manager mounted the stairs to Vito's suite. They stood there for a full minute, their eyes taking in the scene before them. The room was immaculate, nothing out of place.

Ingstad opened the wardrobe door. Vito's clothes hung in a row on their hangers, his shirts and underwear stacked tidily on the shelves. Nielsen opened the desk drawers.

'Nothing here. Just his passport and driving licence.' The sergeant moved round the room opening more drawers. All were empty.

'What about the briefcase?'

Nielsen snapped it open.

'Nothing much. Just a couple of newspapers, sir. Certainly doesn't look as if he's planning to do a runner.'

'He has, though, hasn't he Nielsen?' the Inspector said grumpily.

They fell silent then. Eventually, Ingstad stood by the balcony door, reasoning that if he viewed the room from a different perspective it might awaken some recess in his memory. It did, but initially he could not put his finger on it.

'There's something strange, Nielsen. I can feel it.'

'I know, sir. So can I.'

The Inspector turned to the assistant manager. 'When Vito said he was leaving for Oslo and Copenhagen, who took the call?'

'The receptionist, Inspector. Her name is Berit.'

'Have her come up here straight away.'

Ingstad turned to the sergeant and the manager moved across the room to the telephone.

'You know what strikes me as odd?' Ingstad asked. 'Papers. This is a man who's a senior executive of a multi-national company and yet apart from his passport and driving licence there's not a single document in the entire suite.'

Nielsen nodded. 'You're right. That is odd.' He thought for a moment. 'So if there are no papers here, he either didn't have any - which is inconceivable given his position - or he took them with him. In which case, why did he leave his briefcase behind?'

'Exactly. And if he was going to Oslo or Copenhagen, you'd expect him to take his driving licence and passport with him. Especially his passport. He'd need that to register at an hotel.'

A faint tap on the door interrupted the Inspector's train of thought. Berit, a woman in her early twenties, stood in the doorway. Ingstad adopted his most paternal image.

'*Ja, kom inn*. Berit, isn't it? Tell me, when Mr. Vito telephoned reception yesterday, what exactly did he say?'

The receptionist smiled, her hands clasped loosely in front of her. 'He said that he had come back but that he would be going to Oslo or Copenhagen shortly and might be away for a couple of days.'

'That's all?'

'Yes, Inspector.'

Ingstad gazed out of the window, then turned back to her.

'When he said he'd come back, did he say where from?'

'No sir, but in the morning he rang to order a picnic hamper and said he would be out all day and wouldn't be back until late evening.'

'I see. Anything else?'

'Not really. Except that the chambermaid came down after lunch to say that she hadn't cleaned the suite because there was a "Do Not Disturb" sign on the door. It was a bit funny, that, because she said it hadn't been there first thing. I was a bit surprised because he was supposed to be out, but he must have been there to put the sign up.'

Ingstad nodded. 'Yes, I see what you mean. All right, Berit. That's all. *Mange takk.*'

Ingstad showed her to the door and turned to the assistant manager.

'I have reason to suspect that Mr. Vito has left us,' he said, decisively. 'With your permission, I'd like to search the suite and I'd like you to be present. In the meantime, no one else is to enter this room until I say so.'

Leaving the other man in no doubt that the request was a command, the Inspector nodded to Nielsen. 'Right, let's get on with it.'

They searched then, peering in cupboards and drawers, probing the pockets of Vito's suits, crawling on their hands and knees to check beneath the bed, the assistant manager watching them from the doorway.

'We've got some footprints that don't match here, sir,' Nielsen called from the bedside. Ingstad joined him and stared at the ridged indentations in the carpet. The assistant manager peered over his shoulder.

'Trainers,' he said, tersely. 'The chambermaids are always complaining about them.'

Ingstad glanced up at him, rising to his feet. 'Trainers? You mean for jogging?'

The manager nodded. 'Yes. Trainers, sneakers, whatever you call them. They leave marks everywhere.'

'Not exactly consistent with Vito's image, sir,' Nielsen said, climbing to his feet.

'Or with the rest of his clothing, Sergeant. If he's been wearing trainers for jogging, why doesn't he have any jogging clothes?'

The Inspector wandered into the bathroom. Vito had spaced his shaving tackle and toiletries neatly along the glass shelf above the wash basin. Ingstad unscrewed a bottle of Givenchy aftershave lotion and held it to his nose. Replacing it, he peered into the wash basin and wiped his finger along its surface, examining a thin film of grease, water and talcum powder.

He held the mixture to his nose. The grease was probably hair gel. If Vito was planning to skip the country, he might have used talcum powder to grey his hair. Peering into Vito's wash bag, he was aware of the telephone ringing in the bedroom and Nielsen's voice rising in surprise.

Searching absent-mindedly through the contents of the washbag,

Ingstad picked out a small tube from the jumble of sleeping tablets, extra toothbrushes and nail files. Two words - *Theatrical Gum* leapt at him from the tiny, italic text, demanding attention like diamonds sparkling in mud.

Hurriedly wrapping the tube in tissue paper, he strode into the bedroom. 'I want a check on the registration forms of every hotel in the country, Nielsen,' he ordered. 'The bird has flown.'

The sergeant stood by the telephone, shock written over his features. 'Yes sir. I think ...'

'Switched identities. That's why his passport and driving licence are here.' The Inspector paced up and down, oblivious to Nielsen's distress, speaking his thoughts aloud.

'He'll be wearing a grey moustache and his hair will be grey, too, if my guess is correct, he'll look as unlike George Vito as possible. He's wearing trainers, which means he's probably wearing jeans or a track suit, as well. And he'll be travelling light.' He looked up. 'What's the matter, man? You look as if you've been struck by lightning.'

Nielsen pointed to the telephone. 'That call, sir. It was from the Sheriff's office at Balestrand. It's Tor Falck. He's been found dead in his bath.'

Shortly after ten-fifteen, David woke to find Katrina beside him, her marbled arm and shoulder poking above the duvet, her lean bottom tucked into his groin. At eleven-thirty, when they rose relaxed and pleasured, Katrina checked the moorings and volunteered to cook breakfast while David announced his intention to rename the boat.

'The name's painted in capitals,' he explained. 'All I have to do is paint over the "U" and change the "L" to an "E" - and we have *ERIKA*. And if I paint out the "M" in *MOLDE* and add an "N", you get *OLDEN*.' He grinned. 'I looked it up on the chart. It's a little village at the end of a fjord.'

Unearthing cans of quick-drying paint from the stern locker, he converted *Ulrika* from *Molde* to *Erika* from *Olden* in less than an hour. When he returned below decks, he found Katrina happily folding napkins at a table laden with food. David sat next to her and poured the coffee, his face pensive.

'Has it ever occurred to you, Blue, that there may not be any Viking silver? That Vito might be wrong?'

She looked at him sharply.

'Of course. Nothing in life is certain, but Vito believed it, he had the evidence to support it and the professor believed it, too, I think.'

'But suppose there isn't any? What then?'
'We shall either go to jail or to Paraguay. Stop being so pessimistic.'
'Ay, ay skipper,'
David ate heartily, speaking in monosyllables. Replete, he pushed away his plate, his hands holding his stomach. 'That was some breakfast, Blue.'

'It is the custom in Norway,' Katrina said. 'Big breakfasts to give you energy for the rest of the day. Except that now it is lunchtime.'

'I dunno about energy. I'm so full I have to lie down,' David said, stretching out on the sofa. 'Those hash browns of yours were outa this world.'

She laughed. 'We sail at two o'clock. You may lie down if you wish. If you do, I reserve the right also to lie down' She smiled, teasing him. 'We have a whole hour to ourselves - Mr. Dynamite.'

They lay there then, laughing and talking together of their past lives, Katrina's head in the crook of his arm. Finally, she rose. David reached for a pencil and insisted on drawing a quick sketch of her.

'This is no good, David,' she said eventually. 'We must go.' She moved to the chart table and picked up the dividers. 'It will be a long voyage. If we are to reach Fjærland tomorrow, we must sail through the night.'

She studied the charts, then turned back to him, the skin of her face tight across her cheekbones, her face shiny without make-up.

'You know the boat now, so we will take four hour watches. I will take the first watch and take us round Stadt.' She gestured to the table, smiling. 'You will wash up, I think.'

Plotting a course, she set the waypoints on the Decca Navigator and tuned the VHF. The wind was nor'westerly now, blowing Force Five and decreasing, giving excellent sailing conditions. They weighed anchor at precisely two o'clock. By six, she had successfully negotiated the Stadt peninsular.

Her course took them well out to sea to avoid the confluence of tides that rushed dangerously in and out of a myriad of channels separating the rocky fingers of land.

Although the storm was abating, the swells continued to roll in, growing heavier and more majestic as the seabed shelved, pounding the shoreline with the full weight of the Atlantic behind them.

When Katrina picked up the Kråkenes and Skongness lighthouses, she handed the helm to David and gave him full instructions on the course to follow, pointing out the islands and grounds to avoid. Still tired from the exertions of the previous two days, she retired below fully confident in his sailing abilities. Within minutes, she had succumbed to a deep sleep induced by fresh sea air, contentment and the warmth of the saloon.

David, too, was at ease, threading a course through islands and skerries of granite, the cries of circling seabirds harsh in the silence of mid-evening. His only concern was what might happen on their arrival at Fjærland.

If they could evade the police and find the silver, all their problems would be solved. Quite how they would find it was a mystery to him, and Fjærland was a tiny village; if they were seen, the news would travel fast. Arrest for the second time did not bear contemplating.

Shortly after ten o'clock, Katrina again took the helm. David remained with her on deck to gaze at a sun the colour of molten lava, its rays cast across a northern sky already filled with stars. When the sun finally disappeared beneath the horizon, it veneered the sea with a light of liquid gold.

Only when its rich lustre faded did he go below, leaving Katrina at the helm, one side of her face radiantly reflecting the ebbing glow of daylight, the features of the other diffuse in the gathering darkness.

Throughout the night, they changed watches and slept, *Erika* heeling before a quartering wind, heading towards Sognefjord at a steady eight knots. When Katrina appeared on deck at six a.m., the yawl was accompanied by a flotilla of small boats. Surprised at their numbers, she lowered the sails and gunned the engine. The yawl forged ahead, her diesels throbbing, her bow slicing through the mirror-still waters of the fjord.

David slept fitfully for three hours and did not return on deck until the sun was high in a near cloudless sky.

Staring at the mountain from which he had first seen Sognefjord on the day he had driven up from Bergen with Paul Stryn, he was again consumed with a sense of belonging, as if the brightly-painted frame houses and steepled wooden churches were a part of him. Red and blue national flags hung limply from garden flagstaffs, reminding him of the festivals at Willmar.

Erika forged ahead, her wake washing against the wooden landing stages jutting into the fjord. No boats were moored against them. As David relieved Katrina and steered past Vangsnes towards Balestrand, he realised why. The flotilla had grown into an armada.

'It must be a regatta,' Katrina said, re-emerging from the saloon in borrowed sunglasses, nursing a cup of hot chicken soup. 'I have never seen so many boats here. There are hundreds of them.'

David shook his head. 'Looks as if it's some kind of demonstration.'

He pointed to a fishing boat festooned with Norwegian flags and a banner strung from its black and white hull aft to the tiny wheelhouse. He read aloud the wording and turned to Katrina.

'What the hell's that supposed to mean? "Yanks out. Norway for Norwegians".'

Katrina ignored him, pointing at another banner that read: "No Mine. Norway Ours".

Suddenly, she understood. 'Don't you see? It's a demonstration against the copper mine at Fjærland. Yanks Out. That means Schneider Barr.'

'You mean all these boats are going to Fjærland? Jesus!'

Astern, the deep-throated sound of a siren ricocheted angrily around the fjord. A fishing smack bearing the Planet Watch insignia was mothering a flotilla of ocean-going rubber dinghies bouncing across the bows of a large ship. David pushed his sunglasses onto his forehead and trained his glasses on her.

'*Arctic Constellation*,' he said. 'Looks as if these guys aren't too happy she's here.'

Katrina was not listening. She was at the wheel now, concentrating on avoiding a collision, nosing *Erika* through the Balestrand-Hella gap. Ahead, perhaps two hundred small craft of all types and sizes were strung across the entrance to Fjærlandsfjord, chained together.

David swore and lowered the fenders.

'How the hell are we going to get through that lot?' he shouted.

'Easily,' Katrina said. She nosed gently up to them and hailed a young man standing in the prow of a motorboat.

'*Får vi slutte oss til?*'

'Hurry up then,' he answered, releasing the chain that secured him to the next boat. 'As soon as you're inside the barrier, come about and push your bow in here.'

'Right,' she said, easing through the gap.

'What did you say?' David enquired.

'I asked if we could join them.' She laughed, bending down to give the engine full throttle as they passed through.

'*Tusen takk*,' she shouted, waving. 'A thousand thanks.'

'*Fan!* ' the young man yelled back angrily. '*Din Skitdjevel!*"

Katrina ignored the string of invective. Smiling broadly, she steered *Erika* up the fjord towards Fjærland.

Chapter Nineteen

July 8, 11.50 a.m. - July 9, 00.10 a.m.

All but a handful of the one hundred British miners on board *Arctic Constellation* crowded the foredeck below the bridge, at the same time amused, horrified, confused and incredulous. When they had first sighted the fleet of fishing boats and pleasure craft, many had believed it to be some form of welcome, but as the ship proceeded slowly along Sognefjord its true purpose became more apparent.

Time after time, orange-coloured dinghies and motor boats arced in front of the ship's bows at full speed, their noses pointed skywards in a display of defiance.

'Daft buggers. They need their bloody 'eads testin',' commented one burly Sunderland man. 'Wharra they tryin' to do?'

'I dunno, but if I 'ad my way, I'd run bastards down,' said another, his fists clenched and massive.

'It's them Planet Watch people,' said Bill Ackhurst, pointing to a fishing smack. 'Look, y'can see cameramen on top of deck'ouse. They never go nowhere without television crews, that lot.'

Similar sentiments were voiced a thousand times, not least on the bridge. As the ship steered towards Balestrand, the blasts of her siren echoing around the fjord, her captain's blood pressure was rising rapidly. He had long since telegraphed "Dead Slow" to the engine room, but despite every precaution, an accident of some kind seemed increasingly likely - and no doubt, he would be the one held to account.

The entire fjord was alive with small boats. Bunting fluttered from mastheads. Families waved their fists and shouted slogans. Motor launches crowded with press photographers and television camera crews buzzed about the fjord like wasps in wine.

Police helicopters circled overhead, the officers on board filming secretly. A senior police officer on the afterdeck of a police launch cruising off *Arctic Constellation's* starboard bow held a megaphone to his mouth, repeatedly ordering the Planet Watch fishing smack and her attendant dinghies to disperse. No one took any notice.

'*Legg bi. Dere er under arrest!*'

The helmsman cocked an ear. 'What's 'e sayin'?' he asked.

'I don't know,' said the man next to him. 'Sounded like he's arresting them, I think.'

Arctic Constellation's captain gazed through the angled windows of the bridge. He had given up trying to count the number of boats in the fjord, but with a corner of his mind half preparing for what he suspected might have to be a formal report, he estimated the number of craft at about twelve to fifteen hundred.

Passing through the Balestrand-Hella gap, he rounded the headland to starboard and gaped in astonishment at the line of ships spanning the entrance to Fjærlandsfjord. Outraged, he peered through his binoculars. He estimated them to be no more than three hundred yards away.

'Good God, they're chained together,' he yelled.

Angrily, he rang for "Stop Engines". He was particularly incensed at the demonstrators' overall lack of seamanship and the dangers to which they had subjected his ship and passengers, not to mention themselves.

'Reverse Thrust. Zero-niner-zero,' he ordered, hoping to turn the ship round. But a ship the size of *Arctic Constellation* took time to answer such commands and she continued to surge towards the line of boats spanning the fjord, her officers leaning helplessly over the wings of the bridge.

Not for some minutes did the ship answer the helm, her bows swinging round slowly. By the time her engines had shifted into reverse thrust and the propellers were churning the surface to froth, *Arctic Constellation* was no more than twenty yards from the boats dwarfed beneath her and the closest demonstrators were shrieking and diving without a second thought into the glacial waters of the fjord.

Unaware of the drama behind them, Katrina and David moored *Erika* close to the picnic area at the head of Fjærlandsfjord, deliberately avoiding the hotel in case Vito was still there. Still wearing waterproof trousers and thick sweaters, they walked unseen to Katrina's house at Bøyaøyri. The red Mitsubishi was still parked in the drive, but the house seemed unfamiliar. So much had happened during her absence that time had warped. It was as if she had been away forever.

Unlocking the door with a spare key hidden beneath a stone in the garden, she stepped inside. The house was exactly as she had left it. There was more dust. The lilies and roses had withered in their vases and, annoyingly, the fridge had defrosted, its door inadvertently left open during their hasty retreat three days previously.

'We must 'phone Tor and Paul,' she said, wiping the shelves. 'They must be wondering what on earth has happened to us.'

David looked at her sharply.

'No, Blue. Not yet. Let's find the silver first, huh?' He stood awkwardly by the door.

Katrina hesitated, but decided not to argue. Instead, she retrieved a large scale map from a writing desk in the sitting room and, returning to the kitchen, spread it over the pine table. She pointed to Fjærland.

'Fjærlandsfjord and the Bøya and Supphelle valleys are like a letter "Y",' she explained. 'The lefthand arm is Bøya valley, the Supphelle valley runs to the right and Skarestad - the old Viking settlement of Indre Moa - is at the intersection.'

'And the silver can't be south of Skarestad because in Viking times it was at the water's edge, right?'

'Right.' Katrina smiled, pleased that he had remembered. 'So the *moulins*, or potholes, must be somewhere close to the present edge of the ice because the climate today is relatively mild, similar to that in Viking times.' She glanced at him, stabbing her finger at the map.

'Here, just below the Supphelle glacier. I have seen them - at the foot of this mountain. And look closely, David. The mountain is called Vetle.'

David whistled. 'Vetle, that was the name on the runestone. Blue, you're a genius. What are we waiting for? Let's go.'

Katrina laughed and fished an ice axe from the stand in the hall. For the next hour, they strode along the narrow dirt road towards Supphellebreen, both glad of the chance to stretch their legs after the confinement of the boat. They saw no one, nor were they recognised.

The *moulins* were set in the lower skirts of the mountain, shallow indentations in the rock unrecognisable to anyone unfamiliar with the actions of the glacier. Katrina wasted no time, scrabbling frenetically at the surface with her ice axe. Beside her, David scooped out the soil with a flat slab of stone to a depth of three feet, his muscles rippling. Eventually, Katrina handed the ice axe to him, her chest heaving.

'There is nothing. Try that one,' she said, panting, her nostrils tingling in the clean, glacial air.

David systematically searched two more potholes, but after removing the dirt from the fourth and last, he stood up and arched his back.

'No use, Blue. It's not here.'

'It must be here,' she answered testily. 'Where else could he have put it?'

'Maybe there are more potholes someplace?'

A shout further down the valley interrupted them. Glancing back down the valley, Katrina saw two men, then more, holding what appeared to be metal detectors. In all, there were eight of them. And they were no more than three hundred yards away.

'David, they've seen us,' she said, gripping his arm. 'They must be Vito's men. He must have found out about Indre Moa. They are searching the same area.'

One of the men was speaking into what appeared to be a portable telephone. David swore, his mind revving.

'Is there another way out of the valley?'

Katrina pointed to a narrow track leading upwards through a jumble of fallen boulders. 'We could go up to *Flatbrehytta*. It is a mountain hut. My father used it many times.' She squatted beside him, behind a massive boulder coated in moss. 'It is a popular starting point for glacier tours. It would be easy to lose them up there.'

David looked at her uneasily. 'I get a distinct feeling of *dèja vu* here, Blue. We're not going to wind up walking over that glacier again are we?'

'Of course not,' Katrina replied. 'Please, do not be ridiculous.'

'I hope you're right. You know what I'm like on mountains.'

Katrina pointed back down the valley. The men had dropped their metal detectors and were huddled together, pointing in their direction. One, who looked suspiciously like Centaur, was studying them through a pair of binoculars.

'Damn them,' Katrina murmured. 'Come, we must go.'

She turned on her heel, doubling back to the track, climbing rapidly. David followed, cursing under his breath. The path was well marked, but as the steep sides of the mountains closed in on them, the incline grew steadily more acute.

Katrina slowed to a more even pace. Twelve hundred feet above the valley floor, the path divided. She waited for David to catch up.

'How far behind are they?' she asked urgently.

'I dunno.'

Katrina looked at him, her eyes reflecting her anxiety. 'Are you all right?'

'Just let's get where we're goin' and stop talkin' about it, okay?'

'Then wait here. I will be back in one minute.'

She swung round, climbing the left hand path rapidly. Taking a handful of tissues from her pocket, she screwed them into a ball and wedged them under a stone, then doubled back to David.

'The left path is very steep. We will take the easier route. The two paths rejoin each other later on, anyway. With luck they will see the tissues and assume that we have gone that way. It will slow them down.'

Setting off again, David fixed his eyes firmly on the path two feet in front of him, shielding them with his hand, deliberately shutting the panoramas from view. Climbing steadily for another hour, they reached *Flatbrehytta* nearly three thousand feet above the fjord shortly after six-thirty in the evening.

Vito's men were approximately seven hundred feet below them. Katrina pushed open the door to the tiny log cabin. It was exactly as she remembered it. Small and functional. Designed as a base rather than for comfort.

Crossing the tiny room, she unhooked two worn anoraks from a line of pegs on the wall.

'Here, put this on,' she ordered, taking one for herself. 'You will need it.'

'Blue ...'

'David, please don't argue. We must hide on the glacier. It is our only chance of avoiding them. There is nowhere else to go.'

David groaned. 'Of course we're not going to wind up walking over the glacier again,' he mimicked. 'Please, do not be ridiculous.'

Katrina ignored him. Opening a large box in the corner of the hut, she selected from the tangle of equipment a coil of rope, two body harnesses and crampons.

'With crampons, you will have no difficulty walking on the ice,' she said. 'Try them for size. We will put them on later at the edge of the ice, but we must hurry. There is much to explain.'

She was in command now. This was her world, her territory. Going into the tortured ice of Supphellebreen was risky, especially as David was a novice. Nonetheless, from the way he had so readily adapted to sailing, she was confident that she could teach him the basics of glacier walking in the time available.

'We will hide the rest of the equipment away from the hut,' she said, attaching an array of pitons and karabiners to the waistband of her harness. 'With luck, they will see us walking onto the glacier. If they follow, they will have no chance of survival. Not without special equipment.'

Looping a rope through her harness, she attached the other end to David and handed him a stainless steel flange, one foot long, shaped like a shovel.

'Clip this onto your harness. It is a snow anchor. It will hold your weight if you fall.' She looked at him anxiously, aware of his fears. 'Be under no illusions, David - the glacier is dangerous. If you fall, you will thank God for that snow anchor.' She handed him two ice axes. 'You will need these also.'

'You're a great comfort, Blue,' he said sardonically.

'She smiled. 'I'm sorry. I don't mean to make it worse for you, but it is better that you are aware of the dangers. Come, now we must go.'

Opening the door, she peered outside cautiously. There was no sign of Vito's men but she could hear them shouting lower down the mountain. Motioning urgently to David, she helped him drag the box of equipment out of the cabin. Together, they covered it with stones and sods of mossy grass. That done, they walked towards the edge of the ice, Katrina talking rapidly, explaining the techniques of climbing with two ice axes and crampons.

'It is not difficult. The worst danger is the cold,' she said. 'It is as if the ice is wrapped in cold air. When you are in a crevasse, it sucks the warmth from your body very quickly. As it does so, the ice melts and your clothes become wet.' She glanced at him, her eyes filled with anxiety.

'Hypothermia sets in very quickly then. You will be stiff and cold and unable to move. My father once rescued a man thirty minutes after he had fallen into a crevasse - only to find that he was dead.'

'Jesus, Blue. Do I need to know that?'

She shrugged and laughed, a tiny, forced laugh that caught in her throat. 'I am sorry, but if I do not tell you a horror story, how will you understand? As long as you are careful and treat the ice with respect, you will have nothing to fear.'

'Blue,' David said simply, savouring the word and shaking his head. 'Sure was a great name for you. Cool as ice.'

She tossed her head and smiled wickedly.

'As long as you remember it is the blue ice that is the most dangerous.'

Stepping gingerly onto the glacier, David stamped his feet experimentally, testing the efficiency of his crampons. The surface crystals reminded him of his ice crusher back home in Willmar, except that this ice was fouled with viscid, black droplets half the size of his little fingernail.

'What's this? Oil?'

'Not oil,' Katrina said tersely. 'Sand, organic matter and ten per cent industrial pollution from Europe and Russia.'

'Pollution, in a place like this? Jeez.'

She shrugged. 'What do you think those people are doing down in the fjord? They are fighting to preserve our countryside in the only way they know how, but they are the ones being arrested. Not Schneider Barr or others like them.'

Moving up the slope, she threaded a route through the ice, chipping steps with her ice axe when necessary.

David followed silently. Glad of the sunglasses he had taken from the yacht, he found himself unable to tear his gaze from the ice field. Utterly fascinated by its chaotic beauty, he was soon gaining confidence on his crampons. More importantly, he was actually enjoying ice climbing.

Securely anchored with the axes and crampons on a forty-five degree slope, he fought off a brief wave of nausea and paid out more line as Katrina traversed above him. Below, the slope sheered precipitously into a pit of ice nearly a hundred feet deep.

Unusually, he found that he was able to look down into it without becoming disoriented. It was as if his exposure to heights on Marabreen and the track leading up to *Flatbrehytta* had in some way diminished his acrophobia.

He forced himself to gaze into the depths of the pit. The ice glistening menacingly, an intense turquoise blue. What was it that he had learned at school? Something about ice absorbing more of the yellow and red parts of the spectrum than blue, so the thicker the ice, the deeper the blue. He pushed the thought from his mind.

Chipping steps with his axe, he soon realised that the combination of toe spikes and two axes made climbing even the sheerest ice slopes comparatively easy. All you needed was caution and strength - and he had plenty of both.

The sound of a distant curse cut into his thoughts, signalling that Vito's men had arrived at the hut. Katrina paused and turned, the early evening sun glinting in her glasses.

'They have seen us. That is good,' she shouted, securing herself with an axe, ready for the challenge. David drew level with her.

'No Blue. It's not good. Do you hear what I hear?'

They listened. Between the gusts of wind, a faint but familiar thwacking echoed across the glacier. Moments later, the source of the noise appeared five hundred feet below them, its fuselage bright yellow against the brilliance of the ice and the dull grey-greens of the mountainside. Slowly, the machine turned, hovering above *Flatbrehytta*.

'They got another chopper. They must have radioed the pilot when they first saw us,' David said.

Katrina pointed to a pinnacle twisted grotesquely by the wind, a giant finger of ice stabbing at a yellowing sky.

'We will climb there. It is not far,' she said. 'There is cover there.'

Easing her axe out of the ice, she continued into the heart of the glacier, setting a punishing pace. David followed, surprised by their speed. Watching Katrina leap from one ridge to another, it seemed as if she had been born on the glacier.

Within minutes, the helicopter was upon them, its turbines whining, rotors clattering noisily in the echo chambers created by the ice. Glancing upwards, David saw the machine diving onto them in a ninety degree turn.

Vito was sitting by the open doorway.

David knew it was Vito despite his altered appearance. The shape of the man's head and the way he held his shoulders left him in no doubt about it. He had drawn his portrait back in Willmar. Artists remembered details like that.

A firebomb burst in a sheet of flame, despatching splinters of ice in all directions. David leapt sideways, dragging Katrina with him. Together, they slithered down the slope until, jamming their axes into the ice, they brought themselves to a halt. From the corner of his eye, David saw the men below walking onto the ice.

'They've found the equipment box,' he yelled, but Katrina had no time in which to answer. The helicopter came in for another run, banking steeply. Vito lobbed a second fire bomb at them, but it skidded off the ice, exploding deep inside a crevasse.

Again the helicopter returned, its yellow underbelly only yards away. Now, it was hovering fifty feet above them, the down draught impeding their progress. David watched in morbid fascination as the figure in the rear seat - Centaur - aimed a crossbow at him.

Hurling himself sideways, he rolled down the slope towards a crevasse, ice axes flailing. In the same instant, Katrina employed her snow anchor and leapt backwards over the lip of the chasm.

A bolt from the crossbow ricocheted harmlessly off the ice as David fell, dragged by the weight of Katrina's body. Desperately, he sought a hold, the blades of his axes scraping the surface. Not until he was half way over the edge did he secure a firm hold.

Below him, Katrina was swinging back and forth, trying to reach the overhang.

'I'm okay. Pull the rope. Tight,' she shouted, her voice taut and determined.

With his legs dangling over the edge of the crevasse, David secured his axes and hauled himself back onto the slope. Crouching now, his feet dug in firmly, he gripped the rope and swung her inwards. Another firebomb exploded above him, showering him with ice and broken glass.

Simultaneously, Katrina drove the pick of her axe into the ice wall and found a toe hold with her crampon. The helicopter manoeuvred above them, turning for a better aim.

Another bolt pinged across the ice, but David was so intent on what he was doing that he was aware of it only in the periphery of his mind. He peered over the edge. Katrina looked up at him, her face intense and strained.

'I am secure now. Can you come down without using your snow anchor?'

David nodded. The helicopter slowly swivelled round, almost on top of him. Clutching both axes tightly, he lay on his stomach and kicked his legs over the edge, desperately seeking a hold with his crampons as the downdraught tore at his clothing.

Thirty feet above him, David could see Vito braced against the rear seat of the helicopter, both hands clutching the butt of a Magnum revolver. Strangely fascinated, David watched him take aim, as if the action was in some way alienated from his own world.

The next second proved otherwise. Showering him with ice, the .44 shell blasted a crater a foot wide just ten feet from his face. Desperately, he manoeuvred himself over the lip of the crevasse, struggling for a toe hold.

Vito dropped another firebomb, but it, too, fell harmlessly into the depths. David jammed his right toe spike into the ice wall below him, using his axes alternately to lower himself over the edge.

He was breathing heavily now, sweat breaking out on his forehead, his shirt damp beneath the heavy windproof anorak and harness.

With only his left arm and head above the rim of the crevasse, he was too busy seeking a firmer footing to feel the steel bolt pierce his left arm. He was aware only of an instant numbness in his hand, mildly surprised to see the steel shaft protruding from his forearm, like an Apache arrow pinioning him to the ice.

Suddenly, he was unable to grip the axe, his left hand useless. He shouted to Katrina, securely anchored a few feet below him.

'I'm hit,' he shouted. Pain seared through his shoulders and neck.

Fear spread across her features. 'Are you hurt badly?' she shouted.

'Yeah. My arm ... I can't move my fingers.'

'I'll come up to you. Wait.'

She climbed fast and expertly, joined him directly below the lip of the ice. Here, they hung for a moment silently taking stock. On seeing the bolt protruding from his arm, her eyes widened with horror.

'*Herre Gud*,' she gasped, the blood draining from her face. 'David ... I had no idea.'

'You have to support me while I use my other arm to free myself,' he said, his voice hard and determined. He slammed each foot into the ice, one after the other, to improve his foothold.

Katrina pushed his body as best she could against the ice. David secured his ice axe, then eased the fingers of his right hand underneath his left forearm. Gripping the bolt, he eased it out of the ice, freeing his arm.

Holding his left arm above his head to slow the blood flow, he tightened his grip on the right hand axe and nodded. 'Okay, let's get the hell outa here.'

'There is a ledge behind you,' she said, guiding him. 'It leads to a narrow bridge.' She indicated a point over his shoulder. 'Beyond that is an ice tunnel. When we reach it, we will see how bad your wound is.'

'It's bad.' His arm was throbbing now, shock taking its toll. The ledge was twenty feet away. With a malfunctioning arm it seemed a mile.

'Wait. I will climb past you,' Katrina said. Quickly, she clambered across his body until the line of her snow anchor was taut. 'I shall have to abandon the anchor now,' she said. 'So, for God's sake, make sure you always have a firm hold. If we fall here, we will die.'

David swore. 'For Chrissakes, Blue, will you stop telling me I'm about to die? I have enough problems without that.'

She shivered and apologised, but he did not respond, aware only of the numbness and the blood staining the sleeve of his anorak. Gradually, they descended into the crevasse, the ice deadening all sounds except the chip of ice axes and the sound of its own creaking.

Above them, the overhang and a curve along the rim of the crevasse obscured all but a narrow strip of sky. David crabbed left, a spasm of pain shooting to his neck and shoulder. Wincing, he moved forward again, gritting his teeth.

'David, are you sure you are all right?' Katrina's edged closer to him.

'I will be if I can stop the blood flow,' he muttered. 'But we have to stop soon. I'm losing too much blood too fast.'

Hammering a piton into the ice, she snapped on a karabiner and fed the rope through it, then repeated the action to fashion a handrail. Inch by inch, she led him towards the ledge.

David felt his legs weaken and a wave of dizziness sweep over him. He paused, clutching his arm, worried that the bolt had severed an artery, then moved forwards again.

Stepping into the ice tunnel, he sank onto the ice and examined his arm, thinking rapidly.

The hole in his anorak was five times the diameter of the bolt. Almost certainly, that meant it was fitted with a broadhead. The bolt would have to be pushed through his arm rather than retrieved. For now, he would have to leave it where it was. He couldn't afford to lose more blood.

Recalling his Delta training, he knew that the attacks of nausea and dizziness signalled a loss of more than a pint of blood. It was essential to stem the flow quickly.

'Cut me a length of rope, Blue. About four feet. Quickly,' he ordered, his voice crisply efficient, but showing signs of desperation.

Holding a thumb and forefinger to his throat, he checked his pulse. One hundred and ten. Not much faster than normal, given their recent exertions. That meant he had lost less than two pints. With Katrina's help, he bound the rope tightly over his sleeve.

The bolt had penetrated the centre of his forearm and from the tear in his anorak he judged the broadhead to be about an inch in diameter. It looked as if it had missed the Radial and Ulnar arteries, but it was close.

The slightest jar could sever them. His shirt, sweater and anorak would have to serve as a bandage until he could make it back to *Flatbrehytta*.

Katrina looked at him helplessly, frightened now and shivering.

'We must get back to *Flatbrehytta*. There is a first aid box there.'

'Best leave the wound alone. Leave it to the medics.' He attempted a smile. 'If I pass out, remember to tell 'em on no account to try to pull the bolt out. It's very important. They have to push it through.' He pointed to the coil of rope. 'Give me another three feet of that, huh?'

Struggling to his feet, he raised his left arm to keep the wound elevated and instructed her to tie one end to his left wrist, wind the rope round the back of his neck and secure it by looping it over and under his right shoulder. It would put a helluva strain on the back of his neck but at least it would help keep the blood flow under control.

'Okay, let's get outa here,' he said. 'We're gettin' cold and our clothes are wet.'

Slowly and with infinite caution, they moved along the tunnel until its pale blue walls began to open to a sky coloured with the first blush of evening. At the far end, the passage split into several gullies formed by soft mounds of ice rising one upon the other.

David gazed out from the tunnel and wondered whether he would make it. They were completely surrounded by massive towers and pinnacles of ice eroded by wind and sun into strange troll-like shapes.

He was so entranced by this weird, iridescent landscape that he did not see the figure clad in black looking down on them. He heard only the sudden burst of gunfire and Katrina yelling as she shoved him into a gully wall.

Pain seared through his upper body and he felt his knees sagging. Pain, he remembered from distant training, is an attitude of mind. He forced himself to concentrate. Knowing that their lives depended on it.

Squatting, he scanned the contours of the ice. The gunman was standing on an ice bridge a hundred and fifty feet off to the right, sheltering beneath twin towers of ice interwoven like crossed fingers.

Katrina nudged him. 'I have a plan,' she whispered. 'If I can climb round him, onto the tower. Could you distract him … ?'

Sure,' he said brusquely, his face pale and strained. 'But for Chrissakes, Blue, take care. I don't want to spend the night alone in this hellhole.'

She untied his arm so that he could ease the binding when necessary and left him, working her way along a gully to their right. He did not see her again for a full fifteen minutes, until she was silhouetted directly above the gunman, the reddening sun directly behind her.

David poked his ice axe above the buttress of ice that sheltered him, drawing another short burst of fire.

Hidden from the gunman's view, Katrina chipped a horizontal "V" five feet from the tip of the tower, gradually forming a chunk of ice the size of an armchair. When she had finished, she waited until the patrolling target was directly beneath her, then drove the axe hard into the ice.

Alarmed by the noise, the gunman spun round, firing his assault rifle at random. In the same instant, the massive head of ice tottered, crashing down beside him, its weight collapsing the ice bridge upon which the gunman was standing.

After the scream, there was only silence. Then came the thwack of the helicopter's rotors. The machine appeared from somewhere behind David, its occupants still searching, slowly and systematically.

Abseiling down the remains of the tower, Katrina took cover in the chaotic ice below. For long moments, she disappeared from view. When David next saw her, she was scrambling towards the gunman's body.

He did not see her again until he heard the crunch of her crampons in the gully behind him, an AK47 assault rifle and several clips slung from her harness.

'I thought it would be good to have this,' she said, grinning. 'How is your arm?'

He nodded at the Kalashnikov. 'A helluva lot better now we have that.'

Taking it from her, he laid it on the ice and with his good hand switched the setting from automatic to safe, at the same time explaining the mechanics of the weapon.

'I know,' she said. 'You forget that in Norway we combine skiing and shooting. We call it *skiskyting*.' She picked up the Kalashnikov, drew a new magazine from her anorak and snapped it in place.

'I am not familiar with this particular weapon, but guns are mostly the same - and I am an excellent shot.'

'Then here's what you do,' he said.

They took cover separately then and waited for the helicopter to return, Katrina's anorak spread across a mound of ice as bait. David heard the chatter of the AK47 before he saw the helicopter coming in slowly from his right, flying low.

In the same instant, he saw Centaur topple forwards and rebound off the helicopter's skis. As the pilot wheeled away, David broke cover, crouching, running awkwardly. He reached Centaur's body seconds after it smashed into the ice.

His neck was broken, his sunglasses twisted grotesquely around his ears. Rivulets of blood seeped onto the ice, trickling from a line of bullet wounds that stretched from his thigh to his shoulder. Katrina had done well. She had not been boasting when she'd said she was a good shot.

Leaning over the body, he saw Katrina's face reflected in the mirrored lenses of the dead man's glasses as she peered over his shoulder.

Reaching past him, she unhooked the plastic yellow frames from the dead man's ears and dropped them onto the ice. Then, quite deliberately, she ceremoniously ground them into the ice with her heel.

Wincing with pain, David dragged the Magnum from Centaur's shoulder holster, checked that it was loaded, then turned to Katrina.

'Okay, Blue,' he said. 'You take the AK - I'll stick with this little beauty. I think now maybe we can do some business with these bastards.'

Hurriedly discussing a plan of action, he followed Katrina to the collapsed ice bridge where she had found the Kalashnikov. Here, he took cover in the confusion of ice. The helicopter was cruising cautiously two hundred yards away, off to their left.

Handing her anorak to David, Katrina climbed onto a ledge, openly attracting the pilot's attention, waving her arms urgently, hoping that her dark clothing would lure Vito into thinking she was one of his own men.

Edging forward warily, the helicopter nosed in their direction, but the ruse was only partially successful. Not easily fooled, Vito must have recognised her. The pilot veered away, climbing fast. Then, he turned the machine on its head and dived straight for them.

Another firebomb exploded nearby, the blast echoing thunderously among the chasms of ice. At the same moment, David fired a single-handed shot with the Magnum, aiming at the fuel tank, the recoil nearly taking off his good arm.

Katrina leapt sideways and disappeared from view, the AK47 blazing. Quite who shot the helicopter down was uncertain, but it was academic because one of them had hit the tail rotor. Aerodynamics did the rest.

The machine spun out of control, flinging Vito and his box of firebombs in all directions.

The helicopter's impact with the ice was spectacular, a succession of small explosions followed by a single, massive blast that set the entire glacier trembling, a wall of pure heat scorching along the crevasses, collapsing blocks of ice the size of skyscrapers.

When the rumbling had subsided, the only sounds were those of the ice cracking and water cascading. Gradually, the glacier reverted to its normal state. It was as if Vito and his men had never existed.

David and Katrina made their way cautiously back to *Flatbrehytta*, David repeatedly calling a halt. Cold and shaken, he became increasingly concerned about his loss of blood and the waves of dizziness that swept over him.

It was after nine o'clock when they reached the hut, the sun sinking to the horizon. They saw no more of Vito's men. For all they knew or cared, they were either dead or injured and gradually freezing to death.

Either way, they were destined to remain where they were, eventually to be crushed and frozen into the ice, perhaps for a thousand years before the glacier finally disgorged their remains onto the head of the fjord.

Katrina wrapped David in a foil blanket from the emergency first aid chest and, suspending his arm to the window sill, left him to fetch help in the gathering darkness.

Alone, he drifted into semi-consciousness, remembering periodically to loosen the binding on his arm.

When he awoke, it was after midnight. His breathing was heavy and his pulse high from the loss of blood. Confused, he thought he heard Vito's helicopter returning. It was not until he saw Katrina burst through the door with the police that he realised that help had finally arrived. By then he scarcely cared.

He remembered only the cold as they carried him to the helicopter. By the time the pilot had set course for Bergen, he had slipped once more into unconsciousness.

Chapter Twenty

July 10, 6 a.m - Sept 13, 2.30 p.m.

When David woke two days later, he knew only that he was in hospital, that it was six o'clock in the morning and that he wanted to be asleep. An internal steam hammer was pounding inside his head and his arm was in plaster, suspended on a stand next to the bed. A grey-haired woman with a kindly face pushed a trolley to the bedside.

'What gives, nurse? Where am I?'

'You are in hospital - Haukeland Sykehus in Bergen.' She handed him a selection of pills from a tray. 'Painkillers. You will need them. That … that thing, it was horrible.' She sighed heavily. 'I don't know. So much violence. But you are young and strong. You will live.'

She puffed his pillows and he dozed again, flitting between wakefulness and sleep, the effects of the anaesthetic still blurring his mind. He had slept almost continuously since his arrival.

Waking only for the surgeon's round and for lunch, he gathered that they had flown him directly to the hospital and given him a blood transfusion immediately on arrival. The surgeon had removed the crossbow bolt in a four-hour operation the previous afternoon.'

'*Ja*, it was a success, but you must not expect miracles,' the surgeon said, folding his arms and cupping his chin in his hand. 'Young men like you are too impatient and recovery will be slow, I think. This - how do you say? - this weapon has damaged most severely the muscles controlling your finger movements.'

His speech was soft and musical, the end of each sentence rising up the musical scale. 'If you regain eighty per cent movement within a year, I think you have good luck.'

'You're a real bundle of fun, doc. When are you goin' to let me outa here?'

'Perhaps the day after tomorrow. Maybe at the end of the week. That will depend on the gentleman who is waiting to see you, I think.'

The gentleman introduced himself as Sergeant Nielsen.

'You may remember we met just over a week ago,' he said, fishing a notebook from his pocket. 'When you first arrived in Norway.'

'I'm not likely to forget, sergeant.'

'Most meetings with the police are memorable, sir.'

Explaining courteously that he was under arrest, Nielsen listed the charges as stealing and destroying a motor home, a seaplane and a helicopter, as well as a police vehicle, not to mention evading arrest and stealing a yacht.

'That means holding you on what we call *varetektsfengsling*. You would call it being remanded in custody. No correspondence or visits allowed, I'm afraid, sir.'

Suddenly, the sergeant grinned. 'Mind if I sit down? It's been a long night.'

'Sure, go ahead. What's so funny?'

'You've had quite a time of it, haven't you sir? The joke is that you needn't have committed these offences at all. You see, as soon as we discovered that Mr. Vito's helicopter had been repainted and the forensic boys analysed the undercoat, we knew that he was the man we were looking for, not you. It proved that he was directly involved in the Fjærland bombings.'

David shifted his position, struggling to sit up.

'It would have been good to know that a little earlier. All I heard was how I was supposed to have kidnapped Katrina - Katrina Hagen, that I ...'

'Yes, a pity about that. It was your Delta Force training, you see. Being an expert in helicopter warfare and explosives - that sort of thing. It set us off on the wrong track.' The sergeant shrugged. 'Anyway, the body on Marabreen, eye witness accounts of the shooting at Skei and the theft of a Citröen car at *Trollstigen* - not to mention your aerial battle there - they all pointed to Mr. Vito, not you.'

'Great - and where does that leave me now, sergeant?'

Nielsen chuckled. 'Well, normally, you'd be held under custodial arrest and required to appear in court within twenty-four hours, but in your case that wasn't possible so your lawyer, Mr. Stryn, represented you.'

David nodded thoughtfully.

'Represented - in the past tense? How come?'

'The hearing was yesterday afternoon. We arrested you formally in the hut at *Flatbrehytta*, but you weren't exactly paying attention. Anyway, sir, in Norwegian law the police must show just cause for keeping you in custody, incriminating evidence for example.' He laughed. 'Not that there's any shortage of that. However, if we fail to show just cause to the court, we are obliged to release you.' He paused and smiled. 'Inspector Ingstad sends his regards and says he hopes you appreciate his failure, sir.'

'You mean, you're deliberately letting me off the hook?'

'That's right. We had to arrest you, of course, but we realised that you wouldn't have committed these offences if it hadn't been for us.'

Nielsen held out his hand.

'So, provided you relinquish all claims to compensation from the authorities, sir, you're a free man.'

David sank back onto the pillows and sighed. 'What about the owners of the motor home and the seaplane?'

'Not forgetting the police vehicle, sir. That, I'm afraid, is something you'll have to sort out in the civil courts.'

David yawned. 'As you probably know, sergeant, I inherited a considerable sum of money when my grandfather died. I'd be grateful if you' could pass on my apologies to everyone concerned. I'll instruct Paul Stryn to pay any damage claims in full from my grandfather's estate.'

'Very good, sir. Will that include the police patrol vehicle as well?'

David did not answer. He had fallen asleep again.

Katrina came to visit him in the late afternoon, laden with flowers, grapes and chocolate, bubbling over with news of events in Sognefjord.

'It was quite incredible,' she said, drawing up a chair. 'The police chartered a ferry and sent hundreds of policemen to break up the demonstrations. You've never seen so many boats. The court at Balestrand has been sitting non-stop, handing out automatic fines.' She laughed. 'Some of the demonstrators walked straight from the courtroom to rejoin the protest, but now it is all over.'

David smiled, eyeing her appreciatively, aware of her perfume. Gone were the corduroys and sweater. Now, she was wearing an elegant suit, blouse and brightly coloured cravat. Her hair was styled the way he liked it, long on one side, shorter on the other.

'You look sensational,' he said. As an afterthought, he added:. 'Guess I prefer the way you looked on board *Ulrika*, though.'

She tossed her head and kissed him. 'That is enough of that, Mr. Dynamite. When will they release you?'

'In a couple of days, I guess.'

She fell silent then, her manner strained, her taut little smile fading into seriousness. David studied her, mentally drawing the shadows of her face.

'What's up, Blue? You look as if you're about to start blubbering.'

She sighed, her eyes watering.

'It is just ... that there has been so much violence and death. Seven people killed in the bombing, five more on the glacier the other night. And for what? Nothing.' She dabbed an eye with her handkerchief. 'Tor is dead, too,' she said softly.

'Tor? Why? How?'

'An accident ... He was drunk, I think.'

'I'm sorry, Blue.' He fell silent for a moment. 'I guess you were pretty fond of him, huh?'

She nodded silently.

'Once we were very close, but the bombings changed him. Suddenly, the story was more important than me. For a woman, that is not so easy to understand.' She laid a hand on his arm and smiled, her eyes sad. 'I suppose you will go home to Willmar now?'

'I guess so, Blue. I have to go sometime.'

'Will you come back?'

'Sure I'll come back. As sure as you'll never get me up on that glacier again.'

Not even the most senior reporters among the Norwegian media could remember a story that had generated so much news as the Fjærland saga. Hardly a day passed when its many facets did not warrant a multi-page spread. The morning of July the eleventh was no different.

Editors devoted most of the morning editions to the events on the glacier and the unprecedented police action in Sognefjord. In all, six hundred policemen had been shipped to the scene.

Nonetheless, the Planet Watch campaign to halt the mining project at Fjærland was a resounding success, at least from Johan Michelsen's viewpoint.

One protestor had drowned and sixteen people were injured. Police had arrested hundreds of demonstrators. The courts were filled to capacity and *Arctic Constellation* had been stopped in her tracks. More importantly, the campaign had touched a national nerve and, as a result, erupted into a major political row.

Political commentators demanded to know not only why the Ministry of Industry had approved a copper mine in such a sensitive area, but why, if the exploitation rights had to be granted at all, they had not been given to a Norwegian company.

Did the government have so little faith in Norwegian industry, they asked? And why had the mining rights to a vast Norwegian fortune been given to an American multi-national corporation with a proven record of environmental nonchalance, if not negligence?

It was suggested that Schneider Barr's offer to finance the building of the Skei-Fjærland tunnel was nothing less than bribery and corruption. Surely, the outraged leader writers and opposition politicians argued, if such a tunnel were to be constructed, it should be financed in the normal way - not by a foreign company whose morals were best illustrated by the murderous antics on the Jostedal glacier. Antics in which none other than Mr. George Vito, the Personal Assistant to the President of Schneider Barr, had participated.

Demands were made both in the media and in parliament for heads to roll. The most vociferous politicians and commentators called for the immediate resignation of the government.

At ten-thirty that morning, following consultations with the police and the Minister for Industry, the Prime Minister's spokesperson announced that the government was suspending the Fjærland mining concessions with immediate effect.

The statement revealed further that the government had set up an all-party parliamentary committee to examine the possibility of extending the national park to include Fjærlandsfjord.

As an entirely separate matter, it added, the Minister for Industry had tendered his resignation, giving as his reason the desire to see more of his family.

This, he said to the amusement of the assembled reporters, was a move that had been long planned and the Prime Minister had accepted it only after lengthy consideration and with the greatest reluctance.

David and Katrina heard the news on the one o'clock radio bulletin a few minutes after arriving back at the Glacier Hotel. The doctors had released David from hospital earlier than he had anticipated and after visiting Paul Stryn briefly at his office in Bergen, he and Katrina had driven directly back to Fjærland. After a late lunch, they retreated into Katrina's office, where she retrieved Sheet 1317 of the 1:50,000 Norwegian Geographic Survey maps.

Spreading it across her desk, she pointed to a footpath marked in red, leading to *Flatbrehytta..*

'This is where we found the potholes, just below the edge of Supphellebreen, directly beneath the mountain. See? It is marked: Vetle, 845 metres.'

David leaned over her shoulder and kissed the back of her neck, stirred by her perfume. 'Sure,' he said, forcing himself to concentrate. 'Unfortunately Ejulf Deathsword didn't bury his silver there, so it's not much use to us.'

She smiled up at him. 'No, but while you were sleeping your life away in hospital, I have been doing some serious thinking. We have made a stupid assumption, I think.'

'Not you Blue, surely?' He sat on the edge of the desk and laughed.

'Yes, me - and you, too. We both assumed that because five shiploads of silver would be very heavy, the Vikings would hide the silver as near to Skarestad, or Indre Moa, as possible.' She leaned back in her chair. 'But Ejulf Deathsword had just brought the silver back from Gotland on the east coast of Sweden. Before that Swedish Vikings had dragged it half way across Kazakhstan and the Ukraine to the Baltic. A couple of extra kilometres would have made no difference at all.'

Picking up a pencil, she pointed to the map. 'I knew there were potholes in the Supphelle valley and we assumed ...'

'You assumed,' he teased gently.

She laughed. 'All right, *I* assumed that because they were directly beneath a mountain called Vetle, the silver must be buried there. But look! There are several *moulins* here, too.' She tapped the map with her pencil, her eyes gleaming with excitement. 'In the Bøya Valley - on the left bank of the lake.'

David studied the map. 'Below Marabreen. If you think I'm goin' up there again ...'

'No, no. There is no need ...'

'Don't be ridiculous,' he chided.

She grinned sheepishly, then turned back to the map, her pencil underlining a name printed in smaller letters. 'It is also below Vetlebreen. *That's* where Deathsword hid his silver. I'm sure of it'

David nodded thoughtfully. 'You could be right at that'

'And I will bet you a million *kroner* that if archaeologists were to dig near those huts, they would find another Viking settlement. Almost certainly, it would have been called Øvre Moa. Or Upper Moa to you.'

He whistled softly, then strode to the door and held it open. 'There's only one way to find out, Blue. We'll find nothing sitting around here all day.'

She folded the map and slid it into a drawer. 'We will go home first - to my house. There are axes and a spade there.'

They hurried away then, reaching the entrance to the Fjærland tunnel shortly after three o'clock.

Katrina parked in a lay-by and together they walked along the dirt road leading to the Bøya Glacier. Despite the heat of July sun, the banks of the lake were wrapped in the cold air expelled by rushing meltwater through ice tunnels at the base of the glacier.

Katrina led the way through fields of coarse grass to the base of the slope, the ground rougher and wetter now, a marshland strewn with small boulders and arctic cotton grass.

Hopping and jumping from one tussock to another, they finally reached the edge of the slope and Katrina began to climb, using her ice axe as a walking stick. David hesitated.

'Blue, there is no way I am going up on that glacier again ...'

Gaily, she tossed her head and laughed, a sound as clear and pure as the air itself. 'There is no need. We are here now. Look.'

She pointed at the ground, where the grass gave way to rock. At first, David could see nothing, but gradually he discerned faint indentations in the ground, irregular circles and ovals. Katrina was already attacking the surface with the spade. David took her ice axe and scraped the topsoil away as best he could with one arm in a sling.

For an hour they toiled without success, excavating the *moulins* one by one. As they dug, the earth seemed looser, more like clinker than soil. By four-thirty, they had cleared five potholes and sat down to rest.

'Doesn't look too good, Blue.'

'It *must* be here. Where else *can* it be?' she asked in exasperation, her forehead streaked with perspiration.

David kicked the ground idly. 'I dunno. Maybe there isn't any silver ...' Suddenly, he paused and leaned forward. 'Hold on a minute ...' Quickly, he scooped up a handful of earth and examined it closely, then began laughing.

'David what is it?' Katrina looked at him, her expression puzzled, hopeful.

'We've found it! We've been digging the goddam stuff up for the past ten minutes and not even realised it. Look.' He showed her a handful of stones. 'I thought they were pebbles ... Where's that ice axe?'

Placing a small stone on the rock, he chipped at it until gradually the hard outer coating fell away, revealing a small coin.

They dug frenziedly then until early evening, scooping out the pebbles and oddly shaped stones. Three feet down, they came across piles of coins, rings, necklaces and pendants, and bracelets and brooches carved exquisitely with the heads of snakes and dragons - some silver, some gold. All covered with the grime of centuries.

Beneath these were ingots of solid silver, stacked neatly one on top of the other, and old bones scored with runes.

When they had excavated three more *moulins*, they returned to dig more deeply into the potholes they had previously abandoned. Here, too, they found more of Deathsword's silver. Finally, they sat down together, bemused but euphoric, surveying the horde until the chill air brought them back to reality.

Scarcely able to believe their find, they scooped the piles of coins and jewellery back into the moulins, covering them with the branches of a young birch nearby, and drove back to the hotel, each taking with them a selection of coins and jewellery.

'We must telephone Paul Stryn immediately,' Katrina said. 'I expect we shall have to make a formal claim. It must be worth a fortune.'

'If I know governments, they sure aren't goin' to let us keep it. Why don't we put a little aside first, huh?'

'Perhaps, but let us not eat the icing before we have made the cake. First we will telephone Paul. Then we will drink champagne.'

Stryn was still in his office, catching up on the work that had piled up during his absence.

'*Hej Katrina. Hvordan står det til?*'

'*Bra, takk.* And you - you are well?'

They exchanged more pleasantries and Katrina explained how they had found the silver. Stryn bid her wait while he unearthed a law book.

'Of course, you are quite right when you say you must lodge a formal claim with the government. It is too late now, but I will do it first thing in the morning.' He paused and she could hear him riffling through the pages of a book.

'Ah yes! According to the Cultural Relics Law Number 50 of June 9, 1978, amended on April 21, 1989, the coins belong to the state because they were minted and buried before 1537. However, the law says that the finder shall be compensated at the value of the metal by weight plus an additional sum which shall be no less than ten per cent of the metal value.'

Katrina gasped. 'By weight? But there are tons of it.'

'If that is true, you will be a rich woman, Katrina. As legal advisor to both of you, I suggest most strongly that you both sign an agreement immediately, specifying how the state compensation should be divided between you. I think perhaps I should come to Fjærland immediately.'

Katrina laughed, teasing him. 'You just want to see Hanna again, Paul. I have heard all about you, taking her out for walks. It is not good for staff to be seen consorting with guests.'

'You know about us?'

'Of course. I am very upset. I thought I was the only woman in the world for you.'

He sighed. '*Ja, det er sant.* But you are never there, Katrina. And now, Hanna and me - we are very close.'

'I am happy for you. Come soon.' She replaced the receiver and turned to David.

'He says we will be very rich. We must agree how to divide the silver between us.'

'Right down the middle, Blue.' He stood behind her, massaging her neck with his good hand. 'What are you going to do with your half?'

She smiled. 'My dream - it has always been to have a museum dedicated to the glacier - in memory of my father and the other glacier guides. Perhaps now I can afford to have it built. We shall see. And you?'

'First, there is the minor matter of a motor home, a seaplane and a police car. Then I guess I'll go see the manager of the First Kandiyohi

Lakeside Bank and pay off a few debts. Then, who knows? Buy a new car, a yacht maybe ...'

Arctic Constellation manoeuvred slowly into Ro-Ro Three Wharf on Tyneside, the sun sinking morosely into an industrial haze behind the dockside cranes and blocks of apartments in the west. They stood dark and grim, a symbol of the mood of the miners on board.

The ship had stood off Balestrand for several hours while hordes of police dispersed the demonstrators. Then, the captain announced that the Norwegian government had withdrawn the mining concession and, after more hours of negotiation, a coastguard vessel had escorted them back into international waters.

The return passage had been smooth enough, which was as well given that the miners' frame of mind was bloody and most of them had devoted the entire thirty-six hour voyage to drinking.

When the ship docked soon after nine-thirty, Jimmie Hargreaves was so inebriated he could scarcely stand, but somehow he managed to make his way home to Peterlee. Doris put him to bed, soothing him, distressed to see him in such a state.

In the morning, she brought him a mug of instant coffee and two headache pills for breakfast, sitting on the edge of the bed holding his hand. Gloomily, he recounted the events in Sognefjord, then slept for the rest of the morning.

At lunchtime, he returned to the miners' club and by late afternoon, he had again drunk more than was good for him, shouting at the boys when they came home from school. When Doris returned home from the shop in Sunderland, he was snoring in front of the television.

Quietly, she cooked his supper, understanding his torment. He was a good and proud man. They were all proud men, the miners, and she was no different from any other miner's wife in Peterlee. They were all in the same boat.

The future had looked bleak and Jimmie was not the only one who had started drinking. Still, at least now there was hope for the future. She shook him gently.

'Jimmie, your supper. Tha' can 'ave it on a tray, luv, in front of television, like.'

He stirred and she sat next to him.

'I doan't know, lass. I'm not 'ungry, some'ow.'

'Try an' eat somethin', Jimmie,' she pleaded. She laid a hand on his knee. 'I know 'ow tha must feel, luv.' She fell silent for a moment, then leaned against his shoulder. 'But it's goin' t' be all right. We've got each other. Any'ow,' she said, her face brightening, 'while you've been away, there's been such a row in parliament over t' closures - they're talkin' about keepin' some of pits open now. They say they'd rather subsidise coal than unemployment - so' it looks as if Easington pit 's goin' to survive.' She nudged him gently. 'So tomorrow, y' can keep that promise y'made.'

Jimmie sighed deeply, fiddling with his food. 'What promise is that, our Doris?'

'Y'said you'd tek me dancin'. Y'know, like we used to.'

From the moment the Northwestern Airlines flight to Minneapolis touched down a week after David and Katrina had found the silver, David knew that he would return to Fjærland. Driving along U.S. Route 12 to Willmar in a rented Chevrolet, he was estranged in his own country, the rolling prairies and farmland strangely flat after the mountains of Norway.

His desire to return was reinforced when he swung into the driveway of his home on Quincy Avenue and opened the front door, for among the pile of mail that had accumulated during his three-week absence was a brief note from the manager of the First Kandiyohi Lakeside Bank.

Dated two days previously, it advised him that as the payments on his loan were now seriously overdue, the bank would have no option but to freeze both his personal account and that of his demolition company unless they heard from him within seven days. David tossed the letter in the waste bin.

By nature, he was not a smug individual, but the following morning he was unable to resist allowing the bank manager to lecture him before disclosing the details of his imminent wealth.

The manager droned on about his inability to repay the loan and his apparent reluctance to produce the quarterly accounts as requested, and brusquely advised him that there was no alternative but to call in the loan. If necessary, he added, the bank would issue a court order. The manager gave him one month in which to repay the loan in full.

Only then did David reveal that following the death of his grandfather he had inherited assets worth approximately $670,000. He added that owing to a stroke of good fortune while in Norway, he also expected to receive a sum notably greater than that within the next two or three months. He rose then, nodded curtly and advised the dumbstruck manager that he would contact him in due course, pay off the loan at his own convenience and then close the account.

Three days later, David received a postcard from Katrina. Depicting the Glacier Hotel, its message was brief. "Dearest David. Cold as ice - remember? Need warming. Much love, Blue."

He smiled, placed it on the hall table and opened another missive from the bank.

"In view of your anticipated transfer of funds from Norway," it read, "the manager asks me to inform you that he is happy to permit the loan to proceed for a further three months …"

Each day, David pounced on the mail as soon as it arrived, but not until early August did he receive the letter for which he had been waiting so impatiently. The Bergen postmark set his heart racing.

The letter, from Paul Stryn, began with news of the lawyer's engagement to Hanna, but David's eye quickly isolated the paragraphs that would propel him into a month of frenetic activity and decide his entire future.

"I have now received an answer from the Norwegian government regarding your claim to the silver discovered in the Bøya valley," Stryn wrote. "This claim has been formally confirmed and I am delighted to inform you that the value of the silver by weight has been established as NOK 42,184,023. As you are aware, you are entitled to an additional ten per cent on this sum, which brings the total to NOK 46.402,426. At today's rates, this is equivalent to US$ 7,919,347. This amount has now been transferred to your Norwegian account. Additionally, your grandfather's estate has been valued at NOK 4,012,223 (US$684,679)."

David whistled quietly, the beginnings of a grin spreading across his face. Then, he punched the air and emitted a long, gurgling whoop for joy, startling Septimus who sprang from the sofa and darted into the kitchen. David sank into the sofa and returned to Stryn's letter:

"As your find is considered by experts to be one of the greatest Viking discoveries of all time, you will also be pleased to hear that the Norwegian government has acceded to your specific request to be allowed to keep two pieces of the Viking jewellery, namely a gold ring and the large circular brooch fashioned in silver, with rilled edging and interwoven Borre-style ornamentation. The proviso is that these remain within the territory of Norway.

"In view of this latter condition, I should be most grateful if you could advise me whether you intend to return to Norway - especially as in order to retain ownership of your grandfather's land, you would - as I explained some weeks ago - be obliged to take up Norwegian citizenship. I look forward to receiving your instructions in due course.

"Incidentally, Katrina asks me to tell you that a team of archaeologists from the University of Oslo arrived in Fjærland last week. Apparently, they have unearthed evidence of another Viking settlement in the Bøya valley. She says that you will be keen to know that they have named it Øvre Moa".

David walked through to the kitchen and, opening the fridge door, reached for a packet of ham. Rolling two slices for himself, he cut another two slices into small segments and tossed them to Septimus, who sat expectantly by his feet.

'Septimus, old buddy, you're gonna to be one rich cat,' he said, picking him up and cradled him, 'but I guess you're gonna have to live with Pete Henriksen from here on in.'

Septimus growled and struggled to escape, intent on retrieving a piece of ham that remained on the floor.

'Okay, cat. Be like that,' David said. 'I'm still gonna miss you.'

Two weeks later, a red and white seaplane taxied from the jetty at Hermansverk into the Sognefjord. The air was colder now and the birch leaves were turning. Bright yellows and reds against the sombre green of the spruce.

Climbing to four thousand feet, the 'plane banked to the northwest, flying low over the mountains before descending into Fjærlandsfjord.

Scanning the instrument panel, David's eyes flicked over the dials. Speed one hundred and ten knots. Attitude normal. Altitude fifteen hundred feet. He grinned, confident now that he had won his pilot's licence. It had been a hectic but satisfying month.

Apart from taking intensive flying lessons, he had closed his account at the First Kandiyohi Lakeside Bank, placed his Quincy Avenue home on the market and deposited $50,000 into his company account, signing the business and all its assets over to Pete Henriksen on the condition that he cared for Septimus for the rest of the cat's natural life.

As the little plane flew between the high cliffs of the fjord, David knew that he had come home. The sense of belonging that he had experienced when he first saw Sognefjord with Paul Stryn was as deep as ever.

Ahead, to his left, he could see the Fjærland ferry stage and the white frame building that was the Glacier Hotel, the patch of lawn by the waterside a reminder of the first time he had seen Vito and Centaur together.

He flew on until he reached Skarestad and the Skeisnipa massif, then banked into a tight left-hand turn, heading back towards the village of Fjærland, buzzing the hotel and the steepled wooden church nearby. Briefly, he noted the fresh mounds of earth in the graveyard marking the graves of those who had died in the Fjærland bombings and on the glacier.

Banking steeply for his final approach, he eased back the throttle and lowered the flaps, reflecting on the irony that his grandfather and the others had all died for nothing.

The crazy thing was that there had been no need for the killings or the murderous attempts to acquire his land because Deathsword's silver had not been buried on his grandfather's land at all.

He feathered the plane gently onto the fjord and taxied slowly to the jetty by the hotel. As he cut the engine, he saw Katrina standing on the hotel steps and reached for the briefcase strapped into the passenger seat. Inside it were two boxes, one containing a Viking ring, the other a circular brooch one thousand years old.

Opening the cockpit door, he filled his lungs with the cool September air and waved to her, watching her run full tilt down the slope to the water's edge. And only then did he realise, for the first time, that his grandfather had not died in vain.

AUTHOR'S NOTE

Balestrand, Fjærland and Fjærlandsfjord all exist as described, as do all the locations in the book, including the Glacier Hotel, which I have renamed. The tunnel between Fjærland and Lunde was completed in 1986 and was in use long before the idea for this book emerged. In all other respects the details about the tunnel's construction, cost and equipment used is correct. The Glacier Museum also exists and was in place before I conceived the idea for my story.

There is, to my knowledge, no copper and zinc deposit on Skeisnipa. Nor was any Viking silver found there, although some years ago, I believe the remains of a Viking ship were discovered at Skarestad. Ejulf Deathsword is a figment of my imagination. The aquisition of his secret wealth, however, is entirely credible. Swedish Vikings did travel to the Arab Emirate - as far east as Samarkand, Tashkent and Bokhara. They returned to Gotland and elsewhere in Scandinavia with large amounts of silver and gold. Norwegian Vikings also sailed to Gotland and, given the chance, would doubtless have stolen the silver as described.

Many people have contributed to time and effort to this book, but my good friend and former colleague, Michael Brady in Oslo, deserves special thanks for his boundless enthusiasm. His sleuthing skills into subjects ranging from Norwegian law relating to the discovery of treasure trove to the art of tunnelling have been an enormous contribution to the book. Without his suggestions and research, this story would have been very much the poorer.

Camille Mellor's encouragement and eagle-eyed assistance in reviewing the script was equally of great value.

Thanks are also due to Gunnar Thesen and Jan Olav Aamlid of Oslo Mynthandel, which can be found as described in the book, and to Gunnar Lotsberg, of the Norwegian Roads Directorate office at Hermansverk, Sogn & Fjordane for his assistance through Michael Brady with information on the construction of the Fjærland tunnel.

John Dobson gave me expert help on handguns and their likely effects while George Kelson, Chief Flying instructor, Dennis Kenyon and Steve Wood of Starline Helicopters at Redhill Aerodrome, Surrey, were equally helpful in teaching me to "fly" a helicopter.

Similarly, Peter Heron of British Coal, North-east region, was most helpful in describing so graphically the plight of British miners and the effects on towns affected by pit closures. The picture he portrayed was supplemented by the views of many miners themselves.

To Trygve and Anny Berge in Molde, my grateful thanks for the provision of sleeping bag, sea charts, advice on the treachery of the west Norwegian coast and their hospitality. John and Angela Weaver, together with Roger Bradley, helped me to plot a course for *Ulrika* along the west coast of Norway, and their advice on sailing in adverse weather was invaluable.

The weather off Stadt is frequently as described and I am grateful to Mike Wood of The Met. Office Archives at Bracknell for his efforts in tracking down a system of plausible fronts and weather patterns.

I am also grateful for the assistance of Tim Simon, my solicitor, and David Ing of Downs of Dorking, who kindly advised me on hypothetical legal dilemmas. Similarly, Roger Large, Graham Andrews, Vilhelm Bunderman and most particularly Joe Reilley deserve thanks for their help with the more technical aspects of mining.

Finally, I am particularly indebted to one Fjærland resident who prefers to remain anonymous. Her patience and help with my incessant questions concerning Fjærland and the glaciers were invaluable in lending to the book authenticity and credibility.

Many other people, of course, helped with the research for this book and although they are too numerous to mention individually, my thanks go to all of them.